SHADOWS OF THE MOUNTAIN

by

Robert Prince

Published by Robert D Prince

Robertprince67@bigpond.com

This is a work of historical fiction set in the Mossman River valley, North Queensland, Australia 1874 to 1974. Names, characters, places and incidents are the product of the author's imagination or are used fictitiously.

ISBN 978-0-9944708-2-9

Cover art and design: Glen Holman www.glenholman.com
Editing and interior design: Philip Newey http://www.philipnewey.com/All-read-E

Another historical novel by the same author: *The Farrier's Son*

To all fair-minded people

An Aboriginal warrior with spears in hand stands on the grassy summit of Mount Beaufort surveying the country. To the north, Daintree and Cape Tribulation lie within view of the mysterious Thornton Peak. To seaward lies Port Douglas, jutting into the Pacific Ocean. To the south stretches the hunting ground of Cassowary Range, and to the west stands Mount Demi, protector of his people, the Aborigines of the Mossman River valley. Below him the Mossman River, with its corridor of tropical rainforest, meanders across the valley floor from the towering mountains to the glittering sea.

Never could he imagine that one day his tribal land would be occupied by Europeans and the traditions and practices of his people gone forever. Furthermore, it is strange that the social catastrophe of his valley has, till now, never been told. The author, drawing on seventy years of close association with the valley and extensive research, portrays what happened to the Aborigines during this epic period in the history of Northern Australia. The author's contact includes riding his horse to King Diamond's camp in his youth and playing in the river with the tribal chief's children.

In the story Marku, a noble Aboriginal woman and central character, witnesses events from pre-European times to the eventual destruction of her culture. Midst all the turmoil she falls in love with James, allowing her to experience both cultures.

The portrayal is typical of the events that occurred during European settlement of Aboriginal tribal lands in Australia. The setting of this story in the Mossman River valley in no way suggests that the settlers of this district were any more intrusive than those who settled elsewhere in the Australian colonies. Indeed, apart from intruding on tribal lands, some settlers of the

Mossman River district showed a genuine interest in the welfare of the Aborigines.

Words used to describe people of varying ethnicity are consistent with usage at the time of the story. References considered to be offensive have been avoided. Any perceived misrepresentation of culture is not intended.

CONTENTS:

PROLOGUE

Bajal's birth had not been easy. Old Kija, midwife to his mother, Marku, had told of the ordeal. Kija and two other women of the tribe secreted Marku to a secluded place on the Mossman River. A place well upstream, away from biting insects and the sea tides that brought crocodiles; a hideaway where the stream ran cool and a light breeze drifted through the trees. Apart from the safety of this site Marku chose it for a spiritual reason. She believed that, if she gave birth under the water cherry tree, here by the river, her child would grow up to be strong and wise. Though Marku's labour had begun the previous evening her delivery remained stalled. Now weakened and fearful of dying in childbirth she asked to be taken to the water where she could ask the water spirit for help. The women lifted her to her feet and assisted her to the stream. She then lay, transfixed as the spirit of the passing stream brought fresh hope and renewed strength. With the women assisting she tried anew and soon delivered a healthy baby. Upon hearing its cry and being told it was a boy she cried tears of joy. She remained seated in the cool stream and, with the breeze whispering in the leaves above, placed the babe to her full breast. Upon returning to Jinkalmu, their home village in the shadow of Mount Demi, a celebration marked the birth. The men daubed themselves with ochre clay and the women adorned themselves with shell necklaces, some of which had been traded from as far away as Torres Strait. While a wallaby roasted on the communal fire the clan honoured Marku and the new arrival with ritual song and dance.

Bajal's first memory of his childhood remained with him. While the men were away hunting the women took the children swimming at a pool on the north branch of the river. The women sat by a smouldering fire on a sandbar making dilly bags till one of them suddenly screamed, 'Bilngkumu!' Sand, ash and dilly bags scattered as the women grabbed their digging sticks and scrambled to save the children. As a front they rushed to the water's edge shouting at the crocodile. They risked their lives, entering the water to waist deep, yelling and slapping the water with their sticks. The crocodile turned its attention to the women, changing direction, making a bow wave as it charged towards them. The women, knowing that unity of strength was their only hope, stood their ground, screaming and pounding the water. The crocodile advanced to within a few yards of them and then wavered, turned tail and swam to the deep, where it disappeared from sight. Marku spun around to make sure all the children had made it to safety and then rushed from the water to clutch Bajal. That night she slept on her bed of animal skins with Bajal in her arms. Bajal, though only five years old at the time, remembered her gazing at the stars, thanking the spirits.

At this age Bajal realised he was different from the other children. While the others shared a bed with their parents and sat as a family by the fire, he had no father and most times sat alone with his mother. He thought little of this at the time but when he reached his early teens and was old enough to go fishing with the other boys their talk made him wonder.

Bajal's grandfather, Bujur, sat cross-legged beside the embers of a camp fire. Though almost blinded by ash and smoke his mind remained nimble. He sensed Bajal's approach, turned his head and greeted him with a nod. Bajal sat beside Bujur and placed a hand on his bony knee. Moments of silent reverence followed, with each thinking of the other—the old man with his wisdom and Bajal his youth. The old man knew that Bajal had come to learn more about Aboriginal legend. He remained still and quiet, slowly drifting into a trance, and then began to tell the story of Mount Demi that overlooks the Mossman River and its valley.

In the Dreamtime of long ago spirits rose from a flat earth to form the landscape and all life, including human. These spirits—some good, some bad—often quarrelled and fought. The people of the valley were persecuted by a bad spirit till a good spirit overpowered it and set them free. Since that time Mount Demi, the totem of the good spirit, has stood, guarding them against evil. Bujur went further, speaking in a quiet, monotone voice, interpreting the deep meaning behind the legend. After he finished the story and the fire burnt to ash Marku came forward carrying a baler shell of water. The old man, now tired and thirsty, took her hands in his and lifted the shell to his mouth. When he had finished she sat beside him, clasped his hands in hers and comforted him into the night. Bujur's weak condition remained a constant concern for Marku and she wondered how many more seasons would pass before he departed to the spirit world. She knew, as Bujur did, that when a warrior is reduced to roasting nuts on a fire and weaving baskets his time was near. If only she could get him to the healing spring in the mountains! Its special powers would bring relief and maybe heal his limbs so he could again join the men in the hunt. When Bujur began to doze Marku cradled him in her arms. When he was asleep she laid him down with his head resting on a soft, possum-skin pelt. Back at her hut she found Bajal also asleep, curled up with Murramu, his dingo puppy.

Marku took Bajal to the river, dug for worms and settled him on the bank with a twine fishing line in hand. While keeping him in sight she moved upstream to a backwater that pooled beside the bank. Here she sat, peering down at her own reflection in the water. She remained still, admiring her nakedness and thinking about what the future might hold. Her beauty, both of body and spirit, captivated men, with many having offered her a place in their huts. So far she had declined, shielding behind Dari, who was Bujur's second wife and her stepmother. Hurtful memories came to mind of the time when, little more than a child, she attended a corrobboree at the Mowbray River and was raped at spear point by a man from a tribe to the south. Marku had never since taken a man and had no intention of doing so.

Bajal sat naked on a rock, drying himself in the sun after having bathed in the river by the village. He shook his mop of black, curly hair, sprinkling drops of water into the bright sunlight. As he raised his head he caught a glimpse of a young village girl spying on him from across the river. He turned his head aside, pretending not to see her, waited for a while and then casually rose and walked back to the village. He knew Nganka well by sight but had seldom spoken with her. Her parents, for some reason, shepherded her away each time they came close. He thought of her often during the next few weeks and smiled each time he recalled her pretty face peeping at him by the river. He asked Bujur what he should do. Bujur told him that Nganka was betrothed and by tribal law she could not be his wife. In spite of this objection the young couple became friends and, with time, almost inseparable. They swam and hunted together, venturing through the forest naked and carefree, with Nganka, a slip of a girl with budding breasts, walking behind Bajal admiring his youthful body. Relatives of the husband-to-be became suspicious and took exception. They stalked the young couple and spread whispers around the village to disgrace them. Before long they were ostracised by many and subjected to constant harassment. Bajal and Nganka coped with the situation till, one morning, relatives of the betrothed man sooled their wild dogs upon Nganka, mauling her badly. The ordeal terrified Nganka and left her so shaken that she and Bajal decided to leave. They gathered their few possession, said their goodbyes and set out to make a fresh start downstream at an old fishing site on the north branch of the river. They slept under the stars in a pocket of open forest till completing a thatched hut and then, with Murramu by their side, they settled in for what they thought would be a quiet life, living off the land in the solitude of the wild as their ancestors had done for thousands of years.

PART ONE

THE CEDAR GETTERS

Cedar getters camp on the Mossman River 1870s. The first non-Aboriginal people to settle in the Mossman River Valley.

CHAPTER 1

Nganka stood by the riverside at their camp gazing thoughtfully at the river. Water grass, lush and sprawling, covered the bank and spilt across the water below. A pearly-white sandbar on the opposite bank lay between the water's edge and the tropical rainforest that had flourished for millennia. Nganka's thoughts flickered, causing her to raise her head and look into the distance. *Manjal Dimbi*, Mount Demi, with its rock formation of a spiritual parent caring for a child, stood as her people's guardian. *Wundu*, Thornton Peak, shrouded in misty cloud and home to a cloud forest, held secrets of the past. *Jalkaraburr*, Mount Beaufort, with its all-round view of the valley, drew her attention. Since early childhood she had joined in its wallaby hunts; exciting times when the women and children beat the grass to herd wallabies into the pathway of armed tribesmen. Bajal and Murramu came into view after having been for their morning walk. As they approached, Nganka thought how lucky she was to have them; Bajal the one she loved and Murramu a faithful companion. When Bajal came near she took him into her arms and pressed her breasts to his bare chest. Their embrace soon clouded all thoughts that had gone before. They hugged, searched each other's eyes momentarily and then, hand in hand, turned and entered the hut.

Their decision to leave the tribe some months before had been vindicated. They lived a carefree lifestyle; playing in the river, hunting and gathering, preparing favourite foods, sitting by the fire at evening time and loving tenderly by night. They visited Marku and Dari often and sometimes surprised them with fresh fruit and game. An understanding evolved with the tribespeople whereby they associated with those who were friendly and ignored those who sought revenge. Most surprisingly, the tribal elders, the wise old men who ruled the tribe, accepted their decision.

Their blissful lovemaking was not without purpose. Ever since they first made love Nganka yearned to have Bajal's baby; to cradle a child made of their image, to nurture the young spirit to become strong, to be someone that would make her and Bajal proud. Nganka lay exhausted and panting beside Bajal, hoping that the spirit child of her hope had been planted. Bajal understood Nganka as she understood him and believed that their union would eventually fulfil their dream of having a piccaninny who could hunt with them and share the fire in the quiet of night.

They basked in the afterglow till Murramu began to whine. Bajal called for him to come in but when he continued whining Bajal went to investigate. To his surprise he found Murramu sitting on the riverbank, peering downstream. Nganka soon appeared from the doorway and joined them.

'He can hear something downstream,' whispered Bajal.

Nganka took Bajal's hand, cocked an ear and together they listened, trying to identify Murramu's concern. Suddenly, they heard *clink*, followed by another sound. They had no idea what it could be and shot each other a questioning glance. Soon it became a rhythmic *clink, clink, clink* ... Murramu bristled and fidgeted, ready to leap from the embankment. All three waited, mesmerised, until from around the corner appeared a boat carrying three strange-looking men. Nganka thought of lights she had seen sailing across the cosmos at night and how she had imagined them to be people moving between the constellations. Bajal, locked into his earthly existence, saw them as members of the spirit world, transformed from stone into human form to deliver them a message. Either way, confusing as it may be, both accepted the appearance as a friendly visit and stood to their feet.

Those in the whaleboat, two men handling an ore each and James Partridge, the boss, standing at the stern, responded, with the oarsmen resting their oars and James waving. Nganka instinctively waved back. They then rowed closer, with the rowlocks clinking in their metal keepers with each stroke. More could be seen of them, with their beards, shoulder-length hair, bushman's clothing, bare feet and seasoned looks. They pulled over to the sandbar where James dipped a bucket into the stream and lifted it high to show that it held water. He repeated the motion a few times and then held it out as a gift. With gift giving common within their tribe Bajal and Nganka had no hesitation in coming forward. Bajal picked up a spear and, with Nganka and Murramu following, made down the steep track to the water's edge and waded across. Although Bajal and Nganka were oblivious to their nakedness, Nganka's sensuous form was a distraction to these men who had not seen civilisation for a month. After handing them the bucket, James took a chip of wood from a pouch strapped around his waist and, using sign language, enquired whether they knew of the tree. Bajal recognised it at once as a cedar tree, the same tree they used for making dug-out canoes. With further gestures James asked if Bajal could show him some trees. Bajal nodded and led the way into the rainforest, with Nganka and the others following. With little effort they found several of high quality. When ready to leave, James treated them to English handshakes and, although they had no idea of its significance, it conveyed a sense of warmth that lingered with them.

The men returned downstream to their camp at a deep-water landing where they had been set ashore from a schooner. By the fire that evening James noted the discovery in his diary.

4th April 1874: I have struck Red Gold. A magnificent stand of red cedar trees that will make me a fortune in the southern market! The Mossman River, only recently explored and named, is in North Queensland on the eastern coast of northern Australia. Apart from Cooktown that services the Palmer River gold rush there are no seaboard towns for hundreds of miles. I know the dangers are many but I can't let the opportunity pass me by. Although we are the first I have heard that more will soon join us. I have two reliable men who are working on a share basis …

As Bajal and Nganka anticipated, the men appeared again the next morning with the whaleboat loaded with goods. A wave from James brought them across and soon they stood in awe at the items being unloaded: tents, rifles and ammunition, timber-getting equipment, sleeping swags, clothing, food, cooking utensils and personal items. James took care of a tin trunk that contained his diary and a goat-skin satchel filled with money and papers. Bajal watched closely as James took the trunk from the boat and placed it carefully to one side. Bajal guessed that it was something important and wondered if it contained items for making magic. James then introduced himself as James Partridge and the others as Walt and Alex. Bajal and Nganka similarly introduced themselves. James and his men carried the shipment of goods to a sandbank set well back from the water's edge and then busied themselves, erecting tents and stretching a tarpaulin over a ridge pole for outdoor living. Once done Walt and Alex rowed back to the landing to get the food stores which, in addition to local game, would last them for three months.

When the men disappeared from sight James opened a trunk and took out two sets of clothes. He passed them to Bajal and Nganka, gesturing for them to dress. The pair giggled as they fumbled to dress themselves for the first time. When dressed, Nganka, like a girl seeking approval of her new ball gown, stepped back and twirled around on the sand. Bajal began clapping, followed by James, and the more they clapped the higher she stepped. She twirled gleefully till dizziness pulled her to a halt. They joined in laughter, capturing this moment that would seal their loyalty long into the future.

Although James had laid claim to the best stand of cedar on the river there lay before him the difficult and dangerous tasks of felling, logging and rafting the timber to cargo ships stationed out at sea. Also, until a bullock team came to the district they would be restricted to harvesting trees close to the river where they could be cut into lengths and rolled on skids to the river's edge.

With time at a premium work began the following day. Bajal and Nganka were not satisfied just sitting and watching from the opposite bank and, after carrying their new clothes across the river, they dressed and presented themselves. James welcomed their arrival and soon put them to work. Within a few weeks a routine evolved whereby Bajal and Nganka, when it suited them, would assist with clearing tracks in return for lunch and sometimes a little extra to take home to their camp.

The first time James fired a rifle Bajal and Nganka froze with fear as the sound ricocheted across the river to their camp. The rest of the tribe first became aware of the European's presence when further gun shots echoed up the river. One old man said the sound was so loud that it shook the dew from the grass. Another tribesman reported that he had seen one of the strangers kill a wallaby at one hundred paces by pointing a magic stick. Since then a few hunting parties had passed close by but so far none had dared make an approach.

Bajal and Nganka now crossed the river most days to lend a hand with the logging. While Nganka remained content clearing tracks and laying logs as skids, Bajal soon mastered the art of tree felling and felled as many trees as the other men. The mature trees, some one hundred feet high, crashed to the ground, taking a swathe of forest trees and wildlife in their wake. The moment the tangled mass settled on the forest floor Murramu dashed in to ferret for animals. Bajal and Nganka followed with machetes, killing possums, snakes and whatever else moved. They saw this as a bounty, an easy way to hunt, and looked forward to each day a giant of the rainforest was felled. For the men, each tree meant more money to buy provisions, enabling them to extend their stay on the river.

The rainforest began to retreat for the cool months of the year. The growth of foliage slowed, leaves fell to the ground, leaf litter dried underfoot and visibility improved, making it easier for the team to move about. The men were about to saw a tree into lengths when Nganka rushed to their side, almost hysterical and heaving for breath.

'Nganka! What is it! What's wrong!' asked James, taking her by the arm.

Walt and Alex, believing it to be the first of the inevitable native attacks, took up axes.

After a brief exchange they followed Nganka to the sandbar and found a man casually looking about the camp.

'Hello there,' called James, stepping into the open.

The Scotsman turned and returned the greeting. After introductions were passed around James quickly staked his territory.

'My claim stretches downstream for two bends, upstream for three and back to where the rainforest joins the open forest country. The perimeter is clearly marked.'

Dougal McEwan, dressed in flannel and boots, wanted to stay shy of any disagreement. 'Not a problem. Where do you suggest I set up camp?'

'Just downstream of my marker. There's good timber and it's still well above the tide margin …'

During the talk that followed Dougal revealed that he had a crew of four including himself, ample equipment and enough provisions to last four months.

James noted his interest in Bajal and Nganka and, as he was about to leave, cautioned him, 'They're not all as friendly as these two. Best to make friends rather than foes.'

James routinely took his diary from the tin trunk and updated it before breakfast. Even if he had nothing of importance to note he placed a tick to keep tally of the date. He conducted business with the outside world through the Bank of New South Wales and Pacific Stevedoring in Cooktown and needed to keep track of the date to meet scheduled visits by supply vessels and cargo ships that freighted cedar logs south.

Dougal McEwan visited again, this time to express a concern.

'A new crew arrived on the river last week. Their overseer has staked a claim downriver from me and says they're going to log the whole river. Says they're backed by venture capitalists in Sydney, that they have experience on the Clarence and other rivers in New South Wales. Apparently he has a big camp with several axemen and a cook. I'm worried he might try to push me out.'

'He can't do that!' interjected James. 'Crown land is up for grabs to whoever makes the first claim. That is, providing they've paid their licence fee.'

'I paid mine at Cooktown,' Dougal hastened to say.

'Then you have no problem. Have you marked your boundary?'

'That I have.'

'Well, tell him to go to blazes.'

'But it's my four against his eight and I imagine they're well armed!'

'Your four and my five gives us nine, which will be a fair match. And I might be able to muster some reinforcements,' he said, referring to Bajal's tribe in an offhanded manner. 'I expect this capitalist stooge has pulled his men out of Sydney and, if so, most of them will be tossers who'll run at the first shot. Our best bet is to join forces and let him know we're watching.'

Dougal, a hardy Highlander, knew he was in the right company and readily agreed to the pact.

CHAPTER 2

James woke to a clear, crisp Sabbath morning with gaily coloured parrots chattering in the blossoms of the trees above. He kindled the fire, put a billy on to boil and set about trimming his beard by the reflection in a mirror, tinged with yellow. He recalled earlier days and questioned how life's journey had brought him to one of the most remote places in the Australian colonies.

He brought to mind an early memory when, as a six-year-old, Selene, his sixteen-year-old live-in governess, brushed his auburn locks, morning, noon and night. So gentle, so caring. He touched his hair with the tips of his fingers. Even at that tender age, he had loved her. Selene devoted herself to his care till, at the age of twelve, he, James Partridge, an only child, was sent to King's College, Sydney, to receive the best education and to be groomed as one of the gentry. Although only a carriage ride from his home and Selene, no visits home were allowed till the end of the first term. The moment the carriage drew to a halt he rushed inside, greeted his parents with the formality they expected and then asked for Selene. His father, William Partridge, owner of the prestigious Partridge & Company, Timber Merchants, anticipated the request and took James aside. He explained that Selene was now a parlour maid and that he expected him not to associate with her. James took exception, disobeyed his father and next morning found Selene alone, polishing silver candlesticks in the sun room. At his approach she looked downwards to avoid his advance.

'Selene!' he almost shouted as he rushed forward. 'Selene, I love you,' he murmured, putting his arms around her and pressing his face against her cheek.

Selene had been forbidden to speak to James and, as the sole provider for her mother and five siblings, she needed to heed the master's word. She held James' hands tenderly and explained the situation. James remained incredulous that his father could not understand the depth of his feeling for Selene. The vacation remained one of torment, with his hatred of his father growing by the day. When he returned to school he kept the dream alive night and day and ignored his school studies as a means of retribution against his father. Each vacation thereafter was met by his father's reminder and Selene's explanation of why she could not show affection towards him. At age fifteen, James returned home at the end of the first term to find that Selene's employment had been terminated. He confronted his father, demanding Selene's home address, and when his father refused he struck him across the head with a fire poker and fled, never to return. He hated his father and, as he had done since the day of his departure, wished his father was dead.

Now in his early thirties James still dreamed of her. The image he had formed as a child remained indelibly imprinted in his mind. Since leaving home other women had made approaches, only to be brushed aside. This fixation had stifled his life and it seemed he was destined to remain a recluse, hiding away in rough timber camps. Sadly, his mother, Marie, also remained unreconciled. All she wanted for James was happiness and cared not that Selene was a member of the lower class. She thought Selene to be of good character and had never forgiven William for his action. James had left without a parting word and she stilled pined to hear his voice.

Laughter from across the river stirred James from his wistful thoughts. There were four black people: Bajal, Nganka and two strangers giggling like children by the hut. The visitors were both women and naked except for a headband holding their hair in place. At seeing James, Nganka waved for him to join them. He waved back, bundled two sets of clothes under his arm and crossed the river. The greetings were profuse, with Nganka introducing Marku and Dari with the intimacy that attaches to special friends. The newcomers obviously had knowledge of him because curiosity rather than fear framed their expressions. The women came close and, when Marku touched his white skin, James felt a desire to reach out for her but quickly covered himself by handing them the clothing. With Nganka's help they slid into the clothes and thanked him with their poses and gleeful smiles. Nganka, using English words she had learned from James, explained the family relationship between them.

James set about establishing a rapport that he hoped would eventually extend to the whole tribe and place him in a commanding position in the valley. Using sign language and Nganka as a vocal intermediary, they managed a meaningful interchange. In fact it became clear that both parties wanted to foster a lasting friendship. A large *jadi*, sand goanna, that the women had caught somewhere along the track lay roasting on the coals, and at lunchtime Nganka expertly carved the white flesh and served it with *dukal* fruit and *kalirr* bush cherries. Following lunch they moved to the shade of a tree where James learned more about the tribe: its size, location of camps and possible attitude towards the presence of white people. Marku engaged James constantly and would have stayed the night if Dari had not insisted they return home before dark.

When they entered their tribal village a commotion erupted as tribespeople, young and old, gathered about to inspect the mysterious regalia worn by the women. While most realised that the garments had come from the white-coloured people cutting the logs, their curiosity extended to who or what were these beings that had suddenly appeared in their valley. Marku and Dari set about allaying their fears, telling that the newcomers had the blessing of the spirits. They paraded their newfound clothes as proof of their goodness and told of other treasures they had seen at Nganka's camp and on the sandbar across the river. Marku lived in her clothes almost constantly, day and night, often pressing her face to a shirt sleeve to remind her of James. Dari, savvy in the ways of women and courtship, encouraged Marku to explore her feelings and perhaps arrange another meeting with James. Talk of *waybala*, white person, now became a theme of conversation amongst members of the community.

CHAPTER 3

James, with his rifle in hand, crossed the river, spoke to Bajal and Nganka and then continued downstream to make himself known to the overseer of the new gang of cutters whom he called the Capitalist. He left the open gum forest of Bajal's camp, entered the nearby rainforest and followed the river, passing through a mosaic of shadows. He paused opposite Dougal's camp and peered through the foliage to check Dougal's progress. Several logs lay on the sandbar ready for rafting and James guessed that Dougal would soon have enough for a shipment. He continued on to the Capitalist's territory and halted when opposite his camp, where a shirtless man, presumably the cook, knelt by the river cleaning a pot. James called an 'Ahoy there' to alert him and then crossed. The cook had met Dougal previously and guessed the visitor must be the cutter from further upstream. He seemed pleased to see a new face and spoke freely of the headway his gang had made since arrival. James declined a cup of tea and, after gathering all the information he thought the man could provide, asked of the overseer's whereabouts. The cook pointed to a track leading into the rainforest and said the men were up there 'rolling logs'. James found them wrestling with a huge log and wondered if, by manpower alone, they would manage to get it to the river. When the overseer came over, James introduced himself.

'I'm James from upriver. Guess you're the overseer?'

'That's right. Bill Rowland.' He extended a hand of friendship.

'Nice log.' James pointed to the rich red grain of its butt end.

'Only one of many to come. This country will be cleaned out by the time we're finished,' said the overseer, gloating about his intentions.

'Where will you log next?' queried James.

'Oh, downstream to the landing and then upstream from your camp. We've got to fell it before others arrive, otherwise there'll be strife. Too many logging the same patch never works. That happened on the Clarence; cutters poaching and setting rafts adrift … Then there's the blacks. They never learn and we've had to shoot them in the past. Not sure what they're like here but we're ready for them if they want trouble—'

James cut short the overseer's unwanted comments. 'When do you plan to send your first consignment?'

'Probably in a couple of weeks' time and monthly after that. What's your plan?'

'I've arranged for a lighter to tow our first lot out of the heads and load to the *Aquarius* on the thirtieth of the month. She's a 180-ton steamer and usually runs to schedule.'

The overseer then let slip something of interest. 'We're financed by Matheson and Son, wholesale timber merchants of Sydney. They're good operators and pay well.'

James took the opportunity to ask, 'Have you heard of Partridge & Co, Timber Merchants?'

'Yeah. The old geezer is filthy rich. He and his wife are perched up on the North Shore with no one to leave it to.'

James, for the first time since fleeing his parent's home and forgoing the fortune he would have inherited, felt a pang of regret; not for his father or the money but for his mother's sake. He struggled with the thought for a few moments while the overseer took time out to lift his trouser leg and scrape a leech from his shin with the blade of a machete.

Their attention then turned to the men handling the big log. James thought they looked a motley lot. The man closest, raw boned and underfed, wheezed each time he took weight on his bar; the scantily clad man next to him bore scars from the prison lash. The third along had long suffered a travesty of birth with a liver-coloured birth mark covering most of his face. The fourth, a gaunt little man with glassy eyes and a tobacco-stained beard, appeared ready for the bone yard, while the fifth, a strapping brute of a man with a scowl, bowed his bar with each lift. A self-appointed foreman with a throaty voice stood at the far end, calling instructions and grunting each time the men took the strain. The overseer, one of those brash and demanding men, offered no help and watched while the log was manoeuvred into position. James acknowledged the men's effort with a nod, told the overseer he would be in touch and headed back across the river. As he walked the path homewards he considered Matheson and Son's gang of men. No doubt for one reason or another most, if not all, were social outcasts; people squeezed from society and seeking refuge in obscurity. He retracted his notion of them being tossers and instead saw them as men of broken spirit who posed no threat to his or Dougal McEwan's interests.

The first ever consignment of red cedar logs lay ready to be shipped from the Mossman River. The sawn logs strewn on the sandbar at James' camp represented three months' work. Walt and Alex branded the ends of the logs with the letters 'J P'. Next morning the rafting began. Logs were rolled into the river, chained together and set afloat. With Murramu standing at the bow of the whaleboat the team, rowing and poling, managed to raft the first load to the landing where a ship waited.

'Ahoy there,' shouted James when the skipper appeared. All went aboard the steamer and were greeted by him and his crew of two. The skipper, equipped for rafting, supplied additional chains needed for rafting at sea. They also borrowed his row boat and, within an hour, headed back up the river. The team worked as two crews, with Walt and Alex manning the whaleboat and James, together with Bajal and Nganka, using the row boat. As the bundles of logs arrived the ship's crew tethered them to trees on the bank. During the day and a half it took to shift the full load, those at Dougal McEwan's and the Capitalist's camps watched keenly. The landing, two miles upstream from the river's mouth and tidal, had never before been used as a wharf. Prior to the timber cutters the only white visitors had been a couple of explorers who made brief visits. The high south bank, treed with wattle, became the first established access point to the valley. Both James and Walt had rafted cedar on the Tweed River in northern New South Wales and began assembling the rafts. The largest logs were laid side by side, smaller ones crossways, and then another layer of large logs on top. Chains were wrapped around each raft and twitched tightly. Murramu, sensing the presence of a crocodile, whined each time Bajal dived under a raft to pass a chain. That night the whites slept on the foredeck under the cover of a tarpaulin while Bajal, Nganka and Murramu slept under the stars on the bare boards of the aft deck.

The skipper woke to a bright moon at 4.00 am and sounded reveille with a brisk call. He had not slept well and held concerns about hauling several large rafts to sea in rough weather. With a steamer appointed to be at Snapper Island to take the cargo, a change of plan could only be made if the conditions became impossible. Bajal ignored the roar from a crocodile nearby and volunteered to step to the rafts and secure them to the ship's stern. The *chug, chug* of the ship as it steamed downstream at dawn woke the whole river, including a mob of Aborigines camped on a sandbar at its mouth. Upon rounding the last corner the skipper spotted them, called an alarm and then raced to the wheel house and grabbed his rifle.

'Take cover!' he shouted, putting the rifle to his shoulder.

'No! Wait! Stop!' screamed Nganka.

James took her cue. 'Hold your fire, Skip!'

With the strong current pushing the rafts towards the stern there could be no turning back. The skipper yelled to the engineman, 'Hold your speed o'wise we'll be smashed.' He turned to the helmsman. 'Stay your course!'

Nganka, now hysterical, pleaded, 'No shoot my people!'

Some of the men among the family group on the sandbar raised their spears which, if thrown, could well make the distance to the ship. It seemed there would be carnage with deaths on both sides and the rafting aborted with the rafts floating out to sea. Nganka heard her people's excited voices and shouted for them to stay calm. James, understanding a few words of what she said, appealed to the skipper to hold his fire. Nganka then took the initiative. She ran along the deck to the skipper and bravely put her hand over the muzzle of the rifle barrel. The blacks, all relatives of Nganka, heeded her action, with the men easing their stance. The engineman held the speed, with the propeller churning the water to froth and the helmsman holding his course as they sailed through the heads. The blacks watched incredulously as this magic of the white man towed logs to the open sea and set a course northwards. James thanked Nganka for her action which he believed had prevented a bloodbath.

Before the silhouettes of the blacks fell from sight a new threat arose. The south-easterly trade wind began blowing a gale. White caps, far out to sea, told of a huge swell. The skipper kept to himself for a few minutes and then spoke with James. His thoughts were twofold: to try to re-enter the river, risking the wild surf crashing the rafts into the ship, or chance a crossing to Snapper Island? James wished to continue but left the decision to the skipper. The skipper cast the helmsman a glance and received a shrug in reply.

The trip that normally took four hours developed into a nightmare. The engineman, a seasoned seaman, made a run for the island. He stoked the furnace, raised the steam pressure as high as he dared and fully released steam to the pistons. The *thump, thump* of the pistons rattled the engine on its blocks, threatening to topple it into the bilge. The packing gland on the propeller shaft ran hot, and each time the propeller lifted above the surf it roared a hideous howl. The engineman knew well the dangers but they were beyond the point of return. The helmsman held tight to the wheel, struggling to hold the rudder against the undercurrent of the ten-foot swell. Breaking waves crashed broadside into the ship, causing it to tilt precariously. Sea spray smashed against the wheelhouse glass. The rafts, being dragged to the portside by the surge of the swell, made it nigh on impossible to hold the ship on course. Each time the ship crested a wave and then fell into the trough, the planking of the hull groaned from the impact. James' crew, with Bajal clutching Murramu, huddled behind the wheelhouse, holding a lifeline. They battled for four hours into the journey with no reprieve. If the rafts were cut loose their chances of survival would increase tenfold.

James shouted to the skipper above the siren of the wind, the crashing sea and the roar of the engine, 'Cut them loose. Let them go, Skip!'

The skipper made his way forward, grappling a lifeline to stay upright. To go aft and release the chains held its own danger. They could lose a man overboard. The skipper withheld his reply till the ship rode the crest of a wave and then called back, 'We'll take the chance! This old girl's got enough grunt!'

After they had battled the treacherous conditions for six hours, Snapper Island loomed large before them. The skipper took the ship to seaward of the island rather than risk the passage between it and the mainland. He navigated past the island and, when entering the calm water on its northern side, the engineman throttled back the engine. The helmsman hung to the wheel exhausted and the chains holding the rafts slackened. In a sheltered cove lay a steamer, anchored in deep water, ready to load James' cargo and ship it to Sydney. Loading continued throughout the night and by midday the next day the cargo had been made safe on board. Documents were exchanged and both vessels set sail in fair weather.

CHAPTER 4

Following dispatch of the first load of logs James left Bajal and Nganka at the camp while he, together with Walt and Alex, rowed downstream to meet a supply ship. Upon arrival he left the men to wait for the ship and set out to explore the countryside. With a rifle in his hand and a long bush knife hanging from his belt, he stepped ashore and disappeared into the scrubby mulga. A flight of ducks caught his attention, leading him to a lagoon brimming with wildlife. Ducks paddled amongst the water weed, ducking their heads and feeding. Rather than having a shot James leant against a paperbark tree, watching the ripples and sparkles. Waterlilies lay open, bearing their petals to the sun, while dragonflies rested on lily pads. A jabiru, with patience found only in nature, stalked small fish in the shallows. James stood absorbed in this wonderland of nature until a flock of sulphur-crested cockatoos settled in the treetops above and screeched their raucous call. On lifting his hand from the paperbark he noticed that the Aborigines had judiciously harvested strips of its bark for making gunyahs. As he turned to leave, two white cranes lifted off and settled a few paces further away. It was noontime and, being thirsty, James moved up the bank and dug a hole in the sandy soil with his bush knife. He then brushed his hair aside, cupped his hands, and drank from the pooled water. For lunch he ate a piece of corned meat he took from his shirt pocket.

He left the lagoon and trekked towards the mountain range to the west. After skirting a high peak he crossed a freshly burnt area that the blacks had burnt while hunting and then ascended a ridge. At the top a panoramic view of the valley stretched before him. The patchwork of the valley floor exceeded his expectations, with thousands of acres of fertile agricultural and grazing land lying before him. More astounding was the fact that he was the first non-Aboriginal person to command this view. He breathed deeply to appreciate this unique moment. In his exuberance he began partitioning the landscape, imagining where the town and farms might be and a network of roads connecting people. *James Partridge,* he thought, *explorer and business man. This is your place in the world. From here you can build to great heights and earn a name.* He even thought of names for the town: Jamestown, Partridgeville.

He stood there as a thirty-three-year-old, dressed in rags, casting back to earlier times when he had struggled to convince bank managers to finance his forays into the timber industry. He could now fulfil his ambition, aspire to heights of wealth equal to that of Partridge & Company, Timber Merchants. He let escape from his mind all the tough times and near failures he had experienced. There could be no mistaking it this time. This was *his* valley, the gateway to his life's dreams. In his reverie he thought of Selene, of how he could send for her, bring her to his side, and how they could live together happily in this tropical paradise. Every person in the Bank of New South Wales holding the position of senior clerk or above would have knowledge of Partridge & Company and, as a courtesy, could trace Selene's whereabouts if she held an account with them. He had resisted this avenue in the past due to his utter contempt for his father but now considered making an enquiry. His blue eyes twinkled in the stardust of his dreams. He remained locked into this flight of fancy until he realised the lateness of the hour. The schooner would have berthed and his men and the ship's crew would be supping from a keg of rum. Sure enough, upon his return to the landing he found them inebriated and full of merriment. He joined them for a drink or two and then retired to his swag to savour his discovery.

Walt, Alex and the ship's crew presented themselves as a dreary lot the next morning. However, with the need to catch the tide the men unloaded the cargo early while James and the skipper attended to the paper work. James handed the skipper cheques for the supplies and shipping plus a sealed envelope addressed to the manager of the Bank of New South Wales, Cooktown.

Dougal's gang was the next to send a shipment, followed soon after by the Capitalist. Thereafter, regular consignments of log cedar were exported to destinations as far away as London. Mossman River cedar became known for its close grain and intense colour and the cutters earned reputations as dependable suppliers. By the onset of the storm season hundreds of thousands of super feet of log timber had been felled and shipped. James made the following entry in his diary:

22nd December 1874: We are busy putting together the last shipment for the year. The summer rain will soon be here and we'll not be able to work for three months. Apparently the river rages with flood waters and any logs left will be swept away. The natives have been peaceable and the young native couple working for me have been particularly helpful. The boy's mother visits regularly and seems keen to join their camp. I plan to move my camp across the river to high ground for the wet season. Will visit the bank manager in Cooktown to sort the finances. Expect to find a healthy balance in the account.

Alex gave notice that he would not be returning the following year. He enjoyed the work and the challenge but had difficulty coping with the isolation and lack of social contact. Walt, a confirmed bachelor, agreed to stay on. James spoke with Bajal and Nganka, who wished to continue working for food and handy items, and accepted them as a replacement for Alex. When it came time for the men to leave he wrote each of them a handsome cheque. Walt would stay in Cooktown till the end of March and then return. Alex thought he might try his hand at prospecting for gold on the Palmer River goldfield. Bajal and Nganka accompanied James to the landing to take delivery of supplies that would last the three of them till the end of March.

By coincidence or otherwise, Marku and Dari arrived early on the morning that James proposed shifting camp across the river and erecting his tent beside Bajal and Nganka's hut. They brought their clothes tucked under their arm and carried dilly bags of food. They then dressed, with Dari paying little attention to her appearance. Marku, on the other hand, took time to dress. She pulled on the trousers, carefully tucked the shirt under the waist band and then pulled the belt tight about her slim waist. Dari helped with her head band, drawing Marku's hair back from her face and placing the band snugly across her forehead. Dari then took Marku's hands, stood at arm's length and admired her stepdaughter, whose dark eyes revealed a woman in love.

All joined in the shift across the river. Several loads of camp items and timber equipment were ferried across in the boat and hauled up the steep bank. By lunchtime three calico tents with heavy tarpaulins above for added protection had been erected—one for James' sleeping quarters and two to house the provisions. They hoisted another tarpaulin to cover a dining area, set with a tea chest as a table and packing crates as chairs. That afternoon they all went fishing, using hooks, lines and sinkers from stock brought across the river. James thoroughly enjoyed himself. These carefree people accepted him as family, showing him their way of life and sharing the experience with the occasional smile and giggle.

For the evening meal the girls prepared fish, eel and turtle, while James cooked fire-baked bread called damper and served it with syrup. James filled a kerosene lamp, lit the wick and hung it above the makeshift table as a special treat. However the others, wary of the shaded light that burnt with a strange smell, sat cross-legged around the open fire. James happily joined in and for the first time felt a true nearness to these people. Later, after relishing the damper and syrup, they sat till late, talking, humming traditional tunes and sometimes just sitting in silence. When Bajal and Nganka retired to their hut, Marku and Dari settled by the fire. James lay awake on his swag in his tent till the early hours of the morning, sorting the thoughts passing through his mind. The next day Marku and Dari left it till the last moment before leaving for the Jinkalmu village. With the evening shadows beginning to fall they bid goodbye, with Marku casting James a longing look and shedding tears as she hugged Bajal and Nganka. Dari then shepherded Marku away in her arms.

The schooner *Pearl Shell*, under full sail, set a brisk pace as it passed Snapper Island, slicing through a slight ocean swell. A pod of dolphins came alongside and followed the ship till their interest took them elsewhere. James stood on the foredeck and contemplated the business he would have to attend to when ashore at Cooktown.

Upon arrival he hailed a coach driver who recommended a hotel close to the business centre. The receptionist, buxom and cheap, thought him a grubby bushman and booked him into a cheap room at the rear of the hotel and insisted he pay in advance. James settled into the room and then took a hot tub in the bathroom allocated to those in the lower-class rooms. He didn't care that the tin-clad bathroom had no roof and only a hessian drape for a door. His first hot bath for nearly twelve months felt so good that he refilled the tub and soaked while musing about his time on the river.

For the evening meal and breakfast he sat at the worker's table at the rear of the hotel. With plenty of barber shops in the main street of this frontier town he soon found himself shorn of his sprawling hair and his beard removed. Further down the street the owner of a workman's clothing shop greeted him with a big smile as he entered, looking tattered and torn. Within an hour the owner had outfitted him with new shirts, trousers, boots and bathroom needs. James scouted about the town, lunched in the shade of a tree by the harbour, and then set out to buy a suit to wear when visiting the bank manager.

Sedgwick & Co, stockists of gentleman's wear, lured him inside with their display of mannequins dressed with the latest European fashions. The attendant thought him a man of empty pockets but gave of his time. To his surprise James took the lead, sorting through the garments and asking discerning questions. The attendant agreed with James' choice of a fawn corduroy suit, white cotton shirts, blue cravat and black shoes. He was even more surprised when James paid him with musty £10 notes. At the sight of the money he suggested James might like a hat to accompany his apparel. James declined. He had not worn a hat since leaving King's College.

Upon returning to the hotel James entered by the rear tradesman gate rather than the main hallway. He sat on his bed and chewed soft pumice stone to clean his teeth. At mealtime he styled his hair with a comb and donned his best wear. The waiter in the first-class dining room received him as one of the gentry, pulling his chair back and placing a napkin on his lap. He chose an expensive wine from the list, ate heartily and paid the waiter, placing an extra shilling in his hand. The female staff serving breakfast the next morning were drawn by his cultured appearance. They whispered in the kitchen, wondering if he travelled alone and was in need of company. He bought a copy of the *Cooktown Herald* and read about strife on the goldfield and the mounted police using gunfire to disperse Aborigines in the region.

After wandering the ant-bed pavements for a couple of hours, James entered the Bank of New South Wales. The middle-aged bank clerk brought the appointments book to the counter, but when James gave his name as James Partridge he excused himself and soon returned, saying that the manager would see him now. The manager, having met James before, greeted him with gusto.

'Pleased to see you, James. How was the trip?'

'Fine. Fair skies and a sober skipper always makes a difference.'

The manager waved him over to the ledger desk where a large, leather-bound ledger lay open at James' page. They traced through the transactions since his last visit, checking if the amounts deposited by wholesale merchants in Sydney agreed with James' estimates.

'They've left me short on every transaction,' said James, taking his diary from his satchel. 'Look at this. In every instance they've underpaid me by about ten percent.'

'How is that?' queried the manager.

James explained that the amount payable was calculated by taking the length of a log and the average diameter and applying a standard formula.

'Then how?' asked the manager.

'Because they're robbers. The price per cube is set, but they crib on the measurements, and once the log is milled or on sold there's no come back. And to make things worse I've already paid my two workers their share based on my calculation.'

The banker thought for a moment and then suggested hiring an independent assessor. James cast him a glance which clearly told that one fox in the henhouse was enough.

'Then, should we take them to task about the payments?' he asked.

'No, that would be throwing good money to the wind,' countered James. He put forward an alternative. 'For years I've thought of marketing the logs myself; either store them in a logging yard and go to Sydney once a year to supervise the sale or, better still, get a buyer to come north. The Mossman River cedar is superior to most other that is being logged at present and should command a premium. This in itself should be enough inducement for them to send a buyer. They're filthy rich as you well know!'

The banker, taking the last comment as a reference to Partridge & Company, abided by the bank's policy of not divulging information about account holders. Instead he reiterated the bank's offer to help where it could. James understood and digressed to other matters, such as letters of credit and what he expected to harvest next season. They conversed at length and James invited the manager to lunch with him at his hotel. They enjoyed an extended lunch at a corner table, consuming a few bottles of wine before the manager excused himself. James stayed on, drinking alone till soon after the evening meal when he put himself to bed.

Next morning he visited Pacific Stevedoring to be greeted by the manager sitting on a stack of barrels. Business had been good both ways, with all provisions arriving safely and prompt payment being made. James told of the new arrangement, with two natives replacing Alex, and that he might hire more natives, so the amounts ordered might fluctuate.

James left Pacific Stevedoring and set about finalising his shopping. He bought a new diary and pen and ink for himself and then thought of his friends back at the camp. For Nganka, Marku and Dari he bought shirts and trousers, hair clips and a mirror each. With Bajal showing so much interest in axes he bought him the best axe available.

At first light the following morning he sauntered down to the wharf, carrying his trunk on his shoulder, and boarded the *Pearl Shell*. When sailing to Cooktown a downwind had delivered them to the port before nightfall but returning against a headwind they had to overnight at Snapper Island. James could not believe his luck when he found the beach strewn with pieces of coral and old shells washed in from the Great Barrier Reef. He pawed through the mass of marine remnants, scraping up handfuls of exquisitely shaped shells, and filled a large sack. Although many of the shells were pitted and broken, most were types not found on mainland beaches. This collection would give the women countless hours of pleasure, making adornments for themselves and others. The shells, not available to others in the valley, would elevate their status and provide material they could trade.

CHAPTER 5

While Christmas was blessed with fine weather, the new year brought three months of relentless rain, creating havoc for cedar getting on the Mossman River—rain that was measured in feet rather than inches. In the wake of the annual monsoon rains the mighty north branch of the river roared from the mountain gorge, cascading seawards. The south branch, crazed by swirling currents, spread across the landscape as a sea of muddy brown. Wildlife scattered, scrambling to treetops and racing to high ground. Thanks to Bajal's long-range weather forecast James' last consignment of logs had been shipped and he moved to Bajal's side of the river a few days before the first flood. Dougal McEwan also took Bajal's advice and sent his logs the same time as James. The Capitalist, following greed rather than taking the word of a black man, found himself caught with £17,000 of log timber still on the riverbank. The sudden rise of the river caught him by surprise, leaving barely enough time to move his camp to high ground. Most of the logs were swept to sea, while those that were left lay tangled in the rainforest.

Bajal and Nganka's camp, although well above flood height, did not escape unscathed. James' tent, beside their hut, became sodden during heavy downpours, making it necessary for him to sleep beneath their thatched roof some nights. A third of the flour and rice was lost, and with no scheduled shipments to the river till after the wet season they had to live off the land for much of the time. On sunny days when the rain eased and the sun beat down, the three of them busied themselves hunting, gathering and preparing food for storage. Marku and Dari visited occasionally on fine days but, given the uncertainty of the weather, seldom stayed the night. During this time of sitting out the wet James learned the value of *just being* and not feeling the need to make every moment count. James and Nganka continued practising their language skills, playing games of who could remember what of each other's language, while Bajal remained content to hone the blade of his axe.

The beginning of April signalled the end of the wet, and the moment the river level fell low enough James moved camp back across the river and the ringing of axes sounded in the rainforest. Walt arrived soon after, and then Dougal and his original crew a few days later. The Capitalist, arriving late and with five replacement men, grumbled about his bad luck and the reprimand he had received from head office. Before long the camps were re-established, with the routine of felling, logging and shipping in full swing and good money being made.

On a cool morning in May Nganka called to James to come quickly and see. A burly man with a forest of red hair and a full beard stepped from a row boat at James' camp. A lad, fifteen years of age, sat at the stern.

'Top of the day to you,' called the visitor as he came across the sand in blucher boots only partly laced. His smiling face showed a man of heart.

'And to you,' replied James with a note of pleasure at meeting a man with such an open expression.

'That's my boy,' he said when James glanced towards the boat. 'Shaun!' he called, 'Come along.'

The lad, followed by a crossbred collie-wolfhound dog, leapt from the boat and hurried to the Irishman's side. James introduced himself and Nganka. The Irishman did likewise, introducing himself as Alroy Higgins and insisting that Shaun shake hands with James.

'I'm looking for work,' he explained. 'Have a bullock team as strong as anything in the colony. Eight pairs of sturdy bullocks in good condition. I have them in Cooktown at present, but if there's work to be had me and Shaun can float them down on a ship.'

James wanted to hug the man because with a bullock team they could haul logs from deep within the forest. This boisterous Irishman, his son, the son's dog and the sixteen bullocks were a blessing. Nganka had the good sense to stir the fire and brew a billycan of tea for the men while they sat on a log discussing the proposal.

'You're the furthest up the river so I seen you last. The others think that five shillings a cubic yard is fair.'

James, having experience in logging with bullocks on the Tweed River, readily accepted the deal. He shook Alroy's hand and could hardly keep the smile from his face.

They continued the discussion into the evening and spoke of, among other things, the need for a paddock to graze the bullocks. James told of a place upstream that might suit and agreed to take Alroy there in the morning. Alroy snored so loud during the night that James and Walt had to shift their swags to the other end of the sandbar.

Bajal and Nganka came across early and, after sharing breakfast, Nganka asked Shaun, 'Your dog. Name.'

Shaun whistled his dog as a shepherd would and introduced him as Cobber. With Bajal in the lead the party followed a path upstream, swiping at overhanging branches with machetes as they went. Within a mile they came to a well-grassed clearing. Alroy scouted about and then reported with a note of jubilation, 'This is perfect. Three hundred acres, well grassed and boxed in by a deep water hole at the river end, thick rainforest along one side and a scrubby creek on the other. We can set up camp at the narrow neck leading to the open country, and with the bells on no bullock will be able to slip by unnoticed.'

Alroy returned from Cooktown two weeks later with his and Shaun's worldly possessions and sixteen bullocks aboard a lighter. This was the biggest development since the cutters' arrival on the river, and all three camps pitched in to help. Alroy and Shaun unloaded the bullocks across rickety planking. Their camp equipment and three months' provisions, together with yokes and chains for the bullocks, were loaded into whaleboats.

Alroy spoke to Shaun about overlanding the bullocks to the camp and then joined those in the boats. Shaun, with self-confidence unsurpassed by anybody his age, looped a rope around a bullock's neck and handed it to Bajal to take the lead. He and Nganka would follow behind the mob. Bajal, never having seen anything larger than a wallaby, hesitated till Shaun crawled between the bullock's legs to show he had nothing to fear. Bajal chose the route, picking his way around patches of rainforest and cutting across open woodlands. The camp lay on the other side of the river, so the bullocks crossed at a natural ford a little downstream from the camp. The cloven hoof prints they left behind would soon become of interest to the local Aborigines. By the time of their arrival the men had assembled the camp. They departed soon after, leaving Alroy and Shaun to put bells on the cattle and bed them down. Cobber barked during the night when the restless cattle came close to the camp.

Production tripled, with Alroy, Shaun and the team arriving early and leaving late six days a week while logging James' patch. Alroy told James not once but a dozen times, 'Be Jesus, this is good business!'

Shaun loved his dog and the bullocks and immersed himself in their company. When a bullock lay down to rest Shaun would lie beside it with his head resting on its flank. He and Cobber would rise before first light, follow the ringing of the bells and have the bullocks in the camp by the time Alroy had prepared breakfast. When talking to others, Alroy always referred to Shaun as 'my boy' but the truth was otherwise. Alroy held a secret so close to his heart that not even Shaun knew.

With the shipments of logs becoming more regular and logs from deep within the rainforest being larger and of better quality, the reputation of Mossman River red cedar became a topic of conversation amongst the southern merchants. Marie Partridge, wife of William Partridge, turned pale when she unwittingly heard that her son, James Partridge, was one of the cedar getters on the Mossman River. Since the day James had left at age fifteen she had received no word of him. She grieved the loss every day and prayed for his return every night. She wished to send a message, and even wrote a note, but eventually tossed it into the hearth and watched her words burn to tinder.

William Partridge's iron grip on family affairs choked her every attempt at raising the matter. He must surely know because others in the timber trade know. How can a father turn his back on his only son? Is he blind or has he not the courage to face the truth? From that day Marie kept her own watch, buying newspapers, reading every mention of cedar and cedar getters and secretly storing items that referred to the Mossman River.

Bujur, Marku's warrior father, passed away sooner than expected and, after a grieving period, Marku and Dari found themselves drifting from the tribe. Although they followed the others on their annual walkabout they frequently visited Bajal and Nganka's camp, which was no more than a few hours walk from any of the tribe's scattered camps.

They generally stayed for two or three days and spent most of their time at James' camp across the river. With Nganka and the men working full time to meet their quota of logs there was always plenty of cooking and washing to be done. Washing James' clothes became a labour of love for Marku. She looked forward to taking a tub to the riverside, washing and scrubbing his clothes and then hanging them on bushes to dry. Later in the day she would take them to his tent where she would sit on his swag, fold each garment neatly and hold it to her cheek before putting it away. When finished she often lay in the tent alone, imagining that James was there and that they were making love.

Dari understood Marku's need and stayed clear, busying herself cooking and cleaning. When James twisted his ankle and had to rest, the full extent of her devotion became apparent to the others by the way she nursed and comforted him. She made it known to James that she wanted to stay in his tent at night but he thought it better she sleep in the hut at Bajal's camp across the river. Walt, who had worked with James for years, knew him well but could not understand why he had not taken a woman in all that time. For his part, three months in Cooktown during the wet season, though leaving him almost penniless, saw him return a rejuvenated man. He noted that when Marku and Dari shamelessly stripped off their clothes to swim and frolic in the river James turned the other way. He hoped that James would let go of his inhibitions and take Marku as his lover.

CHAPTER 6

Shaun jerked into life when he heard a commotion outside the tent. Cowbells rattled and Cobber barked. He scrambled in the dark to find a rifle and pushed the tent flap open to step into the moonlight. He shouted to wake Alroy and then headed towards the river, fearing a pack of dingos was attacking the bullocks.

Alroy, still half asleep, bumbled about pulling on his boots as Shaun careered across the paddock towards the sound of the bells. As he drew close he saw the bullocks stampeding his way, with Cobber criss-crossing in front of them, trying to steady their pace. He shouted to Cobber who returned a bark without turning his head. If the bullocks were to break through the narrow neck of the paddock then, in their state of panic, they might never be seen again. Shaun fired a shot to try to head them off. He then raced towards the mob, shouting commands to Cobber as he went. Cobber understood, chopping and weaving and snapping at the muzzles of the leaders, exposing himself to being trampled underfoot. As they approached the camp at full gallop Alroy stood in their path and, in the half dark, risked being crushed. Cobber, who had been trained to work cattle without barking, suddenly barked wildly, giving all to steady the herd before they raged through the camp in their blind rush to escape. Alroy stood defiant as the lead bullock charged towards him. 'Father, have mercy!' he bellowed, thinking his time had come. Fortunately, the big roan bullock recognised the voice and swerved to the left, taking the herd with him. Cobber, knowing that once the lead turned the herd would follow, stretched himself to his full extent, hardly touching the ground as he fleeted through the moonlight trying to save the herd.

'Bend them. Bring them around. Bring them around, boy,' screamed Shaun to Cobber as he followed up the rear. Cobber heard Shaun, swung to the outside and worked the bullocks wide, bringing them around in a full arc. Cobber had saved the herd and Alroy's livelihood for, if they had escaped, they would have surely been lost.

Shaun called to Cobber and when he heard no bark in reply he ran to where he had last seen him. Cobber lay on the ground with blood oozing from a gash in his neck. They carried him back to the camp and, by the light of a lamp, discovered that the top of his neck had been sheared by a spear.

'Father, have mercy on him,' whispered Alroy through clenched teeth.

Shaun cradled Cobber and, through his tears, murmured, 'Don't die. Please don't die.'

As the breaking dawn cast the first light of day they gave Cobber water to drink.

'The bullocks, Dad,' said Shaun with a grimace. 'Have they killed the bullocks?'

Alroy insisted Shaun stay with Cobber and went to investigate. He found the mob, frightened and huddled in a corner of the paddock. He spoke to them as he approached, letting them know that the danger had passed. He counted them in the gathering light and could only account for fifteen. He sorted through them by name and found that Taurus was missing. Alroy cried when, an hour later, he found Taurus speared and partly butchered. He vowed vengeance for the barbaric act. Shaun wept inconsolably when Alroy, still shaking with grief and vengeance, took Shaun in his arms and told of the death.

The next day Alroy and Shaun walked to James' camp where Alroy told what had happened and that he planned to bring in the mounted police. James listened patiently but made little comment except to sympathise with the loss of the bullock and Cobber's injury. He thought that, with time, Alroy would settle and they could get on with the logging. However, within a few days Alroy announced that he was going to Cooktown on the next boat out and that he would leave Shaun in charge of the bullocks.

'You can't leave Shaun there on his own,' said James.

'Why not?'

'Because there could be more trouble. It's not fair on him.'

Alroy hit back. 'If they touch my boy then I'll kill the lot—police or no police. Nobody touches my boy!'

On hearing this Nganka offered to stay with Shaun during Alroy's absence. 'Bajal stay here to cut logs. I go with Shaun.'

Bajal, revealing that he had learned more of the language than James realised, objected vehemently, saying, 'No, Nganka. Not safe for you. Old man from the village still want to kill you for not marry his son.'

Marku and Dari heard of this and, agreeing with Bajal, said that they would camp with Shaun while Alroy was away. Alroy, bearing no malice towards those in James' camp and trusting James' judgement, agreed with the proposal. Shaun welcomed the idea, saying that, since Cobber was still recovering, they could care for him while he shepherded the bullocks.

Arrangements were soon made, with Marku and Dari moving in with Shaun, and Alroy boarding a schooner bound for Cooktown. Alroy stood on the deck gazing towards the hazy horizon. Shaun would soon be a man and should be told the truth. Alroy's wife and four-year-old son had died of consumption in Ballarat one cold winter. How he had grieved and prayed! Soon after, a nun from his Catholic parish had called at his lonely shack by the river. They sat on boxes by a wooden bench as she spoke.

'Mr Higgins, we have a boy at the orphanage we are trying to place. If you could take him for a wee while it might help with your loss. He is four years old and we have named him Shaun.'

Alroy agreed, and with no formal arrangements in place Shaun came into Alroy's temporary care. He was a likable child with a lively personality and quickly found a place in Alroy's heart. They became inseparable. Shaun helped Alroy with his bullocks rather than attending school. They kept to themselves, leading a cloistered life except for church on Sundays.

During one of the nun's occasional visits she took Alroy aside and reminded him that as a widowed man he could not adopt Shaun and that Shaun remained a ward of the state. At hearing those words Alroy became flustered, burst into tears and told her that Shaun was his own flesh and blood and that the government had no place meddling with his son. The nun, duty bound by the rules of the orphanage, tried to explain, but Alroy became so agitated and hostile that she left with the matter unresolved. From that day Alroy ceased attending church and when, out of concern, the nun called by she was met with the windows of the shack boarded and no sign of Alroy or Shaun. Alroy had absconded with Shaun, leaving no trace and never to return.

He became paranoid, thinking the law was shadowing him. This fear consumed his life, forcing him to hide Shaun from society and keep on the move. They lived in timber camps and though conditions were often tough and unrewarding the lifestyle provided a means of remaining anonymous. Alroy had taken Shaun as a surrogate for his deceased child and the son of his dear departed wife.

When the schooner berthed at Cooktown and Alroy stepped ashore these thoughts made him apprehensive about lodging a complaint with the police. However, he did lodge the complaint and, after making hasty arrangements about the next shipment of provisions, he set sail and returned to the river.

The first indication of a response from the police came when two police whaleboats landed at James' camp at lunchtime on a busy day. Eight men in blue police uniforms manned the oars of the boats while a sub-inspector with a pith helmet sat at the stern of the second boat. The troopers stepped ashore with cartridge belts strung across their chests and rifles at the ready. The sub-inspector waited till they pulled the stern around to the sandbar before stepping ashore in his polished jackboots. They were met by James' full team, including Marku and Dari together with Alroy and Shaun, who were logging at the site. The sub-inspector introduced himself and advised that he had spoken to members of the other two camps on the river. He then explained that his instructions were to assess the situation and, if need be, to bring in mounted troopers to, as he put it, 'Teach the blacks a lesson.'

During the discussion it became apparent that Alroy and the Capitalist wanted punitive action against the blacks while James and Dougal thought a warning might be enough. James involved Nganka by asking for her opinion. She really did not know but reeled at the idea of killing members of her tribe. The sub-inspector noted the look of horror in her eyes as she stumbled for words to express her view. Having made his point the sub-inspector and his contingent sailed away without the river people knowing if they would be back next week, next month or not at all. Word did filter through to the tribe that if they killed any more bullocks then the white men would come with their magic sticks and kill them.

During the months ahead logging continued as usual with no further attacks by the blacks or police intervention. As Christmas approached, the camps shipped the last of the logs for the season and left their riverside camps before the river flooded.

On Christmas Day James always thought of his mother and this Christmas was no different. Sitting on a crate under the tarpaulin, he wrote in his diary:

25th December 1875: The year has been eventful and good. Between the three camps on the river we have shipped over a million super feet of log timber. However, after paying the costs of men, shipping, provisions and incidentals there isn't much left in the bank account. I visited the banker in Cooktown and found that the merchants are still cheating me on the measurements of the logs. Another concern is that a recent dispute with some natives could lead to trouble with the whole tribe. My blacks are fine. They work hard and cause me no trouble. I am camped with them at present for the wet season …

He signed off with, *Love you Mum.*

CHAPTER 7

The wet season, apart from the usual sogginess and influx of snakes, passed uneventfully. Walt arrived back after his three months' spree in Cooktown. James shifted camp back over to the sandbar. Marku and Dari, as planned, finally separated from the tribe and built a hut next to Bajal and Nganka's. James set Marku and Dari to work, planting corn, sweet potatoes, pumpkins and garden vegetables. With Nganka occupied full time with logging, Marku and Dari undertook to do all the cooking and cleaning for the team. Dougal and the Capitalist returned, determined to make this the best year yet. Alroy and Shaun had stayed on during the wet and put the bullocks to good use. With an old ploughshare, bolts and carpentry tools they transformed the fork of a tree trunk into a plough and, with hard work, had three acres of corn sprouting from the ground by mid-April. Alroy saw a future for himself and Shaun in the valley with corn being essential to feed his bullocks during the dry time. The season moved forward, with the cooler months bringing relief from the steamy, summer conditions in the rainforest.

~

Marku and Dari heard curses and cusses coming from downstream of the camp. Dari hid in the rainforest nearby to keep watch while Marku raced for help. She soon returned with James and the crew to find four men in a whaleboat poling the craft towards the sandbar at the camp. The craft, piled high with logging equipment and camp needs, laboured through the water as the men, with no room to sit and row, stood, using the oars as poles. James made no approach to welcome them and, when a brawny man with a brash voice stepped from the boat and shouted a greeting littered with expletives,

42

James kept his distance. The rowdy newcomer then waved his men ashore and together they came close, inviting themselves into James' camp. One carried a gallon keg of rum and another a pannikin half full of the vile brew. It soon became apparent that the men were unfamiliar with logging and were not suited to life on the river. The boss man, with a smile that revealed his nasty side, asked where he might set up camp. James quickly laid down the rules of the river telling him, among other things, he would have to go upstream at least three bends and cut beyond his boundary. The boss seemed more interested in talking about the natives than discussing protocols of the river. He asked about the tribe and its location and, when he expressed a fancy for the women, his crew sniggered behind their grimy beards. James persevered with the unwanted conversation till the boss commented, 'Looks like you've got plenty of black company here. I've got a keg of rum if you're interested in a trade.'

James, hiding his exasperation, terminated the meeting with, 'You'd better move on and make camp before nightfall.' When they disappeared from sight James explained to the women that they were bad men and if they approached to run away. 'The drunks' as Alroy called them began cutting just upstream from his paddock. He reported to James that what the men cut in the first month he and Shaun could have cut in half the time. He also told of their messy camp and complained of the gunfire that often startled his bullocks.

Marku waited on James, doing almost everything that a wife would. She became his handmaid, devoting all her attention to him and leaving Dari to attend to Walt's washing and meals. She sometimes tried to coax James away, suggesting they go for a walk in the bush or a swim, but he always found an excuse, feeble as it might be, to escape a situation that might lead to a compromise. He accepted her trimming his hair and beard and later allowed her to shave his face.

Marku, with the passion of a woman deeply in love, insisted on shaving him every Sunday morning. From one week to the next she counted the days, becoming dizzier with desire as each Sunday approached. With her hands trembling with excitement she would spend an hour shaving his face with the razor and shaping his side whiskers with scissors. When she had finished and

James looked in the mirror Marku always thought she could have done better and apologised unnecessarily.

This morning James put his hand on her shoulder and, although falling short of telling her he loved her, he clearly expressed the thought. Marku engaged him with a smile as sweet as summertime honey and an expression as soft as the morning dew. James put a hand to her face, gently brushed aside strands of her silky hair and leant forward, only to turn his lips aside at the last moment. Selene, as she had done for the past twenty years, still commanded his heart.

Strange as it may seem James remained locked into a moment in time. As a child his household had been torrid, with his demanding father berating him at every move and his mother not game to intervene for fear of receiving another hiding. While his father portrayed himself to the outside world as a caring husband and father, those employed there had heard the shouts, the beatings and the sobs. During childhood James lived a tormented existence, fearing for himself and his mother, and if it had not been for the security provided by Selene he doubted he would have survived. Whenever his father tore into him about his conduct Selene had almost always appeared in time to save him from the strap. She would excuse herself and James from William's presence and take James to a quiet room where she consoled him. James had become dependent on Selene, so dependant that, since leaving home, he still clung to her memory. As he had done when approached by women in the past he turned Marku away in the false belief that only Selene could bring him happiness.

James had been giving reasons, almost excuses, as to why he needed to visit Cooktown. He again raised the matter with Walt. 'I best be going to Cooktown soon. Need to sort some business about Sydney …'

Walt listened, as he had done for the past month, to James' talk of Cooktown and his mentions of attending to, as yet, unspecified business. Though he and James had worked and lived together for many years he knew little of James' early days. On occasions, when conversation led down this path, James invariably digressed, taking the discussion elsewhere. *Business about Sydney,* thought Walt, and he pondered what else, apart from dealing with timber merchants, James would be concerned with in a city he said he hated. He could ask James outright but this was not the nature of their relationship. Each had a past private life not fully disclosed. Walt had no knowledge, not an inkling, of James' connection to the socialites of Sydney and if he were told he would have difficulty believing it.

Marku also noticed James' restlessness and, when told of his plan to sail to Cooktown, she worried whether he would return. 'There's no reason for him to go away,' she told Dari before becoming tearful. Dari consoled her, saying that it would be secret men's business and not to worry. To which Marku replied, 'I think he has missus in Cooktown.' Dari, with the wisdom of a sage, knew better and told Marku to be patient and all would be well. The night James left and the nights after Marku cried herself to sleep. She could think of no explanation other than that James had a sweetheart in Cooktown.

James stood stoically on the foredeck of the *Pearl Shell* as she crested the waves, pushing towards Cooktown. He ignored the skipper's suggestion of moving aft, preferring to take the pounding dealt when the bow plunged into the troughs of the swell. Sea spray showered overhead, drenching him each time a breaking wave caught the starboard side. *A troubled man*, thought the skipper as he watched from the wheelhouse. When they berthed in the harbour James made arrangements with the skipper for the return journey, took his trunk and walked to the hotel where he had lodged previously. The receptionist, now knowing him as a man of means, leant across the counter with her breasts bursting from her loosely laced bodice and booked him into the best room in the house. She followed with the offer, '… anything at all, Sir. I can make myself available for room service at a time of your choosing.' James hardly heard her words. He gave her a blank look, lifted his trunk and proceeded to his room.

The clerk at the Bank of New South Wales recognised him immediately when he presented himself in a suit and cravat the following morning. Within a few minutes of waiting the clerk ushered him to the manager's office.

'Always good to see you,' said the manager who then followed with his standard line, 'How was the trip?'

They pawed over James' ledger account, trying to reconcile James' diary record with the amounts in the ledger. As on previous inspections they found that the ledger amounts for each consignment of logs showed less than the amounts in James' diary.

'Not good,' said James, turning away from the ledger and returning to his seat.

'They all do it,' replied the manager. 'It's a constant complaint from our account holders. Some have switched merchants to find they are worse off. The practice is widespread.'

They spent the next hour discussing measures that might be taken to stop the skulduggery practised by the timber merchants and, after weighing the options, James decided not to change merchants for the time being.

James fidgeted for a moment and then turned to the main purpose of his visit. He began with a preamble about being raised in Sydney and attending King's College and then queried the manager, 'I don't quite know how to put this, but I'm asking a favour.'

The manager nodded and leaned back in his chair, encouraging James to tell more.

'Have you heard of a Sydney timber company named Partridge & Company?'

The manager smiled knowingly and replied, 'Yes, James, quite a lot.'

'Then you know who I am?'

'Yes, but I thought it best not to mention it.'

'And my father?'

'Yes, both your father and mother. I've spoken with them at charity events. If you'd like me to have a word with them I can arrange that.'

'No, it's not about money. It's a personal matter. You probably know that I'm not in touch with them.'

'Yes, I've heard a little.'

'Well, this goes back to before I left home. I had a governess by the name of Selene and I want to contact her ...' James spoke on, telling that Selene was a dear friend, that they had lost contact and that he wished to reacquaint with her.

The manager listened carefully and when James finished he asked, 'And you're wondering if she might be an account holder with the bank?'

'Yes. It's a long shot but I have nowhere else to turn.'

'And your parents?'

'They are not to know. It must be kept confidential.'

The manager agreed, took a pencil and paper, asked questions and made notes:

- Selene Montigue
- Now aged 45
- Employed as a governess by Partridge & Company 1847 to 1856
- Parents unknown
- Address unknown
- No contact since 1856

'I'll ask about and get back to you before Christmas. No promises though.'

James added a postscript to his request. 'If you receive word before I'm next in would you please send a note via Pacific Stevedoring who ship our supplies.'

The manager, wishing to please the son of one of the bank's wealthiest clients, said he would attend to the matter forthwith and forward a reply the moment it came to hand

CHAPTER 8

'W'ait on,' said James to Nganka, 'say that again.'

'White man kill!'

Bajal, Nganka, Marku and Dari had crossed the river and now stood before James and Walt as a deputation. Nganka, the spokesperson, trembled as she explained, 'Kill em with rifle!'

'What men?' quizzed James.

'Upstream ones.'

'You sure?'

'Yes, tribe men come to camp last night and tell us.'

'How? When? Tell me, Nganka.'

Nganka told how two white men had ambushed five naked women while they sat fishing by the river. They exposed themselves and made signs wanting sex. The women panicked and scattered but the white men caught one and pulled her to the ground. Her screams brought back two of the women who hit the men with sticks. The men shot one women, the other escaped and when they had finished with the first woman they shot her dead. She followed on by saying that the tribesmen were planning revenge.

James set to cool the situation. He spoke quietly, assuring Nganka and the others they were safe from the bad men upriver and said he would deal with them.

James had a vision for the valley: a place where Aborigines and Europeans lived together in harmony, sharing the land. He also harboured a dream whereby he played a prominent role in bringing the cultures together. During his fifteen years of timber getting in frontier districts he had been witness to many attempts at bringing the groups together and while there had been some successes most were dismal failures. Time and again he had seen

Aborigines denied access to their traditional lands and means of living. He knew of police brutality and believed that if the police ruled the valley then these consequences would soon follow. These were the thoughts that brought James to the conclusion that the police should not be involved.

Next morning he left Walt in charge and followed a track upstream where he found the gang of bad men working in a patch of rainforest. He called the boss man aside and accused him of the murders.

'Not me,' the man replied with a shrug.

'If not you then two of your men.'

'Maybe.'

'You realise that this is police a matter?'

'Police. What police? There's no police in this territory.'

'No, but I can soon call them in.'

'For what? There's no proof.'

'Yes there is. I have witnesses.'

'What, a mob of gibbering blacks?'

'No, a linguist in my camp who can take their testimony.'

'Come on, you're joking.'

'No joke. She's fluent in English and the local dialect.'

The boss held his look of indifference and called James' bluff. 'Go ahead. Call them in.'

James paused for effect before replying, 'Very well, I'll do that.' Then as an afterthought he added, 'The sooner the better, before the blacks get you.'

'Not with this,' shot back the boss, pointing to his rifle.

James gave half a laugh. 'You won't even see them coming. They'll ambush you in the forest or pepper your tent with spears.'

At this suggestion the boss became unsure of his position and, after more talk, suggested a deal whereby James appease the blacks in return for a load of logs. James declined the offer and departed with no intention of calling the police and leaving the boss man to ponder the consequences of an Aboriginal attack.

Apart from contact with Bajal and those in his camp, James knew very little about the local tribe. With fierce fighting being reported between the mounted police and the Aborigines of the Cooktown and Palmer River region, he held reservations about the prospect of talking peace with the tribe. These tribesmen were kings of the valley and not likely to accept a flagrant violation of their women. Any approach would need the support of Bajal and his family and with this in mind he crossed the river to their camp just after dawn. He found the trauma of the event still raw, with Nganka slipping into her hut to avoid him. Bajal stayed clear, chopping firewood, and if Marku and Dari had not come forward then he might have let the matter pass. Marku smiled sweetly as she always did when James visited. Dari, a dependable woman in times of trouble, issued a cheery greeting and then hinted that they should talk. James took the opportunity and suggested a cup of tea. Marku brewed a billycan of tea and, when they sat by the fire, Dari called Nganka and Bajal.

James spoke at length, explaining that rape and murder were unacceptable in white man's law, that he understood how the tribe felt and that the bad men should be punished. He then outlined how he planned to resolve the matter. He told of the warning he had given the bad men and that if they interfered with any more of the tribe's women he would call in the police. He also explained that under white man's law it was equally unacceptable for members of the tribe to kill the bad men, and if they did then the police would shoot them with their magic sticks. He said he wished to meet with the tribal elders to ask that they not initiate a reprisal attack. Dari, more so than the others, understood the reasoning and engaged with the others in a dialect that James only partly understood. They eventually reached a consensus that supported James' idea and agreed to arrange a meeting. Bajal undertook to be courier, left immediately and returned the next day with confirmation that the parties would meet at Kababina, the water-lily lagoon, at midday the following day.

James regarded this meeting as historic and, rather than approaching it with trepidation, he saw it as an opportunity to establish an accord with the tribespeople of the valley. Unarmed and in good spirits he and his four companions arrived at the lagoon to find seven of the senior tribesmen waiting. Greetings by way of nods, hand gestures and words of introduction, not understood by the other party, were passed around. They then sat in the shade of a sprawling paperbark tree to begin the first formal meeting between Europeans and the Aborigines of the Mossman River valley. Nganka, as the interpreter, found herself at the centre of the discussion, translating back and forth. Three hours of talk resulted in a better understanding of each other's point of view, and, indeed, they agreed on the basic precepts of law concerning rape and murder. However, the Aborigines would not accept James' petitioning on behalf of the bad men and held to their view that the murder of the two women should be avenged by killing all four of the accused. That night James lay in his swag going over what had been said and came to the view that peace was possible even if it meant that the bad men had to mysteriously disappear.

Walt and Bajal rowed down to the landing, collected a load of provisions and now, with the help of the others, carried them to the stores tent.

'A letter for you, James,' said Walt, taking an envelope from his pocket.

James took the envelope and turned it in his hands. The plain cover with no return address and a common wax seal on the back aroused his curiosity. Guessing that the letter would be of a private nature, he excused himself and went to his tent. He again tumbled the envelope before breaking the seal and removing the one-page letter.

28th October 1876

Dear James,

I have received word back from Sydney and advise as follows.

Upon termination of employment with your parents in 1856 Selene Montigue worked as a governess for two years before contracting diphtheria.

She passed away in August 1858, unmarried and childless.

She banked with Bank NSW and as she died intestate the bank required Grant of Probate which is still on record.

Please accept my sympathy.

Yours sincerely
David Bloom
Manager
Bank NSW, Cooktown

The news shattered James. Selene could not be deceased. No such thought had ever occurred to him. In disbelief he stood in the tent with the letter quivering in his hand. His face drained to the colour of the calico tent above him. His blue eyes welled with tears and as he wiped them away more streamed forth. He wept inconsolably, holding head in hands, unable to comprehend the loss. The letter, stained from the tears, fell from his hand to rest on his swag. Nothing made any sense. The knowledge that Selene would never be by his side was beyond his grasp. Those outside heard his crying and stood anxious and mystified. Dari took Marku's hand and held it tightly. Nganka and Bajal moved close together and whispered to each other, searching for an explanation. Walt, guessing that the letter bore sad tidings, bowed his head in sympathy. James fell to his knees, took the pillow from his swag and clutched it in his arms. He looked at the swag, the one he dreamed of sharing with Selene one day. He visualised her there with her arms outstretched, reaching for him. So serene, so calm, beckoning him to lie with her. He lay down with the pillow against his cheek and cradled her as he had imagined so many times before. He felt her warmth, her tender touch, a nearness he wished to cling to forever. James, in his shocked state, consoled himself by lying there in the comfort of her arms till the stifling summer heat in the closed tent suffocated his thoughts and forced him to rise to his feet and move outside.

He ignored his friends, turned the other way and disappeared along a logging track into the rainforest. Here, in the stillness of a cathedral of tall trees, he knelt and prayed, seeking salvation for Selene. The prayers eased his numbness, allowing some awareness to creep in. Filtered light from above played on delicate ferns, reminding him of his childhood and Selene holding his hand when they ventured into the fairy dell at the bottom of the garden. He fancied that she was with him now and spoke aloud, recalling memories long forgotten. He needed this alone time and stayed till the fading light forced him to return to camp.

Walt, not knowing what to say, sat alone by the fire as James approached and sat on a box opposite him. Both gazed into the fire in silence until James spoke in a soft voice, 'Walt, there's been a death in my family.'

'I'm sorry,' replied Walt, toying with the cracked enamel on his mug. 'Will you need to go away for a while?'

'No. She's gone and there's nothing I can do. One day I'll visit her grave and pay my respects.'

'Your mother?'

'No, but someone very dear to me.'

Walt, not wishing to pry, let the matter lie and set about preparing tea. James declined to eat and stayed by the fire till very late.

Next morning Marku came across the river just as James put a damper, a cabbage, ammunition and a tin of wax matches into a bag. Marku knew that the message on the paper had brought bad news but had no idea of its nature. She wished to comfort him with a hug but his solemn mood held her back.

'I'm going away for a couple of days,' he told Walt and Marku.

'Any idea where you might go?' asked Walt, concerned about James' state of mind.

'No, I just need a couple of days to think things through.'

Walt could do no more, and when James set to leave with rifle, bush knife and the bag he wished him well. Marku contained herself till he disappeared from sight and then cried as she had done when he last went to Cooktown.

James headed east, cutting cross-country in the hot sun till he reached the wildlife lagoon he had visited on an earlier occasion. The long walk did nothing to relieve his grief and despair. Thoughts of silencing himself forever remained foremost in his mind. To his bereaved mind it would be easier to take his own life than continue living. Who would care? Who would miss him apart from Walt and his river friends? All so easy. One shot by a lonely lagoon and his remains never found. The temptation plagued his every attempt at thought. The afternoon clouded over early, banking against the ranges, building to a storm front. After nightfall the landscape descended into total darkness except for the glow of James' fire and lightning sheeting the sky. The roll of the thunder came and went as storms rumbled through the mountains. James, suffering from the exhaustion of the past two days, eventually lay down, made himself comfortable on the ground and slept for a few hours.

At first light he felt an urgency to walk, no matter to where, just walk to wherever his feet would take him. Armed with the rifle and knife he wandered for hours, circling the lagoon and then walking the long distance to the beach and back. The disbelief of earlier turned to questioning the truth of the advice he had received. He considered that there could be more than one Selene Montigue and that it could be a case of mistaken identity. However, the bank manager had cited a Grant of Probate document that identified a Selene

Montigue who the bank identified as having once worked for the Partridge family. There could be no mistake.

At lunchtime he munched some dry damper and a slice from the head of cabbage and then rested in the shade. Fleeting thoughts shadowed his restless attempt at sleep. The urge to be with her challenged him again, forcing him to put a bullet into the breech of the rifle. *So easy, so certain*, he thought. *One squeeze of the trigger and my pain will be gone.* This impasse held him at bay till late afternoon when another storm gathered and lit the sky with flashes of lightning and drum rolls of thunder. It broke soon after dark, pelting down and stinging James' skin. The discomfort of sleeping in wet clothes on wet ground hardly registered; his emotional pain ran far deeper.

For breakfast he swallowed some sodden damper and chewed at the head of cabbage. The repetitive need to extend himself over a long distance drove him to walk south for many miles and then backtrack to the lagoon. Weariness, both physical and emotional, began to take hold, relieving his anxiety and placing a semblance of order into his thoughts. The evening brought a calm and for the first time since arriving he lay beneath the stars listening to the nightlife of the lagoon.

At piccaninny daylight he took his few possessions and headed for home, feeling secure in the thought that he would be safe in the hands of his friends.

CHAPTER 9

❧

James' loss caused difficulties in the camp. He became reclusive, keeping to himself rather than sharing with the others. Walt would never have thought that his long-time friend could suddenly lose interest and talk of selling the business. James even spoke of the recent gold rush at the Hodgkinson River to the west and how he might leave everything behind and try his luck as a miner.

James had not shaved since receiving the news and looked like a man from the wild. He remained confused, unable to fathom the feelings that tugged at his emotions; one day frustrated and irritable, the next not caring if another log ever reached the river. The most telling times were when, overwhelmed by grief, he walked off with hardly a word and hiked for miles through the bush without a rifle for protection. It seemed that nothing mattered, even his life.

Marku, more so than any other, felt the pain. She empathised with James, reading his emotions and enduring the moments and days of his torment. When the last shipment of logs for the year needed to be assembled Walt took the lead and, together with the others, managed to meet the shipment quota. He then helped James shift across the river to where he would camp with Bajal's family till the end of the wet season.

Walt, though unable to get any firm commitment from James, decided to follow his routine of revelling with the girls in Cooktown and return in the new year. The bad men from upriver left soon after James' last load, oaring down the river with the boat full of personal possessions. An inspection of their site by James and Bajal revealed logs and equipment still lying about and they wondered if the men planned to return. Dougal fared well, leaving no logs behind and moving his equipment to high ground before he and his crew took their leave before the wet weather arrived. The Capitalist struggled with manpower shortages and just managed to raft his last load and secure his camp before the first of the monsoon rain flooded the river.

On rainy days James brooded, reliving the fantasy of his unrequited love. When the sun shone his mind eased, allowing thoughts of the present and glimpses of the future to soothe his sorrow. This conflict stayed with him till Alroy passed by the camp one day and, during the course of conversation, offered him work on a time-in-lieu basis, where hours worked would be compensated for by haulage with his bullocks. James agreed and Alroy explained his plan. The immediate tasks were to place a post-and-rail fence across the neck of his paddock to fence in the bullocks, and then clear more land for growing corn. Later, when settlers came and the land was surveyed, he would purchase the land he had improved.

He also talked of 'finding a place' for Shaun. He followed with, 'No matter he can't read and write. A strong back in a free land is all that's needed.'

The others in James' camp thought well of the work arrangement. Their enduring patience, a trait of the Aborigine, had helped James, and being put to work would assist. James recognised their support and promised himself that he would, somehow, someday, repay them for their loyalty.

James worked for Alroy for the next six weeks and during this time they became confidants. As for Shaun, he saw him as a willing worker but a person with a wavering temperament. He learned of the death of Alroy's wife, which occurred more than a decade earlier, and how Alroy, in moments of quiet solitude, still grieved for her. He confided to Alroy the circumstance of his own lost love and, following a discussion where they compared notes, James realised that he was not alone in experiencing such a loss. Alroy, with his willingness to speak freely about matters of the heart, led James forward, and by the time the work had been completed James realised that Selene was gone forever.

Bajal now considered himself a sharp-shooter with the rifle, felling wallabies with head shots at eighty yards. This morning he again scored a direct hit, dropping one to the ground with a single shot. James, with his bush knife in hand, quickly bled the animal by cutting its throat and pumping its body with his foot. When the last of the blood pooled on the ground he gutted the animal and then turned to Bajal and jested, 'You always pick off the biggest and leave me to drag it home!'

Bajal threw back a rude remark in his own dialect, handed James the rifle and took the wallaby by the tail. Bajal knew that, apart from keeping his wife happy, the next best thing he could do for the family was to bring home a big, fat wallaby. With James in the lead Bajal struggled, dragging the carcass through long grass, across gullies and over logs. The tree line of the river and then smoke from the camp fire came into view, pressing the men to hurry home to brag about their catch. James, rather than walk around a charred log, jumped over it and, unfortunately, landed beside a taipan snake. The startled snake whipped around and struck. James, unable to avoid its strike, felt the snake hit the cuff of his trousers and its fangs pierce his heel. He yelled, drawing Bajal's attention in time for him to see the snake slither away into the long grass. Bajal, knowing the consequence of a taipan bite, raced to James' side and confirmed the puncture wounds.

'Cut it! Cut it!' roared James, pulling the bush knife from its sheath.

Bajal knelt and slid the sharp blade across the wounds, drawing blood.

'Here, rip my shirt!' James shouted, pulling the shirt tail from under his belt. 'Tie it around my leg and twitch it!'

Bajal did as instructed, tying a strip of shirt about James' thigh and twitching it tight with a piece of stick. They left the wallaby and rifle behind and made for the camp with James dizzy and hobbling and Bajal supporting him with a shoulder under his arm.

When the camp came into view Bajal called *jarba*, snake! The three women rushed forward and together they carried the now failing James to his tent and laid him down, hardly conscious and beginning to convulse. Marku became hysterical, screamed and fled outside with head in hands. Nganka followed and took Marku in her arms. Dari insisted that Bajal stay and help. With James' leg turning blue from the pressure of the tourniquet she eased the pressure a little at a time till it was fully released. He vomited, choking on the spew till they turned him on his side. Dari stayed with James, murmuring to the spirits for help, while Bajal dashed off to get Jajin, the medicine man.

By the time Jajin arrived that evening the convulsions had ceased but James' breathing had become erratic; laboured one minute and hardly a breath the next. Jajin knelt down, turned James' eyelid up with a finger and then turned to Dari and shook his head. Tears wet Dari's cheeks and breasts as she implored Jajin to stay the night. He stayed, waving a string of magic beads back and forth while chanting incantations.

James' condition changed little during the night and at first light Jajin sent Bajal to collect buds from the *dukunjaka* medicine tree. He mashed these with a little water and instructed Dari to tip a few drops at a time into James' mouth.

Nganka, wanting a white man present, raced to Alroy's camp and told him that James was dying. Alroy and Shaun followed her back at a hefty pace. Alroy then joined Jajin in the tent and together they prayed and chanted, asking that James be spared. Dari and the others sat alongside them, swaying to Jajin's chants. Shaun, feeling uncomfortable with the display of emotion, stayed outside with Cobber and Murramu.

James lay almost motionless throughout the day and, although his breathing had become steady, he looked pallid and ready for the grave. The occasional flicker of an eyelid was all that gave those there some hope that he might survive.

The possibility that James might die tormented Marku's every thought. She could not bear to contemplate life without him. Even if he would not take her as his lover, to be his handmaid would give her purpose to continue living.

Jajin stayed for another two days and then departed, leaving James in a critical but stable state. Alroy visited daily, sitting with James and filling in time about the camp. Marku kept her vigil, staying with James day and night. Every two hours she would place James' head on her lap, part his lips and feed him the medicine drip by drip. On the fifth day she became excited when he gulped the medicine and opened his mouth for more. She lifted him upright with his head against her breast and held a mug of water to his mouth. With his eyes still closed he gulped the water down and motioned for more. She held another cup to his lips and spoke, openly declaring her love for him. He heard and opened his eyes just long enough to capture her smile and then lapsed back into unconsciousness.

Marku cradled him in her arms like a child in a mother's care. In the early hours of the next morning she felt him stir and feel about for her. She rolled over, almost covering his body with hers, and put her head on his chest. He squeezed her hand, signalling his love for her. James took only fluids for the next two days and then progressed to a few spoons of oatmeal porridge. Thereafter his health improved rapidly, with him regaining weight daily. When his recovery seemed certain Alroy declared, 'To be sure 'tis his strength of body and mind and a little help from the Lord.'

Jajin visited two weeks later and, after a dignified ritual, inducted James into the brotherhood of the tribe.

Bajal sat cross-legged cleaning his rifle, Nganka played with Murramu, and Dari attended to a pot of wallaby stew. James sat on a log as Marku prepared to tidy his hair and bushy beard for the first time since receiving the news of Selene's death. She snipped his hair and beard with scissors and soaped his face. As she began to shave, James placed his hands on her hips to steady himself. She smiled and trembled at his touch, hardly able to hold the razor steady. When finished she dabbed his face with a wet cloth and gazed into his twinkling blue eyes. He returned the gaze, exchanging thoughts of love. After lunch he took her by the hand and suggested they go for a swim. Dari smiled to herself when Marku said they would not be gone long.

The romance of the river took on a new meaning, with this couple from different cultures hugging each other as they made their way along the cool, leafy pathway by the river. They spoke in both his and her dialects, teasing each other with words of courtship. The forest stood as a silent witness when Marku stopped James by a quiet pool, turned to him and suggestively undid the buttons of her shirt. James stood star-struck when she continued, shedding her clothes and posing before jumping into the river. 'Come in,' she called with girlish glee after shaking the water from her hair.

James smiled and paused momentarily before removing his shirt and trousers. Upon seeing his naked manliness she stood tall, fully exposing herself. At her second call for him to come in James stepped forward, dived in and rose by her side. With no words spoken he took her in his arms and embraced her in the way of his culture, kissing and holding their lips together. Marku answered his call, clinging to him tightly and returning the kisses. She trembled and James' heart pounded as, hand in hand, they waded to a sandy cove in the shade of a water cherry tree. They embraced again, sharing kisses and murmuring words of love. Bliss overtook them when they knelt on the sand and fondled the softness of each other's body. Marku surrendered first, lying on her back and reaching for him. He gazed at her in wonder, fondled her some more and then lay between her thighs. Her willingness and his gentleness soon brought them together in perfect harmony. They lay entwined for what seemed forever and, when James rolled onto his back, they held hands and silently gave thanks for the moment. James thought he had conquered all, and now, with Marku by his side, nothing could stand in his way. Marku hoped that her wish had been granted, and that a spirit child had been planted in her womb.

CHAPTER 10

James provided everything needed by Bajal's camp during the next wet season. They became family. Everything except some personal items and their private lives was shared. When the wet season finished James shifted his logging camp back across the river to the sandbar, with Marku sharing his tent. Bajal, Nganka and Dari remained in their camp on the other side. Walt returned from his escapade in Cooktown, happy to be home and pleased to find James and Marku living as a couple. The moment the ground dried James' team recommenced, falling trees larger than ever.

Alroy's bullocks, refreshed and ready for work, willingly leaned into the yokes, hauling the heavy logs to the river ready for rafting. He and Shaun worked well together, with Alroy managing the bullocks and Shaun handling the chains. Shaun, now sixteen years of age, took interest in the young native girls that occasionally visited Bajal and his family. Dari expressed concern, telling him that most of the girls were betrothed.

Dougal kept his homecoming quiet, steering away from James' camp till he sent his first shipment of logs. According to what the Capitalist told James, Dougal had been before the magistrate in Cooktown for underpaying his men. The magistrate berated him, denigrating cedar getters as scurrilous and that they were mistaken if they thought they could escape the law by hiding away in cedar camps. He fined Dougal £20 and garnisheed his first consignment of logs to make restitution to the men. Needless to say, two of the three terminated their arrangement, leaving Dougal the difficulty of finding experienced replacements. When James visited Dougal he made no mention of the incident.

The Capitalist had problems of his own. The venture capitalists financing his operation complained about the costs he had incurred last season. In particular the amount paid for stores. In a letter they said, 'Are you feeding all the blacks on Cape York!' His personal life fell into disrepute when a brothel keeper in Cooktown banned him from her establishment and passed the word to the other madams profiting from the gold rush. Apparently his sexual preferences and strange antics were too much for the girls of the gold port.

The bad men who had murdered the two Aboriginal women were never heard of again. Their logs washed out to sea and their equipment lay buried beneath the sand of last wet season. James lamented the loss of dozens of logs worth hundreds of pounds as log timber and thousands of pounds as turned furniture. He surmised that they thought it better to forfeit the timber than be speared.

The season progressed well, with fair weather, no onsite mishaps, shipping schedules on time and presumably payments going into James' bank account. He had not contacted the bank manager since receiving his letter. His mixed feelings at losing Selene and pairing with Marku had him finding excuses for not visiting. He and Marku sometimes left the camp in the care of the others and visited family groups who could be found at various places on their walkabout. James never ceased to be surprised by how Marku knew where they would be and wondered even more about how those in the camp knew they were arriving. A bright greeting always welcomed them into the camps. Though Marku tried to explain her family relationships, much of it remained vague and sometimes disconnected. It seemed that Marku was related to almost everybody by family linkages, either close or distant. If Marku were to have a child all the senior women on her maternal side would be called 'Mother'. James mused to himself about the possibility of his child being passed around amongst the women. Some women commented privately about the union, thinking Marku lucky and James a handsome warrior.

Towards the end of the year a corroboree to be held at a location known as Wonga became a topic of constant discussion. The Wonga beach area marked the tribal boundary between the Mossman River tribe and the Daintree River tribe to their north. Though they spoke different dialects they could communicate. With regular corroborees being held and intermarriages common, the tribes had kinship connections that kept them from warring— politics Aboriginal style. James also learned that cousins from the Bloomfield River tribe further north would be attending. They were also of the same language group, speaking a third dialect that could be understood by all; something of a grand gathering of related souls. The site with a sandy bora ground served the purpose well. Food and water were plentiful, with freshwater springs, a large lagoon, an inshore reef and forest animals to be hunted. The mile-long seaside camp site could accommodate upward of two hundred people in shelters made from palms fronds and the bark of paperbark trees. The four-day event provided an opportunity for the collective to trade goods, sing and dance, swap notes, court partners and sometimes settle disputes. James had begun to understand the depth of this fascinating culture and wanted to learn more. He told those in the camps they visited that he and Marku would be attending and that while there they would live as true Aborigines, using traditional methods and living off the land.

The men on the river found that for freight purposes it paid to use one vessel to ship in all their supplies. Two weeks before the corrobboree it arrived and stayed overnight, so as to catch the sea breeze back to Cooktown the following day. The men usually took this opportunity to socialise and, with swags on board, rowed down to the landing at mid-afternoon. The skipper and his crew of two helped with the transfer of goods and then they all set up camp on the high bank. Over a pot of stew and a few rums the skipper gave an update on the outside world, including a report of murders committed by Aborigines on the Daintree River. He spoke of 'murderous bastards', and how the police had responded with a 'punitive raid'. Being unaware of James' connection to Marku and her family, he continued with his scathing attack on the natives till the Capitalist interrupted with, 'How did it happen?'

The skipper swilled down a mouthful of rum and explained. 'Tom Hanley and John Rogan, together with an offsider, were cutting a patch of cedar up on the main branch of the river. Tom and his missus lived downstream, and when he didn't come home she hailed a passing boat owner, a chap named McKeown. He mustered a few men together and they went to investigate. They found the camp a mess with belongings scattered everywhere. They then hunted about and found the men's bodies in the rainforest. They had been speared and mutilated in cold-blooded murder!'

'Bastards!' interjected the Capitalist. 'They ought to do what we did on the Clarence, shoot them on sight.'

'Yeah, I agree,' replied the skipper. 'I've told my crew to have a rifle handy at all times. You never know when they'll shower you with spears. We've seen them on the river in their canoes but so far have left them alone. It's spooked some cutters, with them not game to go back to their patch even though they have logs on the ground. The worry is that if they go unchecked there'll be further attacks. Sub-Inspector Shillington and his troopers are on the river now, launching a raid.'

The Capitalist, a pugnacious man without a shred of empathy, drew another draught of rum from the keg and added, 'There's no room for them and us. If the inspector wants to come down here then I'll gladly join his party to clean them out.'

James remained silent while the men spoke, describing the Aborigines as savages. Dougal, wanting only to profit from the river, said he 'couldn't care less what happened to them'. Walt, knowing something of what James would be thinking and sharing the same view, refrained from comment. James slept little that night, tossing in his swag, fearing that a police presence would soon destroy tribal life as it had been for millennia. When rowing back up the river the next morning James and Walt remained quiet, reflecting on what had been said and contemplating what the future held for the Aborigines of the valley.

James told Marku and the others of the incident and that it would be best if he did not attend the corrobboree. Marku, in particular, found this difficult to accept and when James suggested that she and the others go without him she began to cry. She so wished to be seen in his company as his wife, to show all the tribespeople that she had partnered someone extra special. The adornments she had made for each of them lay in a corner of the tent. She also intended surprising James by wearing a dress rather than shirt and trousers while at the Wonga camp. The realisation that this, her big outing, was not to be, left her disappointed and dismally sad up to the time of the corrobboree and for days after.

CHAPTER 11

The year 1878 brought fresh promise to the young colony of Queensland. The Great Barrier Reef fishery provided seafood for the local market, and bêche-de-mer and shark fins for trade with Asia. Coastal rivers echoed to the sound of axes as timber getters stripped them of red cedar and other timbers. Gold seekers, after routing southern Queensland of gold, scrambled to new deposits discovered in the northern inland. They blazed trails from Charters Towers north to the Gilbert and Etheridge Rivers, and then to the Palmer River. The pastoralists followed close behind, pushing their herds ever further north into fresh pastures. The Palmer River strike of 1873, manned by 30,000 people at its height, waned, and by 1878 a surplus of labour existed in the north of the colony. These gold seekers, mostly from the dispossessed class of colonial rule, dared not return south. Instead they sought a new life in the wilderness of tropical Australia. With a swag on their shoulder and a billycan in hand they trudged the north, seeking opportunity and a place to settle. From all walks of life they came together to form small communities along the coast and inland. The government, in its rush to populate this vast chunk of the continent, granted licences to those willing to take risks.

Closer to the Mossman River and James Partridge's camp the race to develop the country forged ahead at a breathtaking pace. The Hodgkinson River gold rush, only sixty miles to the west, desperately needed a supply line to transport goods in and gold out. The 150-mile track from Cooktown proved unsatisfactory, and the government offered a reward to anyone who found a shorter route from the field to the coast. In 1877, an intrepid explorer by the name of Christie Palmerston blazed a trail across the rugged Great Dividing Range to link the field with the coast. Within months this port of entry had been named Port Douglas and surveyed as a town. Teamsters arrived, ready to share in the gold by hauling heavy loads across the range to the miners. Commercial men, seeking to capitalise on the rewards of gold, flocked to the port to engage in trade. The government, seeing an opportunity for advancement, provided the administrative framework needed to service the fledgling community. Within no time private individuals built wharves and cleared the track to the Hodgkinson. Remarkably this all took place just a few miles south of the Mossman River. In fact, the wharf facilities and some of the buildings could be seen from the river's mouth.

James thought he had another three years of cedar left to cut and entered 1878 with zeal. With Bajal and the girls now competent cedar loggers he planned to engage Aborigines from the local tribe to increase production. He spoke to the Aborigines towards the end of the wet season and offered them produce, including flour, sugar and tea, in exchange for work. They appeared enthusiastic but when the rain eased and the earth dried they marched off on their walkabout, leaving him short. Undaunted, he spoke to Walt and the others about bringing European workers into the camp. They disagreed vehemently and instead promised to work harder. While Walt received a share of the proceeds, the others were happy to work for their benevolent boss for tucker. In the first three months they outstripped the other two camps, felling more trees and sending more shipments. However, the situation changed when, one day, a stranger appeared from around the corner of a logging track.

'Good afternoon!' he called as he came forward, trampling twigs underfoot like a man familiar with the outdoors. James and Walt were two springboards high and scarfing a cedar tree when they heard the call. Bajal and company, standing nearby, were unsure what to make of this man who, to them, looked too cocky. James and Walt, bare chested and wearing only trousers, rested their axe heads on their boards when he called again.

'I say, chaps, are you able to spare a few moments.'

The men on the boards, savvy of each other's thinking, exchanged cautionary glances before lowering themselves to the ground and fronting the newcomer.

'Ashton's the name. Jonathan Ashton …' and as he continued, listing his pedigree and credentials, James made his own assessment. To be sure this thirty-year-old man of dapper appearance belonged to the landed gentry: soft, linen shirt buttoned at the cuffs, bright-red cravat, tailored riding breeches, polished cavalry boots, chamois gloves tucked under his leather belt and riding cap in hand. The dark curls springing from his crown and tumbling across his forehead did little to distract from the intensity of his piercing eyes and their glint of greed.

'How did you come in?' asked James.

'Up the river. I've a row boat and two oarsmen.'

'Just passing through?'

'No. I intend buying this selection; the one you're felling.'

James could not believe what he heard. He had never envisaged anyone selecting the property. He surmised it to be a ploy and pushed back. 'There's only three gangs on the river. You would have passed their camps. There's nobody else apart from a teamster and his son.'

'I know. I spoke with the Scotsman downriver. But one can't pass on land at 2s 6d per acre.'

'Who says?' asked James.

'It's in the Queensland Government *Gazette*. Thirty-year leasehold land with an option to purchase on the Mossman River at 2s 6d per acre in lots up to 640 acres. Apparently they're trying to attract people from New South Wales to Queensland. I've explored the river up as far as I can go and found this to be the best section. The block has about a mile of river frontage and goes well back into the forest country. I've already registered my interest. I'll have government surveyors here within a month and expect to have leasehold title within two months of the survey being completed.'

'How did you hear of the land sale?'

'It was advertised in the *Goulburn Herald*. My family runs 15,000 head of sheep in the district. We also have Merino and Thoroughbred studs.'

'Quite a business,' said James, being polite.

'Yes, I'm third generation. Each generation makes a move and this seemed a good opportunity to expand the business.'

He prattled on, oblivious to the fact that James and his five helpers were eking a living from the patch he intended sequestering from them. 'I'll use this local timber to build a homestead and then send for my wife. I have big plans, a mix of grazing and agriculture with shipments direct south from Port Douglas. There'll be lots of clearing and planting to be done and harvesting. Maybe you and your crew could work for me?' He then looked at Nganka suggestively and said, 'I'll need house help to get things in order for when the wife arrives.'

He took his time, engaging them all with his talk, asking about the lay of the land, the Aborigines as a source of labour, shipping movements and the like. When leaving he added, almost offhandedly, 'Of course you'll have to cease cutting once the paperwork is completed.'

At lunchtime James kept to himself, sitting on a log by the river. Never could he have conceived that all he had built during the past four years could be thrown into jeopardy by the intrusion of a southern land-grabber. Sure, he could move to another patch on the river, but it would not be the same without Bajal's camp directly across the river. This was home, the first real home since leaving Sydney. No matter that he and his friends lived in isolation and in conditions that city dwellers would consider unimaginable. To his mind the love and respect they all shared counted for more than anything else. He remained seated, locked into these gloomy thoughts, till Walt came to his side and spoke reassuringly.

'James, don't take it too hard. We have months to go yet. I reckon we should fell as many trees as possible before that miserable bastard comes back. The law says that trees felled on unoccupied land belong to the cutter. It could be months before he returns and by then we could have a year's supply on the ground.'

James appreciated the support and roused from his misery. That evening, by Bajal's fire, James explained the situation. His friends, unsure what to say, listened in silence till Dari spoke for them and pledged their loyalty by saying, 'Boss, we stay with you.'

CHAPTER 12

Word of Ashton's intentions passed to the other camps, upsetting their mood and pressing them to log their cedar before more of the squattocracy moved in. Alroy, with ample work to keep him and Shaun occupied, favoured more settlers because it would bring regular shipping services. As he said, 'I'm tired of tossing out mouldy flour and sorting weevils from the rice.' While the men of the river speculated about change, none of them could have foreseen the seismic shift that was about to happen.

With Port Douglas now a vibrant community and an important port of call, word soon spread through the colonies about the fabled river land that lay only a day's travel from its wharfs. The new Government Lands Office at Port Douglas was inundated with enquiries. The river became busy, with hardly a day passing without people plying its course and stopping to enquire about the availability of land. James found himself at a crossroads for if he wished to take up land then he must act immediately, otherwise all the river frontage would be taken. He anguished day and night, tossing thoughts about, trying to decide. With his savings and the backing of the bank he could purchase a block large enough to feed his family and show a profit. He and Marku also planned to have children, making it more imperative that he buy land.

However, all this changed when, one night, he had a strange turn of mind that made him feel guilty about harvesting trees that he now thought belonged to the natives. How, then, could he cut down and burn hundreds of acres of their forest, furrow it with a plough, grow crops and sell the produce to outsiders? To his mind this would be sacrilege and, if anything, he should resist any such move. His mind became a mire of confusion, grinding thought and action nearly to a halt.

He spoke to Walt who listened carefully before putting his view that James' notions amounted to unrealistic idealism. He tried to explain that for his own sake and that of the family he should set aside his idealism and live life the European way. He even went so far as to suggest that James had lost touch and maybe it would be best if he and Marku took themselves away from the isolation and settled in a white community. While James agreed with the thrust of Walt's argument he still could not bring himself to truly believe it. The fortunate aspect of all this toing and froing was that James and Walt remained stout friends, accepting the other's right to differ.

Although James did not discuss the matter in detail with Marku and the others they sensed the nature of the problem and resolved to continue as normal—chopping trees, logging and rafting.

Walt again took the lead, organising the harvesting and, given the circumstances, kept morale high. James, as he had done following word of Selene's death, often needed to walk off the site and trek for miles through the open bush to ease the anxiety that at times almost drove him to distraction. Everybody understood his situation, and each time he returned Marku took him in her arms and held him tightly.

During the next two months production remained at a steady level, with consignments being shipped and presumably payments being deposited to James' bank account. James concluded that, before he could seriously consider any substantial purchase, he needed to visit the bank, inspect his account and, if necessary, discuss loan arrangements. As always he was welcome aboard the schooner *Pearl Shell* and stepped to the deck dressed for the occasion. He booked into the same hotel where the same buxom receptionist indicated that she would entertain him for a night at half the going rate. James politely declined and took three bottles of wine to his room and latched the door. The middle-aged clerk at the bank counter advised that the manager was busy with shipping contracts and could not meet with James till the following morning. This suited James as he needed to meet with Pacific Stevedoring to discuss the supply of his camp stores. As usual Jake, the manager, had all the information at his finger tips and once that was sorted they sat on bags of corn and discussed current matters. Jake told how Port Douglas was drawing business from Cooktown and, with alluvial gold becoming scarce on the Palmer River, the future prospects for Cooktown were not good. At a mention of James' appointment with the bank Jake advised that the Bank of New South Wales would soon open a branch in Port Douglas. 'When the banks decide to move in there's money to be had,' he said, throwing James an enquiring glance.

Next morning he dressed in his gentleman's clothes and arrived at the bank with a copy of the *Cooktown Herald* under his arm. The manager welcomed him with a cheery greeting. He then showed him to the ledger room where he opened a large ledger book and turned the page to James' account. Within moments of perusing the inked entries James became dismayed and said, 'There's money missing. Lots of it. There's even a full shipment not paid for.' The manager called in the ledger keeper and, after a thorough investigation, concluded that their records were correct. Possibilities for the shortfall were passed around, with the consensus being that James had been swindled by the merchant receiving the logs.

'James, I think this is a matter for the police. We have our own lawyers and, for the sake of the bank's reputation, we often initiate police investigations on behalf of clients. The merchant's name and the copy of the consignment note signed by the ship's officer will give us a good start.'

James, feeling sickened from the shock, motioned to chairs by a desk. When seated he expressed doubt as to the success of any search. 'All my logs are branded but this doesn't mean they'll be traceable. It's easy enough to remove brands and, once milled, all the evidence is gone. As to bills-of-lading signed by ship captains and receipts issued by merchants, it's anything goes. They collaborate, with graft money passing hands and, in the event of court action, false testimonies are tendered. I know how they work.'

The manager asked the ledger keeper to excuse himself and pulled his chair closer to James. 'James, apart from any legalities, this pilfering has to stop, otherwise you'll be short of funds. The account balance is already low and any more losses could see you in strife. To be realistic I think you should consign the logs to Partridge & Co. That way you'll be assured of receiving the correct payment.'

James stiffened at the mention of his parents' name and shook his head, without giving the suggestion any real thought. The manager, knowing something of James' estrangement from his family, continued, 'I know it's your business and your decision, but forgiveness is often the best remedy in these situations. We can make the contact.'

The pressing silence that ensued lasted a minute or more before James replied. 'No, that's not an option. There are some things that can never be forgiven. You might have some insight into my family but the truth is buried deep.' James then digressed. 'I have another idea. With Port Douglas booming it won't be long before cedar is shipped from there. Although Snapper Island has the advantages of deep water and being close to the shipping lane, Port Douglas is a lot closer to the river and has wharf facilities. I'm not sending any more on consignment. From now on I'm going to sell direct. There's enough local cedar to attract buyers. They've had it too good for too long.'

After further discussion the manager concurred with the idea and offered to 'scout about' for a suitable buyer. He also informed James that he would be manager of the new branch of the bank when it opened in Port Douglas in September. When James was about to leave the manager wished him well and said, 'Stay in touch.'

As James trudged along the main thoroughfare of Cooktown all he could see before him was gloom. He saw himself a failure, a man with a life unfulfilled, one destined to living the life of a pauper and maybe even buried in a pauper's grave. He bought another three bottles of wine and retreated to the solitude of his room where he sat in the dark till, inebriated and exhausted, he lay back and descended into a hell hole of nightmares that lasted till he was woken by the sound of street traffic.

He breakfasted at a stall in China Town and then made for the wharf where he spoke to the skipper of the *Pearl Shell* and cancelled his return passage to the river. He spent the remainder of the day in his room with a wine bottle to his lips, trying to allay the despair that beckoned him to end his life. That night took forever to pass, with the same harrowing nightmares plaguing his every attempt at sleep.

He rose before the sun, staggered from his room and left via the tradesmen's entrance to avoid being seen. He visited the same Chinese stall and sat on the ground, feeding himself from a bowl with his fingers. He had not changed since visiting the bank and now, ragged and dirty, took to the slopes of nearby Grassy Hill. He pushed through the long grass, stumbling over rocks as he made his ascent. At the top the blistering sun cut into his eyes and parched his throat, forcing him to return to the town below. He shunned passers-by who cast him a sympathetic look; even a lady who touched him on the shoulder and asked if he was all right. He rummaged in his pockets, pulling out notes and spilling coin when he bought a half dozen bottles of wine. He carried them, three clutched in each arm, and followed the sandy track to Finch

Bay. Here, he sat on the beach, defying the rising tide as he guzzled more. The sea overcame him, washing about his feet and then rising to his waist before he retreated to a sandy headland. This was the last he remembered before waking to the morning sun and dragging himself back to the hotel.

He sat on his bed with the door wide open, wondering where he had been and what had happened during the past days. He tugged at the grimy cuffs of his shirt and looked at his ruined shoes. Recollections remained scant, with his last clear memory being the bottles of wine he carried in his arms. He gradually remembered where he was and that he had loved ones waiting for him on the river. He felt no pain, no remorse, only a numbness as he packed his trunk, left a £1 note on the bed to pay for his lodgings and headed towards the wharf. Fortunately, he found a vessel making ready to sail to Port Douglas on the next tide and, for an extra £1, the skipper agreed to divert and take him to the landing on the Mossman River. They sailed part way, sheltered in an estuary overnight and completed the journey the following morning, reaching the landing at midday. James, hungry and exhausted, walked upstream along a well-worn path to arrive at Bajal's camp late in the afternoon.

Upon sighting him, Marku fell to her knees and sobbed into her hands. She thought that James had deserted her and the others of the camp. She had not believed Walt's assurance that he would return. James took her in his arms and cried, spilling tears down her bare breasts. Dari, Nganka and Bajal, trying to hide their doubts that he would return, hugged him with affection. Walt stood clear till the sentiment settled and then stepped forward, shook James' hand and said, 'Welcome back.' Dari jested that she knew he was coming back because she had cooked a curried wallaby stew and rice. That night James tried to explain to Marku but she put a finger to his lips, laid him down and kept watch over him while he slept.

CHAPTER 13

A couple of days after James returned Walt took him aside to discuss an event that had occurred during his absence.

'James, three surveyors called here when you were away. They oared up the river with a dinghy full of gear in tow. Said they finished surveying Ashton's block a while ago, have two more to do upstream and then they're going to survey the block where Bajal is camped.'

'They can't do that. It's Bajal's home!'

'I agree, but what can he do. If he doesn't move the police will come and burn his camp to the ground.'

'Who's taking up his block?'

'A man from Sydney. They didn't give his name, only that he comes from Sydney. He's selected 300 acres with a fair amount of river frontage.'

'How would he know what to select?'

'Not sure. I think it's the surveyors. Have heard stories of them making money on the side by selling information.'

'And his arrival?'

'Don't know. As soon as he has title I suppose. Probably just before the wet or soon after.'

James, hardly recovered from his binge in Cooktown, wavered in his thoughts and then asked about Ashton. 'When's Ashton moving in?'

'They reckon he'll be here in two to three months. Apparently he's based in Port Douglas and has been prowling about the place. Haven't seen him, so he's probably avoiding us till the title comes through. He's bragging about it at Port. Says it's the best block on the river. He's arranged for Alroy to shift two drays of equipment when it's shipped in. He has a few men to help him get started. He plans to build a post-and-rail fence to paddock draught animals, clear some forest for crops and pit-saw timber to build a house. They say he has a wife …'

The surveyors kept their distance from the camp, with the first indication of the survey of Bajal's block being a steel peg driven into the riverbank upstream and another downstream. James and his team continued on, putting their shoulder into the logging, stacking as many logs as possible for a big rafting to Port Douglas. The bank manager had sent a letter from his new office in Port Douglas, advising that a cedar buyer would be in Port from the eighth to the sixteenth of October and that the buyer would take all the quality cedar that could be supplied. This gave James an objective to work towards and could be the beginning of his financial recovery. These positive thoughts occupied his mind and eased his anxiety.

All went well till one Sunday, their day of rest. A tradition had evolved whereby Dari, the self-appointed chief cook, prepared a special Sunday lunch which they all shared at Bajal's camp. This day, under James' guidance, she had made plum pudding and custard to accompany the wild-duck stew that had been simmering since the previous evening. With the meal finished and due compliments passed to Dari, Murramu suddenly leapt to his feet, raced to the edge of the camp, whined and then stood, transfixed, staring into the bush. Bajal, knowing that this meant trouble, ran to his side, knelt and placed a hand on his shoulders. He felt Murramu's quivering and the reverberation of his whines through his body. He followed Murramu's gaze, peering into the open forest, looking for danger. The others, sitting cross-legged in the shade of a tree, craned their necks to see. Nothing came into view and it appeared to be a false alarm until, suddenly, Bajal spotted shadowy shapes heading his way from trees in the far distance. He turned, gave the others a petrified look and then waved for James to come to his side. James' worst fear had been realised. Through the forest haze he saw the shapes of mounted police coming their way. He gathered everybody about him and, in a few words, told them that bad men were coming, to stay calm and let him do the talking. The patrol, following the smoke from the fire, approached at a steady trot with rifles drawn.

Upon sighting the camp the eight mounted troopers broke into a canter and then a gallop, charging what they thought was an Aboriginal camp. Upon closing in on the camp they were surprised to find two white men shielding four Aborigines. The officer in charge, bearing braided epaulets, reigned to a halt a few feet from James and Walt. After a cautionary glance about, he holstered his rifle and motioned his men to do likewise. Walt feared the worst, believing they might be about to arrest him for a murder he had committed in New South Wales many years ago. The incident occurred before meeting James and, though he planned to confide in James, the matter, as yet, lay undisclosed. The police contingent—four white troopers and four native police—had between them only two packhorses that carried food rations, ground sheets, ammunition, marching chains and spare horseshoes. From the trooper's weathered look and the drawn flanks of the horses James deduced that they had been on patrol for several days and that today's charge had not been the first. While the officer knew of the logging activity on the river he was completely unaware that whites were living with blacks. He dismounted and introduced himself to James and Walt.

'Sub-Inspector Morgan,' he announced, without extending a hand of friendship.

James responded, giving his name and then pointing to Walt and stating his. James made no attempt to acknowledge the others of his camp. He wished to keep them anonymous and not indicate a close connection. When the officer pointed to them James quickly replied, 'We picked them up as help. Get a bit of work out of them for flour and tobacco.'

Morgan had been seconded from Cooktown to 'stamp out the blacks' in the hinterland of Port Douglas. His mission was to locate, harass and disperse the natives of the valley. He was well known on the Palmer River goldfield for his absolute intolerance of black people and readiness to shoot them on sight.

As he strode about the camp, kicking at everyday items and peeping into huts, it became apparent to James that he did not believe James' inference that there was no cohabitation with the black women. He came back to James, pointed to Marku and said, 'Who's she?'

'Oh, something of a roustabout; does cooking and washing.'

'And this one,' he asked, pointing to Dari.

'She's this one's mother,' he said, pointing to Marku.

'And this buck. What's he doing here?'

'He's a cousin and this is his woman,' he said, including Nganka. 'They give a hand with the logging.'

Morgan, disbelieving almost every word James had said, grunted and asked, 'Where's the rest of the tribe?'

'Don't know. We seldom see them.'

Morgan darted him a look. 'I hope you aren't withholding information. We take a dim view of sympathisers.'

'Not me. I'm only here for the timber. If they pester me I hit them with a scatter gun.' James knew his lie was as unconvincing as his earlier comments and that Morgan now had him as a marked man.

Morgan then turned on Walt. 'Where do you fit in? Which black woman are you sleeping with?' Walt, though wanting to break Morgan's neck with his bare hands, held his composure and replied. 'None. I have a wife and child in Cooktown.'

Morgan hit back. 'Is that so? So tell me, what's her address?'

Walt, not being very familiar with Cooktown, gave the address of his regular prostitute. Morgan, who knew the address well, gave Walt a look that told James that Walt was also a marked man.

Morgan did not bother to seek an opinion from the other white officers. His own opinion and, if need be, testimony would be sufficient to have most white men jailed and individual blacks disappear without question. In fact, he was chief slaughterman for the force, with his practices condoned by both senior officers of the force and government officials. He reported when and how he liked.

Morgan, having accomplished his purpose of instilling fear into the natives and their sympathisers, signalled to his troopers to prepare to depart. He then, without speaking a single word of goodwill during his visit, mounted, turned his back on the camp and rode off.

CHAPTER 14

With the date of the first shipment to Port Douglas nearly upon them the camp rallied to send their largest shipment to date. The logs, cut into lengths, lay by the water's edge and stretched the full length of the sandbar. Four days before the arrival of the steamship they began floating them down to the landing where they sorted and chained them as sea-going rafts. The steamer arrived at the appointed time and, with the rafts in tow, James and Walt joined the crew and sailed to the river mouth. From here they sailed across the bay to Port Douglas and completed the four-nautical-mile journey without incident. The harbour, on the lee side of a windswept promontory, proved perfect for docking, with the rafts being secured to large trees on the bank of the inlet. James visited his bank manager to make sure the arrangements with the buyer were in place. He and Walt then scoured the dusty streets of the town before settling into a crowded hotel bar where they stayed till after dark. They found their swags where they had left them and curled up by the inlet for the night. The owner of a slipway close by offered them an early cup of tea and breakfast.

'Lugger's my name. Fifteen years pearling on luggers in the Torres Strait earned me that. Best lifestyle but when you get to forty diving becomes too dangerous so running a slipway is the next best thing. There's no end to the work. I could work day and night if I wanted. What brings you pair to town?'

'Cedar,' said James. 'We're cutting on the Mossman. Brought rafts over yesterday and due to see a buyer later this morning.'

Lugger, dressed in shorts only, displayed the hallmarks of a seafarer: burnt brown and wiry, agile as a cat and with an opalescent pearl shell hanging from his neck. He was one of those personalities who could win favour in any company. He chattered incessantly while cooking, and when a fried egg fell to the floor he flipped it back into the pan without a flinch. He invited the boys to stay in his shed while in port and suggested they put their swags inside, away from the sun.

The buyer, a tubby man who, from his appearance, would surely stay in the best accommodation while in town, knew his business and struck a fair deal. He simply cast his practised eye across the rafts, counted the number of logs and did a quick calculation. To James' surprise his offer exceeded James' expectation by £40. He also banked at the Bank of New South Wales and by noon the manager had the money deposited to James' account.

This called for a celebration so they checked with Lugger and then bought a carton of top-shelf wine and fresh seafood and settled into the slipway shed for a party. Lugger, though small in stature, drank like a buccaneer on a spree, keeping them awake till past midnight. During the evening James warmed to his generous personality and thought that maybe there could be a place here for him and Marku. They missed a schooner returning to the river on the early morning tide so stayed at Lugger's open-air shed for another night. Lugger sold them a row boat that somebody had forfeited for non-payment of the repairs. Though it would fetch £8 on the open market he insisted they take it for £3, the cost of the repairs. They left on an incoming tide so that if the current became too strong while crossing the bay they would be washed inshore rather than out to sea. Taking turns to row they reached the mouth of the river in good time. So good that they considered rowing across when stores were needed, staying a night with Lugger and rowing home with the stores the following day.

Given the success of the Port Douglas sale, James decided to fell as many trees as possible before Ashton arrived. Dari took full charge of the camp while the others worked from daylight to dark dropping trees. This morning she collected vegetables from the garden, took a piece of salted wallaby from a brine cask and set to preparing a hearty lunch to keep the workers well fed.

'You cook too good,' said Walt, patting his belly after lunch.

'Me fix up man,' replied Dari, getting her words a little mixed.

James laughed aloud and, to show his appreciation, stepped close and kissed her on the cheek. Dari let fly with some crude remark that set Bajal, Nganka and Marku giggling.

'What did she say?' asked James, turning to Nganka.

'White man mind his own business!' she jested, telling a half-truth.

'Well tell Dari—'

James cut short his reply when Murramu jumped to his feet, bristled and whined. All followed his line of sight, and within moments Ashton and an aide appeared at the far end of the sandbar. Ashton waved and then came forward. He carried a stout riding crop as an accompaniment to his flashy riding attire. His aide, dressed in calico trousers and shabby boots, carried a rifle in hand and a cartridge belt strung across his hairy chest.

James, wishing to meet Ashton on gentlemanly terms, greeted him with a warm handshake.

'Seems you've been making hay while I've been away?'

'Trying to log as much as I can before the wet,' replied James. 'Once the wet comes that will be the end for the season.'

Ashton nodded and then explained, 'I'll be moving on site as soon as the teamster can wagon in the equipment and supplies. Plan to settle in the forest uphill from the river. Easier to clear the open forest than the riverside. I have men digging a well up there now; need to find water before building.'

James, accepting the inevitable, replied in a conciliatory tone. 'Once we've shifted the logs we'll be out of here.'

'What's your plan?' asked Ashton with a hint of self-interest.

'Not sure. Might log another patch.'

'Interested in working the land?'

'Could do, but there's other options.'

'Like?' quizzed Ashton.

'Port Douglas is booming. Plenty of opportunities over there. It's a place where a man can make money.'

'True,' conceded Ashton with another nod. He then tossed a suggestion. 'If you like I can lease you a few acres of my place. Plenty of room for you and your gang. I'd be happy to employ you and your crew till you get established.'

James, though feeling a loss of dignity at the suggestion, replied politely, 'I'll keep it in mind.'

'I can offer good terms,' added Ashton, not wanting to lose the opportunity of ready labour. He quickly followed with, 'Could also work out a deal for your white mate.'

Walt stayed quiet, his mind reeling with contempt. Never would he work for a blood-sucking overlord. He also took exception to Ashton's glances at Nganka.

In the discussion that followed Ashton made further reference to his offer, trying to persuade James to make his pool of labour available. James, for his part, had no intention of doing so and continued sidestepping the suggestions. When Ashton left, Walt, a staunch anti-royalist, launched a tirade of insults about the man and said that if he came to their camp again he would 'dunk him in the river'.

Much needed to be done. Bajal's weather forecast predicted a flood in mid-January. While many trees had been felled none had been sawn or hauled to the river. The team worked harder than ever, filling a quota of work each day to meet the target date. No Sunday rest days were taken and Christmas day passed as a work day. This test of strength, resilience and loyalty proved its worth when James sat with his friends the night before the rafting and announced, 'We have succeeded! This would not have been possible without your help.' He then became quiet and, in the silence, by the glow from the fire, he began to cry. He wept tears as he tried to further explain his gratitude. Marku, sitting beside him, took him in her arms and cuddled him, while Dari put a billy of water on the fire to make tea.

James and Walt accompanied the rafts to Port Douglas with their rowboat in tow and bunked with Lugger at his slipway. The buyer commented that the logs were equal to the best he had seen and paid James accordingly. After completing the transaction at the bank James wrote Walt a cheque that included a very generous bonus. They decided to have a party but did not realise that Lugger's idea of a party lasted three days. During the days of inebriation James spoke as never before, telling Walt and Lugger of his past, of Selene and the estrangement from his family. At the mention of Marku, Lugger told of his escapades with native women of the Torres Strait and of his children born to them. As to what he might do now that Ashton had taken over his patch James spoke of possibilities that included him and Marku coming to Port to live. He paraphrased the reason by saying, 'I've had enough of the river and Marku deserves a chance.'

Through their clouded thoughts of alcoholic euphoria James and Lugger stitched together a plan whereby James and Marku could build an extension to the slipway shed and open a ships chandlery business. Shipping needs were growing by the day and the business would complement Lugger's business of ship repairs. They spoke of including Walt but he had other plans. He revealed that, like James, he wanted to leave the river behind and make a new start. He would settle in Port, work for wages and maybe find a wife.

In accordance with James' policy, no alcohol was taken back to camp. Instead he bought bundles of clothing, jewellery, fishing tackle and assorted items that he thought those at the camp would appreciate. He bought a great pile of groceries, including enough to fill Lugger's bare pantry.

Those at the camp, knowing the importance of the sale, expected the men to celebrate and that they might arrive home a few days late. Their shouts and the joy in their expressions upon seeing the men row up the river even brought tears to Walt's eyes. The women rummaged through the bags of girlish things while Bajal toyed with the fishing tackle. Their infectious excitement extended to Murramu, sending him into a spin, trying to catch his tail. That night they feasted as never before: seafood, cream cakes and cordial, together with other tasty bits. When Marku and James retired to bed she cradled him and made him promise to deliver her a spirit child.

CHAPTER 15

With the logging finished Walt moved to Port Douglas and the camp shifted back across the river to the high ground. The summer storms had quenched the thirst of the landscape and soon the river would flood, washing away forever any evidence that once a cedar getter's camp had been on the sandbar. James and Marku were washing clothes by the river when a solitary oarsman appeared from around the corner. He stood upright in the boat, rowing steadily. Though he could see them he gave them no acknowledgement. He hardly made a ripple with the oars as he came closer, revealing himself as an athletic man dressed in trousers and a black hat. They thought he would pass them by until, little more than a boat length away, he nodded and skulled their way.

'Good morning,' he said with a cultured voice.

'Hello there,' replied James, somewhat mystified by this character alone on the river.

Without further words he stepped ashore, tied the boat to a tree and introduced himself as Winston Ambrose.

'Been on the river long?' he asked.

James took the opportunity to make conversation. He told how he camped there with Aborigines and invited him for a cup of tea. The stranger took a seat, and then removed his hat, revealing the fullness of his kindly expression. James tried to fathom the man's past. To be sure he had led a life of labour, but there were signs of his having come from a good home. They talked on, and from the questions being asked it became apparent that the man had a purpose in mind. Though he had not visited the river previously he knew a lot about the geography, particularly the riverside land and it's potential for farming.

James eventually asked, 'What brings you here?'

'Land,' replied the stranger without a ruffle. 'You'll be interested to know that I have selected this block where we're sitting; 300 acres in all. You've probably seen the pegs.'

While James knew that this day would inevitably come the unexpected announcement from such an unlikely source shocked him.

'When might you move in?' he asked, almost feverishly.

'Hopefully tomorrow. My food and equipment are at the landing and I don't want to leave it unattended. I've come up to have a look around and find a place to pitch my tent.'

James' curiosity deepened. Why would a man in his thirties want to live alone, in a tent, on a riverbank, in the backwoods?

'Would you like to show me about,' asked the newcomer, rising from his seat and stretching his long legs.

'Well, yes,' said James, feeling obliged.

They wandered the property, found the other survey pegs, and then returned to the riverside near Bajal's camp. The newcomer looked about briefly and announced that he would pitch his tent where they stood.

'I guess we'll have to leave?' asked James, desperate to settle the matter.

The man took his gaze from the river below, turned to James and quietly said, 'Your friends are my friends. I'd like you to stay.'

Those few words, spoken almost with melancholy in the stranger's voice, stayed with James ever after.

Winston's presence transformed the camp. Together with the others he battled the drenching rain, raging river, leeches and other deprivations brought about by the annual monsoon rains. Throughout the wet they persevered with logging and pit-sawing timber to build bush dwellings. Though roughly hewn, these first-ever European constructions in the valley, with their timber walls, tin roofs, earthen floors and rainwater tanks, marked the beginning of white intrusion into a land that for millennia had housed only native people in gunyahs and grass huts.

Winston and James pooled their resources, buying in and setting up everything needed for a well-equipped bush camp. Dari now had an annex to shield her from the sun while cooking. A sealed shed kept rodents from the food stores, a screened butcher shop stored cuts of salted meat, a pit closet provided convenience, and a clothesline replaced the practice of tossing clothes over bushes. Livestock found a place: two nanny goats and a buck that would provide milk and meat, a sow ready to drop her litter, hens and a rooster that made a welcome change from trapping wild turkeys and scratching about in leaf mould for their eggs. Ducks that swam in the river and returned home at evening to be fed.

At the close of the wet season Winston set to growing vegetables to supply the Port Douglas market. With the willing help of his friends, he began clearing land and planting market-garden crops to be shipped across the bay.

Winston, an accomplished seaman, bought a small sailing boat that he used to ferry the produce to market. He journeyed alone except for the occasions when James needed to visit for business. James always visited Lugger and with each visit the idea of he and Marku establishing a chandlery at his slipway firmed. One day, there by the seashore, he read a recent edition of *The Queenslander*.

He dwelt on an item that read:

The blacks are assuming the offensive, and several horses have been speared within the last eight or ten days on the road between Port Douglas and the Hodgkinson goldfield. I am informed by a settler named Molloy that he has twice come upon mobs of Aboriginals sneaking round his place, and on one occasion he discovered them only in time to save his horses. His wife also has seen them at some distance from the house during her husband's absence. Four loaded teams were despatched this week to the Hodgkinson, as well as a large number of packhorses. The gold escort arrived this morning, in charge of Sub-Inspector Icely, bringing 9000 oz. of gold. The *Lovett Peacock* and *Harriet Armitage* have completed loading their cargoes of cedar for the southern market ...

James sat and deliberated with mixed feelings. His earlier concern of leaving those at the river at the mercy of the whites had been allayed with the arrival of Winston. They were now well established and, God willing, their future secure. If he were to make a break, now was the time, while Port Douglas bubbled with opportunities. On the other hand he worried about Marku. How she would settle into a society foreign to her ways, with acceptance or otherwise by the white community. He spoke further with

Lugger, sailed back to the camp and announced to Winston his intention to leave the river and try his hand at town life. Winston, though surprised, understood and readily accepted his decision. He added, 'If it doesn't suit you, you can always come home.'

Those at the camp took time to accept the idea. Although Port Douglas formed the southern extremity of their tribal land and Marku had fished there as a child, much had changed since the arrival of the whites. Marku expressed enthusiasm but the others held back, not wishing to split the family and worrying about how Marku would cope. Dari made the decision for them when, at breakfast one morning, she said to all present, 'James and Marku can go so long as they promise to visit often.' From that moment relief spread through the camp and preparations were made for the shift.

CHAPTER 16

James visited Port Douglas, sealed the deal with Lugger, whereby James would build a shed adjoining Lugger's slipway and each would assist the other with no money passing hands. James also called on his bank manager to tell of his plan and placed an order with a merchant in Sydney for stocks of chandlery and fishing equipment. They pit-sawed red cedar boards at the camp, shipped them across the bay, sourced hardwood poles locally, built the shop and within two months were ready to open for business.

James and Marku, travelling as husband and wife, said their goodbyes and rowed across the bay to Port Douglas which, for convenience, people now simply referred to as Port. Once at sea the reality of leaving behind all that Marku knew and beginning a new life took hold. She looked landward, identifying the almond trees at the tribe's beach camp, the mangrove fringe at the end of the beach that held so many memories, and Muddy Creek where one of her near relatives had been taken by a crocodile. So near yet so far, the memories of her past almost within hand's reach but not within grasp. James, seeing the longing in her eyes, did most of the rowing, leaving Marku to gaze out across her people's land. She could never have guessed that this peaceful place in paradise would, within a few years, be transformed into a place where she and her people were not welcome.

Upon stepping ashore Marku was suddenly overcome by a feeling of dread. She felt a compulsion to rush into the sea and wade towards home. No matter about the crocodiles or the impossibility of swimming that far. None of that mattered. The separation from family and the security they provided tore at her emotions and, when James rushed forward and prevented her from swimming into the blue yonder, she became distraught, shaking and crying uncontrollably. James put his arms around her, led her to their new home and laid her on their swag. He sat, holding her hand, reassuring her that all would be well while, at the same time, agonising whether they should stay or return to the river. That night they made love and he promised her that if she wanted to leave then he would leave the building behind and go back to logging on the river. Marku, having made a commitment and knowing of James' ambition, dried her tears and told him that she would follow him wherever he went, no matter what the journey or destination. In reality she wanted nothing more than to be with him, to admire and wait on him day and night. James took her in his arms again and, as they lay in an embrace, she accepted James' promise of caring for her forever.

James wished to explore the new settlement and, within a few days of arrival, he left the shop in Lugger's care while he and Marku scouted the district. The portside town, a narrow strip squeezed between a barren hillside and a tidal saltpan, bustled with activity. Frontier men, eager to be on their way, loaded wagons destined for the Hodgkinson goldfield. Others, trading locally, advertised their wares and services from newly built shop fronts and tents. 'Nothing wrong with calico,' called a tobacconist when questioned whether his tent was waterproof. Shanties and a sprawl of makeshift camps spread about the township and along the teamster's track leading westward. The track, cut through scrubby mulga, followed a sand dune ridge for three miles and then opened into forest land. This open space where the packers and teamsters spelled their horse and bullock teams became known as Craiglie. By day men moved about with a spring in their step, making ready before attempting the gruelling climb over the Great Dividing Range where sparks flew from horse's shoes and blood dripped from bullock's yokes. Blacksmiths and farriers did a roaring trade, often making more money than those hardy men who risked all to push through to the Hodgkinson. Even at night the rattle of bells could be heard as teamsters mustered their teams to leave by moonlight to avoid the blazing sun. The grazing land extended a couple of miles to the Mowbray River and its valley, where running water made a welcome change from the stale water in the soaks and shallow wells at Craiglie. Every man carried a rifle and often travelled in the company of others to protect himself and his team from marauding Aborigines. Only a few white women had crossed these rugged mountains and ventured into the wilderness beyond.

While James thought all of this interesting Marku saw it differently. Ships crammed the inlet where she and members of her tribe had fished. The barren hill by the township, a place of spiritual significance, now flew flags that signalled ship arrivals. The sandy mulga that teamsters often cursed was no longer home to bush turkeys. Craiglie, once a quiet Aboriginal camping ground, had become a rowdy marshalling yard. The Mowbray, the home of their southern corrobboree ground and its bora ring, was now grazing land for the white man. No longer would the Mossman River tribe be able to meet with the Barron River and Hinterland tribes for their annual celebration. The native trading route over the mountains that the Aboriginals had shown to the white men could no longer be used for fear of being shot. The lust for gold had taken priority over native tradition. All of this Marku understood as she stood, shocked and dismayed, looking at the tribal bora ground trampled by the teamster's livestock.

Portside Chandlery soon become known and well patronised. Apart from the Hodgkinson track all goods came by sea. Seamen called regularly to purchase replacements and spares for their boats and fishing equipment. Marku, still shy of white men, busied herself outside under a sail sheet repairing sails and making fishing nets. As an aside she made mother-of-pearl jewellery from pearl shells Lugger sourced from the Torres Strait. These were sold in the shop and James encouraged her to come inside and attend to customers that showed interest. She prided herself in her work and would have given the pieces away if James had not insisted on taking money. Nobody would ever have guessed that they lived under the sail sheet by day and moved their swag inside the shop each night. James tidied his appearance with a regular haircut, beard trim and by wearing a shirt. Marku likewise cut and styled her hair and took a liking to wearing kaki shirt and trousers. Nobody cared that neither of them wore shoes. Lugger, apart from the occasional binge, played his hand well, doing quality work and building a clientele.

James bought a small sailing boat that he and Marku used to visit those on the river. While Winston provided all the provisions for Bajal's camp, Marku always took lollies and biscuits. On return trips they loaded the boat with firewood for cooking and some red cedar offcuts that Marku sculpted for sale in the shop. Visits were generally for three nights giving them ample time to discuss river gossip. Two more gangs of cedar cutters now worked on the river, with one gang bringing their own bullock team. More free settlers selected acreage in the district, while some destitute Chinese miners from the dwindling Palmer River gold rush drifted in to squat by the river, grow vegetables and live off the land. Ashton stayed on his side of the river but Bajal sneaked across and reported that the house was nearly finished. Alroy's son, Shaun, became infatuated with one of the young native girls that visited Bajal's camp and could soon find himself in strife. Christmas Day proved to be a bonzer event, with many from the tribe walking cross-country to share in a pig roasted on a spit. Of course Dari strutted about, claiming credit for the cooking. Winston enjoyed the company and made a speech, thanking everybody for their help during the year.

PART TWO

COLONIAL OPPRESSION OF THE ABORIGINES

European police officer and native police apprehending Aborigines in North Queensland 1890s.

CHAPTER 17

Another wet season came and went, washing the river clean, greening the forest and replenishing the grassland. Winston and his team seeded their crops early, tended them carefully and were the first to supply Port Douglas with new-season vegetables. He was standing by a maturing crop of corn, musing about his success, when Jonathan Ashton rode into view astride a thoroughbred stallion. Although Winston had not previously met Ashton there could be no mistaking the posh gent who carried a riding crop.

'Good day to you, Sir,' called Jonathan, while taking the liberty of dismounting before being invited.

'And to you,' replied Winston, taking off his black hat.

'Jonathan Ashton,' he announced in an affable tone.

'Winston Ambrose.' The men greeted each other with a handshake.

'Seems you're well ahead with clearing and cropping,' said Ashton. 'I have five men working six days a week cutting trees and burning. Virgin land is always the best, I say. My crops are growing like topsy and with about two thousand people in and around Port, and that many again on the Hodgkinson, there's a ready market for all I can grow. Livestock is a problem, though, with the blacks prowling about. Haven't had any trouble yet but if I do I have a couple of Rottweilers chained at the house. If there's any pilfering or killing of livestock I'll let them loose. You've probably heard them bark …'

'We're safe here,' commented Winston, pointing to Bajal and Nganka who were chipping weeds nearby. 'I have a good relationship with them and don't expect any trouble.'

'Interesting,' said Jonathan with a shrewd edge to his voice. 'Can they be picked up easily?'

'Don't think so. I was lucky to inherit these from a logger who camped here.'

'Trustworthy?'

'I'd stake my life on this lot. They've picked up the white man's ways and fit in well.'

'And the old girl chopping wood by the fire?'

'Oh, Dari. Wouldn't be without her. She's something of a matriarch and keeps them in order.'

'Could you spare her for a month or two? My wife's arrived from Goulburn and she's wary of the blacks. If I introduced her through a half-civilised one then maybe she'll settle.'

'Don't think so. They're tribal by nature and don't take well to being singled out.'

'Well, maybe part-time housekeeping. What about the young one?' and he looked towards Nganka. 'Maybe she could come over some days. I would pay her well with produce and meat.'

Winston gave the matter quick consideration and replied, 'I could ask. She's a smart girl and likes to associate with whites.'

'What if we ask her now?'

'No. They don't like to be pounced on. I'll ask her later and let you know.' Winston then added, 'I'd expect her to be treated right.'

'No problem. I'm sure she and my wife Ellen would get along fine.'

They remained there in the warmth of the winter sun discussing matters of common interest till Jonathan excused himself. He mounted and, as he turned to leave, called, 'I'll be back in the morning for an answer.'

Dari, wanting to know what the cocky man from over the river wanted, called everyone for a cup of tea, hot damper and syrup. Winston took his time, talking around the point, giving all time to grasp the detail. When finished he signalled his own approval by turning to Nganka and saying, 'If you go over there you won't be able to sit on the ground like that.' Nganka quickly scrambled to her knees and, with a gleeful look, said she would do everything right. Bajal, also curious about the white man's big camp, thought it might open an opportunity for him to visit and readily agreed. Dari, with her frown that could mean anything from slight disapproval to impending doom, expressed caution saying, 'Dem white fella like black girl.'

Jonathan arrived next morning and, in anticipation of agreement, brought a batch of scones baked by Ellen. Dari took charge of them, chewed at one with her gapped teeth and asked for the recipe. Since Dari could neither read nor write Jonathan suggested that Ellen teach Nganka how to cook them in their wood oven. Dari replied with a look that suggested she should be the one to learn from Ellen. They settled on one day a week housework, and in return Nganka could take home whatever she liked from the garden and meat when available.

Nganka busied herself like a girl preparing for her first outing. She boiled her shirts and trousers in the copper boiler for hours, brushed her hair often, cleaned her teeth, laid jewellery on a wallaby hide in her hut and admired herself in a mirror. She thought it would be like stepping into wonderland; seeing a flash white man's camp, meeting a white woman, the workers, the animals and the dogs she had heard barking. On the first morning she hugged everyone in her camp, stepped out confidently and waved to them when she had crossed the river. A shortcut leading through the rainforest soon brought her to the open country of Jonathan's property. There before her, set high on a slope, stood a home like nothing she had ever imagined. The home, with brick chimney and sprawling verandahs, covered an area the size of Winston's camp. Plants and shrubs never before seen grew in splendour behind a white-picket fence wrapped around the house. Outbuildings, yards and pens to store equipment and house livestock stood in stark contrast to the huts and gunyahs she knew. A cluster of slab huts with thatched roofs seemed grand residences for the labourers who worked the land. In the distance men could be seen tending the crops and orchard.

Nganka approached the home cautiously, hoping someone would see her and extend a welcome. She opened the picket gate, stepped to the wide verandah and called, 'You there, Ma'am. It's me, Nganka.' Within moments a lady appeared at the doorway dressed in a white bodice that neatly covered her breasts and a long skirt. Her skin, soft and pale except for the tincture of pink colouring her cheeks, and the golden locks spilling about her shoulders, held Nganka spellbound. Never could she have visualised that a woman could be so beautiful.

'Ellen,' said the lady, introducing herself with a gentle smile. 'Come in.'

With grace that would be envied by most of the aristocracy she took Nganka's hand and guided her through the house room by room, explaining a little about each as they entered: the living room with polished floor, red cedar walls and high ceiling; the spacious kitchen and fully stocked pantry; steps leading downstairs to conveniences; a drawing room, sewing room and four guest rooms with satin bedspreads and expensive window drapes. She kept till last the master bedroom where a lavish four-poster bed stood centrepiece to a room adorned with lace and fine furnishings. Ellen paused here and almost in a whisper said, 'This is where Jonathan and I sleep.' Her voice carried no joy, only the melancholy of a lonely bride.

'Nganka,' she said, 'I don't expect you to work hard. It's company I seek. I'm the only white woman on the river.'

Nganka, thinking she understood what was said but unsure of the meaning, replied calmly, 'Yes, Ma'am.'

Nganka followed her to the kitchen where they made a pot of tea, took biscuits from a canister and sat together by a small table on the verandah. Ellen expressed interest in Nganka's personal life, asking if she were married, loved her husband and were there children. Nganka proved to be good company, listening, saying little and not being judgemental. To break a long pause Ellen placed her hands on the table, spread her delicate fingers and hesitated as though in anticipation that Nganka would place her hands on hers. Nganka stayed shy of what she thought was the suggestion, keeping her hands to herself. Ellen, with resignation in her voice, then said quietly, 'Best we have you do something so as to be able to tell Jonathan.'

With a bucket of water and a brush Nganka knelt on her knees and began scrubbing the verandah floor. She recalled Winston telling her that she must keep her clothes clean to make a good impression and to this end she stripped off her shirt and trousers, leaving her naked to continue scrubbing. When, some distance along the side verandah, Ellen suddenly appeared, wide-eyed and surprised, Nganka immediately stood and, unaware of the significance of her nakedness, began to tell Ellen the reason her clothes were hanging on the verandah rail. Ellen seemed not to want an explanation and, with Nganka standing before her, she undid the tie of her bodice, stepped forward, took Nganka in her arms and kissed the cleavage of Nganka's breasts.

Nganka continued visiting once a week when, most times, they had the house to themselves. Work and pleasure were mixed and Nganka always arrived home with a selection of vegetables, a live goat strung across her shoulders or a leg of smoked ham. Nobody asked questions and everybody remained happy.

Rumours of strife between blacks and whites circulated about the district, with mentions being made daily in the streets of Port Douglas. A contingent of native mounted police, now stationed at Mowbray, meant that local Aborigines could be tracked and gunned down more easily. During James' last visit to the river Winston told how three ill-fated Chinamen had been attacked upstream from his camp. One fled and the bodies of the other two had not been found. Within days of the murders mounted police called at Winston's camp and interrogated Bajal. He remained quiet and uncooperative until the officer in charge took chains from his saddle bag and threatened to march him overland to Port Douglas and put him in the lockup. Bajal surprised Winston by convincing the police he had no knowledge of the incident when, in fact, Winston was aware that Bajal knew the names of the perpetrators and where they were camped. Though Bajal lived apart from his tribe the bush telegraph, an Aboriginal way of spreading word by way of mouth, kept him well informed of tribal matters. After all, they were family, and why should he not lie to protect his kin? James nodded agreement when told and recalled reading a particularly nasty item in the *Port Douglas Gazette.*

> The blacks of the Mossman, the Daintree, Saltwater and Mowbray Rivers are as dangerous as they are numerous. They appear to have a special liking for spearing horses and cattle. While they have no objection to turning their hands to cutting the throats of white people, they will do so if they think they can without being 'dispersed' by a bullet through their heads. We are reminded by our new contemporary of the killing and hacking into mincemeat of Hanley and his two mates. During the last two months three horses belonging to Mr. Moffatt (one of them worth £50), were speared within a mile of the town, two of them mortally, while a fourth is missing. Mr. C. Emerson lost two horses and a foal, and Mr. Price a couple, all speared. Not long ago Mr. Jones a settler on the Mossman found he had a horse killed, and a week or so since, he found that a valuable horse and three cows had been speared to death close to his homestead, while others had been driven away …

> We should be sorry to see a second edition of old times, when 'Notices' were revolvers—and when settlers met together for the purpose of enjoying a day's 'turkey shooting'.

CHAPTER 18

The year 1881 brought an influx of Europeans and Chinese to the river valley. With most of the Palmer River alluvial gold mined, men deserted the diggings in hordes and passed through the port of Cooktown seeking a life elsewhere. With the Mossman River and its fertile land only a day's sailing south of Cooktown, they flocked to the district. Men arrived in steamships and sail boats, with many vessels being hardly seaworthy. Some miners even walked the distance through rugged, scrub-clad ranges, taking a chance that their meagre provisions would last the distance and that natives would not cross their path. Stories of escaping from Aboriginal attacks and others of Aborigines saving lives were told around camp fires. It seemed that if the natives had been harassed by whites previously then a hostile reception could be expected and, if not, a friendly greeting might be extended. A tide of humanity surged into Port Douglas, with people sleeping in swags and sheltering under tent flies. Gaunt men, wearing nothing more than tattered trousers or loin cloths, begged for work in exchange for food. Many passed through to the Hodgkinson gold field while others stayed local or crossed the bay to the Mossman River. River traffic increased daily, with sail and rowboats navigating to the upper reaches of the river, and those offloaded at the lower landing trudging their way upriver to find an unoccupied space. Both branches of the river and tributary creeks echoed to the shouts of men.

The early selectors, having suffered from labour shortages, welcomed the Chinese labourers, with some even giving thanks in their prayers. Cheap labour to clear the land and grow crops drew moneyed selectors from the south. Men queued at the Port Douglas lands office, anxious to stake their claim. The man behind might be applying for the same slice of land! Their camps were no more than a clearing in the bush with a smouldering fire. Swags and hand tools dotted the landscape in the rush. Land, thought to be the enduring resource, replaced the lust for gold and red cedar. With food scarce they shot everything within sight and fished the river, pillaging the food stocks of the Aborigines. When a succession of rifle shots were heard, men stiffened their spines, thinking it an Aboriginal attack and that they might be next.

As the settlers forged ahead, plumes of smoke spiralled into the sky as the pristine forest was cut, piled high and set alight. The smell of smoke lingered in the air at night, and when the morning sea breeze strengthened, fanning the fires, fresh clouds of smoke filled the sky, blanketing the sun. Wildlife stood no chance, scurrying before the flames, with those escaping often blinded or maimed to die a cruel death. The land clearing decimated animal habitats and populations, leaving those that survived with little space to shelter and forage. Flowering trees frequented by honey bees fell victim to axemen. Lagoons that had survived the clearing were commandeered by the whites as watering points for livestock, turning once productive food sources into mud holes.

An overland track, cut through the bush from Port Douglas to the Mossman River, brought more men, wagons and equipment. Horse teams, shipped in from the south, strained at chains to remove stumps to leave the land bare and vulnerable to the torrential rain of the wet season. Horse-drawn ploughs then turned the soil, destroying its structure and the soil-borne life necessary for its health. Whichever way they turned the whites took to the task diligently, destroying all that had been set in place over thousands of years. The more heavily vegetated the land, the more fertile the soil, so men leant on tree stumps and smoked pipes while sizing how best to fell and destroy the towering rainforest.

Huge swathes of forest country were cleared, animal populations reduced to remnants, soil degraded and Aborigines deprived of food. Not to mention the loss of their way of life and places of spiritual significance. Yes, the white men had arrived and, by whatever means necessary, they were here to stay.

Nganka crossed the river, followed the evergreen path through the rainforest, skirted around Jonathan's grove of papaya trees, crossed a small field where saddle horses grazed, opened the picket gate and skipped up the steps to the verandah.

'Ma'am,' she called from the doorway, and when no reply came she called louder, 'Ma'am.' Still no answer. Nganka became curious. Ellen always met her at the door to signal if Jonathan was nearby. She quietly stepped into the living room and called again.

'Here, Nganka,' came a muffled reply from the bedroom. Nganka, barefoot and still unaware of Jonathan's whereabouts, slipped along the corridor to find Ellen lying on the bed covers dressed in a light nightdress. Ellen beckoned her closer and held out her hands. Nganka crossed the polished floor, took Ellen in her arms and kissed her on the lips.

'Thank goodness you came. I was beginning to worry,' she whispered when their lips parted. She then patted the bed for Nganka to sit by her side. Nganka, mystified to find Ellen still in bed, put a hand to her forehead to check for a fever.

'No illness. Just morning sickness,' she said, placing Nganka's hand on her tummy.

'Morning sick?'

'Yes, I'm going to have a baby and this is what happens. Girls get sick some mornings. After a while it goes away.'

Nganka, thinking that somehow she had planted a spirit child into Ellen, patted her tummy to feel for the child.

'No. Not yet. Probably seven months away. I've told Jonathan. He's pleased and hopes it's a boy.'

Nganka, having no knowledge of biology and believing that an unborn child came from the spirit world after a mating, asked, 'Spirit child from me or Jonathan?'

'From Jonathan. It can't be from you.' She kissed Nganka's hand to avoid any embarrassment. 'Here,' and she made room for Nganka to snuggle beside her. 'Jonathan's ridden off and won't be home for hours.'

They hugged and cuddled, tossing their clothes and the bed covers aside in their excitement. Ellen, yearning to be loved, lay naked and giving as Nganka fondled. They took turns until Ellen, exhausted and perspiring, turned the other way. Nganka propped herself against the bedhead and looked Ellen's way. Ellen stared at the wall as if somehow distracted and, when Nganka placed a hand on her shoulder, she asked, 'Nganka, do you love me?'

Nganka, unsure what to say, remained silent.

Ellen then turned to Nganka and revealed herself by saying, 'I love you. I truly do.' She continued, 'If it weren't for you I wouldn't still be here.'

Nganka lay down, kissed Ellen and with a knowing smile waited for her to say more.

'Jonathan's a good man from a good family, but our marriage was a mistake. My parents are grocers in Goulburn and I grew up helping in the shop, knowing everybody in the town and playing with friends. Without realising it these people filled my need for company. People were kind and considerate and when I was sad someone would always give me a hug to lift my spirits. I knew no different. Somebody was always there to care for and comfort me. There were times when I tried to hide my emotions but there was always someone who understood and came to the rescue.

'When Jonathan proposed to me I thought I was the luckiest girl in the world, marrying into a good family that owned the largest estate in the district. In the early days of our marriage there were no problems because I still had my friends and Jonathan had no objection to my going to town visiting. We did want children. Especially his mother who I can remember saying "their pedigree lines are well matched". We tried for a few years but his interest slowly waned and our bedroom routine suffered. So much so that I had to nearly beg him to make love to me.

'He has always needed to prove himself and, without considering me, announced that we were going to northern Australia to open new land. Believe me, I have never been so shocked in all my life. What, leave my friends and family to come to this place? He seemed not to care what I thought or felt. He simply made the arrangements and told me we were going.

'Imagine how I felt, leaving everything behind to come to this godforsaken place where I'm the only white woman. Since arriving he's become more obsessive, worrying more about his crops and the men than me. There's nothing between us anymore.'

Ellen paused and became teary, leaning into Nganka for comfort. Nganka cradled her, kissing her damp forehead and soothing her with soft words. Ellen struggled to regain control because she had more to say.

'Nganka, I was about to leave him when you came along. Don't know how I was going to book passage but I had written to my parents telling them all and of my decision to leave. I have received no reply and feel that they think I should stay and be loyal to my husband. It seems that now, nobody but you understands me. You are all I have.'

Ellen put her hands to her face and sobbed, crying out for understanding and help. Nganka became entwined in Ellen's emotion, shaking, sweating and weeping. They sat there, naked on the bed in each other's arms, till Ellen said, 'Nganka, if you don't love me then please say so and I will understand.' She then lifted her head and, with pleading eyes, asked, 'Do you love me?'

Nganka for the first time admitted to herself that she loved Ellen and spoke with sincerity when she said, 'Yes, I love you. I love you very much.'

'And of Bajal?' asked Ellen.

'Yes, I love him too. I love you both and will always be with you and Bajal.'

They cuddled further, reaffirming their love for one another till a whinny from the horse stalls had them scramble to dress.

CHAPTER 19

James received the following note via a messenger:

Tuesday

Jajin the medicine man has died.
Please come quickly.

Winston

'What is it?' asked Marku, seeing the distress on James' face.

'Jajin has died.'

'How?'

'Don't know. It's a note from Winston telling us to come quickly. I'd say he's been dead for a day.'

'We must go right now!' said Marku.

'Yes, yes. I'll tell Lugger we're going.'

'Be fast. I'll roll our swag,' she called after him.

James spoke to Lugger. 'We've got bad news. One of Marku's people has died and we're going to the funeral.'

'Not by boat I hope?' replied Lugger.

'Why not?'

'The south-easterly is blowing a howler!'

'So?'

'You'd never make it in your sailing boat. You'd be caught in the bay, pushed on to the mud flats of Muddy Creek and be crocodile meat by tomorrow.'

'If we get stuck we can walk the distance.'

Lugger grunted at James' ignorance of the sea and warned, 'You'll be stuck up to your crotch in mud and won't be able to move. Believe me, I've been over there and it's treacherous in a swell like this.'

'Well, we'll walk!'

'That's a better idea. I'll look after the shop while you're gone.'

James turned to Marku and called, 'Leave the swag. We're going on foot.'

They left within minutes, following the wagon track to Craiglie and then heading north till they passed through the gap in Cassowary Range. From here they covered the remainder of the twelve miles at a trot, drawing hard for breath till they reached Winston's camp.

'Winston!' called James, seeing him sitting by the fire.

Winston, who had been waiting anxiously, rose and spun around saying, 'Thank God you're here. The others have gone and I'm left minding the camp.'

'Where to?' asked James, catching his breath.

'To the Jinkalmu village near the Gorge. Apparently his funeral is being held at the ceremonial ground there.'

Marku removed her clothes, revealing her sweaty body that glistened in the sun. 'I must get ready,' she explained, taking a lump of white ochre from a hut and going to the river.

James packed rations in a sack and spoke with Winston till Marku returned. With her naked body now streaked with white she looked more like a wild native than a shop keeper from Port Douglas. After giving Winston a hug and saying a hurried thanks she and James headed upriver, sparing nothing of themselves in the rush to be there in time.

While James had heard of the ceremonial site he had never visited and was surprised to find it a riverside place strewn with gravel and granite rocks.

The wailing and chants were clearly heard from a mile distant and when they broke through the cordon of trees James beheld a sight that would remain with him for the rest of his life. The whole tribe had assembled to pay tribute to Jajin, a man revered by all. The black figures swaying in the smoke haze, stomping, dancing, shouting and crying laments, held James mesmerised till Marku took him by the hand. She led him to her family group gathered by a cluster of bottlebrush trees. The trees, twisted and scarred from the torrents of past floods, displayed tassels of bright, crimson flowers. James saw this ceremony as an expression of unbridled grief, a show of respect equal to anything European culture could offer. To his mind this spectacle represented the pulse of a vibrant culture equal to any other.

Amidst the tears and hugs and the shouts of welcome he received upon arrival he knew that this was his place in life; living with people respectful of the land and its people. Nothing would change his mind. In spite of the deprivations and hardships he had found peace here in the wilderness amongst people who had lived in isolation for 60,000 years. He marvelled at these people who were now his family and smiled at the thought of him and Marku having a child to proudly carry his name forward.

As evening drew near James moved aside and thought reverently about Jajin, the medicine man who had saved his life when he was bitten by a snake, and how Jajin had inducted him into the tribe. He recalled how Jajin had not asked for or expected any thanks in return. To James this was the true meaning of life, to care without expecting any recompense. He slipped into a reverie and when Marku, sweaty and dusty, came to him by the firelight and took his hand, he undressed and joined the throng in song and dance, giving thanks to the guardian spirits of their world.

At first light the next morning James rolled across to Marku and, even though family members lay close by, he and Marku made love on the bare ground with him promising to seed a child. Marku willingly engaged, taking all she could to spawn the child they had both wished for since that first day on the sandbar by the river. Only scraps of food remained after two days of ritual. Even so every last morsel was offered around, with each passing the food to the next in a gesture of goodwill. James and Marku were sitting naked with the others when the thunder of galloping horses descended upon their private gathering. The tribespeople, unarmed due to the ceremony, leapt to their feet, with the more agile dashing towards the river as a contingent of native mounted police, led by a white sergeant, hurtled towards them with gravel flying from their horses' hooves. They fired a volley of shots into the air and then pulled their mounts to a halt by Jajin's corpse, which lay exposed on a thatched mat by the central fire. Those who had not managed to escape froze in fear that any movement would bring a blast their way. The young white officer, too stupid to realise that these people did not speak English, shouted, demanding they lie on the ground, and when nobody moved he became agitated, threatening to shoot them all. James, riled but contained, came forward as a spokesperson. He came right beside the officer's jackboot in the stirrup and spoke quietly.

'Do you have a problem with these people?'

The officer snapped back, 'People. You call them people. They're nothing more than savages. I want them out of here!'

'Then where do you suggest they go,' countered James.

'Away. Take their scabby bodies elsewhere, away from the settlers. They have no right to be here'

'Rights. You talk of rights. What gives you the right to charge into a private funeral service and threaten violence,' said James, becoming hostile.

'I am authorised under the law to keep the peace. These people are a clear threat to peace and must disperse.'

'Are you ordering them to leave now?'

'Yes.'

'And what of the body of the deceased?'

'If they want it, they can drag it away with them!'

If it were not for the six native troopers at the sergeant's flank James would have pulled the officer from his horse and dealt him a flogging. Instead, he turned to his people, spoke fluently in their language, explained the situation and, to avoid a blood bath, asked them to obey the order. He then turned to the officer and said that he personally would attend to the corpse.

The officer, feeling empowered by his position, gave them till midday to clear the site.

After the troop had ridden away James tried to explain but the tribespeople could fathom nothing of the white man's way.

James, having never before attended a native burial, was left aghast when he experienced what was yet to come. As the tribe regrouped the elders met and decided to take Jajin's body to a secret location deep within the rainforest. Young warriors took hold of the mat on which Jajin lay and followed a select group of men and women as they proceeded to the base of Mount Demi and then wound their way along a narrow track to a valley hidden deep within the folds of the mountain. At a clearing which no white man had ever sighted, the final stages of the funeral rites were conducted. While some gathered wood and lit a smoky fire beneath a platform four feet from the ground, others prepared the body for mummification. To chants and at times hysterical gesticulations, appointed members of the tribe began disembowelling the corps, including the heart and lungs. As parts were removed they were held high for all to see before being placed aside in accordance with ritual. With rigor mortis now passed and the muscles again relaxed the body was placed in a sitting position with the legs drawn up against the chest and the hands across the face. Once again, according to status within the tribe, chosen men lifted the body to the platform where it would be smoked till dry and leathery. Once completed the mummy would be stored in a dry place and removed for display on occasions like corroborees.

James, indebted to Jajin for saving his life and having inducted him into the tribe, was expected to take part in the mummification as a mark of respect. Marku explained this to him but, as the natives had not understood him earlier in the day, he struggled to comprehend this situation. He tried to assist but the putrid stench—even the thought of the decomposing corpse—caused such revulsion that he could not bear to look at the sight, let alone handle the deceased's body.

Everybody camped there that night, keeping the fire stoked and chanting to the sound of clap sticks. Next morning James and Marku, together with some others, retraced their steps along the track and broke out into the welcoming glare of the open forest. When back at Winston's camp, James, believing he could still smell the stench, burned his clothes.

CHAPTER 20

Ellen sat on the duchesse stool, admiring herself in the mirror, while Nganka brushed her hair. Her full-length petticoat clung tightly to her breasts, hips and tummy, showing the advanced stage of her pregnancy. Nganka fondled Ellen's silken hair as she brushed and, when finished, put her hands on Ellen's shoulders, kissed her on the cheek and gazed at her reflection in the mirror. Nganka loved Ellen dearly and would do anything for her mistress, but she still called her 'Ma'am'. Ellen lifted a hand, took Nganka's and squeezed it tightly, signalling for them to snuggle into bed.

Jonathan, realising that Ellen needed care and having noted the deep friendship between she and Nganka, actively encouraged Nganka to visit. Those on the other side of the river, though having not yet met Ellen, saw the sparkle in Nganka's eyes and took this to be Nganka's delight at being accepted into a white family. Nganka visited two, sometimes three times a week, leaving after breakfast and returning early afternoon when Ellen rested. She revelled in learning the white man's ways and soon took charge of most household duties, including cooking.

Jonathan spent most of his days in the fields, working beside the Chinese tenant farmers who were clearing his land in return for leasing rights to some of the property. Nganka often stood by the kitchen window watching the Chinese in their conical straw hats labouring to bring the virgin country into production. With sixty acres seeded with an assortment of crops and vegetables, an orchard nearly ready for its first fruiting, and additional land fenced for grazing, it seemed that Jonathan's dream would be fulfilled. He had become softer, more conciliatory and, as Nganka and Ellen had discussed, there was now hope their marriage might survive.

As to a midwife for the birth Nganka wanted she and Dari to attend but Ellen insisted on a white woman from Port Douglas and put the arrangements in place. The moment labour pains became evident one of the Chinese tenants was to drive a buggy to Port Douglas and return with the midwife while Jonathan cared for Ellen. The girls monitored the baby's movements, trying to guess the date of delivery, but, in reality, neither had a clue. When Ellen's tummy distended well down, indicating that the time was near, Nganka lay awake at night, tossing between worrying about the birthing and the joy of having a newborn. Bajal felt the excitement and covered Nganka most nights in the hope she could have a baby of her own.

Nganka now crossed the river daily to check on Ellen and was surprised when one morning she found a horse and buggy hitched to the picket fence. She rushed upstairs and hurried inside without being announced.

'Ma'am,' she called when inside.

'Here, in the bedroom,' called Jonathan.

Nganka hastened to the main bedroom to find Ellen sitting up in bed with a cup of tea, the midwife present and Jonathan standing close by nursing the baby.

Nganka could not contain herself. She peeked at the baby wrapped in a blanket, gave Jonathan a hug with one arm, smiled at the midwife, knelt by the bed, took Ellen's hand and held it to her lips as a show of love and respect. Nobody thought anything of it. Nganka's show of spontaneity showed that she truly cared.

Nganka believed that the baby was a spirit child belonging to her and Ellen and therefore needed to be included in her family across the river. Within a week, everyone in Winston's camp crossed the river to meet Ellen and the baby and enjoy tea and scones. Nganka continued visiting, caring for Ellen, Jonathan and the baby girl they named Frances Marra, with Frances being Jonathan's mother's name and Marra the Aboriginal name for the zamia palm.

After the Sunday service at St Mary's Church, Port Douglas, Matron Duggan of the local hospital took Father O'Malley aside to tell of a concern.

'Father, if you would be so kind as to spare a moment,' she said, stepping aside from the others of the congregation.

'Certainly, Elizabeth.'

'Father, I'm worried about a black lad that has been in the hospital and is now in the lockup ...'

Matron spoke on, explaining that a young Aboriginal man had been apprehended for theft and, during the arrest, the police had hit him over the head with a rifle barrel, gashing his skull and causing concussion. He had been chained to the hospital bed for his four days' stay and during that time ate nothing and did not speak a word. The only response he made was to touch her arm each time she dressed his wound. He was now in the lockup awaiting a hearing and she feared that if the police did not bash him to death then he would starve himself to death or suicide. When she had finished, Father took the details, thanked her and said, 'Leave it with me.'

The next morning the court messenger visited James' chandlery and handed him a message from the magistrate of the court, asking him to call at his office for 'a chat'. As it happened James, wanting to integrate Marku into white society, had encouraged her to take employment as a house keeper, and she occasionally spent a day cleaning the magistrate's house. Thinking the note referred to Marku's cleaning he promptly visited the office. To his surprise the meeting concerned an Aboriginal lad who, Marku later confirmed, was well known to her.

'James, the problem I have as magistrate is that most of these petty offences don't warrant a mention but the police keep making arrests on which I have to adjudicate. This lad has apparently stolen a handful of vegetables, been hit over the head with a rifle and is now in the lockup waiting to be sentenced by me. While I have to be seen to be consistent with sentencing there's a possibility that if the matron and Marku both speak on the lad's behalf he might be excused.'

James, understanding the thread of what was being said, asked, 'If convicted what happens to him?'

'Probably sent to a prison farm down south.'

'What sort of farm?'

'Growing vegetables and the like. Not many return to tell the story.' The magistrate then added, 'It's best he not go.'

'Agreed,' said James. 'What do you want Marku to do?'

'Well, the matron is going to submit that the lad is a little deficient mentally and has suffered enough with the hit to the head. If Marku could support this with a personal character reference this could give me room to move. As you can appreciate I can't be seen to be involved in this, so if Marku is agreeable then the hearing is scheduled for 10.00 am on Thursday.'

Upon being told Marku wrapped some cooked fish and walked the short distance along the foreshore to the police station. As most blacks that came to the police station did so in shackles the officer expressed surprise at her coming to the front desk and requesting to see a prisoner. He escorted her to the jail, let her in, locked the door behind and left. She stood on the meshed deck area and called through the darkened doorway, 'Wadi.' No reply came but a characteristic scent told her that an Aborigine was present. 'It's Marku,' she whispered. A faint scraping sound on the floor drew her to a corner where she found him crouched against the wall. With some blackfellow coaxing and the promise of saltwater fish he eventually came from the dark and sat with her on the rough timber decking. The pitiful sight of the adolescent, stuffing food into his mouth, upset Marku terribly. The once cheerful lad with the hoppy leg seemed detached from everybody and everything. Marku let alone the matter of his arrest and, instead, spoke of family and how she would speak to the *buliman* police the day after next and have him set free. She stayed with him till late and when she had to leave he shook the steel mesh like a caged animal. Marku returned the next day to find that his condition had sunk to that of one condemned. She knew her people and their culture. If he were not released soon he would lie down and die.

Marku and James arrived early and took seats at the front of the near-empty courtroom. The clerk of the court called the court to order as the magistrate entered from a side door. The accused, with no legal representation, stood alone, handcuffed and wearing police-issue trousers to hide his nakedness.

After the standard opening address that included announcing the charge of theft the police prosecutor, with a growl in his voice, gave his version of events and then called on a witness to provide evidence. In essence the prosecution's case relied on the witness seeing the 'hoppy legged' accused fleeing from his vegetable patch by moonlight and the same 'hoppy legged' Aborigine being found on a riverbank the next morning with fresh vegetables in his hands.

The magistrate then asked if there were any submissions in the accused's defence. Matron Duggan, buxom and hardy, told how the accused had been brought to the hospital hardly conscious and bleeding profusely from the scalp. That during the term of his hospitalisation she assessed him as having limited mental capacity due either to the concussion he sustained or a condition inherent since childhood.

Marku followed, rising to her feet and drawing on every shred of self-confidence James had instilled in her. She looked around anxiously till the magistrate caught her eye and nodded for her to commence. She stated her name, her relationship to the accused and told how she had known him as a family member since his birth. She told of Aboriginal culture and the pride attached to being a provider and that Wadi, with his bent leg, could not hunt and had been reduced to doing women's work of picking fruit and digging yams. She became emotional, teetering on the brink of tears, when she told about the tribe's culture of sharing and its necessity for the tribe's survival. She concluded her appeal to the magistrate by saying that in her culture food in the wild belongs to everyone and that there is no such thing as stealing food.

The magistrate thanked her and then asked, 'If the accused were to be placed on a good behaviour bond, would you undertake to provide care and guidance?' Marku responded by nodding in the affirmative. He then asked her to be seated and proceeded with his judgement. He found the accused guilty of theft but quickly followed with placing him on a six-month good-behaviour bond and no conviction to be recorded.

The police un-cuffed Wadi and then, with Marku and James taking an arm each, they ushered him from the courtroom and escorted him back to their chandlery shop. Wadi remained cloistered, taking only a little food and water and huddling between two wooden crates. That night Marku bunked him down inside the shop with her and James but by morning he had decamped and presumably re-joined the tribe. James had heard the door open and close but thought it prudent not to make mention to Marku.

CHAPTER 21

W ith Ellen's baby now six weeks old and a routine set Nganka could devote more time to her own family. She visited relatives often and this morning took herself off to call on those living at a camp downriver. When within hearing range of the camp, the sound of women wailing grabbed her attention and pressed her to hurry forward. Upon entering the camp she found her people in the throes of a funeral rite. A first cousin had died in child birth the previous evening. The body, naked and stained, lay prostrate on the ground with women and men crowding around, chanting to the spirits to accept her into the spirit world. With the ceremony well progressed and many exhausted from a night of purging, Nganka stood aside from the mob, quietly expressing her grief. While weeping she noticed an old lady sitting in the shade of a tree with the newborn on her lap. Nganka, aghast at the sight, rushed to the woman's side, knelt and looked deeply into the woman's eyes, only to be met with a blank stare. Knowing that look of hopelessness, and with no suckling mother in sight, she realised that the baby had not taken milk and would die before the next morning. She took the mite of a child from the lady and pressed it against her face to test for life. She felt its warmth and looked around for support. No one cast her a glance. The baby, like all those before her that had been born into a milk-dry camp, would die and be secreted away, wrapped in bark and placed in the fork of a tree beyond the reach of dingos. This dispossessed child, with its eyes closed, reached up with an open hand asking for help. Nganka, having learned something of the white man's ways, did not accept fate. She held the baby close, rose and without a word to anyone walked from the camp and disappeared into the bush.

Driven by maternal instinct she fleeted upriver, hardly touching the ground, heading to where the child might be saved. To save time she took a shortcut, plunged into a deep river crossing, sank below the surface and resurfaced with the baby still in her clutches. She struggled, holding the baby high, kicking with her legs to push to the other side. As a woman possessed she fled along rainforest paths, jumping logs and tripping on vines. At the sight of Jonathan's paddocks she spared a moment to check that the little one was still alive and then scorched across the open ground to reach the house, exhausted and hysterical.

'Ma'am!' she shouted, and then screamed, 'It's Nganka with a baby!'

Ellen, shocked and frightened by the distressed call, met Nganka in the living room and reached forward to take the baby. Nganka, breathless and panic stricken, could not speak. Ellen instantly recognised the situation, stripped her dress from her breasts and pressed the little one's mouth to her nipple. The child, beyond the instinctive impulse to suck, nuzzled the nipple but would not or could not take it into her mouth. Nganka, once again not prepared to accept fate, drew Ellen's breast, bringing milk to the nipple and squirting it across the baby's face. She then rubbed a finger in the milk and put it into the baby's mouth. They tried for nearly an hour, with Ellen willingly letting milk and Nganka persevering. One small movement of the babe's mouth as she moulded her lips around Nganka's finger brought a cry of joy. At the sight of the baby beginning to suck, Ellen's milk flowed even more freely, wetting her tummy and Nganka's hands. As the babe's suckle strengthened Nganka slipped her on to the nipple. The baby sucked strongly for a minute or two before letting go and falling asleep against Ellen's breast. When Jonathan arrived home he could hardly believe the girls' story. However, he was soon overwhelmed and readily accepted the child into his home.

Nganka raced across the river, told Bajal and the others of the rescue, and returned to spend the night at Ellen's to care for the baby. Neither of the girls slept that night. They kept vigil by lamp light, watching for signs of life and expressing joy at each murmur or movement. By morning the black child, washed and in a white frilly nightdress, woke to the blessing of the girls. Ellen's own daughter had not been forgotten because, as the sun rose above the brow of the hill, Jonathan came inside carrying a jug of fresh goat's milk. Nganka stayed on for another three nights, taking residence in one of the guest rooms.

During the next two months Nganka almost lived at Ellen's. Bajal, with endless patience, encouraged Nganka to stay with the child till it was well and strong. Nganka and Ellen proclaimed themselves to be the parents and christened the child Nyulu Ann, Ann being Ellen's second name and Nyulu the Aboriginal word for feminine. Jonathan had become resigned to the idea that the child was there to stay and let this be known, although he admitted he felt squeamish when he had to write to his parents and tell them he and Ellen had adopted a full-blood Aborigine.

The girls worked in perfect unison, sharing the time and effort needed to care for the two little ones. Dari took to visiting and, on the second visit, declared herself to be Grandma to both children. The Chinese living on the property gradually unravelled the mystery and, though not daring to breathe a word to Jonathan, gave him credit for accepting the situation.

CHAPTER 22

Marku had been accepted by most people on the waterfront of Port Douglas. As the main point of entry for those on the Hodgkinson gold field and the growing number of settlers in the Mossman valley, the government wharf and rickety private jetties bustled with activity. She exchanged greetings with many of the regulars and readily waved to others who looked her way. She became known among the whites as Marku and there were some lonely souls who thought of her in their dreams.

Like all Aborigines she preferred saltwater fish to those caught in the rivers and spent hours patiently fishing from a nearby jetty. One evening she hooked a huge trevally and the squeals of excitement that followed brought James running and onlookers calling for her to hold on tight. That evening she, James and Lugger, together with a couple of Lugger's friends, ate heartily of the fish she baked whole on their cooking fire. One friend predicted that with a north-easterly change coming the weather would be perfect for sailing. As James and Marku were due for a visit to the river they decided by the mellow light of the moon to make sail the next morning.

With the shop left in Lugger's care they made ready early and sailed across the bay in near perfect conditions, with Low Isles and Snapper Island shimmering like mirages on the horizon. The surprise visit drew a chorus of welcome when they reached Winston's camp. Nganka, who had grown more proud of her children across the river by the day, soon suggested that Marku visit. James also expressed interest so Nganka scampered across the river and returned later to say that Jonathan and Ellen were expecting them for morning tea the following day. Old memories came to mind when James and Marku, hand in hand, crossed the river and lingered on the sandbar where they had camped during the logging seasons. 'Come on you two,' called Nganka,

116

anxious to show them the children. Ellen and Jonathan, dressed as though they were about to attend a community outing in Goulburn, welcomed them when they came through the front gate. While James and Marku had met Jonathan previously, the introduction to Ellen was a first. As had Nganka, they both became enthralled with Ellen at first sight. Her effusive femininity, not yet tarnished by the harshness of life in the bush, held sway as they exchanged niceties. Jonathan, eager to show James over the property, suggested the ladies move inside and that the men take tea later.

James soon realised that Jonathan had not been bragging when he had spoken earlier about his intentions to extend the family dynasty into northern Australia. The planning, from the siting of the home and Chinese living quarters to the layout of the fields and the extent of the clearing, clearly showed him as a man capable of fulfilling his dreams. As a courtesy Jonathan introduced James to the Chinese tenant farmers who were weeding a crop of dry-land rice. Though they were only able to speak a few words of English they engaged enthusiastically, nodding agreement more often than required. They appeared a happy lot, thankful to be gainfully employed, living a quiet, communal life and smoking opium at night to help them sleep. They inspected the one hundred acres now cleared, with Jonathan proudly showing the horses and cattle, the crops thriving on the new ground and the mixed orchard by the river.

The ladies, happy to be left alone, enjoyed themselves, with Ellen and Nganka conducting a tour one room at a time and answering Marku's questions, many of which would not occur to a person raised in a white household. Ellen, knowing that the babies would capture Marku's heart, left that room till last. Upon entering the nursery Marku felt a sudden rush, an urge to be blessed with motherhood. The two cots against the far wall, the cradle, change table, stack of folded linen, brightly coloured curtains and a carpet mat on the floor proved to be too much for Marku. She stood misty eyed till Ellen beckoned her to come close to see the two bright-eyed babies. With Nganka shepherding her every move Ellen handed Nyulu to Marku who, after a moment of disbelief, kissed the child on the forehead and held her close. She then looked at the others in a way only a woman could understand and kissed them both on the cheek as a show of gratitude for their having saved a life. Nganka ushered Marku to a chair beside the bay window where she sat while Ellen lifted her own child, moved across the room and handed it to Marku.

With the two children in her arms she beamed with delight. Before now, the nearest she had been to a nursery was to bed a baby down on a possum-skin rug in a thatched hut. Ellen watched as Marku spoke to them in her own language. She marvelled at Marku's care and, for the first time, fully realised that Aborigines were no different from white people.

Morning tea reminded James of his childhood days in Sydney when his mother often hosted morning teas at their Kirribilli home. The refinement of Ellen's and Jonathan's families shone through. The verandah table was covered with an Irish linen cloth and set with fine china. Nganka served the tea and scones, surprising James with her knowledge of the white man's ways of entertaining. The two wee ones, dressed in baby frocks and bonnets, held the women's attention, while the men spoke to one side.

'The river has progressed since I first arrived,' said Jonathan, casting an eye across his selection. 'All the river frontage is taken and the back country is filling by the month. With the cedar logged they're turning their hands to other things. A chap by the name of Andy Creswell called the other day and plans to open a rice mill to take all the local crop. That has the selectors busy, felling and stumping new ground. My Coolies have heard of it through their channels and have asked to lease more of my land. I've told them they can lease up to another 200 acres on a five-year term. Suits me because under the terms of the government lease I have to clear so much a year and make improvements, like buildings and fencing.

'That settler across the river near you has subdivided some of his property for a township. While it hasn't been officially proclaimed a town the Divisional Board have stipulated that he has to make provision for roads and parkland. I've heard that a few families have already moved in. Good to see that sort of settlement; families coming in, adding to the labour supply and maybe some services. Though I can't see many improvements being made in the near future with government funding being administered from Port Douglas. The road to Port is a goat track and will stay that way till the settlers agitate for improvement.

'Winston seems to be doing well with his plantation. Having the blacks there is a clever move. He hasn't had a native attack or any significant pilfering. I have them prowling about here occasionally but the dogs keep them shy of the place. I've heard a whisper that Nyulu's father wants her back. Apparently he rolled into a fire as a child and has a badly scarred shoulder. I don't want to pre-empt anything but if he comes here he'll end up dog's meat.' He then digressed. 'Have you any thoughts about coming back to the river?'

'Sometimes,' replied James. 'I'm happy at Port but Marku has a yen to come back to the river. She misses her family and communal life. Winston's a godsend. He's given my mob a secure home which is more than the other blacks have. The tribe's fragmented. The poor devils don't know which way to turn. The native police are cutting them to ribbons, with most of the butchering not being made public. The way they're going the tribe will soon be extinct.'

'Winston's a mystery man,' commented Jonathan. 'I remember reading about a boxer named Winston Ambrose and wonder if it's the same person. I recall because there was a controversy about him. A title holder who killed a man in a bare-knuckle fight.'

'Could be,' replied James. 'He certainly has the build for it and has a couple of scars on his face. Never says anything about his past and I don't think it's my place to ask. He seems to be attached to black hats and is never without one.'

Nganka interrupted their conversation when she appeared with a fresh pot of tea and offered it all around.

'Thanks, Nganka. You're a gem,' said James, leaning back to make room.

After being served they continued the discussion while the women put the babes down for a nap. The women seemed to take forever and, upon their return, James mentioned that Dari had a special lunch prepared and if they were late she would be cross.

Marku snuggled into James on the way home and, as a playful gesture, coaxed him to carry her across the running river. After lunch she took him by the hand and, with a hint of frivolity in her voice, suggested they go upriver for a swim. James, having intimate knowledge of Marku's ways, happily followed. At the pool where they had first made love she turned to him, cheekily undressed and daringly stripped him of his clothes. With love-light in her eyes she kissed his chest and lips and then dived into the cool stream. James followed and, after some splashing and teasing, they moved to the sandbar where they had first taken of one another. Marku lay down, holding James' hand and taking him with her. She, more so than ever, wished for a second child, this one made in the image of her and James. Eddies in the stream passed by and leaves fell from the trees above as, in blissful solitude, they worked their way to a crescendo and unleashed their passion. They then lay hand in hand till Marku reached across and took him in her arms for a second time.

When the shadows began to lengthen they took a dip in the steam and returned to the camp. Marku felt sure that the spirits had led her to that place for a special purpose and wished to share her emotions with Dari. Dari listened and then took Marku aside and told how she had a recipe that would bring her a spirit child.

Dari always rose before the others, stoked the fire, put a billycan of water on to heat and then rattled about making noise to wake the others. Marku became curious when she woke to find the fire well alight but no sign of Dari. She roused the others who also expressed concern. Marku's anxiety lasted till Dari appeared at mid-morning carrying a rare variety of lily plant that Marku knew was found only in a dark lagoon where a large crocodile lived. Dari washed the lily in a bucket of water, broke off the root and handed it to Marku to eat. Marku, knowing Dari's strange but sage ways, ate the fleshy root, forcing herself to swallow and sometimes choking to get it down. When she had finished Dari explained how the lily draws on the spirits of the earth to make a spirit baby. When Marku and James left for Port later that day Dari insisted, 'Tell me quick when you see a change.' Within a month Winston received a note which read:

Dear Dari,

Marku has asked me to write and tell you that the recipe worked and that we expect a baby after the wet season.
All the best to everybody at the camp.

Love from Marku and James

A selector who laid claim to a large tract of land that included a lagoon watched from the cover of a clump of trees as two Aboriginal lads took wild ducks from a trap they had set using corn from his paddock. After spying on their activity for a second day he went to the police and lodged a complaint of trespass, poaching and stealing. A surly sergeant took interest and assured the selector that the matter would be dealt with promptly. The lads revisited again and were taking ducks from the trap when a troop of mounted police descended on them at full gallop. The lads, naked and shiny black beneath the burning sun, dashed into the lagoon and waded waist deep through the reeds, trying to escape. The troop of four, shouting abuse about 'black bastards', drove their mounts into the water in hot pursuit. The horses floundered in the soft mud and tangle of reeds, with the sergeant's horse falling and tossing him from the saddle. He struggled to his feet and, in a fit of humiliation and outrage, shouted for his men to trample them. The lads, terrified by the sight of police, scrambled to the other side and dashed across the open ground, only to be blocked by the horsemen wielding revolvers. The sergeant staggered from the lagoon, leading his horse, and hurled more abuse as he approached the stricken lads.

'Chain the bastards,' he ordered.

The leading constable, surprised by the instruction, took a marching chain from his saddlebag, shackled the lads by the neck and then mounted with the end of the chain in his hand. The troopers, expecting the sergeant to tow them to the next creek and let them loose, were further taken aback when he proceeded ten miles to Port Douglas, signed them in under dubious names and put them in the lockup.

The magistrate, upon perusing the charge sheet, went to the police station to see for himself. While he stood outside the lockup an officer entered and hustled the lads from the darkness of the cell to the meshed decking. They shivered with fright and cowered, understanding nothing of why they had been taken in or severely beaten. The magistrate, hiding his shock and dismay, referred to the raw chafe marks about their necks and asked, 'What's being done about the abrasions?'

The officer pointed to a bag of salt and a billycan of water against the wall and replied bluntly, 'They've got salt and water to bathe them but are too stupid to savvy.'

The magistrate, utterly disgusted at the sight, held his peace and acknowledged the comment with a wave of his hand.

In his office he wrote a note to James and Marku, explaining the situation and asking if Marku would give character references on behalf of the lads who were to appear at 11.30 the following morning.

Upon receiving the note via a messenger Marku's immediate impulse was to run to the lockup to help but James held her back, telling her that an appearance might connect her to the magistrate and compromise the case. They both lay awake till very late, with Marku worrying about the, as yet, unidentified members of her tribe and James concerned about what effect an upset might have on Marku's advanced state of pregnancy. He reckoned Marku to be in her early forties and was well aware of the problems that often occurred giving birth at that age. James finally drifted off to sleep, leaving Marku to bear the burden of thought.

Sleep evaded her completely so she eventually left James' side, crept outside, lit the fire, put the billy on and made a cup of tea. There in the dark she thought of those in the lockup: who they were, what they had done and what the magistrate would decide. At piccaninny daylight, that first glow of a breaking dawn, she moved from the fire and sat quietly on a log by the slipway. The blush of early dawn soon followed, lighting the sea and surrounding landscape, heralding a day of uncertainty. Her people had suffered enough at the hands of the white man. She reflected on what she had seen and heard in recent years and, as she began to think of the future, a deep resentment of whites crept into her mind. Sure, James, Lugger and friends she had made in Port treated her with respect, but the others, the police and the selectors, understood nothing of her people or their way of life. She saw them as intruders, wielding big sticks, rushing into their camps and beating them into submission. These thoughts, and the bearing they would have on her half-caste child to be, left Marku feeling sorry and confused. She wept silently until James came to her side, sat on the log and comforted her. He had no inkling of her thoughts and Marku, not wanting to cause a rift, kept them to herself.

With Marku now clearly showing, James persuaded her to wear a dress rather than trousers to the court hearing. The courtroom, with its sombre surrounds and officialdom, scared Marku and when she and James entered she began to tremble. To add to her angst, the same police prosecutor as before stood across the aisle, casting threatening glances, trying the white man's dirty trick of intimidation. James, aware of the prosecutor's belittling tactic, held Marku's hand and tossed the prosecutor a confident look. The opening address was carried out with mundane formality, followed by the prisoners being brought in, handcuffed and under police guard. The pathetic sight of the two bewildered Aborigines standing there in police-issue trousers they had been forced to wear drew James' ire and Marku felt his hand clench tightly about her slender fingers.

The prosecutor outlined the charge and gave supporting evidence, citing the selector as a respected gentleman going about his worthy business of tilling the soil for the benefit of the community. He then turned his attention to the prisoners, accusing them of trespassing on private property, poaching the selector's ducks and stealing corn. He spoke at length, trying to cover for what soon became apparent—his star witnesses had failed to show! When asked if he had witnesses to call, the prosecutor put forward the nebulous excuses that the selector was busy harvesting a crop and the sergeant had been called to go on patrol. When summing up, the prosecutor stressed the importance of setting a standard and inferred that the two were of doubtful character and would probably reoffend.

The magistrate paid little heed to the closing comments and said, 'I understand that those charged have somebody to speak on their behalf.' He then turned to Marku, cast her a reassuring look and said, 'Miss Marku, would you like to address the court?' Marku, stiff with fright, remained motionless till James stood and addressed the court. 'Your Honour, Miss Marku is heavily pregnant and is unwell. Could I please stand with her?'

'Approval granted,' replied the magistrate.

James took Marku by the arm and helped her to her feet. Marku remained silent till she heard a whimper from one of the lads. She looked across at him and then directly at the magistrate.

'Mr Your Honour,' she broke out in clear English, 'I know these two boys. They are my cousins from the river tribe.' Marku named them and told how she had known them since birth, and spoke of their parents and their parents' parents. She told of their way of life, explaining their beliefs and connection to the land. She then stared the prosecutor in the face and told him direct that he was an evil spirit, like all the other *bulimen* who rode horses and shot her people. She became impassioned as she spoke, further telling the court how, before the white man came, her people lived in peace and now they lived in fear. With tears streaming down her cheeks and quivering with resentment she turned to the two lads, called them by name and then pleaded with the magistrate, 'My people are starving. The boys have done nothing wrong. Please let them go.'

The magistrate asked Marku to please be seated and then turned to the prosecutor. 'How old do you think the prisoners are?'

The prosecutor, knowing the significance of the question, and with mounting anger, replied, 'Eighteen, Your Honour.'

The magistrate, with disdain in his voice, gave his view. 'I would put them at fourteen.' He then waved his hand for everybody to be seated while he wrote his judgement in the record book. After a few minutes of eerie silence he lifted his head and delivered his judgement by saying, 'Case dismissed.'

The prosecutor looked at him in disbelief and, disregarding the finality of the magistrate's judgement, asked, 'How?'

The magistrate, overlooking the contemptuous remark, shot back with, 'Wouldn't a shotgun blast into the air have been enough to frighten them off?'

The ordeal at the courthouse left Marku shaken. The vision of the boys standing in the courtroom intimidated and defenceless loomed large before her whenever left alone. She, more than ever, needed to return to the river to be with her people. The call of her ancestors beckoned her to roll her swag and leave. The chandlery shop and her jewellery business no longer held importance. Marku found herself torn between her love for her people and

James. Try as she did to keep herself busy, making jewellery and fishing nets, nothing would ease her longing for the past; living off the land and sharing with others by an open camp fire. She wanted to raise her child in the traditional way; to go walkabout, to hunt and fish and build gunyahs. She thought of Dari and Nganka often and how they would be midwives at the birth of her baby. She wanted nothing to do with James' suggestion of having the baby born at Port Douglas with a white woman as midwife. As the weeks passed her focus narrowed and James, try as he did, was unable to lift her spirit.

Marku stood, almost listless, in the shade of the sail sheet by their shop and watched as a two-masted bêche-de-mer sailing boat docked at the jetty nearby. The grubby skipper and his three Chinese crewmen sorted the catch and soon left, with the crew carrying the product in baskets hanging from bamboo poles across their shoulders. They would go as far as the Mowbray River, selling the smoked sea slug delicacy to the Chinese community, and would be away most of the day.

Lugger, seeing Marku standing there and feeling sorry for her, suggested he cast his net for bait and she go fishing. Marku smiled and when the tide washed inshore she took a bucket of bait fish, settled herself on the jetty beside the grubby skipper's boat and tossed in a line. Fishing always soothed her soul and as the hours passed she drifted into a reverie that brought a sense of peace. James looked her way occasionally and, understanding her situation, let her be. She dabbled there by the water, whiling away the time, till the skipper returned and shouted loud abuse. 'You black bitch! Get away from my boat!'

Marku looked around to see the skipper, delirious with rum and rushing her way. The flimsy jetty, made of poles from the mangrove forest further up the inlet, swayed as he pounded his way along its rickety platform. She gathered the hem of her dress and stood to confront his assault. With the swipe of a fist he knocked her to her knees and before she could get up he kicked her in the belly, sending her to the decking, screaming with pain. He continued, stomping on her with his bare feet while accusing her of stealing from his boat. Marku tried to fight back, grabbing at his legs, but each time she got to her knees he struck another blow. James, seeing the attack from the slipway, shouted to Lugger and then raced to the jetty, bypassing the Chinese on the bank and charging towards the skipper. He hurtled headlong into him, lifting him as he went and tumbling him on to the deck of the boat. Before the skipper could scramble to his feet he leapt to the deck and, crazed by anger, set to beat him to a pulp. The Chinese, fearing the ship's master would die, hurried along the jetty with their wooden sandals clattering on the timbers underfoot. They stepped over Marku, boarded the boat and, while two grappled with James, the third went to the galley and returned with a carving knife. Marku, now back on her knees, screamed as Lugger careered towards her carrying an oar. When within striking distance he put the oar to the decking and pole vaulted into the brawl, landing with the oar still in hand. The man with the carving knife raised his hand only to be met with a sharp prod from the ore that snapped his ribs and sent him crashing to the floor. The other two, shocked by the screams from their friend, rose up to find themselves similarly cudgelled, with one being smashed in the side of the head and the other prodded in the buttocks as he went to jump overboard. James, now manic with vengeance, ignored Lugger's shouts to stop and continued beating the skipper until Lugger shoved a bucket over his head. The skipper, badly battered and bleeding from the mouth, lay unconscious as Lugger set the boat free and pushed it out into the receding tide with the oar. Marku, badly injured, lay on the jetty, unable to comprehend the situation. She remained as limp as a rag doll as the men, with an arm each over their shoulder, carried her back to the shop and laid her on a swag.

Throughout the night Marku complained of belly pain and passed blood. James wanted to send Lugger to bring the doctor but Marku refused, saying, 'If white man doctor come, I run away.' She lay there for days, hardly moving, and when able to move about she often sat alone on the foreshore, gazing northwards towards the river.

CHAPTER 24

After three weeks of indecision, and with the birth date drawing ever closer, James and Marku decided she would return to the river while James commuted to and from Port Douglas. With the chandlery business showing a profit and Lugger prepared to open the shop during James' absence, the business could continue supporting them and make a contribution to their family on the river. James managed to cross the bay most weekends, berthing his sailing boat at the landing and walking upstream to the camp. Dari, now the official midwife, monitored the pregnancy and gave James a lecture each time he visited about coming quickly when the baby arrived. Marku wanted to have the baby at the same place as Bajal had been born. 'The spirits were kind to me there. Look at Bajal!' she had said at a tender moment.

Dari chastised Marku one morning for cutting wood with an axe. Soon after Marku held her tummy and called. 'Dari! It's coming!'

'Nganka come quick,' shouted Dari, running to Marku's side.

'Quick, let's go before it's too late!'

With the birth place two miles away and the contractions already severe, Dari doubted they would reach there in time. They were further frustrated when they had to skirt around crops planted by selectors. When approaching the chosen place they found that the selector had recently cut and burned the forest right to the riverbank, leaving them exposed as they crossed the blackened landscape. With the selector's homestead in full view on the ridge, Marku suddenly fell to her knees, clutched her tummy and, after a shriek of pain, lay on the ground. A dog at the homestead barked, bringing chilling memories of others who had been attacked by the white man's vicious dogs.

'I can't,' begged Marku, rolling on the ground and screaming.

127

Dari took charge, ignored Marku's pleas and, with Nganka's assistance, led her to the riverside where Bajal had been born.

'This is the place. The more quick the better with that dog barking,' urged Dari while undressing herself in readiness for a traditional birth. Nganka followed suit, slipping from her shirt and trousers and tossing them aside. Marku, now delirious with pain, fought the girls as they tore her dress aside and dragged her to the shade of a water cherry tree that hung over the river. Dari tried to reason with Marku, calling for her to listen and take deep breaths, but Marku, in the grip of unbelievable pain, curled herself into a ball.

'No, Marku,' pleaded Dari, now herself in tears. 'Nganka, hold her legs for the baby to come out. Try, Marku. You must try!' she almost shouted.

After a few minutes of sustained labour Dari let out a 'whoop' followed by unrestrained emotion. The hardy woman sobbed like a child as she took the emerging child in her weathered hands and delivered it into the world. Marku heard the baby's cry, lifted her head and saw Dari on her knees, holding the child for her to see. Nganka moved behind Marku and held her head and shoulders up for her to take the newborn. With disbelief in her dark eyes she took the babe and held it to her breast. Nganka, who, till now, had remained composed, let go and shed tears of joy. Nganka had wished for motherhood for so long and now, seeing a spirit child born, she wanted nothing more than a baby of her own.

A blissful calm followed, with mother and child, together with her close kin, resting by the cool of the stream. When Marku settled, Dari took the baby girl into the stream where she washed it clean with tender, loving care. She then held the baby above her head to show off the newest member of the family but her expression suddenly turned stony. Nganka and Marku followed her line of sight to the top of the bank from where a selector on horseback watched. Dari clutched the baby tightly to her chest and called, 'No shoot!'

The selector, armed with a rifle and with a dog at heel, made no reply. Instead, he reined his horse their way and forced it down the steep embankment with the dog following. He rode to within a few paces of the women and looked down on them silently like a white overlord inspecting his livestock. Nganka cringed, Dari stood defiantly in the waist-deep water and Marku lay on her back with the stain of afterbirth from her waist down. The dog sniffed about, coming close to Marku before turning to the placenta lying nearby. The settlor watched with interest as the dog dragged the placenta a few feet away, crouched and began to chew the afterbirth. Dari saw this diversion as an opportunity to excuse themselves and called for the other two to join her in the river. Nganka, trembling with fear, helped Marku to her feet and, with a shoulder under one arm, helped her into the water. Without acknowledging the selector Dari motioned to the others to follow and waded to the other side. As they climbed the bank the selector spoke for the first time, shouting, 'And don't come back. You're not wanted here!'

A lad of fifteen, riding a sweaty horse, trotted to the chandlery door and called, 'Thomas Brown with a message.' Upon seeing him James knew it would be word of the baby and almost snatched the envelope from the messenger's hand and fumbled to take out the single-page letter, which read:

James,

Wonderful news. You have a baby daughter. Both well.
Advise by return mail time of your expected arrival.
Marku sends her love

Winston

James scratched a reply on the bottom of the letter:

Best news ever. Will leave by boat immediately.
Expect me after dark today.

Thanks
James

He handed it back to the messenger and asked, 'When will this be delivered?'

'Tonight if I get back to Mossman in time,' replied the lad.

'And if I give you five shillings?'

The lad, thinking he had stumbled upon a money pot, quickly replied, 'Within the hour, Sir!'

'Thanks, but don't push the mare too hard. By dark will be all right.'

The scrawny bush kid, earning more this hour than he had all week, gave thanks, turned the mare on a sixpence and trotted off.

James shouted the news to Lugger and, by the time he had grabbed his hat and swag, Lugger had appeared with a bottle of rum and two pannikins. 'Best we wet the baby's head,' he said while pouring each of them a large slug of rum.

'Just one. I'll hardly reach the river by dark and there's no moon.'

Lugger sat on a stool and watched as James, with a brisk breeze behind him, sliced through the surf under full sail. He mused about the time he had spent with James and Marku and wished them well.

James reached the mouth of the river as darkness fell, navigated mainly by memory along the dark river course, roped the boat to a tree at the landing and fleet footed through the dark corridors of the forest to find everybody awake and waiting for him. They gave a whoop and a cheer when he burst forth into the firelight. Such joy had to be seen to be believed as all, except Marku, shook his hand, slapped his shoulder or hugged him.

Marku stayed aside and when James saw her sitting by the fire, looking sore and sorry, he realised the extent of the suffering she had endured. He fell to his knees beside her and, before taking the baby from her arms, held her tightly and reaffirmed his love for her. That night they spoke again about baby names and chose Juran Marie, with Juran being an Aboriginal name and Marie being the name of James' mother.

Next morning Dari, just as the sun peeped over the ridge, paraded around the camp, beating a kerosene tin to wake everyone. At breakfast Nganka brought out a surprise. Ellen had given Nganka a bundle of 'hand-me-downs' from the babes across the river, who were now more than a year old. Later in the morning Winston produced his own treat of six bottles of warm champagne he had bought from a shanty owner at Mossman, a new settlement being established nearby. Though it only amounted to a bottle each the essence of the drink soon took effect, with Bajal, Nganka and Dari giggling and dancing. James, more so than Marku, could not take his eyes off Juran. He gloated over her all day, whether awake or asleep. He described her colour as bronze but Dari said it looked more like honey. James had intended registering the birth at the court house but, with the prevailing animosity, he instead noted the date in his diary as *25th April 1884*.

CHAPTER 25

Marku settled remarkably well, engaging in light duties while breast feeding. James commuted to and from the chandlery business as planned but found difficulty in adjusting to the new situation of being away from Marku and Juran. He struggled with the routine for a few months, boating across the bay each weekend and leaving before daylight when returning. Eventually he realised that, apart from the separation from Marku and the little one, he preferred to live with Aborigines. He discussed his concerns with Lugger who, being a man for all seasons, readily bought the business from James for the cost price of the stock. James set sail for the last time and, upon reaching the river, thought he had finally come *home* and had no wish to ever leave the river. With Marku's help and Juran propped under the shade of a tree he built a fine, two-room cottage for him and Marku to live and raise their daughter. Winston now had two hundred acres under grazing, cultivation, orchard and market garden, and welcomed the extra help. They lived as a commune, sharing the work and the rewards of their efforts.

Port Douglas began to decline when Cairns, a port to the south, developed as a commercial hub for the inland and enticed businessmen to relocate. Families, left destitute by this drift of business, left Port and moved to Mossman, where they sought employment labouring for the selectors. Large tracts of forest continued to be felled and burned for cropping and grazing and in anticipation of a sugar mill being established. Many of these families decided to settle in Mossman and paid a few pounds for a house allotment. Here they built two-room cottages with cooking annexes, all made of timber and corrugated iron.

Children slept two to a bed and, with schooling being a far-fetched dream, they occupied their days herding goats, collecting firewood and carting water. Boys became men when, at age thirteen, they were put to work grubbing stumps from the ground and stoking fires to clear the land. There were no roads as such; only rutted tracks that clouded with dust in the dry and bogged with mud in the wet. A community spirit held the people together, with neighbours pitching in to help one another and families gathering together for Sunday picnics by the river. The new settlement attracted business and before long enjoyed the services of Chinese street vendors with their sticks and baskets, a butcher, baker, grocer, two shanty hotels, a livery stable and a blacksmith. These traders found themselves well patronised by the town residents, together with visiting teamsters, packers, loggers and those who ferried supplies and produce by sea to and from Port Douglas. The selectors, their tenant farmers and labourers also frequented the town. Drifters, mainly from the northern goldfields, squatted by the river and occasionally came to town to barter vegetables and eggs for tea, sugar, tobacco and meat. The shanty hotels did well, with men congregating to have a yarn and soothe their sorrows with locally made rum.

The Aboriginal people, now scattered, leaderless and hungry, crept into town at night and pilfered food to take back to their families. The townspeople, fearing for their lives and property, sought an increased police presence. The selectors also complained about their crops being pilfered, livestock slaughtered and stores stolen. Their call was partly answered with a police substation being built on the outskirt of the town. This camp, with huts and stables but no holding cell, meant that prisoners were either marched the twelve miles to Port Douglas or chained to trees in the open till processed. This further incursion by the *buliman* into Aboriginal territory provoked the local Aborigines and heightened the prospect of retaliation. The police called at Winston's camp, often under the pretence of wanting information; but all there knew that the prime purpose was to intimidate.

Although Winston's property was referred to as *the blacks' camp*, the locals readily traded with them, exchanging goods and services for fresh farm produce. With a horse and cart James became the delivery man, making regular house calls. He became friendly with Arthur Brown, the blacksmith, and soon began working part time for him. The arrangement worked well, with James juggling the demands of the plantation with Arthur's work load. Arthur's son Thomas, the messenger who had delivered the note to James at Port Douglas, also helped in the smithy shop and became friends with James and those at the camp. He visited often, spending time with Bajal, fishing the river and hunting the rainforest that the selectors had not managed to destroy. Winston told him he could have whatever produce he could find and, after most visits, Thomas could be seen leading his horse home with the split-bag on the horse's back bulging with fruits of the farm. Winston showed interest when, on one occasion, Thomas casually said, 'Did you know that old man Thomson didn't do himself in?'

Winston looked at him questioningly because the common view was that he had committed suicide on his property down near the landing.

'Yeah. It was his wife and her boyfriend that shot him in the head,' continued Thomas while stuffing another orange into the split-bag.

'How do you know this?' asked Winston.

'Oh, I just heard.'

Winston, knowing the lad well enough, thought something amiss and pressed him further. 'You want to be careful about what you say. The word is he took his own life.'

'No way!' replied Thomas with certainty.

'Then—'

'Well, I seen it myself. Writ on the paper.'

'What paper?'

'A piece of paper I found.'

Winston, not accepting this, peppered Thomas with questions till he admitted to reading a message he had delivered from the police station at Mossman to Port Douglas. He continued on and explained that he often read the contents of unsealed envelopes.

Winston cautioned him. 'If the police find out you'll be put in the lockup.'

'I only told you, nobody else.'

'Then best we keep it to ourselves,' said Winston, closing the discussion without realising the future implications of Thomas' reading police correspondence and informing.

If it is possible for animals to love then Murramu loved Juran. Though his eyes were now dim and his joints stiff he remained her constant companion. Bajal, fully aware of Murramu's aged condition and that he had limited time left, happily let him laze about the camp while he worked elsewhere in the plantation. From the moment Juran began to walk Murramu shepherded her about the camp, coming between her and the fire and whining when she went near the steep riverbank. He accepted her crawling over him and pulling his ears and often licked her in return. They were mates, almost inseparable while awake, and when Marku put Juran down for a nap Murramu lay dutifully by her side. All in the camp felt sorry when Murramu suddenly took sick and died soon after. Bajal took him in his arms and sat by the fire in disbelief. His friend had remained loyal to the last moment, licking his hand before closing his eyes for the last time.

Bajal became distraught, wailing and chanting to the spirits to take Murramu into their care. He reverted to tribal custom, grieving openly, scoring his thighs with the sharp edge of an oyster shell. Neither James nor Winston had witnessed this tribal custom before and, thinking it could lead to serious harm, moved to intervene, but were intercepted when Dari said, 'Leave alone. White man no understand.' She then moved forward and rubbed fresh ash into Bajal's wounds. Bajal remained by the fire till the following morning, cradling Murramu. He then rose to his feet and quietly walked away to lay his friend to rest in the bush.

Although the children, Frances and Nyulu, were now running about the house and pulling on Ellen's apron strings, Ellen and Nganka still managed to find time to be alone, sharing their emotions. The loving bond between them had stayed strong and, to their minds, would last forever. Jonathan's dream of extending the family dynasty remained his focus to the exclusion of most other things and Ellen wondered if he would really care if he discovered her and Nganka lovemaking in bed.

Birthday's for the children had become a specialty with each occasion honoured by the families from both sides of the river getting together to celebrate. Today was Juran's third birthday and Nganka crossed the river early for Ellen to fit and stitch one of her dresses for Nganka to wear.

At ten thirty, Ellen, with Frances in her arms and Nganka carrying Nyulu, held their crinoline skirts high and crossed the fields to the riverside where Nganka called to Bajal. As arranged, Bajal rowed across and then, with much ado, helped the ladies and children into the boat. At the other side the boat nearly capsized when Ellen, not used to the outdoors, stumbled and shouted for Bajal to save her. She encountered further difficulty when climbing the steps cut into the riverbank and gave Bajal a gorgeous smile when he took her hand to help. Once in the camp greetings were passed all around with hugs and kisses. Ellen made a point of saying that Jonathan was busy harvesting and sent his love to all.

Gift giving followed with Juran sitting in a deck chair, opening gifts that varied from a beaded necklace wrapped in bark to a bag of home-made sweets sent by Mrs Brown of the smithy shop. Dari, now passed middle age, sweltered in her annexed kitchen, allowing nobody but James to offer advice about how to cook a traditional English lunch. The other women set to, collecting flowers from the garden to decorate the dining table that stood in the shade of a sail sheet strung from trees. With the three little girls following they snipped purple bougainvillea, red hibiscus and yellow frangipani from the garden and spread them full length on the long table. For the salad they took a variety of salad vegetables from the garden and added sunflower oil made in the camp. At lunch time Dari sorted the roast vegetables while James cut the home grown pork and chicken roasts and placed the meat on large platters. He then called to everyone, 'Lunch is served.'

What a feast! Bajal backed up for a second and third helping while the others ran a close second. For sweets they enjoyed a tropical fruit salad made from fruits grown on the plantation. Dari also prepared bananas, smeared with syrup, wrapped in banana leaves and cooked on the coals. Winston made his own contribution by seating Marku, Ellen and Nganka together with a child each on their laps then singing a ditty:

Three little girls, all in a row.
Black, white and brindle, all ready to go.

He then took a harmonica from his pocket and played the little girls a rendition of *My Blue Eyed Doll*. The joyous memories of that day would last while those present lived, but would eventually be lost.

CHAPTER 26

Alroy had done well, purchasing and clearing his selection and putting it under production. He should have felt proud of his achievements, having come from a poor Irish Catholic family, clawed his way through life and become a well-to-do and respected member of the community.

However, he harboured a deep disappointment that played on his ageing mind.

Since the day he had taken Shaun as a young child and absconded, he had promised himself that he would be a good parent and make provision for Shaun's future. After a decade of wandering the timber camps of the southern colonies he and Shaun finally settled on the Mossman River and secured a place they could call home. During those early years, before Shaun began to mature and cavort with Aboriginal girls, all had been fine between them. They lived together as father and son, sharing the good and bad times and being supportive of each other. When Shaun teamed up with the members of Winston's camp Alroy thought it only natural that a young man would want to socialise with others, especially young girls who came his way. The fact that they were Aboriginal caused no particular concern because, since arriving on the river and living amongst them, he had come to regard them as people not much different to himself. While he expected that Shaun might engage with them in his youthful lust for company he never seriously considered Shaun would take one or more as a wife and spawn a brood of half-caste children. To his mind, Shaun possessed the strength of character to stay with his own kind and bear Alroy white grandchildren. He also envisaged a daughter-in-law accustomed to European ways, who could provide adequate care during his twilight years.

Over time the young Aboriginal girls, some seeking a white man, had their way, luring him from Winston's camp and frolicking with him in secluded nooks of the river. Word of these youthful romps became well known in the Aboriginal community and to some of the white settlers. By the time Shaun had reached twenty years of age Alroy knew of three children born to Shaun and rumour had it there were more. Apart from not knowing the exact number of Shaun's offspring he knew none of their given names or whether they carried his family name of Higgins. This secrecy, the holding back of common knowledge, hurt Alroy more than anything.

Added to this disappointment was the realisation that, over time, Shaun had drifted to the Aboriginal way of life, with Alroy now being the forgotten man. While Alroy and Shaun had quarrelled about what Alroy considered to be Shaun's philandering, to his mind there could be no dispute so deep that a kind word could not set it right. However, Shaun saw it differently and now seldom spoke to his father. When they did cross paths Shaun most times offered no more than a nod. Alroy wished with all his heart to set the matter right, to have Shaun and even his women and his brood living on the property. After all, old age was knocking on the door and soon he would no longer be able to attend his orchard, gardens and livestock.

Alroy sat at the bench by his fireplace with these thoughts drifting through his mind when, in the distance, he saw the approaching silhouette of his long-time friend James.

'So pleased to see you,' called Alroy, hobbling towards him.

'And you too,' returned James with an affable smile.

'Here. Have a seat. I'll put the billy on.'

Ever since James had worked for Alroy one wet season many years before they had remained staunch friends. They shared a pot of tea and some boiled fruitcake, with James telling of the latest happenings at his camp and the gossip from Mossman. When he told of Juran's birthday Alroy referred to Shaun's children and asked, 'Tell me. How many children has Shaun got?'

'Not sure. There's three women I know of and about eight kids. Don't see much of him these days. He lives upstream not far from Jinkalmu. What about you?'

'No. Hardly ever see him anymore.'

'He's not the same lad I used to know,' said James. 'That young scallywag of a kid that used to visit our camp showed promise but I'm afraid

I've lost faith in him. He comes by occasionally with his women and kids, moves in for a day or two, makes a mess, then leaves without as much as a thank you. Dari has tried to pull him into line but he's rude to her. Last time he was at the camp she asked him to quieten the kids and he told her to fuck off. For myself, I don't want to fall out with him but I have Juran to consider. He gets drunk on rum and fornicates by the fire at night. I can't have Juran seeing that. If he ever touches her I'll—' James cut short what he was about to say.

Alroy digressed and asked, 'How does he feed them all?'

'Huh, haven't you heard?'

'No, not a thing. Last I heard he was working bullocks.'

'Not anymore. He makes his money from the sly grog trade.'

'What, pedalling it?'

'No, making it. He crushes cane he gets from the selector's plots, distils it and sells it on the black market. I hear the police are watching and it's only a matter of time before he's caught.'

Alroy lifted his elbows from the table and shook his head in dismay. He knew that Shaun had been running wild with the blacks but had heard nothing of his sly grogging.

He sighed and said quietly, 'He *was* a good kid, as you say. What is it that turns them away? We were friendly with the blacks but never overfriendly. The nearest he got to them was visiting your camp.' He then added wistfully, 'Where have I gone wrong?'

Although the conversation continued in the same vein, with both men making frank admissions and expressing views, Alroy made no mention of the fact that he was not Shaun's biological father. James, having heard gossip over time and from his own observations, had concluded that Alroy was not Shaun's real father. What he could not understand was why his close friend could not bring himself to disclose the truth, particularly now that his family name had been tarnished.

The plight of the Aborigines became increasingly desperate, with their numbers dwindling from starvation, introduced diseases and deaths at the hands of the police. Winston's camp did what it could, handing out flour from their storeroom while stocks lasted. Although Nganka and James earned money outside and the camp made a profit from selling produce, they were unable to buy in enough flour to fill the need. When the Aborigines came Winston tried to explain that they could not give away more than they could afford. Yet they came, haggard and with pleading eyes, begging for a little something to carry them through the day. Dari could not bear to see her people dying and sneaked a little extra to starving families when she thought it would not be missed. The tribespeople saw Winston's camp as a saviour with some believing Winston to be an incarnation from the spirit world. However, the local police saw the situation differently. With their aim being to harass and disperse they saw Winston's interference as countering their attempts to scatter the natives into the hills. As a consequence not a week went by without a visit by mounted troopers enquiring about the blacks and their whereabouts. The situation was further provoked when a Chinese man ran into Winston's camp one morning and screamed that a settler had been attacked.

'They kill boss. Black man kill the boss,' he ranted.

The Chinaman, scared out of his wits, stumbled for words as he gibbered, explaining that a mob of Aborigines had ambushed them on Klien's selection. From the garbled message Winston deduced that the three Chinamen had escaped, that Mr Klien had raced to his hut with the Aborigines in pursuit and, from the hideous screams heard, he had been speared.

Winston, realising the implications of the attack, slung a cartridge belt over his shoulder, snatched up a rifle and was about to leave when Bajal stepped forward with a bundle of spears in hand.

'No, Bajal. Best you not come. If the police see you there will be more trouble.'

'But—'

Bajal was overridden by a wave of Winston's hand before he trotted off, taking a path upstream. When opposite Klien's selection, he crossed the river and scrambled through a tangled mass of vines to reach the selector's clearing. He paused, checking the surrounds before approaching the hut. The entrance told a gruesome story with fresh blood splashed across the door. He found the inside of the hut wrecked and the food stores missing. Winston had seen a lot of blood during his career as a boxer but nothing to compare with this carnage. The floor and walls were splattered and a pool of blood in one corner marked where Klien had died. Winston paused in the eerie silence, imagining Klien's struggle and his last moments. He considered the savagery and, for a moment, wondered why he cared about the blacks. Outside, a trail of blood led into the rainforest and disappeared into the dark understorey. A grisly thought crossed his mind as he considered why hungry men would take the body. He could follow the path and probably discover the reason but chose to close his mind to the possibility. Those in his camp would undoubtedly know the perpetrators and they may have even received rations from his store. As to his safety, he held no particular concern because, macabre as this murder was, he knew that the blacks respected him. He needed to think, to re-evaluate his purpose and the contribution he was making to what he had, till now, considered to be the *Black Struggle.*

Later in the day, Bajal tracked his movements and found him sitting on a sandbank, alone and distracted. Winston appreciated Bajal's concern and, after exchanging a few words, followed him back to camp.

Winston sat on the ground by the fire till very late that night. Dari busied herself till the others went to bed and then sat beside him and, for the first time ever, held his arm and leant against him. Winston laid his head against hers and, by the glow from the coals, they comforted one another till Dari drifted off to sleep with her head on his lap. Winston remained unreconciled. He thought he had found a way, a means of bringing black and white together through understanding and goodwill, but the tragedy he had witnessed earlier in the day now put everything in jeopardy. He stroked Dari's hair, feeling a nearness to the Aborigines, and before daybreak came to the conclusion that he must, at all cost, protect Dari and her people.

Early in the morning six mounted troopers, two abreast and with rifles drawn, trotted down the main avenue of the plantation and straight into the camp. Winston signalled to the others to stay aside and stepped forward when Sergeant Caxton, the officer in charge, pulled his mount to a halt. Caxton, obviously rattled by the murder, spoke loudly, demanding to know the whereabouts of the perpetrators. Nobody admitted to any knowledge of the event and the officer, frustrated and disbelieving, left empty handed.

CHAPTER 27

The selectors continued with their relentless advance on the landscape. They felled the rainforest by cutting nicks into the smaller, understorey trees and then felling a large one in their midst which, attached to the others by massive vines, crashed, taking all in its wake to fell an acre at a time. After a few months the tangled mess would take a fire, with the flammable sap burning to a raging inferno. It consumed all, including fine building and cabinet timbers, in its hunger to decimate every last remnant of the forest. The open forest country also fell victim to the insatiable desire to intrude on pristine land and take down what nature had provided. Axemen gloated and boasted to all about the huge swathes of forest they felled and the clean burns of what they called debris. The government lauded these efforts by publishing glowing reports of the rate of clearing, the crops grown, and the imperative of supplying the southern markets. Incentives and dispensations were given to those prepared to attack the native forest and reduce it to embers.

For the Aborigines there was no way out. Their habitat, beneath skies blackened with smoke, shrank by the week, leaving them nowhere to go. While calls about *protecting* the native population were heard in the halls of power, the killing and starvation continued.

Jonathan Ashton made his contribution by extending his cleared area to five hundred acres and with every intention of felling the remainder of his square mile of country within the next two years. He engaged more Chinese tenant farmers, expanding his influence in the district, gaining himself a reputation as a ruthless operator. Nothing, it seemed, could stand in his way. His plan of extending the Ashton empire to the northern reaches of the colony of Queensland would be a dream fulfilled. He cared not about the black children with distended bellies caused by malnutrition, the gaunt figures of men he saw fishing in the river or the women, tired and ragged, carrying listless children on their bony hips. Jonathan had become a man obsessed. To his mind every acre put under production further enhanced his self-worth as a man able to tame the wilderness. His emotions, those tender moments he had spent with Ellen in earlier years, were buried beneath the harshness of what he now considered to be reality. Ellen sought refuge in the company of Nganka, not only seeking passionate embraces but something far more important; the need for a confidant who could keep her sane. Jonathan, in turn, welcomed Nganka's presence, thinking the two shared nothing more than a deep friendship. He even encouraged Nganka to visit more often and paid her handsomely for the time she spent at the house.

Ah Sam, a spokesperson for the twenty or so tenant farmers working Jonathan's property, interrupted Jonathan grooming a horse at the stables.

'Boss. Big trouble in the camp. The blacks speared a horse by the river and my men think they might be next.'

'What horse?'

'The old mare that's in foal.'

'Dead?'

'Yes, Boss. Proper dead.'

'Did you see?'

'No. Must have been soon after dark last night.'

Jonathan flew into a rage, told Ah Sam he would deal with it, and ran to the house. Ellen had seen the men talking and, as Jonathan took his revolver from the kitchen shelf, she asked of the trouble.

'Mongrel blacks have killed Lucy!' he said, seething with anger.

'Are you sure?' replied Ellen.

Jonathan looked at her, astonished that she could be so naïve. He ignored her question and said, 'Stay indoors. They're going to pay for this.'

He took the revolver, a rifle, cartridges and a dagger, and with his two Rottweiler dogs tugging at their choker chains, strode across the field to the brood-mare paddock. The dogs, inflamed by Jonathan's mood, the sight of the dead mare and the smell of blood, pulled at the chains. Lucy, a prize mare he had shipped from Goulburn for breeding purposes, lay butchered, with her bones scraped clean and her unborn foal taken away. She was so quiet that the blacks would have simply walked up to her and plunged a spear into her heart. Jonathan, after a few moments of disbelief, yanked the chains to check the dogs and then set them free. They raced about, picking up one scent and then another, trying to find a lead scent to follow. Jonathan, realising that the blacks had dispersed in different directions to confuse the dogs, called them in. He chained them again and made sweeps, widening the circle from the carcass till a likely scent was found and then followed it to the river with the dogs dragging him forward. Once again the blacks had deceived the dogs by entering the water. He searched till nightfall and then took the dogs home, resolute that someone would pay for the killing.

Ellen said a few words and then stayed clear, leaving his dinner on the table and retiring to the bedroom. The next morning Jonathan left at sunup with the dogs, hoping the blacks might have revisited the carcass to take the bones to smash for the marrow. Nganka, unaware of the incident, visited before Jonathan returned. When Ellen explained the situation she wanted to leave but Ellen pleaded with her to stay, saying Jonathan would only punish the blacks responsible. When Jonathan returned and sat for breakfast he spoke to Nganka in a civil manner, hiding his outrage. Both Nganka and Ellen respected his decency and in consideration of this decided to try to set the matter aside.

Jonathan remained uneasy during the weeks ahead, doing daily rounds of the paddocks with the dogs. Ellen feared for the natives' safety and, contrary to her sense of loyalty to Jonathan, asked Nganka to pass the word around that he was doing regular patrols and for their own safety to stay clear of the property. Another problem arose when a Chinese deputation approached Jonathan and said they were leaving due to fear of an Aboriginal attack. Intense negotiations followed for the next few days with Jonathan offering them more favourable lease terms. A compromise, which included arming them with rifles and ammunition, was finally reached and the tenants continued felling trees.

CHAPTER 28

The evening routine at the Ashton's home followed a familiar pattern. Ellen would have Frances and Nyulu bathed and fed before Jonathan came indoors at dark. As a family they joined in the kitchen with Ellen preparing the adults' meal, Jonathan having a couple of rums and the children playing on the floor. It must be said that Jonathan, although he loathed the presence of the wild blacks, did cherish Nyulu and accepted her as his own. He engaged with the eight-year-olds in games of make-believe, sharing his time equally between the two till supper was served. The children, now able to take a place at the table, watched on as their parents ate by lamplight.

Through Nganka's influence, both children spoke English and the native language. Their conversations drew smiles from both Ellen and Jonathan as they toyed with words, mixing them in wondrous ways. Following mealtime Ellen would put the girls to bed, kiss them goodnight and retire to the master bedroom. Jonathan often stayed up late, drinking rum and thinking about the property and his workforce. Ellen knew the routine well and would lie awake waiting for him to come to bed. Though she wished to engage for his sake, she found no pleasure in taking him and lay passively while he had his way. The most upsetting moment of these evenings was when Jonathan, after having taken her, simply said 'Goodnight' and rolled the other way.

This moonlit night both lay awake on the covers till one and then the other of the Rottweilers began a low, guttural growl. Ellen felt Jonathan slide from the bed in the darkness and heard the click of the door as he left the house. When she heard his muffled voice talking to the dogs she feared the worst and, dressed only in a nightdress, went to the open window. There, by the light of the moon, she saw Jonathan crossing the field with the dogs pulling at the chains. Thoughts of horror flashed through her mind and she hoped that, for the sake of both the blacks and Jonathan, the dogs would not pick up a scent. To ease her concerns she stepped quietly along the dark corridor, stirred the embers in the firebox of the kitchen stove and put a kettle on to heat. Jonathan had taught her how to fire a rifle and instructed her to lock the doors in the event of an attack, but she left the rifle alone and the doors unlatched. To defend herself and maybe shoot someone was unimaginable.

Suddenly, rabid barking filled the night air. Hideous screams then erupted, reaching to every corner of the property and beyond. Nyulu began to cry and Ellen, not wanting her to hear, picked her up and covered her ears. The little one would have enough to cope with as a black child growing up in a racist white society without being traumatised by memories of atrocities. The child, sensing Ellen's upset, called 'Mummy, Mummy' in a soft voice to comfort the one she believed to be her mother.

The barking, shouting and screaming lasted for a few minutes and then stopped as abruptly as it had begun. Livestock moved about restlessly. A lighted lantern appeared at the Chinese quarters. Ellen heard their murmurings and thumps and thuds as they barricaded their huts. After the Chinese had settled she listened for the sound of the dogs returning or a word of command from Jonathan; anything that would tell of his arrival. A sudden yelp from one of the Rottweilers caused her to panic; was it an injured dog struggling home to raise the alarm? Soon after she heard Jonathan talking to them by name and realised he was safe. She put Nyulu to bed, lit a lamp and found Jonathan at the outside laundry bench. As she approached the lamp light revealed him naked, bloodied and washing his clothes. She stood, aghast and horrified, as he soaped and scrubbed the clothes without acknowledging her presence. Never could she have imagined that the man she loved could become so desperate that he would resort to murder. She waited and, when he still paid her no attention, she returned inside, went to the nursery and locked herself inside with the children.

Ellen eventually drifted to sleep to be woken soon after sunrise by the sound of a galloping horse. Still blinded by thoughts of the previous evening she scrambled from the bed and reached the window in time to see Jonathan galloping into the distance. Where he was going, what he intended to do and of his state of mind she had no idea. When he disappeared from sight she stood numb and lost till Frances came to her side and said, 'Good morning, Mummy.' She turned to be greeted by Frances' smiling face and at that moment realised that for her own safety and that of the children they must leave. She dressed them both, filled a suitcase with children's clothes and told them they were going for a holiday to Nganka's house. The children, somewhat mystified, watched as she wrote a note:

Dear Jonathan,

I have gone to live at Nganka's for a while.
Have taken the children with me.

Ellen

She then turned to the children and said, 'Can you run fast!' The children, thinking it to be some sort of game, followed Ellen down the stairs and through the gateway. The Chinese watched as the threesome ran through the corn stubble, stumbling and tripping till they entered the rainforest. When part way along the rainforest path, Ellen suddenly stopped and stood stock-still. Before them stood three naked blacks, armed with spears and clubs. All she could do was fawn and sacrifice herself to their wishes in exchange for freeing the girls. One man with dog bites to his legs stood aside while the others advanced to within arm's reach. They admired Ellen, one touching her lily-white skin and looking at her suggestively. Miraculously, Nyulu began to speak in their native tongue and while Ellen only partly understood the words she fathomed that Nyulu was asking them not to hurt Mummy. The two men looked at Ellen longingly for a minute and then turned to their accomplice. They conferred and, when the injured man nodded agreement, they stood aside and let Ellen and the children pass.

'Hurry, children!' urged Ellen, taking them by the hand and scurrying towards the river. At the sandbar opposite Winston's camp Ellen lost control, became hysterical and yelled as loud as her soft voice would allow.

'Help! Someone help! Nganka, please help!'

Those in the camp were finishing breakfast and jumped from their seats at Ellen's call. Nganka and Bajal reached the riverbank first and, upon seeing Ellen, Nganka took a few steps backwards and then rushed forward and leapt over the thirty-foot embankment, just clearing the ledge below to land in the water grass lining the river. She struggled to free herself from the tangled mass of grass and swam to the other side. Bajal descended the steps to the river, taking them two at a time, and dived into the current. By the time he reached the girls they were in a huddle, with Ellen and Nganka clinging to one another and holding the children close.

The piercing noises the camp had heard during the night were confirmed when Ellen, soaked from crossing the river, told what she knew. Winston and James stepped aside to discuss the situation and decided to leave Jonathan to his own devices. They reasoned that for them to take Jonathan's side would probably jeopardise the camp's relationship with the blacks. The future of the entire tribe took precedence over the safety of one person.

Ellen's anxiety eased after Bajal visited the property and reported that he had seen Jonathan working in the field.

Ellen could never have guessed that she would one day be living in a camp with blacks. Though she had Nganka by her side and knew the others she had difficulty adjusting to the new situation. Dari, having long suspected the unusual relationship between Nganka and Ellen, insisted that Ellen and the children share her hut and not that of Nganka and Bajal. However, Ellen and Nganka continued to meet, rendezvousing away from the camp.

The children saw the change as an extended holiday and a time to play with Juran, whom they regarded as a cousin. At a camp meeting where everybody had their say, they brought forward an earlier decision to build another cottage and, within two months, Ellen and the children moved into a new cottage with a wooden floor.

James introduced Ellen to Mrs Brown of the smithy shop in Mossman and before long the two women formed a friendship, with each visiting the other regularly. James still worked part time at Arthur Brown's shop and, on occasions, Marku and Juran accompanied him. Marku helped by pumping the bellows while the two men shaped red-hot steel at the forge.

Mrs Brown's son Thomas, the messenger for the police in earlier days, had matured into a handsome young man and spent a lot of time at the camp with Bajal. He worked as a farrier at his father's smithy shop, shoeing local horses and those of the police stationed at Mossman. He confided in Bajal telling him, among other things, that the local police operated a racket whereby government flour rations for the blacks were being siphoned off and sold to settlers or bartered for home-made rum.

Winston visited Jonathan occasionally to keep in touch and to report that Ellen and the children were well. Jonathan openly expressed regret for his behaviour and sent a message via Winston, asking Ellen to come home. Ellen, still deeply in love with Jonathan, replied that she was not yet ready to reconcile, though she did keep the line of communication open by always asking Winston to convey her love to him each time he visited.

With time, Ellen became accustomed to camp life and could be seen learning traditional crafts and working in the plantation. The children continued to be a blessing, frolicking in the camp and scampering through the orchard. In keeping with Aboriginal tradition all the women in the camp were regarded as 'Mother', with the children going to any one of them in time of need or just for a cuddle.

The blacks visited regularly for rations and Ellen began to know them by name, even one she identified as being in the party that had intercepted her when bringing the children across to the camp. Every time he visited she wished to ask but refrained, so as not to upset tribal custom—warriors were warriors, often keeping their deeds and actions to themselves

Ever since the discussion with James about Shaun's wayward behaviour Alroy had questioned himself, trying to come to terms with what he now believed to be his failure as a father. Sure, he and Shaun had lived a rough life and Shaun had been deprived of a mother figure, but Alroy knew of others in similar circumstances who had raised children to become respected members of the community. Try as he might he could not fathom how, ten years ago, Shaun had left home as a bright and enthusiastic young man with opportunity before him and now lived the life of a drunkard who traded illegal rum, lived in sin with three coloured women and had a string of half-caste children at foot. While Alroy's standing within the community appeared not to have suffered he could not help but think that people gossiped behind his back. His dream of Shaun marrying a white woman, having children and settling on the plantation had been shattered. Now in his early seventies and suffering from pleurisy he had given up hope and did little more than potter about the garden and feed the chickens. All livestock, except for a couple of draught horses, had been sold off, the orchard lay in a dismal state and the flower garden struggled as a faint reminder of its former glory. It was no wonder that Alroy jumped from his chair when, one morning, Shaun arrived with his women and children in tow and announced that he had come to manage the plantation.

Alroy did what he could, letting them set up camp within sight of his cottage and accepting the women and the children. He cooked them meals and washed the dishes without receiving a word of thanks. The adults, including Shaun, lay about like dogs during the day and made a ruckus at night. The children, with no understanding of Alroy's aged condition, ran through the cottage, leaving an untidy mess in their wake. He often drew on his meagre savings, went to town with a horse and cart and returned with a load of supplies that, at best, lasted little more than a month. One of the women, only slightly pregnant when she arrived, gave birth by the open fire and, if it were not for a faint cry in the night, Alroy would not have known.

Alroy came to realise that Shaun's promise of attending the orchard was a sham. The nearest Shaun got to the plantation's fruit trees was to pluck fruit to brew wine to supplement the rum he distilled by the river. Shaun ignored Alroy's expressed concerns about the illegal activity and carried on as though he owned the property, with Alroy being the yardman. People of dubious character visited often and departed with a few bottles under their arm or a case on their shoulder. This was no longer Alroy's home. It had become a traffic way for the distribution of sly grog. Each time he heard raised voices he expected it to be the police conducting a raid. Alroy had no idea what Shaun did with his money until one day a Chinaman visited and, from the exchange, realised that Shaun and the women were addicted to opium as well as alcohol.

Alroy managed to keep his silence till one evening the son of a local dignitary called. Alroy watched incredulously as the well-dressed young man shared a pipe of opium with Shaun and handed him money for a supply of rum. *Who else must know?* thought Alroy. *Is it common knowledge that my plantation is being used for illegal purposes?* His reputation was at stake. All the goodwill he had earned through the years was now threatened if not already lost.

Sleep evaded Alroy that night. He sat alone in the dark on the verandah of the cottage, raking over the past, searching for a reason why Shaun had failed so miserably. Next morning he found Shaun and the women lying motionless beside a cold fireplace and some of the children crying. As he had done in the past he made a pot of porridge and fed them. The youngest, who Alroy called Sweetie, cried incessantly till one of the older children roused the babe's mother and put the child to her breast. Alroy could not bear to live this way any longer and at midmorning confronted Shaun.

Shaun, in a half stupor from the opium and alcohol consumed the night before, sat by his family's cooking fire in a dazed state. A woman, suffering delirium tremens, sat nearby, holding Sweetie to her sagging breast. The other two women lay asleep in makeshift gunyahs while their youngsters played in the dirt. The older children, used to fending for themselves, had gone to the river to swim, fish and catch small game for roasting. Shaun ignored Alroy's approach until he came to his side and said, 'Shaun, we must talk. I can't go on like this.'

Shaun raised his head, pulled his matted hair aside, and looked at Alroy as though he were a stranger.

Alroy struggled with his blank stare for a moment and then asked, 'Who was that smoking a pipe with you last night?'

'Grant Messinger.'

'Is he the son of the magistrate?'

'Yeah'

'How does he know you?'

'He's a regular. Comes over from Port once a fortnight for a fix.'

'Does he live at home?'

'Yeah. His old man has threatened to kick him out, but so far so good.'

'What about you? Do people in Port know he comes here?'

'S'pose so. He has friends over there.'

Alroy stood silent, grappling with the implications, till Shaun spoke further. 'The police already know. I supply a couple of them and they're aware of Grant's habit.'

'The police come here!' exclaimed Alroy.

'No, I deal with them downriver, but they know where I live.'

'Shaun, this can't continue,' said Alroy angrily. 'I can't have my name dragged in the mud. You'll have to leave.'

'Why? There's plenty of room here. I'll shift camp down to the river and be out of sight.'

'No. No you won't. You'll leave the property.'

'Where will I go? I have wives and kids.'

'I don't care. Take them to Jinkalmu.'

'I can't.'

'Why not?'

'Because the elders won't let me camp there.

'Why?'

'They say I'm a bad influence.'

'And that you are, Shaun. Look at yourself. Living the life of a derelict and criminal and ruining the lives of those around you!'

Shaun paused, taking in what Alroy had just said and then replied vehemently, 'Don't preach to me. I'm not your son and never have been. You know that!'

The words stormed Alroy's mind. Everything he had done for Shaun, all the sacrifices he had made, now counted for naught. He clenched his fists, grimaced from behind his flaming red beard and shouted, 'Enough! That's enough! Get out of here!'

'What?' asked Shaun, taken aback.

The black women stirred from their inebriated state and took note. Alroy stood over Shaun and, if he were any less of a man, he would have clouted Shaun in the ear with a thunderous blow. Shaun, now realising that the eviction was for real, shuffled beyond Alroy's reach and stood.

Alroy, seething with anger and disgust, shouted for all to hear, 'I want you out. All out before nightfall!'

Shaun, addressing Alroy with a note of contempt, said, 'All right, old man. If that's what you want, we'll leave.'

The situation worsened as they traded more insults, with Shaun blaming Alroy for his station in life and Alroy shouting about the shame Shaun had brought to the name of Higgins.

Alroy eventually picked up an empty rum bottle, threatened Shaun with it and then flung it into the bush. 'Go!' he roared. 'Be out of here by tonight or I'll call the police!'

'Where to?' asked Shaun with a plea in his voice.

'Don't know. Don't care!' replied Alroy with a menacing growl, before turning on his heel and leaving.

As evening drew near Alroy watched with sorrow as Shaun, together with his wives and children, left the property, trudging along the dusty track like a mob of nomads.

This altercation left Alroy very hurt and had lasting effects from which Alroy would never fully recover. He languished there on the property till the chill of one wet season brought his life to an end without having reconciled with Shaun.

CHAPTER 30

The flow of scrawny Aborigines coming by Winston's camp and begging for food swelled so much that he was unable to finance enough flour to feed them all. He began cutting the ration and refusing those who looked to be in good condition, reserving the supply for those in dire need. As the dry season approached the situation became critical. He received reports of men, women and children dying of starvation. To cut costs he began buying local corn and, with the help of those in the camp, ground it to a cornmeal and handed it out by the pannikin full. He also brought in barrels of molasses from a southern sugar mill and made it into a sweet toffee to be handed out as a supplement. One selector, taking pity on the natives, donated an acre of standing corn on the condition that Winston arrange the harvesting. With Bajal as foreman he mustered together a band of blacks who picked and carted the lot within a week. They then stayed at the camp, husking, shelling and grinding the rich food to a rough grade of meal that those dependent could make into cornmeal cakes and cook in the coals of a fire. Winston recognised that this would only bring short-term relief and wrote a letter to the Minister for Native Affairs, pleading for the government to provide a regular supply of flour that he could distribute. By reply mail he received a note saying that an official would call at his riverside address the following month to discuss the matter. All in the camp took heart from this reply and, to tide them over, went to selectors asking if they could help. Two responded, and between them made available three acres of standing corn. When this supply began to dwindle Jonathan came to the fore and relayed a message that Winston's camp could harvest a four-acre paddock by the river. By the time the government official arrived most of this newfound corn had been distributed.

True to the government's word a whaleboat manned by four armed troopers and an official rowed up the river and pulled to shore at Winston's landing. Official visits were a rarity and all in the camp watched on as a trooper climbed the bank and handed Winston a business card and then asked permission for his commanding officer to enter the property to discuss the supply of rations. The card read:

Queensland Government
Office of Native Affairs
Administrator of Stores

Charles Benson

Winston readily agreed and then stood in anticipation as the representative from the Colonial Secretary's office stepped ashore, with troopers standing knee deep in water, holding the boat steady. Dari, Marku, Bajal and Nganka looked in amazement as the corpulent, middle-aged man, clean shaven and with a waxed moustache, stepped from the boat and climbed up the steps. Even Winston thought him overdressed, with white, starched trousers, pleated shirt, silk necktie and bowler hat. When he came into the camp Marku, Dari and Ellen went back to their kitchen chores, while Bajal and Nganka retreated to husking corn under the shade of a tree. The children, curious about this man in fancy costume, stayed just far enough away as not to bring a rebuke from Dari. Charles was equally curious, glimpsing the mix of black and white adults, a black child, a white one and a half-caste. Most of all he could not fathom what a beautiful woman like Ellen was doing living in a black's camp!

Winston introduced James and then offered Charles a seat at the table. When Charles removed his hat Dari, peeping from the kitchen, fell in love with his blond curls. Winston and James, dressed only in trousers, took seats on the opposite side.

Charles opened by explaining that as the Administrator of Stores for the Ministry of Native Affairs he was responsible for all stores issued to Aborigines in Queensland. He referred primarily to food stores, blankets and clothing, and told how distributions were made through mission stations administered by religious groups and the police. He added that Aborigines away from settlements and still roaming in the wild were left to their traditional means of support.

Winston, in turn, gave an account of his situation and impressed on Charles the urgency of getting supplies to the natives. 'The blankets and clothes can be sorted later,' he said to emphasise that food to fill empty bellies took priority. He followed by telling how, before the white man arrived, the tribe numbered more than 300 but now the head count was less than 200.

James, a soft-hearted man with a gentle nature, spoke of the suffering, referring to the Aborigines as though they were his immediate family. He told of how he had come to the river sixteen years ago, fell in love with an Aboriginal woman and had a child; about life on the river as it was then, and his shattered dreams of today. His eyes welled with tears as he told how Bajal had carried home a young malnourished boy, the struggle to try and save him and his recent burial on the property.

Charles was touched by these first-hand accounts and confirmed that he would do whatever he could to help. He then turned the conversation to practical considerations.

'We have distribution points at the Mowbray police camp and the Mossman substation, but acknowledge that reports have been received about police misappropriation of flour, and rations not reaching the natives. This confirms my view that church bodies and private individuals are more effective in providing the service and I'm happy to list you as a distributor. The government considers the flour ration as a supplement only, and it is expected that the natives will, for the most part, forage food from traditional sources.'

This last statement drew comment from Winston who explained that most of the open land had gone under the plough, lagoons and waterways were degraded and the reef near the mouth of the river almost destroyed by silt washed down from the selections. As to the rainforest that remained standing, it provided little compared with the open forest where large game used to roam.

Charles readily acknowledged what he said but came back to the government's viewpoint that there was limited assistance the young colony could provide. After some toing and froing, and given the number of tribespeople expected to call on Winston's camp, they eventually decided upon half a ton of flour per month, with the quota to be reviewed as required. Charles added that he would wire the order south from Port Douglas and that they could expect the first shipment in three weeks.

With the official business sorted Winston and James took Charles on a guided tour of the plantation, wandering amongst groves of fruit trees, inspecting lush market gardens and viewing the livestock grazing in the pastures.

'How do you do it?' asked Charles, believing this to be the most productive settlement he had visited.

'Hard work and trust in our native friends,' replied Winston. 'Without their dedication and hard work this would be wilderness.'

'Do you ever fear for your life?' queried Charles.

'Never. Since James and I have been here there has never been an occasion when we have thought our lives to be at risk. We can wander anywhere in the valley without carrying a rifle.'

'But there have been some occasions when the police have had to repel them with lethal force?' added Charles as a qualification.

'That is so but almost always as a result of police provocation. The police do as they please and only report what suits them. The white officers sool the native troopers forward and let them do the killing. Poor bastards, young men, hoodwinked or coerced, taken away from their family and tribal land and flung into foreign territory. No wonder so many desert the force. Very few return to their homeland. Most become derelicts, living on the fringes of the local native camps. As long as the government has them as attack dogs there will never be any peace!'

The ladies had prepared a delicious meal of corned meat and vegetables and, since it was now lunchtime, they all gathered at the table. Charles made a point of getting to know each of them individually and marvelled at the rapport and conduct of the camp. He saw it as a template of what could be achieved with leadership, guidance and perseverance, and planned to write a report for the minister, telling of the success and recommending it as a model for integration.

The troopers lunched at the water's edge, helping themselves to cold corned meat and the damper they had packed. Charles' attention was diverted when the young girls, hiding in the grass on the high riverbank, popped their heads up and called to the troopers below, 'Crocodile get you!' The troopers, dressed in blue tunic, caps and jackboots, gave them a wave. The girls had fun repeating the warning that Dari had often given when they ventured too close to the river.

Charles felt the same nearness that all the white people before him had felt upon experiencing the goodwill and harmony of the camp. Winston's camp proved to him that a meaningful relationship could exist between the natives and the white settlers and it gave him confidence to press forward with his mission to save what many thought was a doomed race that would be extinct within fifty years.

CHAPTER 31

Mrs Brown regularly bought a copy of the *Port Douglas Times* and when she had read it handed it to Thomas to deliver to Winston's camp.

James enjoyed reading the paper from cover to cover and this morning sat at the table reading while Juran, his half-caste daughter, sat on a log with Marku brushing her hair. He turned the pages casually, savouring the update of local news and that of the outside world till he read a letter to the editor which read:

THE DAINTREE BLACKS.
TO THE EDITOR.

Sir,

In June last a boat was stolen from me on the Daintree by the blacks, and in my endeavour to secure the culprit, I visited many of their camps. In one place I found six of them, three women and three piccaninnies. One of the women was suffering from cancer in the face, and was in a deplorable state; another old crone was in the last stage of decrepitude and exhaustion, and the third appeared to be suffering from consumption, and was much emaciated. The three children, with protuberant stomachs and limbs which appeared too frail to support them, were evidently half starved. They were lying and sitting on the bare ground, with scarcely a rag of clothing among them. Although living in the tropics, the cold at night was extreme, they had no blankets and appeared to be too weak to make gunyahs. Not a vestige of food was anywhere about the place. The consumptive woman was sitting with the tears streaming down her face, and the most aged one was attacked every few minutes by shivering fits which threatened to shake her poor, withered old frame to pieces. I have seen destitute outcasts in the streets

159

and slums of London; I have seen fakirs and beggars in different parts of India and other Asiatic countries; but such a spectacle of utter hopeless misery and disease as those poor creatures presented I have never witnessed before.

Yours faithfully
Jack Arnold
Daintree

James paused and, with his arms holding the open paper on the table, looked across at Marku and Juran with a heavy heart. These people he had just read about were their cousins and, although somewhat distant, they shared the same blood lines, language and culture. Further, as husband to Marku and father of Juran he was part of the extended family. He cast his mind back to the time of his arrival on the river and recalled the life the tribe lived as hunters and gathers before European interference. They were a proud people, practising a rich culture and living lives with purpose. At that time they were blessed with fine physiques, clean skin, sharp eyes and strong teeth. Now, most of those of the Daintree and the Mossman were nothing more than pitiful remnants of a once great people. James criticised himself for his part in leading the charge into the region by being the first person to settle on the river. He unfairly berated himself for the harm he thought he had caused and as the thoughts twisted in his mind he became more unsettled. He stood up from the table and moved away, letting the pages of the paper blow in the wind.

Marku, now braiding Juran's hair, watched with concern as James went to the cottage, slipped a bush knife into his belt and left without a goodbye. The moment he disappeared into the orchard she panicked and raced after him only to discover from his footprints that he had broken into a trot that Aborigines adopt when hurrying to cover ground. She followed for a short distance and then, realising he was heading to Mossman, she stopped, not wanting to be seen following her man into town.

Upon returning she found Winston collecting sheets of the newspaper strewn about the camp. She tried to cover for James, saying he left in a hurry to attend to business in town, but Winston surmised differently and soon Marku told what she had seen and of her worry. Winston sorted the sheets of paper and read till he came to the letter. Marku looked on anxiously as he read it aloud. Winston, aware of James' sympathy for the Aborigines, told Marku that James most likely became upset after reading about the situation on the Daintree. As to why he might go to town, Winston offered no explanation.

Marku kept to herself during the afternoon, watching and waiting for him to return. By suppertime all in the camp shared her concern and they ate almost in silence, listening for a call or the fall of his footsteps. Winston told those at the table that he could go to town and enquire but followed by saying that maybe it was best to let James sort his own mind. Marku sat by the fire till late, struggling to stay awake. In her darkest moments she thought that James might have found another woman while working at Arthur Brown's smithy shop. Another damming thought was that James might have switched sides, preferring to live with the settlers. She felt abandoned and held Juran close, trying not to believe the possibilities that came to mind.

When the first peep of daylight lit the eastern sky a faint sound roused Marku from her nightmares. Thinking it was James she jerked her head up and looked around, only to see the dark outline of a tribesman coming her way. He stepped cautiously and when close Marku recognised him as a clan leader and a man of repute. He signalled with a finger to his lips for her to stay hushed and then whispered in her ear that he had found the 'white boss man'. Marku laid Juran on the ground and scrambled to her feet. In blind haste she followed the black figure into the bush. With her eyes clouded by tears she kept pace with the fleet-footed warrior till he stopped and pointed to a figure lying on a sandbar. Marku, not knowing if he was alive or dead, froze where she stood, leaving it to the warrior to check for signs of life. He approached timidly, knelt and felt for body warmth. Then, as he turned the man on his back, James groaned. Marku let out a shriek, rushed forward, crouching down and taking James' head in her hands. The warrior cast her a glance in the breaking dawn, stood and within moments found two empty bottles that stank of rum. He tossed them beside Marku and said, 'Boss man. He drunk.'

Marku roused James to consciousness and then, with an arm each, she and the warrior lifted him to his feet and limped back to camp where they put him to bed. The warrior accepted Marku's gratitude and thanks and, when Winston handed him a bag full of rations, he returned the compliment. James lay in a delirium during the day with Marku by his side. Though exhausted she continued her vigil throughout the night and collapsed when Dari came knocking at first light.

James later explained to Marku that in his younger days he had had a problem with alcohol but had reformed himself, except for times when he came under stress. Marku, without a word of criticism, smiled that knowing smile to which James responded with a loving touch.

CHAPTER 32

Although James had left school at an early age after the altercation with his father, he had received a good grounding and knew the value of education. He was also of the firm belief that, if the Aboriginal people were to advance, they must be educated. To this end he had, during the past four years, devoted time to the three girls, teaching reading, writing and arithmetic and the value of money. Ellen, likewise, played word and number games, encouraging them to learn. Those in the camp never ceased to be amazed when the children read them comic books while showing the pictures.

'If you get your spellings right you can have whatever you like from the garden,' said James. The inducement worked every time.

'And the strawberries?' asked Frances.

'Yes, anything you like.'

The girls chatted amongst themselves for a few moments, planning how they would raid the garden, and then settled for the spelling test. All three showed a remarkable degree of skill, scoring high, with only a few points between them. When the class finished they skipped off holding hands, heading to the strawberry patch hidden behind a stand of custard apple trees. No one in the camp gave them a further thought till the children's screams brought them rushing. They found Frances and Juran but not Nyulu.

'Where! What happened!' shouted Nganka who was first on the scene.

The girls, stricken with fright, could only say, 'Black man take Nyulu!'

'Where. What black man?' urged Nganka.

Ellen arrived at that moment, took Frances by the shoulders and said, 'Frances. Frances, look at me.' Frances turned her way and then, between sobs, told how a black man with spears had pounced on them and dragged Nyulu away. She pointed to the bushland, showing where they had gone.

'What man. Have you seen him before?'

'No. Never!'

'Are you sure?'

'Yes. The man had scars on his shoulder like he'd been in a fire.'

Nganka screamed and threw her hands to her face. 'Mawal. It's Mawal, Nyulu's father. He's come to get her!'

'Does she know who he is?' asked Ellen.

'Yes. She's never seen him but she knows he's the man with the scars.'

While the women comforted the children the men made quick decisions: Bajal and Winston would track him; James would cross the river and tell Jonathan that his daughter was missing. After a quick word to the women James rushed to the river. Bajal and Winston left with spears and a rifle.

Ellen, Nganka and Dari, with the children clutching their skirts, moved to the riverbank where they waited for a sign of James' return.

The first they heard was the howl of the Rottweiler dogs. As the sound came closer Ellen shuddered and lifted Frances to her hip. When they broke through the forest to the sandbar Ellen grimaced at the sight. Jonathan looked worse than had been reported. With his hair and beard as long and rough as that of a native, and wearing shorts and no boots, she could hardly believe it was the man she once knew. With the dogs still restrained Jonathan led the way, splashing across the river and leaping up the bank.

'Where to?' shouted Jonathan, glimpsing Frances and engaging Ellen's anxious look.

'Here. This way,' urged Nganka, heading to the orchard.

The two men, though short of breath, took chase. When the dogs found the scent and began barking Jonathan lengthened his stride with the dogs pulling him forward.

The women, terrified of the consequences, stayed silent, each thinking the worst. Ellen, shocked with disbelief, trembled. Frances, who had hardly seen her father during the past few years, remained confused. Marku sat with Juran, telling her that Daddy would bring Nyulu back and everything would be all right. Dari held Nganka by the wrist, refusing to let her take chase. The barking and howling could still be heard even though they were now miles away.

While everybody imagined Nyulu to be filled with terror the situation could be otherwise. Those in the camp had overlooked the fact that Nyulu was a full-blood Aborigine with close heredity ties to Mawal. Who knew what they might be saying along the way?

At a scrubby creek the dogs lost the scent and whimpered to be set loose. Jonathan jerked them to heel while James skipped across the creek to inspect. Within moments he called, 'They've gone this way. There's lots of tracks so Bajal and Winston are not far behind him. He's heading towards the river mouth.'

'Will he swim?' yelled Jonathan.

'Think so. It's his only chance of heading off the dogs.'

While Jonathan understood the threat posed by sharks and crocodiles in the river he dared not set the dogs loose for fear of them attacking Bajal or Winston or, God forbid, Nyulu. They pressed forward, leaping in bounds across the rugged terrain, closing to where they hoped to corner Mawal.

At the beach they scrambled through sand dune mulga to be met by gale-force winds sweeping the coast. Foam from the crashing sea streaked the foreshore, grains of sand cut into the men's eyes and the wind whistled in the treetops. In the distance they saw Mawal and Nyulu at the south head of the river with Bajal and Winston standing thirty paces back. The men hesitated, not sure what to do. When the dogs began barking Bajal turned their way. They heard him shout but could not understand a word above the roar of the wind.

'What's he saying?' called Jonathan, now struggling to stop the dogs from breaking loose.

'Not sure. Something about us staying back.'

'Staying back. I'll tear that black bastard apart if he hurts Nyulu!' shouted Jonathan.

'Agreed, but maybe Bajal can talk him around. He's probably panicking more about us whites than anything else.'

Bajal shouted again. This time the strain of his voice filtered through the coursing wind, 'He'll swim. If you come close he'll swim!'

Bajal then turned to Mawal and spoke to him again in his native language. 'Mawal, you won't make it. The current's too strong.'

Mawal, naked except for a tie around his waist, stood exposed with the horrific scars from his childhood accident in full view. How he had survived was a mystery to the few white men who had caught fleeting glimpses of him. According to the Aborigines, the medicine man had applied honey to the ghastly burns to guard against infection and for pain relief he sang chants that put Mawal into a trance. Bajal knew this and also that the disfigurement had made Mawal's life a misery. He was considered an outcast by many and lived alone on the fringes of camps. To deny him custody of his own daughter would surely push him beyond the brink.

Mawal, having regained his daughter after years of watching and waiting, stood defiant, clutching Nyulu to his side.

Though well within rifle range Winston had not fired a shot for fear the bullet might stray and hit Nyulu.

Bajal continued his efforts to have Nyulu released but his negotiations seemed to be going nowhere.

Jonathan, impatient and not prepared to wait any longer, let the dogs drag him forward.

Mawal, who had been savaged in the dog attack on Jonathan's property years ago, broke into a rant as the dogs came closer.

Bajal looked behind, waved his hands and yelled to Jonathan and James to keep back.

Winston, trembling, found it increasingly difficult to hold a steady aim.

The clouds, skating across the sky, cast moving shadows on the spectacle unfolding at the river mouth. Surely one or more would die. There would be no compromise. Brute force would determine the outcome. One or the other would have custody or, worse, Nyulu would die in the melee and everyone would lose. James recognised this and, in the crossfire of shouts, appealed to Nyulu as an intermediary.

'Nyulu,' he called in a voice she was accustomed to, 'tell your father we don't want to harm him. Tell him to let you go and we'll leave.'

Nyulu turned to Mawal for guidance. With tears trickling from his beard he looked at her and held her gaze. The pain of all those years of wanting to hear her voice, hold her and call her his own was expressed on his weathered face. Nyulu at that moment realised the depth of love Mawal held for her. She had been led to believe that he was a Myall, a wild black man who could not be trusted. She now knew that nothing could be further from the truth; that he loved her and was prepared to sacrifice his life for her.

Nyulu called to James, 'Take the dogs away. Go away!'

James, thinking that Mawal had coerced her during those moments of engagement, called back, 'Stay there. We'll rescue you!'

'No! No!' she cried. She took Mawal's hand and together they turned to face the treacherous river crossing.

James, sure of what was about to happen, pleaded for Nyulu not to swim. Bajal also begged them not to chance the crossing. Jonathan, in a tangle with the chains, struggled to contain the dogs, now salivating and baying for blood. Winston wavered, trying to keep the rifle barrel steady in the strong wind.

Nyulu, as a twelve-year-old, could not possibly swim the distance against the current, and although Mawal was muscular and strong the chances of him dragging her across were slim.

James knew this, and in a frantic attempt to save Nyulu he broke free, careering towards the couple, shouting as he went. The familiarity of his voice caused a flicker in Nyulu's mind, and she turned her head. The sight of him running her way with outstretched arms held Nyulu's attention for a brief moment, during which Mawal let go of her and turned. With only a few paces now separating the two men, Mawal instinctively raised a spear above his head.

In the same instant the crack of a rifle shot creased the air. Mawal dropped his spear, clutched his chest and staggered. Nyulu tried to hold him up but he fell to the ground, gurgling blood.

Nyulu screamed, fell to her knees and pulled Mawal's hands from his chest to reveal a gaping hole. As the blood bubbled from his mouth Mawal managed a few words that reaffirmed his love for Nyulu. When his eyes closed and his body went limp Nyulu became hysterical, screaming and cradling his bloodied body.

James knelt by Nyulu to console her while Bajal stood in stark disbelief. Jonathan and Winston stood aside, wondering if they had acted too hastily.

They dragged the body to a sheltered place behind the sand dune where it lay till tribesmen retrieved it the following day. Such were the circumstances of Mawal's death that no whites dared to attend the funeral.

Nyulu, at her tender age, was confused, unable to reconcile the circumstances of her father's death. The loving exchange that had passed between them at the river led her to believe that he would not have thrown the spear. On the other hand, had Winston not fired that shot, what would have been the outcome?

CHAPTER 33

While the others soon settled back into the camp routine Ellen and Nyulu remained unsettled. Nyulu needed loving care and Ellen's mind kept drifting across the river to Jonathan and the property. The sight of him dishevelled, and looking like a man from the wild had made her feel guilty. She visualised him at home alone, toiling in the fields by day and sitting alone by lamplight at night. Then there were Frances and Nyulu to consider. They were as much his children as hers. She now wanted to reach out to him, to be by his side, to share and care. She tussled with these thoughts for days till, eventually, she approached Winston by the wood heap and made mention of returning to Jonathan. Winston buried the axe blade into a billet of wood, sighed and said, 'I thought this day might come. Here, take a seat.'

Ellen could never have envisaged that one day she would be sitting on a block of wood on a riverbank, telling of her past and discussing her future. She spoke easily, telling of her innocence at the time of her marriage, her time with Jonathan, their estrangement, the past few years in the camp and now her wish to return.

Winston also had a story to tell of a lost love but that would have to wait till another time. He spoke lovingly, telling Ellen he understood and offering to speak with Jonathan. He concluded by saying, 'I'll go across and see him in the morning. In the meantime sleep well.'

The following morning Winston, armed with a sealed envelope from Ellen and a batch of hot scones baked by Dari, waded across the river, followed the path through the rainforest, stepped into a corn field, continued through the orchard and arrived at the house where an eerie silence greeted him. Normally the dogs barked but today all he found was an empty kennel. He entered the back door, placed the letter and scones on the kitchen table and then, after searching about, found Jonathan and a few tenant farmers chipping weeds in a potato patch. Jonathan welcomed his arrival and soon they were back at the house, seated at the kitchen table. Jonathan turned the envelope over a couple of times before opening it. Winston watched in anticipation as Jonathan read the note, paused and then quietly passed it to him. The message, beautifully scripted, read:

Dear Jonathan,

I don't know what to say except that I love you and want to come home.
I realise it has been a long time and you may not want me. If you wish we can meet on the sandbar at ten o'clock tomorrow morning. Please forgive me if I have done wrong.

The children send their love.

Your loving wife.
Ellen

Jonathan had waited for this moment since the day he had found the note saying she had left. Ellen's absence had taught him much about life and the need to have her by his side. He confirmed with Winston that he would meet as arranged and then babbled, asking after Ellen and the children. They spoke on over a cup of tea and when Winston left Jonathan thanked him for his care and promised to make it up to him. As Winston pulled the garden gate shut he asked, 'Where are the dogs?'

Jonathan replied, 'That's another thing I've learned. Dogs like that have no place with family. I've had them put down.'

Late that evening Ellen invited Nganka into her cottage and, with the children asleep in the next room, she sat with her and told of her plan to return to Jonathan. Nganka, while aware of the possibility, had never believed it would come to pass. She became upset and wept by the lamplight, feeling rejected and lost. All this time, since Ellen had crossed the river, she had believed that she was the favoured one. Ellen reached across and took Nganka's hands. They then sat in silence till Nganka lifted her head and searched Ellen's eyes. Ellen responded by whispering, 'I love you, Nganka, and nothing will ever set us apart. We can carry on as before with you visiting.'

Nganka, in a haze of thought, believed Ellen and squeezed her hands. Ellen, now emotionally adrift, doused the lamp, rose and led Nganka to the bedside where they kissed and undressed. At the risk of being intruded upon by Bajal or others they lay down and took of each other, sharing every emotional embrace possible. When spent, Nganka hugged Ellen, said goodnight and crept to her hut to find Bajal asleep.

By breakfast time the next morning the word had passed around and was met with sincere hopes that the reunion with Jonathan would be lasting. Ellen frisked about, shaking the creases from a girlish skirt, grooming herself and getting about on a high. She told Frances and Nyulu that Mummy was going to meet with Daddy for a talk. Dari played Grandma, occupying the children with cooking their favourite biscuits.

With the men away working in the field Nganka took the opportunity of slipping from the camp without being noticed. She secluded herself in a nearby thicket of rainforest with a clear view of the sandbar. At the appointed time of the meeting Ellen descended the steps to the river landing, removed her clothes to keep them dry and waded across. At seeing her naked, with her breasts fully exposed in the bright sunlight, Nganka anguished that Jonathan would be standing in the shadows and also watching. The moment Ellen dressed, Jonathan appeared, clean shaven and wearing shirt and shorts. Though Nganka could not hear, the body movements and expressions raised her anxiety and aroused her possessiveness. They conversed at length, exploring thoughts and boundaries and then, when Jonathan took Ellen into his arms and she surrendered, Nganka wanted to scream. She had expected a civil meeting, maybe a kiss, with any romantic engagement to follow at a later date. She watched as they entered the seclusion of the rainforest and imagined them undressing and kissing and fondling, before lying on the forest floor to release their passion. The thought of Ellen having taken her the night before and now Jonathan confounded her mind. After so long as Ellen's only partner the pain of sharing tore at her emotions. She thought that once Ellen had experienced Jonathan again, she would no longer want her. Nganka became so traumatised that, at that moment, she considered taking her own life.

Ellen returned late that afternoon, entering the camp with a breezy air that told that she and Jonathan had bridged their differences. During the evening meal she referred to Jonathan often, telling, among other things, that much needed to be done to tidy the house and garden, and that it would take she and

Nganka a week of hard work to restore it to order. The inclusion of Nganka gave a glimmer of hope and partly allayed Nganka's fears. Over the next week, Frances and Nyulu were left in the care of those at the camp while Ellen and Nganka crossed the river daily to scrub and clean. Ellen's move back to Jonathan's with the two children proved to be less traumatic than thought, with them only a short walk away and promises to visit often. James also insisted on regular school classes that made for more contact. Nganka, a giving girl by nature, soon accepted the situation, with she and Ellen remaining part-time lovers.

CHAPTER 34

The road between Port Douglas and Mossman remained hazardous. It was little more than a bush track, with no bridges across the river and creek crossings. Most people made the journey by boat, leaving the wharf at Port Douglas, sailing across Muddy Creek bay and then sailing up the Mossman River to tie-up at the junction of the north and south branches of the river. From there it was a short walk to Mossman. Almost all of the light provisions such as food came via this means, with cartage available from the junction to the town. From the town a web of dirt tracks weaved through the forest to selector's properties spread across the valley. While transport services remained reliable during the dry months of the year, the wet season played havoc, with roadways becoming impassable and the river and creeks flooding. Mossman and the valley properties could expect to be isolated from the outside world for weeks at a time, with packhorses the only means of conveying goods. For weeks on end neither boot nor fetlock were free of mud. Leeches and mosquitoes drew blood and snakes snapped at ankles. Though the times were tough and often disheartening, people persisted because they had no better option or, as some found, they had become part of this cruel but splendid landscape and would not leave for love nor money.

Port Douglas, though still in decline, continued to be the centre of government administration and services. Apart from the police substation and a postal agency at Mossman all other public facilities of the district, including the post office, customs, courthouse, hospital, school and telegraph service, remained at Port Douglas. People from Mossman had to trek twelve miles on foot, horseback, or by horse-drawn vehicle, or sail by boat, to access these services. Even the dead had to be taken to Port Douglas for burial in the only public cemetery. During the tropical monsoon season, when twenty-four inches of rain sometimes fell within twenty-four hours and the journey to Port Douglas was impossible, burials were conducted on properties or on the outskirt of the town. Simple but dignified gatherings of the deceased's few relatives and friends huddled in the rain as a hole was axed in the coffin so it would sink.

Those needing medical attention during the wet season often persevered with the ailment rather than risk the trip to Port Douglas. A local midwife did what she could but often there was little she could do with her bare hands to save a child and in some instances the mother. Many are the stories of hazardous journeys which failed to reach the hospital in time, with bush burial sites being marked by wooden crosses along the way.

After the closure of each wet season the people of the district began life anew, repairing damage to property and planting crops. The town again became vibrant with an infectious spirit of good cheer, pushing unwanted memories aside and planning ahead. Over the years the number of residents increased to the point where Mossman could be called a township. A horse-drawn grader swept the streets clear of ruts. Saddle horses, buggies and the occasional bullock team plied the streets, while people walked the grassy footpaths. Each year saw the establishment of new businesses, with flashy hotels, general stores, a carrying business and a clothing merchant springing to life. The town had its characters. An enterprising Chinese pastry cook who made pastry on his kitchen table and squirted water from between his teeth to dampen it while he rolled. A grubby butcher whose sweat dripped from his nose to the chopping block where he sliced meat. A timber cutter, who police chained to a log for being drunk and disorderly, dragged the log to a local hotel and ordered a drink. The visiting priest who rode over from Port Douglas to conduct services at Mick O'Shannessy's hotel, most times became so drunk that he arrived home a day late.

Family life lay at the heart of the town. Small cottages with picket fences dotted the surrounds. These people of the Victorian era practised a stoic way of life, rising before dawn, labouring all day, and then retiring early at night. They shaped their own hardy and reliable character. Children learned to be diligent and tolerant and to heed the scriptures that were read to them by lamplight at night. They played on the streets, amusing themselves with bat and ball and playing chasing games. These children, free of prejudice, readily mixed with the Aboriginal children who accompanied their mothers to town to do menial work for households or to scrounge for food. Their black faces could be seen looking from kitchen doorways while their mothers scrubbed and cleaned. They played marbles in the dirt with the white kids, showing their skills to be equal to that of their hosts. They taught the white children that a game of marbles was fun and not a conquest. They readily learnt each other's language which helped overcome the divide. It was not unusual for a husband to come home for lunch and find a black child occupying his seat at the kitchen table. The children of both races, naïve and accepting, became go-betweens, helping to smooth relations between the blacks and whites.

The Aborigines that came to town offering their service sometimes became attached to households, with arrangements for regular work. Arthur Brown employed some at his smithy shop in the main street while Mick O'Shannessy of the Shamrock Hotel kept a crew occupied with yard work and domestic duties. The days of Aborigines sneaking in at night, stealing goats and pilfering vegetable gardens, were almost a thing of the past. Men no longer needed to sleep with a rifle by their bed.

Sergeant Caxton, the police officer in charge of the Mossman substation, could not be trusted. Many times he had used his position to thieve or extort. As to race relations, he drove wedges between black and white at every opportunity. With a contingent of twelve officers—four white and eight black native police—he patrolled the district intimidating and, on some unreported occasions, shooting or beating blacks to death. From information passed by Thomas Brown the police farrier, Winston's camp knew of these events and, though Winston had complained to the district sub-inspector at Port Douglas, no action had been taken. It seemed that the sergeant's bogus reports were sufficient to satisfy the requirements of the sub-inspector and his superiors in Brisbane. Regarding the flour trade, where Caxton traded Aboriginal rations for rum and favours, Winston had written directly to Charles Benson, the government stores manager, telling him that the practice continued while the natives were starving to death. Charles responded, saying that the matter was being investigated and that he would call on Winston during his next visit.

Caxton was aware of the objections coming from Winston's camp and planned to silence them. In particular he sought revenge against Bajal who was making packhorse deliveries of the flour Charles Benson supplied direct to Winston's camp. Mick O'Shannessy, the publican, also experienced trouble, with Caxton threatening to have his hotel licence revoked unless he paid a £4 per month extortion fee. Mick told Winston that he had his own means of dealing with the colonial upstart, but as yet nothing had happened.

The selectors in the valley had progressed, replacing the old practice of chipping holes and planting seed between blackened stumps with the improved method of using horse-drawn equipment to clear and cultivate the land. This put money into their pockets and, finding it more convenient to shop at Mossman than travel to Port Douglas, they patronised local businesses. The growing of sugar cane as an industry had been a tease for a decade. An earlier mill venture had failed, causing trepidation, but a new move was afoot to build a co-operative mill financed by a group of sugarcane farmers. Sugar cane, a perennial that once planted could be harvested year after year with minimal attention, presented an opportunity for long term prosperity. Selectors with entrepreneurial skills came forward, planning and negotiating what was to become the mainstay industry of the district.

CHAPTER 35

An inflammatory incident occurred when an Aborigine known to the whites as Billy Salmon got drunk, stole grog from a local hotel and wandered into Winston's camp at first light and called for Dari. Dari, recognising the voice, rushed from her hut and others came outside in time to see her confront him and say, 'What you doing here!'

'Come to see you,' he replied in broken lingo.

'Why for?'

Billy, struggling to stay on his feet, waved a bottle of rum in front of her and said, 'To drink with you.'

'Me no drink!'

'Why for you no drink?'

'Because it's poison. Send you blind.'

'Me no blind.'

Dari, tired of this nonsense, said, 'Go away. Go back to your own camp.'

'Got no camp.'

'Why?'

'Missus kick me out.'

'Kick you out, huh?'

'Yeah. She say Billy no good no more.'

'Why?'

'Dunno. Might be she have another man …'

Billy, needing someone to steady him before he fell, lurched forward and grabbed Dari. She kicked him in the shin, pushed him back and threatened, 'You come near me and I'll roll you in the fire!'

Billy, beyond caring, turned aside, staggered a few paces and then collapsed by the fire. Winston looked at him lying in the dust and thought,

What chance have they got? Their land and culture gone, next to no food, and family scattered all around the countryside? The others, apart from James, seemed less concerned and set about preparing breakfast, stepping over and about Billy while cooking their toast. Winston remained distracted, brooding and mulling over the plight of the Aborigines, more determined than ever to make a stand on their behalf.

By mid-morning the tropical sun had begun to bite so Winston took Billy by the shoulders and dragged him into the shade beside Dari's hut. He again stood silent and pensive, looking down on Billy's small frame, trying to come to terms with the increasing abuse being suffered by his black friends. He thought of Caxton pilfering Aboriginal rations and concluded that if Charles Benson did not arrive soon to sort this mess then he would take it upon himself to send Caxton to the grave. He was snapped out of these thoughts when Marku came running from the orchard, shouting, 'Buliman.'

Hearing the call Dari raced to Billy and took him by the hands. She called to Winston as she dragged him into her hut. 'Wipe tracks away.' Winston, getting the message, quickly followed, brushing dust over the drag marks left by Billy.

The familiar sound of troopers' horses at the trot confirmed Marku's warning and all, except Dari, stood in the open ready to receive the unwelcome intrusion. With Caxton at the lead the troop, comprising three white officers and four native troopers, entered the camp at a brisk pace with Caxton waving for them to search right and left. Winston stepped forward into the pathway of Caxton, putting his hand up to halt the horse. Caxton, with his rifle at the ready, ignored Winston and instead shouted, 'The black bastard's here somewhere!' The troopers rode about the huts and looked over the riverbank and then reined their mounts to centre camp where they halted by Caxton. Caxton's eyes met Winston's and then, with an intimidating threat in his voice, demanded, 'Where is he?'

'Where's who?' replied Winston, standing his ground.

'That drunken black bastard that stole grog from the Cedar Cutter's hotel!'

'Not sure what you're talking about. No drunk blacks have come this way.'

'Don't press me, Ambrose,' said Caxton, referring to Winston by his surname.

Winston, strong enough to down the three white officers in a fair fight, drew his knuckles tight, moved to Caxton's side and, with menace in his voice, said, 'I'll break your fucking neck if you hurt anyone!'

Caxton, meeting the challenge, pointed the rifle at Winston's chest and replied sarcastically, 'Will you now?' He then ordered his senior constable to dismount and search the huts.

James and the others, unarmed and no match for the firepower of the Martini-Henry rifles, remained rigid and silent. Winston, braving Caxton's threat, held his position only an arm's length from the muzzle of Caxton's firearm. All feared that Dari might try to defend Billy and be shot in the scuffle. An eeriness hung over the camp as the constable went methodically from hut to hut and into the cottages with his finger on the trigger. Dari's hut, set to one side, was searched last and when he put his head in the doorway Dari shrieked for all to hear, 'Who's that!'

The officer, taken aback, called back, 'Police!'

'Go away. I sick,' she screamed back at him.

The officer, not believing her, took a pace forward into the dimly lit hut to be met with another shout, 'Go away. I dying.'

'What you dying from?' called the officer.

'The pox!'

'You got the pox?'

'Yes. I catch it from *buliman*!'

The officer, still not satisfied, moved closer to her bunk but was rebuked when Dari, speaking loud enough for those outside to hear, said, 'You want to puck me too?'

'No. No thanks,' replied the officer in a fluster, before retreating outside and reporting to Caxton. 'There's an old girl in there bad with the pox. Do you want to take her to the hospital?'

Caxton, without a trace of empathy, replied, 'No. Let the old bitch die here.'

He then directed the constable to open the door of the building where the government stores of flour and other food was kept. He nudged his horse forward for a better look and then turned to Winston. 'Be careful what you do with government stores, otherwise you might find yourself in trouble.'

Winston, ready for a confrontation, said, 'Safer here than at your depot.'

Caxton, detecting a flashpoint, replied, 'Believe what you want.' He then let the matter rest.

When the troop cantered from sight Winston called to Dari, who came to the door and, with a devilish grin, said, 'Them white bastards gone yet!'

'Where's Billy?' asked Winston hurriedly.

'He's asleep in my bed under the blankets.'

This brought a chorus of laughter from everyone, to which Dari wiggled her hips to show that she knew how to handle a white man. With Dari giving directions they then carried Billy to a hiding place in the nearby rainforest and laid him on a swag.

That evening, by a starlit sky, Winston wondered what would have happened if the police had discovered Billy. He thought of Billy being cuffed, chained to a horse and lugged along the track to Port Douglas. Billy could have fallen down and died or have been murdered, with his body, like others before him, dragged into the bush, piled high with wood and set alight to destroy the evidence. This would add him to the list of Aborigines who had disappeared while in police custody and be a further indictment of the police's rough-shod tactics and total disregard for human dignity or the rights of the individual.

Winston thought more deeply. What chance did an Aborigine have when the only legal representation available was a government duty solicitor who colluded with the police daily? With the assistance of an interpreter the solicitor extracted a name, correctly or incorrectly, from the accused and bundled him before the magistrate in a frightened and confused state. The court then processed him like a beast being pushed through a cattle crush, with the coercive voice of the prosecutor extracting a simple 'Yes' or 'No' that would convict the accused. This was followed by a call of 'next please', and another poor unfortunate would be led into the courtroom to answer a charge as foreign to him as life in another galaxy. Worse still, because Aborigines did not understand the meaning of *swearing on the bible* their evidence was often not accepted. The bias and prejudice practised by the courts to uphold white supremacy was taken for granted. No consideration was given to Aboriginal law and that a sentence according to their sense of justice might be more appropriate. No attempt was made to see the situation from the Aboriginal point of view. The white men had no idea of Aboriginal culture which, at best, puzzled them.

If convicted, then what? Will the accused be fined a sum of money of which he has no concept, or sent away to prison or to a native reserve, never to return? Will relatives be officially informed of the court's decision and the incarceration? Such was the debauched system of justice imposed on the Aborigines.

During the next three weeks Dari, with Juran by her side, attended to Billy, taking him food and drink and keeping him company. Others also visited, and when Billy became stronger Bajal took him fishing and trapping bandicoots.

One school day, when Ellen brought Frances and Nyulu over for lessons, Juran revealed she had a secret and took them to Billy's hideaway. On their next visit Ellen brought a lemon meringue pie and, at the girl's insistence, a large slice found its way to Billy's den.

When Billy recovered and his skin returned to its shiny black he began to pine for his family. He told Dari and Juran that he had been stupid to get drunk and steal the rum and that he would never touch the poison again. He spoke of his wife often, asking if they thought she would take him back.

Unknown to Billy, Dari had visited Billy's camp at Tara Hills, spoken to his wife and she had agreed to take him back, providing he kept away from the grog. At hearing the news Billy let out a whoop that was heard at the camp. When Billy left Winston's camp Bajal accompanied him on foot, leading a packhorse with provisions for his camp. On approaching the camp the voices of women and children, singing and chanting, drifted down the valley, for they knew Billy had returned. When Billy entered the camp his wife came forward and wiped the tears from his cheeks.

CHAPTER 36

Toby, the big draught horse with the white face, wandered the streets of Mossman, making regular calls at cottages and waiting patiently at the front gate till someone came out to feed him a few slices of bread. He had belonged to Alroy and when Alroy died and left his estate to the Catholic Church rather than his son, nobody wanted an aged horse and so he found refuge in the town precinct. He never caused any harm except for the time he leant over Mrs Anderson's fence to pick grass from the watered garden and, in the process, destroyed her petunias. She took to him with a broom and since that day he had bypassed her cottage when doing his rounds. He visited Arthur Brown's smithy shop daily for a handout of corn and Thomas trimmed his hooves when needed. When in his prime no other draught horse could beat him in a scratch pull where two horses were hitched back to back to a log, took the strain and then pulled to test who was the strongest. Alroy Higgins had been known to put a ten-pound note on the bar of the Cedar Getters Hotel when Toby won. Alroy would now be grateful that Toby had friends to care for him in retirement. All the children loved this gentle giant who listened to their stories and carted them around on his back five at a time. Though aged he remained strong and the townspeople put him to use, pulling a water sled down to the river to get water. He readily accepted the harness and took bold steps as he pounded his way along the dirt roadway to the river crossing where he turned in a circle, to set the sled close by the stream. From here men and children would bucket water into a tank on the sled and, when full, signal Toby to take the strain and head for home.

Mick O'Shannessy's rainwater tanks and well were dry and until the first storm came he needed to haul water from the river daily. He generally attended to this himself or directed a roustabout to take charge but today, in a fluster, he hitched Toby and allowed the children to do the run to the river. His two daughters, Kate and Brianna, aged eleven and nine, together with Ben Frankston a fourteen-year-old and three other youngsters set off with Toby to get water from the river crossing. Brianna, thinking her puppy would like a swim, swept him up at the last moment and cuddled him all the way to the river. Ben bucketed water into the tank while the girls spent their time playing in the shallow water. The pup, in a playful mood, jumped about, avoiding Brianna's attempts to grab him. She followed him downstream to where the water deepened and the pup had to swim. Brianna, in a panic, rushed to help and soon went beyond her depth and began to struggle. Kate, seeing the danger, shouted to Ben and then waded after Brianna. Brianna screamed for help as the current dragged her downstream. Ben, an able swimmer, dashed along the bank and dived into the swirling current. He fought the current but, when he was nearly within reach, Brianna's head disappeared beneath the surface. He dived, powering ahead underwater till he saw her movements. Though spent for breath he forced the last few strokes, grabbed hold and emerged with both their heads above water. Briana gurgled and spluttered and then screamed. Ben held firm and, with frog-leg movements and paddling with his free arm, he made it safely to a sandbar on the far bank. No sooner had he dragged her ashore than one of the other children cried, 'Kate's missing!'

Ben looked across but could see no sign of her. He raced to the riverside and peered into the shadows cast by the rainforest on the other side.

'Where is she!' he yelled. 'I can't see her!'

Toby, sensing the strife, fidgeted, looking a long way downstream with his ears pricked.

Ben yelled again, 'Toby, where is she?'

Toby stamped his feet and whinnied while continuing to gaze well downstream. He tugged at the trace chains, trying to pull free. The other children clutched one another anxiously, fearing that Kate had drowned. Suddenly, a loud splash sounded downstream, the sound a crocodile makes when diving from a high bank to capture prey. Ben stiffened in terror, his thoughts chaotic as he imagined Kate being eaten alive. He ran along the sandbar to tackle the crocodile barehanded but halted when from the water rose an Aboriginal man holding Kate high above his head. He reached the rescuer just as he emerged from the water. Kate, blue and lifeless, lolled like a jelly in his arms. The Aborigine, tall and lithe, held Kate upside down and thumped her back with his open palm. He ignored Ben while he continued administering black medicine to the young girl. Kate's body jerked once and then twice. The man laid her down side-on with her head facing downhill to the river. Slowly, ever so slowly, Kate began to breathe. First, a few jerky breaths, and then steady movements. Ben looked in wonder into the Aborigine's eyes and, in response, the warrior, with initiation marks on his chest and wearing threadbare trousers, gave a quiet smile. With sign language he offered to carry Kate back to the sled where he laid her on the tank. With a wave of his hand, he sent them on their way home with Briana holding the puppy that had managed to save itself. When free of the river Ben looked back but all he saw was the dark forest and shimmering water.

Mick O'Shannessy could not sleep. He sat in the dark at the bar of his hotel, remorseful about how irresponsible he had been. Kate was now out of mortal danger, safe in bed, but he could not forgive himself. If he had lost his two daughters he would have been found hanging from a rafter of the bar room. In the wee hours his wife Claire came to his side with a lighted candle, placed it on the bar and sat close to him. Mick took her hand and thanked God once again for saving the children and for blessing him with a good wife. They sat almost motionless by the tint of light till Mick turned her way and said, 'Who was he?'

'Don't know. The children had never seen him before. He just appeared, took Kate from the water and disappeared.'

'We must find him, Claire. Find him and repay the debt.'

Claire now smiled for she loved Mick, no matter his ways or temper, for he had a tender heart and an honest spirit.

'Yes, we will. To be sure we'll find him,' she said reassuringly.

'But how? All we know is that he's black.'

'There'll be a way. The Lord knows and will show the way,' she replied, trusting in faith.

Word of the incident passed around quickly and later that morning Winston and Bajal visited Mick. It seemed that the Lord had worked through the night and when Bajal told him the black man's name was Bularr, Mick shook his head in wonder and asked, 'Certain?'

'Yes, the bush telegraph tells us so,' said Winston. 'He was passing by and saw the whole thing.'

'Where is he? Claire and I want to repay him. We'll throw a party here at the pub. What say next Saturday?'

While parties with community engagement were frequent, never before had the town hosted a party with an Aborigine as the guest of honour. When Winston commented that police approval might be needed to allow a mob of blacks into the town Mick quickly put the matter to rest, saying, 'The police can go to blazes!'

The following day Bajal and Nganka visited Bularr's camp, hidden away at the headwaters of Saltwater Creek. Bajal had visited previously, delivering provisions, and felt that he could persuade Bularr and family to attend. At hearing that Mick planned to roast a pig on a spit and that all blacks were invited he turned to his wife who insisted he accept. They agreed to meet at Winston's camp early on the appointed day. Bajal and Nganka then scouted the other camps and reported to Mick that he could expect twenty to thirty blacks. Jonathan, Ellen and the children accepted their invitation, with Ellen slipping into town to speak to Claire about helping with the catering. Apparently Mrs Brown already had the matter in hand and word was that many of the townsfolk would attend. Marku, Nganka, Dari and Juran spent days sorting their clothes and jewellery and preparing traditional food.

On Saturday morning, Bularr and family, dressed in rags except for his wife who had come by a nice dress, arrived soon after sunrise to the smell of bacon and eggs. Bularr's children, curious and wide eyed, explored the camp with Juran as guide. Bajal hitched the horse to the cart, loaded the food and young children and then, as a troop of fifteen, they descended on the Shamrock Hotel. The other invited tribespeople appeared as if from nowhere. Mick took exception when Sergeant Caxton instructed him that only whites were allowed to consume alcohol. 'Security reasons,' he said when Mick barked that if a black man is good enough to save his child then he's good enough to drink his beer. By lunchtime thirty blacks and sixty whites had assembled in the backyard of the hotel. Mick called the throng to attention, made a rousing speech, thanked Bularr and presented him with a sparkling piece of Waterford crystal. The guests then stayed on, chatting and enjoying the lunchtime meal till Caxton and his mounted troopers arrived. The blacks, fearing they were the target, stayed a little longer and then dispersed with the troopers riding close behind. Although no incidents were reported, Caxton had sent a clear message that the assembly of blacks in the town would not be tolerated.

The *Port Douglas Times* featured a front page item, headlined *Aborigine Saves White Child*. The article told of the rescue and complimented Mick and Claire for the respect shown. Winston and James borrowed Arthur Brown's buggy, went to Port Douglas and presented the sub-inspector with a petition requesting that the government present Bularr with a medal of commendation. The sub-inspector, recognising this as a new approach to native pacification, endorsed the petition with a recommendation to the Commissioner of Police that it be forwarded to the Colonial Secretary for his consideration.

CHAPTER 37

Life at the Ashton's home had returned to normal, back to the days when Jonathan admired Ellen each time she entered the kitchen, and those tender moments in the bedroom when they murmured words of love. Frances and Nyulu, now in their fourteenth year, lived in true colonial style, surrounded by opulence common to the landed gentry. Nganka still visited a few times a week to clean the house, care for the children and find time to be alone with Ellen. This morning, Jonathan, dressed in dapper style, gathered the horses to harness and drove the open carriage from the stable to the picket gate where he called, 'All set to go!'

Ellen and the children, all dressed in white crinoline, came to the verandah carrying baskets of food and a bunch of roses the children had picked for Dari. They stepped aboard with Ellen taking the front seat of the carriage and the children the rear seat where they could see the two horses clopping ahead of them. They basked in the sun, beneath a pacific blue sky, as they whisked along the roadway where hardly a puff of dust rose in the still morning. To be free, to be going out together as a family, always brought joy to Ellen's heart. Her dreams were coming true with a kind and devoted husband, two beautiful daughters and a future for all. Jonathan, feeling the power of the two magnificent horses under his command, dreamt of one day becoming a member of parliament. The children, thankful that they had not been sent away to boarding school, relished the nearness of their parents and the smell of the Australian bush.

At the junction of the main roadway Jonathan, with words and a light touch of the reins, turned the horses towards Mossman. They splashed through the water at the river crossing and, when clear of its rainforest fringe, Frances asked, 'Where are we going, Daddy?'

'To Juran's.'

'What for, Daddy?'

'We are to meet a very important man.'

Frances paused momentarily. 'What man?'

'A man from the government, coming from Brisbane, coming to talk to us about the Aborigines.'

At hearing the mention of Aborigines Nyulu shifted her gaze from the silhouette of Mount Demi, her people's spiritual protector, the mountain with the twin peaks that stood prominent on the mountain range. She moved to the front seat, knelt beside Ellen to be close to Jonathan and asked, 'Is he your friend, Daddy?'

'I haven't met him yet but he's a friend of those at Winston's. He's the man in charge of food for the Aborigines and wants to help more.'

'Will we help, Daddy?'

'Of course we will, darling. That's why we're going to meet with him.'

'And Mummy?'

Ellen stroked Nyulu's dark, curly locks. 'We're going do all we can to help the Aborigines. Daddy and I and those at Winston's …'

They passed a grove of pines planted each side of the entrance to Winston's property and then followed the avenue flanked by fruit trees to make a grand entry to the camp. Juran, wearing a dress provided by Ellen, raced forward and scrambled into the carriage before the others could step down. In her excitement she hugged Ellen and the girls and when Jonathan put a cheek her way she gave him a kiss.

'We're the first here!' called Jonathan, stepping down from his seat.

'Yes, but they won't be long,' said Winston. 'They're expected at any moment.'

Those in the camp, dressed to their best, exchanged greetings with the new arrivals and then chattered, forgetting that they had spoken with one another only a week before.

'You've been busy,' said Ellen, referring to the swept ground and the sprays of brightly coloured bougainvillea wound around the poles of the dining area.

This meeting was probably more important to Bajal than the others because, when making deliveries of food to the camps, he had seen, first hand, the deprivation and suffering. He stood, somewhat anxious, waiting for the arrival of the official guest and when he heard the clatter of hooves he called the others to attention. Charles Benson had left Port Douglas earlier in the morning and arrived with a white officer at the reins and four white officers flanking the buggy. Some of the welcoming party noted the absence of native police. Charles, dressed as though he was about to meet the Governor, greeted them as old friends. Dari, dressed in a floral dress she and Nganka had chosen from a shop in Mossman and with her hair in braids, hugged Charles rather than shake his hand as James had instructed. The escort officers settled themselves by the buggy and were served a billycan of tea and scones. The children needed no encouragement to go and play and occupied themselves raking through Marku's jewellery and parading themselves for all to see. The others, with additional stools arranged for the occasion, sat under cover of the sail sheet at the long dinner table. After a few preliminary comments the group got down to business. Surprisingly, Bajal, a normally reserved person, led the way, speaking with passion, giving a graphic description of the conditions in the Aboriginal camps, the number of people in need, the location of the camps and the amount of food required. As Bajal spoke Charles made notes and asked questions for clarification. Dari had seated Charles at one end of the dining table with Winston at the other and while it looked impressive it would have made more sense for those most involved to be seated at one end and the others further along. However, nobody was game to suggest otherwise so they managed by raising their voices.

At the conclusion of Bajal's report Charles complimented him and also thanked Winston for his previous correspondence. He then outlined a proposal that he thought would solve the problem. He referred to his earlier discussion with Sub-Inspector McIntosh at Port Douglas, the man in charge of the Port Douglas to Daintree district. For the natives in the Mowbray River district, distributions would be made by police at the Mowbray police camp. For those on the Daintree River, police from Port Douglas would ship supplies up the river and distribute food from designated landings. As for Mossman, distribution of food from the Mossman substation would cease immediately. He added, 'Indeed, McIntosh's men are there now advising Sergeant Caxton of the change and removing the stores.'

Charles paused, sipped his tea and then told of the alternative arrangement for the Mossman natives. 'As from today responsibility for distributions will be with your camp. All rations presently allocated to the substation will be allocated to what will be officially known as "Winston's Camp on the Mossman". Winston is the man in charge and will be responsible for overseeing the operation.'

Charles looked across at Winston for confirmation and Winston nodded. 'Thanks, Winston. I have every confidence that it will be a success.' He then paused while Jonathan led the way with applause.

He continued, 'The provisions will include flour, sugar, rice, tinned meat, blankets and clothing. The amounts supplied to be on the basis of need, with Winston assessing needs and submitting requests to my office. As to payment for services an amount of £10 per month will be paid to Winston.'

Charles then turned to Bajal. 'We understand that some natives, due to bad experiences, are reluctant to come near white administrators, and if Bajal is agreeable he will be paid £4 a month to distribute provisions to those not willing to come in. Further, the head of the department would appreciate it if Bajal reported instances of sickness or physical abuse to the doctor at Port Douglas.' Bajal hesitated behind his modesty but was spoken for when Nganka took his hand and raised it to signal his acceptance. Charles concluded by saying that, while regular matters would be dealt with by correspondence, emergency calls could be made from the telegraph office at Port Douglas.

Lunch followed with a spread of food equal to anything available to the gentry of George Street. Dari excelled, serving a variety of dishes and waiting on Charles as though he were the Governor himself. The police officers enjoyed the pot of stew and damper she served to them. She was especially proud when one of them commented loudly, 'Best food ever. You can come and cook for me anytime!'

While the ladies attended to clearing the table and washing the dishes the men discussed the new program in more detail, working through the best way of tapping all of the family groups and ensuring an equitable distribution of the stores. The dialogue inevitably led to talk of police abuse and, in particular, Sergeant Caxton's record of maltreatment.

Charles, well aware of the problem, spoke candidly. 'There's talk within government circles of introducing an Aboriginal Protection Act to better care for the Aborigines and stop the abuse.'

James showed particular interest in the idea of a Protection Act and asked when it might be introduced. 'It's sometime off yet but the Minister for Native

Affairs has commissioned two reports into the Aboriginal situation and, once these are tabled, parliament will debate the issues.'

Jonathan, with his budding interest in politics, also asked about the Protection Act and, in passing, said he would support any initiative to assist the Aborigines.

CHAPTER 38

The support pledged by Charles and the idea of an Act of parliament to protect the Aborigines stirred passion and strengthened the camp's commitment to saving the tribe. They believed in the tribespeople, in themselves, and set to prove the naysayers wrong who thought the tribe was destined for extinction. As to those who simply wanted the blacks gone they had news for them—the blacks were not going anywhere.

Jonathan and Ellen became actively involved, handing out produce, employing some and offering them a camp site by the river. Ellen and Nganka learned how to harness horses, drive a buggy and provided an ambulance service whereby the sick and injured were ferried to the hospital at Port Douglas. They won favour with the doctor and staff who encouraged them to present those in need of medical attention. Many of the Aborigines, still locked into traditional medicine and belief in the medicine man, refused assistance, with many dying unnecessarily.

Bajal expanded his delivery service, covering many miles a week, leading a packhorse laden with rations direct from the government stores. Nganka, now fully literate, took charge of ordering the stores and mailed requisition forms regularly from the postal agency at Mossman. On occasions, when a dire shortage arose, Bajal and his white mate, Thomas Brown, went to Port Douglas where they telegraphed an urgent wire to Charles Benson. Bajal became something of a missionary, preaching that the white man was good and trying to bring black and white together. Many of those in the Aboriginal camps believed him and trusted that the white man acted in good faith. However, in spite of this spirit of goodwill, a number of Aborigines remained sceptical and continued hiding in the bush, believing the rations were bait to lure them into the open where the *buliman* would either shoot them or take them away in chains.

The rainy seasons proved particularly difficult for Bajal, trudging through torrential rain, leading a packhorse that floundered in the mud to deliver urgent supplies. With native foods being particularly scarce during the wet months Bajal often found groups of cold and hungry blacks sheltering under leaky gunyahs. On leaving these destitute people he would cry, with his tears indistinguishable from the falling rain. Yet, difficult as these missions were, he drew heart from the knowledge that those back in the camp understood and were doing their part in the supply line.

Thomas Brown often accompanied him, being away for a night or two and staying in native camps. Having a white man by Bajal's side further strengthened the rapport between black and white. Thomas became known as the *White Fella*, and one that could be trusted. Thomas also acted as a go-between with the selectors, visiting with Bajal and being offered a cup of tea. Most recognised the value of his and Bajal's work with some encouraging Bajal to visit when making deliveries by himself. Selectors offered fruit that would otherwise perish and, over time, invited the natives to visit and ask when they saw fruit dropping to the ground. This interaction further soothed relations and fostered trust on both sides. So, from Bajal's delivery service grew the first real rapport between the selectors and the natives. Those in Mossman came to learn of *Bajal's Run*, as it was called, and Bajal became a household name throughout the district. Charles Benson even heard of the success and sent Bajal a personal note of thanks that Nganka had to read to him. The softly spoken Bajal received this recognition as a humble servant of the people, politely thanking those who made comment.

Why Sergeant Caxton had not been replaced nobody could really say. During the time of Sub-Inspector McPherson's command some restraint had been shown but now, with a new sub-inspector stationed at Port Douglas, he roamed the district almost as a law unto himself. Some said that the new sub-inspector lacked competence while others took the view that Caxton's effectiveness in subduing the natives found favour with the sub-inspector, who sought promotion by quelling the frontier. Though the days of the frontier were fast disappearing there were some senior officers in the police hierarchy who failed to fully realise that co-operation was replacing the old practice of dispersal by gunfire. Though many complaints had been lodged against Caxton, to date there had been no mention of a transfer or of him being discharged from the force.

Of particular concern to Winston's camp was Caxton's continued harassment of Bajal. Since the furore about the flour trade that resulted in Caxton losing control of the distribution of rations to the blacks, those of Winston's camp feared for Bajal's safety. Several times over the past few years Bajal had been intercepted by the police when making deliveries to the camps. Mounted native police, sometimes unaccompanied by a white officer, appeared as though from nowhere, badgered him for no good reason and then rode away. A recent incident in which the officer in charge of a patrol accused Bajal of carrying rum and made him unpack the pack saddles riled Winston and brought him to the conclusion that, one way or another, Caxton must go.

Another telling incident was reported to Winston when Bajal and Thomas returned home after being away for a two-day delivery trip.

'Did you see anything of Caxton?' asked Winston when speaking with Thomas.

'No, but he's causing trouble with the blacks upriver.'

'What sort of trouble?'

'Do you know an old girl called Lulu who lives in the camp just up from the rapids?'

'Yes, though I haven't seen her for ages.'

'Well, Caxton's been poking her. She's addicted to rum and she can't resist when he shows up with a bottle.'

'Nothing unusual about that. All those troopers are into the black women,' commented Winston.

'That's right, but he's also poking her seventeen-year-old daughter who's betrothed.'

'Are you sure?'

'Yes. There's big trouble in the camp, with some of the men threatening to kill him.'

'Pity they didn't,' replied Winston.

'I agree, but he's told them that if anything happens to him the native troopers will raid the camp and shoot everyone in sight.'

'Why don't they shift?'

'That won't help because those blacktrackers of his will find them within a day or two. It's got to a stage now when he comes to the camp, gives Lulu a bottle, takes the girl away and pokes her.'

'What about the girl?'

'She's got no say in it. Lulu just hands her over when he passes her a bottle.'

Though Winston appeared to make light of the matter it further convinced him that Caxton must be put down, and the sooner the better.

A month later those in the camp were startled when Thomas galloped in, shouting, 'Bajal's been arrested. The police have taken him to Port!'

Winston rushed forward, put a hand on the horse's wither and spoke for all there, 'What's happened!'

'Not sure. The word is that he's raped Mrs Wilkinson of Killarney Estate!'

Horror and disbelief crossed the faces of all there. It could not be true. There must be some mistake. Bajal would never make an approach to anyone except Nganka.

'Who says!' shouted Winston above Nganka's screams.

'Not sure. I went to the police station to shoe a horse and a trooper told me.'

'When!'

'Half an hour ago.'

Bajal had been busy the past few days and, yes, he had passed through Killarney Estate yesterday while making a delivery. Winston turned to Nganka, pulled her hands from her face and demanded to know, 'Did Bajal say? Do you know anything?'

Nganka raised her head, opened her eyes and pleaded, 'He wouldn't do anything wrong. You know he wouldn't.'

James came to the fore and spoke more calmly. 'Tell us what you know, Thomas.'

Thomas explained that a white officer had told him in confidence that Bajal had raped Mrs Wilkinson yesterday afternoon and that the police tracked and arrested him at Shannonvale a few hours ago. He added, 'He'll be in the Port lockup by now.'

'Was Caxton at the arrest?' interrupted Winston.

'Yes. The officer said it occurred yesterday, and, since Bajal had been seen near Killarney, Caxton presumed it was him.'

'Codswallop,' said Winston. 'Everybody, including Caxton, knows that Bajal wouldn't do anything like that. It's Caxton trying to frame him!'

After a few more words they set to, making hasty arrangements. Winston and Thomas were to proceed to Port Douglas on horseback while James drove a buggy to Mrs Wilkinson's to get her account of the incident. Marku, Dari, Nganka and Juran would stay at the camp.

Winston and Thomas arrived at the Port Douglas police station with their horses in a lather of sweat, hitched them outside and confronted the duty officer. When told that the sub-inspector was busy Winston threatened to tear the door from his office. The sub-inspector heard the ruckus, opened his door and came to the counter. He recognised Winston and invited him and Thomas into his office and closed the door. The duty officer, curious to hear the conversation, moved to the bench near the door and listened. He strained to hear more when the inspector said, 'There's doubt about the truth of the allegation but you'll appreciate we have to follow protocol.' Whatever was said appeased Winston because he spoke to the duty officer in a civil manner when being escorted to the lockup. Bajal, upon seeing them, held on to the steel mesh of the cell and began to cry. This upset the men who, while not allowed into the cell, told Bajal of their discussion with the inspector and that the charge would be withdrawn. To reassure Bajal, Thomas stayed the night, sleeping on the ground by the cell, while Winston returned to Mossman to liaise with James.

James bounced along the dusty track to Killarney Estate to be met by Ted Wilkinson at the house. Ted, anticipating the purpose of the visit, called Mrs Wilkinson as James stepped through the gate. She appeared tired and dishevelled as she took James' hand to welcome him. They sat on the verandah and soon into the discussion it became apparent that the offender was not Bajal but another blackfellow unknown to Mrs Wilkinson. She knew Bajal well and explained that she had told Sergeant Caxton she had never seen the offending black man before. Mr Wilkinson also said that they planned to be at the police station at 10.00 am the following day to give a sworn statement. James thanked them, said he and Winston would be there and left, raising a cloud of dust as he hurried home to break the promising news.

The next morning Nganka insisted on accompanying the others to Port so, with James and Nganka in the camp's buggy and Winston driving one borrowed from Arthur Brown, they passed through Mossman and wound their way through the wooded forest to Port Douglas. Nganka ran straight to Bajal's cell while the others went to the office where they were told that the Wilkinsons had arrived earlier and were in discussion with the sub-inspector. They waited anxiously on the verandah and, when the Wilkinsons appeared, Mrs Wilkinson, pale and fragile, wept as she told James and Winston that the inspector accepted her version of events and that the charge was being withdrawn as she spoke. She insisted on seeing Bajal upon his release. They hugged in public view, displaying the respect each held for the other. Bajal, though battered and bruised from the flogging he had received when arrested, put his people first and vowed to continue with his deliveries.

After Bajal's arrest, Thomas made enquiries while shoeing at the Mossman substation and reported to Winston. Though Caxton received a severe reprimand from the sub-inspector he continued with his ways, including taking advantage of Lulu's daughter.

'When does he visit her,' asked Winston while alone with Thomas.

'On the weekends. Usually goes early afternoon on Saturday and home by daylight on Sunday.'

'Does he go alone?'

'Seems that way. Bertie, the trooper I'm friendly with, didn't mention anybody else. Bertie thinks it's a bit rough, poking a girl of that age.'

'How does he get there?'

'There's a track from the back of the station that goes to the river and crosses just below the camp. He travels barefoot so as not to leave boot marks.' He continued, 'You thinking of giving him a hammering?'

'Maybe, but keep it to yourself.'

'Sure thing. I know Lulu and the others would appreciate it. Be careful, though. He carries a revolver.'

Winston patted Thomas on the shoulder. 'Good man. Keep your ear to the ground and keep me posted. Remember, not a word to anyone.'

CHAPTER 39

Dari noticed a change in Winston's mood and when he slipped away before midday the following Saturday without making mention she became curious. At the evening meal she covered for him by telling the others she saw him head upriver with a fishing line. Nobody took particular notice and by nine o'clock all but Dari were asleep in their bunks. Winston's lateness worried Dari and, as she sat by the fire in the shadowy moonlight, a horrid thought crossed her mind. With all the women now in Mossman, had he found himself a white woman or, worse, a river girl? She refused to sleep, sitting upright and tossing another stick of wood on the coals each time she felt herself drifting.

Winston had gone upstream but not for the purpose of fishing. His bare torso flexed as he swung a machete, cutting vines and overhanging branches on a less-used path through the rainforest. He struck at a fifteen-foot python rearing up before him and severed its head with one swipe. He was in no mood for compromise, and beware anybody or thing that crossed his path. He moved carelessly, pushing against a dreaded wait-a-while vine. Its sharp hooks tore at the flesh of his arm.

Nearing the rapids, where native fish traps were set, he slowed his pace and moved cautiously. A family group sat by a fire on the other side, talking amongst themselves while cooking fish. He recognised the family, an old family unit that had stayed together in spite of attempts by the police to fracture and destroy tribal life. They seemed not to notice him till a young, newly initiated warrior went to the river to fill a billycan of water. After his return and the exchange of a few words the family members quietly rose to their feet, entered the forest and faded from view like disappearing apparitions. Winston knew he had been sighted and, for the sake of his mission, hoped they had not recognised him and that they would not alert those of Lulu's camp further upstream. He felt confident they would not return and entered the shallow water above the rapids where he washed the blood from his arm and torn trousers. A scrawny dingo, taking advantage of the family's retreat, pawed at the embers of the fire, scraping a fish from the hot coals with its nails. It fled at Winston's approach, fearing the white man's scent.

Winston, now close to Lulu's camp, steadied his pace and moved stealthily along the bank opposite her camp site. While he had learned to hunt and stalk game from his black friends, he could never match their uncanny ability to sense the presence of people unseen. Add to this the camp dingos' sense of smell and the blacks' capacity to detect any slight change in their mood; he would have to conceal himself in a hide downwind of the camp. Yet, at the same time, he needed to be close enough to see the arrival and departure of any strangers. He watched their movement from a distance and then crawled close and hid behind the buttress of a large fig tree. He expected his quarry would arrive because the lure of sex has more pull than a team of yoked bullocks.

When a call from a member of the camp signalled Caxton's approach most of the young girls vanished from sight. Older women dug their thighs into the sand and the men stood aside, wary of the *buliman*. Caxton came into the camp with a bottle of rum in his hand and a revolver strapped to his hip. He expected a greeting of some kind but when no one gave him more than a glance he crossed the sand to where Lulu and her daughter Kaba sat in the shade of a tree. He sat beside them, pulled the cork from the bottle, took a swig and passed it to Lulu. Lulu accepted and before long they were drinking, with one then the other putting the bottle to their lips. Kaba, knowing Caxton's intention, sat quiet and fearful. Caxton soon moved closer, began fondling Kaba's shoulders and then slipped a hand to her bare breasts. She objected, squirming and moving close to her mother for support, but Lulu, now under the influence of liquor, simply patted Kaba on her bare thigh and nodded towards Caxton. Kaba, obeying her mother, turned his way. Caxton then rose to his feet, took Kaba by the hand and led her away from the camp. The moment they disappeared from sight Winston sheathed his machete and hurried off to follow. Unknown to Caxton or Winston, an eighteen-year-old lad betrothed to Kaba also followed along with a spear in hand.

Caxton and Kaba walked a mile and, when nearing a dry creek, Kaba began to hold back, pulling against Caxton's grip. He held tightly and dragged her the last few paces to the sandy bed of the creek. To dissuade her from trying to escape he took the revolver from its holster and waved it in front of her as a threat. She stood helpless, watching, as he removed his belt, shirt and trousers and flashed his huge phallus before her. She became mortified when he took her into his arms, felt her all over with his grubby hands and rubbed himself against her naked body. He drew pleasure from prolonging his sordid notion of foreplay and continued violating Kaba for what seemed to her an eternity. He then pushed her to the ground and, instead of lying face up she sprawled face down for protection. She heard him laugh and then felt his toes in her ribs as he forced her to roll over, leaving herself fully exposed.

Caxton had raped her consistently for months, sometimes as much as once a week. His monstrous behaviour had injured Kaba both physically and mentally, with her experiencing continual belly pain and living a life of torment and fear. The routine suited Caxton fine, taking Kaba at his leisure and releasing his lust with impunity. As he had done before he ignored the look of terror in her eyes and knelt beside her. He then held her wrists to the ground and put a knee between her thighs, forcing her legs apart. Kaba tried to resist, wriggling her frail body, but was no match for his punishing strength. She lay sacrificial as he kneed her more, spreading her legs further. She felt his weight as he sank on her thighs and began to thrust. Finding it difficult to penetrate, he cussed about her dryness, spat on his hand and wet her crotch. He then took his throbbing penis in his hand and set to punish her for what he took to be a refusal. Kaba, now in a state of total distraction, felt the entry and then the tearing pain as his bestial thrust tore at her insides. She screamed and as he tightened his buttocks for another shove she lifted her head and sank her teeth into one of his biceps, tearing the muscle. Caxton shrieked and in agonising pain pulled himself free and jumped to his feet. He abused Kaba, calling her a filthy slut, and kicked her in the ribs before grabbing his revolver. Kaba hesitated momentarily and then, ignoring his threat, she, as instructed by an old woman of the camp, scooped up a handful of sand and stuffed it hard up between her legs, pushing it as far as her fingers would reach. Caxton, incensed by the audacity of the move, kicked her again and then cocked his revolver.

'You're finished, you worthless slut!' he shouted while trembling with rage and holding the revolver barrel within inches of her face.

Meanwhile, Winston had crossed the river near Lulu's, searched for Caxton's tracks but missed them in his haste. He set to reorientate himself and when looking towards the mountains caught sight of what appeared to be a moving shadow behind a clump of trees. There, it moved again; only slightly but enough to confirm that it was an Aborigine stalking him. The mystery man, realising he had been spotted, stood perfectly still. Winston, well known to all the blacks on the river, hesitated and then called, 'Who's there?' A few moments later the shadowy figure called back and came forward to reveal himself as Kaba's betrothed.

Following a brief exchange the young native said, 'Longa this way.'

Winston, trusting the black lad, drew his machete and said, 'I'll follow.'

The lad soon found the tracks in the sandy country and then hurried, following the footprints till, suddenly, he halted at a gully leading to a dry creek. He paused and then spoke softly, 'They bin there.'

'Where?' whispered Winston.

'In creek,' he said pointing with his spear.

'Sure?'

'Plurry oath. That white cockatoo has spotted something,' he said pointing to a sulphur-crested cockatoo screeching in a treetop ahead.

'All right. You go upstream. I'll go down this gully.'

Winston stepped into the gully, bent low and crept forward. The drumming sound of cicadas in the trees muffled any sounds from underfoot. As he moved closer he heard Caxton's distinctive voice above their chorus. He had envisaged surprising Caxton at close quarters and settling the score with bare knuckles but now, with the possibility of confronting him in the open, he wished he had armed himself with more than a machete. He followed the gully's turns till it opened into the creek from where he saw the pair on the other side some fifty yards distant. Caxton, still naked and with his back to Winston, continued talking loudly, venting his frustration and anger.

Kaba craned her neck at seeing Winston, and to keep her silent Winston put his hands over his eyes. Kaba, knowing this to be the Aboriginal hunting signal to stay quiet and hidden, turned her attention back to Caxton.

Winston crouched behind a stump and scanned the tree line for the lad. The lad, now upstream on Caxton's side of the creek, indicated with a flash of his spear shaft when Winston looked his way.

Caxton had stalled with his threat to kill, making a lot of noise but hesitant to pull the trigger. He seemed reluctant to murder the lass who had satisfied his deviant need so many times in the past.

Winston caught another glimpse of the spear shaft catching the sun, this time further downstream and closer to Caxton's position. Winston signalled back with a wave of his machete.

Kaba also caught sight of the machete and, guessing a rescue was at hand, she bought time by speaking to Caxton in a lingo he understood. Caxton, still standing over her, engaged, and to further distract his attention she rose to her knees, bringing her breasts within reach.

The lad made full use of the distraction, slithering from bush to bush, bringing himself within spear range. He could throw but if the spear fell short then Kaba might become the target.

Winston, knowing this and that police issue revolvers were inaccurate at fifty yards, stood up and took a chance by bravely shouting, 'Caxton!'

Caxton, taken wholly by surprise, spun around to confront him.

'So, we meet again,' called Winston, buying precious moments of diversion.

'I'll take you down!' bellowed Caxton, levelling the revolver.

'I don't think so,' replied Winston, holding Caxton's attention while Kaba scrambled clear.

Caxton held the revolver with both hands and as he steadied his aim the lad shrieked a war whoop from behind. Caxton turned to fire but the lad's spear, already quivering through the air, struck him in the chest. Caxton gasped, pulled the spear free, picked up his revolver and fired at the lad. Though now giddy and wavering he tried for another shot only to be brought down by Winston's tackle. He fell, lying on his back, and soon blood ran down his side, turning the pearly white sand to a bright red. Winston, Kaba and her betrothed came close and watched as Caxton struggled for a couple of minutes and then convulsed and died. They decided not to hide the body because the blacktrackers would inevitably make the discovery. After making a pact to remain silent the young couple left hand in hand with the spear, and Winston headed homeward with his machete.

Winston cut cross-country rather than using tracks where he might be seen by the police or settlers. He stopped by a lagoon and sat, thinking about Caxton's death and the ramifications that would follow upon discovery of his body. He expected trouble but dismissed any serious thought of the possible consequences because, to his mind, Caxton had to go whatever the cost. The punitive police raids, the starvation, the deprivation being suffered by the blacks must stop, and if he had to be the one to bring it to an end then so be it. He sat there stoically till evening fell and the moon rose high in the sky. He then made his way home.

Dari was roused from her vigil by the fire when she heard a sound near Winston's cottage. She scanned the puddles of moonlight between the shadows and made out the figure of a man at the wash stand. If it were Winston he would surely have come over to tell her where he had been. She called quietly, 'Is that you, Winston?'

The figure paused momentarily and then replied, 'Yes.'

She waited, watching his shadowy movements till he finished washing himself and came to the fire. Where he had been and what he had done she did not know but she sensed trouble. He stood, solemn and expressionless, by the firelight for a minute and then sat down and held her hand. She let him settle and then asked, 'What is it?'

'Caxton's dead,' he replied without elaborating.

Dari understood. Her mind filled with thoughts of police reprisal and Winston going to the gallows. As a show of support she hugged him and said in a soft voice, 'I love you.' Winston, moved by her emotion, wrapped an arm about her shoulders and replied, 'And I love you too, my darling.'

CHAPTER 40

By nine o'clock the next morning Caxton's speared body had been discovered and a trooper galloped towards Port Douglas to alert the sub-inspector. The word spread around Mossman, with people guessing the identity of the perpetrator. All in the town knew of Caxton's ruthless treatment of the blacks and his molestation of black women. While some were aghast that such a crime could be committed so close to town, most welcomed it as a release from Caxton's cruel policing. Thomas Brown stirred Winston's camp when he cantered in and announced, 'Caxton's been murdered!' Winston and Dari, having overslept, heard the ruckus and came to the doors of their huts to see him telling the others how Caxton had been speared to death upriver.

'Who did it?' asked James as Thomas settled his fidgeting horse.

'Not sure. There's talk it was Lulu's camp.'

'What are the police doing?'

'They're on their way. All hell's going to break loose! The blacks don't stand a chance. The river's going to run red with blood.'

'You're right. They've been waiting for an excuse and with their blacktrackers the blacks don't stand a chance.'

Bajal spoke up. 'I'll go to Lulu's and warn them. They can spread the word from there.'

James thought differently. 'They might do a sweep from Port, blasting everyone in sight. We'll all have to warn all the camps.'

James then detailed a rescue plan. 'Bajal, you go to Lulu's. Dari, you and Juran warn those camped over at Jonathan's. Tell Jonathan to go and warn those on Saltwater Creek. You and Juran then stay with Ellen. Nganka, cover the camps down to the river mouth and then tell those on the beach front.

Marku, you do the south branch of the river and I'll head to the home village near the Gorge. Tell them to send runners to the outlying camps.'

James, recalling Winston's absence last night and knowing his view of Caxton, turned his way and cast him a glance. Winston, now armed with a rifle and cartridge belt, strode into their midst and added, 'Thomas and I will head towards Port, clearing the way and maybe heading off the police. If it's trouble they want then we can give them plenty.' He then turned to Thomas. 'You right with that?'

'Sure am. I'll bridle your horse while you get me a rifle and shot.'

They dispersed, covering the rough country faster than a man could on horseback, running into camps and shouting that the *buliman* was coming and to head for the hills. Winston and Thomas took native tracks, short-cutting till they reached the pass where the road threaded through the gap in Cassowary Range. They spurred their horses up the steep hillside to have a commanding view of the road towards both Port Douglas and Mossman. A trail of dust from the direction of Port alerted them to travelling horses and before long a dozen mounted troopers approached at a measured trot. Thomas wanted to fire a shot to draw then away from their mission. His plan was to lead the troopers on a chase along the foothills of Cassowary Range and then swim their horses at a tidal section of the river known to be infested with crocodiles. While some of the white troopers might not hesitate he knew that the native blacktrackers would baulk at being eaten alive. This delay in making a crossing would give him and Winston time to mix with Sullivan's cattle on the north side and cover their tracks.

Winston stayed Thomas' intention by reaching out and pushing the barrel of his rifle aside. He thought it better to shadow the troop and launch a diversionary attack if the troopers cornered a mob of blacks and set to blast them out of existence.

'Hold your fire till needed. We can take down half of these bastards before we get hit!' he said in a low tone.

They shadowed the troop at a safe distance, moving stealthily through heavily timbered country.

The townspeople, with concerns similar to those of Winston's camp, gathered at Mick O'Shannessy's hotel. Mick stood on a barrel on the street front with Arthur Brown by his side, shouting rallying calls that could be heard across Mossman.

'Caxton is dead!' he chorused. He incited the people to stand up against police brutality of Aborigines. 'Let's lay siege to the station before the others arrive. Arm yourselves, my friends, and join me. The Lord is with us!'

Most of the adults armed themselves with an assortment of weaponry and marched towards the local police garrison. The troopers, caught unawares, fired several warning shots in the direction of the crowd and then barricaded themselves inside their barracks. The sub-inspector's troop, now only a mile from the township, heard the shots, broke formation and galloped headlong towards the commotion. A bystander caught sight of them and shouted, 'They're coming. The troopers are coming!'

The crowd, fearing they would be shot or trampled to death, milled around in confusion until Mick broke from the crowd, bellowed obscenities about the British and then confronted the advancing troop.

He knelt, put a rifle to his shoulder, steadied his aim and pulled the trigger. Although the bullet fell short it downed the sub-inspector's horse, with the sub-inspector being flung from the saddle and dislocating his shoulder. Mick quickly reloaded and fired a second shot aimlessly into the charge. The troop, now without their commanding officer, began firing indiscriminately. It seemed that a massacre, not of the blacks but of the white community, was about to occur. However, the situation suddenly changed when two gunshots from behind the troop felled a native trooper and wounded a white officer. The sound of the shots and the sight of the troopers falling from their saddles drew a cry from the crowd. More shots followed and when word spread that it was Winston and Thomas some in the crowd fired at the police. The troop, now caught in a crossfire and with two more wounded, fell into disarray. With their horses panicking they found it almost impossible to hold their seats in the saddle and reload.

Mick O'Shannessy took advantage of the confusion. He dropped his rifle and, with a revolver in hand, raced to the sub-inspector, dragged him to his feet, held the revolver to his head and threatened to execute him. The possibility of a public execution brought horror to the faces of both the townspeople and the police. No one there, except Mick's wife Claire, could have imagined that their affable innkeeper was capable of committing such an outrage.

Mick held his post fearlessly till a sergeant, the second-in-command, shouted to Mick from behind a wood heap, 'Drop the weapon or you'll hang!'

Mick, with vivid recall of his father being murdered by the British constabulary, challenged the sergeant, 'Come out into the open, you English pig!'

'It'll do you no good, O'Shannessy,' came the reply.

Mick ignored the call and, instead, launched into a tirade about British rule and the oppression of his countrymen of the Emerald Isle. His voice reached everyone there and it soon became clear that if he were to die then at least one British pig would go with him.

Claire, having been part of the history and having witnessed Mick's father gunned down at his doorstep in Dublin, shook herself free from Arthur Brown's grasp and raced to Mick's side. She stood close and pleaded, 'No, Mick. Let it stay in Ireland. We came to make a new start, you and me and now the children. There can be no redemption for cold-blooded murder.'

A hush descended as she spoke further, talking of the future and the futility of revisiting the past. The sweet caress of her voice, as it had done in previous times of crisis, captured Mick's attention and Claire, knowing that Mick would do anything for her and the children, stayed calm and kept talking.

'Mick, we all need you, me, the children and the townsfolk. We promised each other that no matter what, we would do good with our new life. We've been blessed with opportunity. Don't throw it away. Please, please think of the children …

Mrs Brown, who had been restraining Kate and Brianna, let them go. They ran, calling, 'Daddy, Daddy.' Mick looked at his daughters and then back at Claire. He then took a long look at the sub-inspector before handing the revolver to Claire.

The sub-inspector, realising the situation was untenable, gave the order to withdraw. As the troop reassembled and made ready to leave with the wounded officers and the dead native trooper, Arthur Brown spoke to the community, asking them to disperse.

During the following days arrangements were made via the telegraph service to bring in police investigators from Cooktown to conduct interviews with those actively engaged in or having witnessed the rebellion. This was conducted in such a way as to create a sense of impartiality, but throughout the process the reports continually referred to the incident as a riot and not a rebellion. The difference in perception was that while a riot is simply a matter of public disorder and therefore a police matter, a rebellion is armed resistance against the government and therefore would come to the notice of the Colonial Secretary and, in turn, the Home Office in London. With an investigation from London likely to expose gross inadequacies of the administration of the colony, politicians and government administrators alike scrambled to paper over their deficiencies. This deceit even stretched to the evidence from some witnesses being discarded, and some misreporting by police who were involved in the incident. However, newspaper headlines of a 'Rebellion' took their toll and the government was eventually forced to establish a commission of enquiry into the incident.

The commission was flawed from the outset. The terms of reference were so narrow as to exclude any real consideration of police brutality against the Aborigines. Furthermore, they claimed that a scarcity of police resources was to blame for the inadequate policing of the district. To limit the evidence taken they allowed for only a two-day hearing at Port Douglas, and even then the arbitrary selection of witnesses called smelled of a cover-up. The commission's report concluded that the garrisoned police had fired hastily and in so doing unnecessarily exacerbated the situation. Further, the citizens acted in genuine fear for their own lives and the lives of others when responding with gunfire. As this was deemed to be self-defence the report recommended that no charges be laid against individuals. While this meant that Mick escaped charges of incitement, affray and malicious intent and Winston and Thomas avoided prosecution for murder and grievous bodily harm, it did nothing to bring to notice the plight of the Aborigines. The native trooper who sustained a fatal gunshot was simply written off as having absconded and the white police officers wounded during the insurrection were silenced by promises of significant promotions within the force. Overall the process amounted to a whitewash to protect the inadequacy of the government's native policy.

As to Caxton's death, the police conducted an extensive investigation, interviewing both blacks and whites throughout the district. Winston was interviewed in his camp and a second time at Port Douglas where it became obvious they suspected him of being involved but had no evidence. Although no charge was laid a shadow remained over his name.

At a later date an inquest into Caxton's death was held at Port Douglas. Several witnesses were called, with some giving dubious evidence. In summary the magistrate concluded that Sergeant Caxton died as a result of a spear wound to the chest. As to who delivered the blow, that question remained open.

In spite of this inconclusive finding, newspaper reports of Caxton's death and the subsequent inquest did expose abuse of Aborigines and caused ructions within the Department of Native Affairs. Questions were asked. The Colonial Secretary demanded a full report. Sackings occurred within the administration and the sub-inspector was transferred. Native police were withdrawn from Mossman and Port Douglas, leaving only white officers. With the killings at an end the Aborigines, though not entirely free of abuse, now found themselves able to move about the valley more freely.

CHAPTER 41

Mossman celebrated Federation Day in grand style. The *Port Douglas Times*, with patriotic gusto, peppered their pages with articles extolling the virtues of Federation and assuring that statehood for the Colony of Queensland was to everyone's benefit. The coming together of six former colonies to form the Commonwealth of Australia captured people's imagination, so much so that Mossman celebrated 1 January 1901 in regal fashion. Mick O'Shannessy, a native of southern Ireland, set aside his resentment of the British and made his hotel available for a gala ball. When asked if he could accommodate the whole town at his establishment he replied, 'To be sure, with a little help from the Lord we'll all fit.'

The Mossman district had matured in recent years and now boasted a population of 700 non-Aboriginal people. Two main streets bustled with activity, advertising goods and services not previously available. The government, convinced that the district had a future, built a new police station, a courthouse, school and post office. The Postal Directory now listed the town as Mossman rather than the previous loose term of Mossman River via Port Douglas. Transport between Mossman and Port Douglas became more reliable, with an improved road and a puffing-billy train service. The rail service, with open railway wagons, freighted bagged sugar from the newly established Mossman sugar mill to Port Douglas for shipment and carried general goods and passengers between the towns.

While these advances improved the lives of the white settlers they did little to give the Aborigines any hope for the future. They continued doing menial work for food, cast-off clothing and a few shillings while living destitute in rough camps along both branches of the river and at the Jinkalmu village near the Gorge. Interference with Aboriginal women also continued, with bachelor men, now earning good money harvesting sugar cane by hand in the fields and working long hours in the sugar factory, paying the women with coin. Shopkeepers in Mossman came to know which ones were prostituting themselves and pitied them when they handed over their earnings in exchange for goods, without knowing if they received the correct change.

Dari's health became a concern. She continued losing weight and found herself unable to do much except wash a few dishes. So far she had refused to see the white man's doctor, preferring to rely on the medicine man with his beads, chants and potions. After weeks of prompting Dari finally agreed to visit the doctor in Port Douglas, and with Marku as chaperone she set off to travel there by train. Though wise in the ways of tribal custom, Dari had always had difficulty accepting European ways and approached the Mossman train station with trepidation. With the sugar mill belching clouds of smoke from its stack, the machinery rumbling and finally the puffing-billy threatening more chaos, she held Marku's hand tightly as they stepped aboard and sat on deck chairs in an open wagon. After a toot of the whistle and a hiss of steam the train jolted into motion and gathered pace. Dari's face was grim as they rattled along the tramway, whisking past sugarcane fields, passing through forest and sweeping by mangroves as they approached Port Douglas. At the sugar wharf, men busied themselves, shouldering bags of sugar onto a moored ship. Dari and Marku stepped from the carriage and hired a horse cab to take them to the hospital.

Doctor Strenner, a kindly man, examined Dari in a consulting room and diagnosed her condition as anaemia. 'Plenty of red meat and rest is what you need, my darling,' he said, expressing genuine compassion. He guessed that she was in her seventies and that, from the gnarled appearance of her hands, she had worked hard all her life. As they were leaving he caught Marku's eye with a look that told her that he thought Dari's time was limited.

The whole ordeal left Dari shaken. She refused to stay in an accommodation house so Marku bought a loaf of bread and they slept the night on a sand dune by the beach. On the return journey Dari gazed wistfully across what used to be her country, reminiscing about old times and the freedom they had enjoyed. Marku stayed quiet, letting Dari have her moment, for she too thought that Dari's time was near.

With Frances' and Nyulu's birth dates only six weeks apart Ellen and the women in Winston's camp decided to give them a joint eighteenth birthday party. At Frances' insistence the party was to be held on the verandah of her home. Birthdays were always a big occasion and excitement grew as the special day approached. The women in Winston's camp busied themselves making gifts while Ellen and her girls fitted themselves with the latest fashion at La Claire's in Front Street, Mossman.

Dari loved family, and especially birthdays, when everyone joined together to enjoy each other's company. Marku had slipped to town and bought Dari a nice dress and now, seeing the look of delight on Dari's face as she admired herself in the mirror, tears came to Marku's eyes and she had to excuse herself. Outside she wept, knowing that, after so many years of caring, this would probably be the last time Dari celebrated Frances' and Nyulu's birthdays. Bajal, the man with the kindest heart, took charge of Dari when they left to cross the river to the girls' home. He and Winston helped her down the steps of the steep bank, seated her comfortably in a boat and oared across, with her sitting centrepiece like a princess drifting down the Nile. James, together with Marku, Nganka and Juran, followed in a second row boat loaded with gifts and food. Once across, Bajal carried Dari on his back as would a loyal porter, stepping lightly so as not to cause any jolts. At Dari's request they went via the blacks' camp on Jonathan's side to say hello to the members of her family who lived there—something of a final goodbye. Winston offered to take a turn at carrying Dari but Bajal passed it off, saying that Dari was 'light as a feather'.

Those at Jonathan's welcomed them, hugging, kissing and exchanging compliments. When the gifts were being unwrapped Dari held pride of place, sitting at the head of the table in her new dress. As always Winston and James wanted a tour of inspection and when the women took themselves to the kitchen to prepare lunch Jonathan drove them around the property in a buckboard.

Jonathan's ambition of extending the family's dynasty to northern Australia had come to fruition. Almost all of his 640 acres were under production, with sugar cane and cattle the main focus. The days of growing corn and dry-land rice were now only a distant memory. He spoke of his progress to date and plans for the future, lauding the virtue of hard work as the way to success. At lunchtime the ladies served a variety of dishes that would be the envy of the southern aristocracy. During lunch Winston reflected about the past: his arrival on the river, his friends becoming his family, the births of the three girls, their childhood and now Frances and Nyulu celebrating their eighteenth birthday. For the first time he fully recognised them as individuals in their own right.

Frances, dressed in a long crinoline dress and high collar, carried herself with the grace found amongst the gentry. She had already won the admiration of Gerald Rubenstein, the son of the wealthiest sugar planter in the district and, from snippets that Winston had heard, marriage was a strong possibility. Nyulu, though raised as the daughter of Jonathan and Ellen, exhibited traits of her native heritage, being somewhat subdued and accepting life with a degree of fatalism. With a sarong wrapped around her bust line she sat on the verandah railing with her back against a post. Juran, now seventeen years of age, sat dressed in shorts and a colourful blouse. She played the middle ground between the other girls, presenting herself as neither tightly laced nor loosely fitted. As a part Aborigine she saw herself as a go-between, a mediator between black and white. Winston recalled recent whispers about Juran and Thomas Brown being sweethearts but so far there was no confirmation.

As with every enjoyable outing, closure was inevitable, and when it came time for them to leave Dari held Ellen close and whispered in her ear, 'Take care of Nganka.'

Dari continued wasting away slowly till eventually she had to be fed. Marku slept by her side during the final days, and the morning Marku woke to find her cold and lifeless the camp lamented. Marku cradled Dari's body, refusing to let go till late in the morning. Bajal scored his thighs as he had when Murramu died. Nganka wailed into the night and the next day. Juran sat in disbelief beside the fire place. James, remembering prayers from his schooldays, prayed for her to be received by God. Winston, without ever having consummated the deep affection between him and Dari, left the camp and wandered aimlessly by the river. The tribespeople soon heard of the passing and joined with those of Winston's camp, grieving in the traditional manner of wailing and performing ritual dance to ensure Dari's spirit found its way into the spiritual world. Dari's only wish was to be buried on the plantation, and with dignity the blacks, together with whites from Winston's camp and the town, gathered by her graveside to bid her farewell. Later, Winston erected a wooden cross inscribed 'Dari 1901'

Since the day Alroy had evicted Shaun from his property Shaun and his family had wandered the river as social outcasts. Shaun, now in his early forties, had been convicted for trafficking rum. They camped at Winston's place occasionally and though not welcome they imposed, staying for days at a time, slouching about in a rough camp only a hundred yards from Winston's camp. If it were not for Alroy's help with his bullock team in the early days and his ongoing friendship with Winston and James they would be banned from the plantation. James, in particular, took exception to Shaun. He abhorred Shaun's promiscuous ways and kept close watch over Juran. Juran, for her part, was sweet on Thomas Brown and would have squirmed at the thought of Shaun making an approach.

James and Marku had extended their cottage and Juran, now in the blush of maidenhood, enjoyed her own room. Her terrier, named Bitsa for its odd mix of colours, shared the room and slept on her bed at night. Juran's presence at breakfast always brought joy, and this morning Marku admired her as she and Bitsa played by the door. Juran, with a complexion lighter than the usual dusky half-castes, and with a full bust, trim body and engaging personality, caught the attention of men both young and old.

She turned to Marku and said, 'Mum, Bitsa and I are going to pick some guavas.'

'All right, darling. Pick a basketful and we can stew a pot for the camp.'

'Sure, Mum.'

Juran, dressed in shorts and an open-neck blouse, took a traditional native basket, stepped from the cottage and, with Bitsa by her side, walked leisurely towards the orchard. The mountains in the distance, with their varying hues of blue, caught her attention, casting her thoughts back to the time when her mother's people roamed the valley. Much had changed since James first arrived to cut cedar and it was with mixed feelings that she recollected the past.

The guavas, bright yellow and ready for picking, hung in clusters, with the weight dragging the branches to the ground. 'Here, Bitsa, this way,' called Juran as they left the track to enter the grove. She hummed to herself as she reached for the best fruit and checked them for blemishes before putting them into the basket. Bitsa stayed close, sniffing animal tracks left from the night before. When nearly done Juran sensed the presence of company and turned to see. She was surprised to see Shaun standing only a few paces away.

'Shaun,' she greeted with a wary smile. 'What do you want?'

'That depends,' he replied, stepping closer.

'Would you like some guavas?' she offered, trying not to offend.

'No. Something better than that. You and me.'

Juran, though still a virgin, knew what he meant and tried to ward him off by saying, 'I think you have it wrong.'

'I don't think so. I've watched you for years and now is the time. You and me and not a word to anyone else.'

'No. Go away,' she insisted while bending to pick up the basket.

'No you don't,' said Shaun grabbing her arm.

'Let go! You're hurting.'

'I don't want to hurt you.'

'Then let go.'

'Not unless you say yes.'

'Yes to what?' said Juran indignantly and pulling free of his grip.

'To us making love.'

'What!'

'Yes. You and me.'

Juran stood aghast at hearing the proposition. Her cheeks drained of colour as she said, 'Leave me alone. Go away and leave me alone.'

Shaun looked much older than his age, with his long, matted hair, hollow cheeks and that distant look common to alcoholics. His bushy beard, chest deep and as coarse as horse hair, had been trimmed by one of his women using a lighted stick. His torso and arms showed blotches caused by sleeping on ground infested with tropical fungi. A leather belt around his waist held his shorts up and carried a sheathed bush knife. His sinewy legs carried numerous scars of past injuries. His bare feet, with soles as tough as cattle hide, told more of his native lifestyle.

Though bearing these hostile body marks and with his mind addled by alcohol he still sought the gratification of female company and, what is more, thought himself able to satisfy their needs. He thought that Juran would accept him and pursued his conquest by saying, 'No one will know. We can do it now and be back at camp before anybody realises.'

Juran, now fearful, turned to leave but Shaun grabbed hold, pulled her in close, took hold of her blouse and stripped away the buttons. He groped her bare breasts and when he bent over for a suck she fought back by punching and kicking. He grabbed her wrists and then continued engorging himself till she lowered her head and bit hard into his cheek. He howled with pain, shoved her backwards and drew the bush knife. She froze when he stepped forward and held the point to her throat. While still holding the knife he again fondled her breasts and although Juran was a half-caste he gawked at what he imagined to be the breasts of a young *migaloo* white person.

He made play, drawing the loose garment from her shoulders and tossing it clear and then stroking the inside of her thighs with wandering hands. He petted her as though she was his lover, savouring the moments that he thought would lead to their intimacy. He wanted to see more of her, how a *migaloo* might look undressed, and undid the buttons on her shorts. He felt Juran twitch and, thinking she might make a move, pressed the sharp tip of the blade more firmly as a reminder that he was in control. He found difficulty pulling the shorts down with one hand and when he bent lower in his eagerness, Juran jerked a knee upwards, driving into his lower jaw so hard that she heard teeth snap.

The force flung Shaun backwards but not enough to overbalance. With blood now spewing from his mouth and a menacing look in his eyes he set to rape her as he had done to the black women of his past. 'Try to run and I'll cut you to pieces!' he threatened. Juran, thinking she could be a match for him even though he held a knife, steeled herself for a make-or-break attempt at an escape. Though only young, somewhat naïve and never having felt the thrust of intercourse she thought she would rather die than take his dirty dick. She began to move, edging towards a heavy guava stick left on the ground from last year's pruning. He demanded she stop and when she did not he came closer and swiped the sharp blade close to her face. The threat dented Juran's confidence and she paused, wondering if it would be wiser to accept his filthy grime than be dead. When considering this sickening alternative she realised that Bitsa was nowhere to be seen. *Where has Bitsa gone? What is Bitsa doing? Has my little mate gone for help?* reeled in her mind. Shaun's bloodied mouth worsened, with him spitting clots of blood and becoming increasingly concerned about the injury. Juran decided to play a game of stall in the hope that either help would come or Shaun would quit. She toyed with his emotions, calling his bluff in various ways and then backing off when at the brink.

James, unaware of Juran's danger, finished splitting firewood and returned to the cottage for a cup of tea. 'Where's Juran?' he asked while stirring in the sugar.

'She and Bitsa have gone to pick guavas,' said Marku.

James sat quietly, took a couple of sips of tea, and then rose from the chair and moved to the window. He peered across the open area to Shaun's camp and scanned for a sign of him.

'Have you seen Shaun this morning?' he asked Marku.

'No. Not since yesterday evening.'

James went to the open door for a better view and when he realised that Shaun was missing from his camp he became concerned.

'I'd better go and check,' he said.

'All right. The bread is nearly ready to come out of the oven. I'll be along soon.'

James sat on the back steps and, as he pulled on his boots, Bitsa came running towards him. 'Here, mate. Where have you been?' he called.

Bitsa, panting and with her tongue lolling out from running in the heat, came to James' feet and then crouched.

'Where's Juran?' he asked.

Bitsa looked at James with an understanding gaze and then jumped to her feet, barked and turned towards the orchard.

James hurriedly laced his boots, stood and called to Marku, 'Bitsa is hot and bothered. There's something going on in the orchard. I'll go see.'

Bitsa took the lead, running in front and turning her head now and then to be sure James was following. Halfway along the main avenue she stopped and cocked her ears. James, now anxious and breathing heavily, came to her side and listened. All he could hear was the hum of bees in the nearby blossoms and a bird call. He waited a few seconds and then called, 'Which way, Bitsa?'

Bitsa, having heard something, let out a yap and then rushed off through the orchard, outstripping James who had to push through foliage. He lost her and came to a halt. Though Juran had said she was going to pick guavas she could have diverted and be anywhere. James stood in the still surrounds, trying to map what he thought would be her movements till, suddenly, Bitsa began barking from the direction of the guava grove. From the urgency of the barks he knew something was terribly wrong and imagined Shaun raping his daughter. In a state of panic he took a direct line, crossing rows of trees and tearing away branches in his path; pushing, pushing till he finally broke through and saw Juran topless.

James, now in a state of hysteria, ran forward and lunged at Shaun, crashing him to the ground. Juran screamed and reached for the heavy guava stick while Bitsa attacked, snapping and biting Shaun wherever possible. Shaun pulled himself free, scrambled to his feet and flashed the blade of the knife. Bitsa went in first and received a kick that sent her flying and left her stunned. James, unarmed, and Juran holding the stick, circled Shaun, angling for a chance to strike.

'Dad, leave him to me!' shouted Juran waving the stick.

'No. I'll take him!' called James consumed by anger and revenge.

Shaun, well versed in slaughtering animals, stood ready to stab or slash the first one to come within reach.

Juran struck first, stepping forward without notice and smashing the stick across his back.

James followed, reaching forward to manhandle him, but Shaun, not as badly injured as James thought, managed to jab the knife into his belly. James staggered as the blade was withdrawn and then put his hands to the wound. Juran screamed, dropped the stick and went to his aid. Shaun, realising the implications of what he had done, took the knife and fled.

After checking that James was not in a dire situation Juran raced, half naked, to the camp for help. Within fifteen minutes everyone from the camp arrived, and found James conscious and able to speak. They kept him calm while Winston ran back to the camp and returned with a horse and buckboard.

They whisked him to Port Douglas where the hospital doctor examined the injury and reported that the knife had punctured the belly lining but no organs had been ruptured. After stitching the wound he gave his prognosis, saying he expected a full recovery provided no infection set in.

Due to the travel time from the plantation to Port Douglas, Marku and Juran lodged at a boarding house and visited James each day. James felt well and spoke of being home within a week till, on the fourth day, stomach pain became a concern. The doctor, suspecting peritonitis, took the girls aside and warned that the infection could be fatal. James' condition continued to deteriorate and on the tenth day a local clergyman was called. That night the girls slept at the hospital and just before first light they were woken to be told that James was critical and to come quickly. He died within the hour and when Marku wailed and Juran sobbed, the staff, realising that love transcends colour, comforted them while shedding tears of their own.

With the funeral set for two days' time, word needed to be spread quickly. Thomas and others covered the countryside on horseback while the blacks sent messages via their bush telegraph. A large gathering of people, both black and white, assembled at the plantation and, with the minister from Port Douglas ministering the service, James, the first white person to settle on the river, was respectfully laid to rest.

Marku grieved violently, wailing and searing her back with burning sticks to show her sorrow. Juran, being raised more in the English tradition, prayed for James' salvation and put an obituary in the local paper. To console herself she read passages from James' diary and entered the date of his death as 24th March 1902. She treasured this personal record and reread it when feeling sad. In her twilight years she would pass it to Frances' family for safe keeping.

Shaun eluded the police for three weeks till a police patrol, assisted by blacktrackers, captured him near a spring in the foothills of Mount Beaufort. After a much talked about trial a jury found him guilty of assault, attempted rape and murder for which he was sentenced to life imprisonment. He escaped a sentence of death by hanging by arguing that he stabbed the victim in self-defence.

CHAPTER 43

Four months after James' death Thomas trotted into Winston's camp, hitched his horse to the rail outside of Marku's cottage and called, 'Letter delivery.'

'Hello there,' greeted Marku, wiping her hands on her apron. 'Just in time for a cuppa.'

'Is Juran about?'

'Yes, she saw you coming and is changing into something nice.'

Thomas turned the letter in his hands and said, 'This is a strange one. It's addressed to James Armitage Partridge Esq. and has the old address of Mossman River via Port Douglas. It's post marked Sydney and has a flashy seal on the back.'

'Oh, probably nothing important. Winston's coming over for a cuppa. He might know,' said Marku, not looking away from the batch of scones she had just taken from the oven.

Thomas put the letter on top of a china cabinet filled with items James had collected since coming to the river. He glanced at the portrait of James hanging on the wall above and wondered how Marku must feel now that James was gone. Juran soon appeared, bright and cheery, and when Winston arrived Marku served tea.

They chatted on about the latest happenings and when Marku went to make a fresh pot of tea Thomas jumped to his feet. 'Here, I'll get that. It's the least I can do.' He rummaged about and, when returning with the tea, took the letter from the cabinet, placed it in front of Winston and said, 'What do you make of this?'

Winston looked at the front and back, held it to the light to better see the seal and said, 'Interesting.'

'Here, give me a look,' said Juran, reaching across the table. She took particular note of the word 'Solicitors' in the imprint of the seal. 'It's from a solicitor. What would Dad be doing with a solicitor?' She turned to Marku. 'Mum, do you know if Dad had any dealings with a solicitor in Sydney?'

'No. I sent Dad's death certificate and his will to the solicitor in Port Douglas but have heard nothing back.'

'Well, let's have a look while we're all here.' Juran took a bread knife, carefully opened the envelope and handed it to Winston. 'Here, you'll understand it better than me.'

Winston removed an official document and a sheet of letter paper. He unfolded the letter, glanced at it and said, 'Glory be. I'd better read this to you.' He paused and then began to read:

Howarth Partners
Solicitors
28 O'Connell Street
Sydney

10th July 1902
Mr. James Armitage Partridge Esq.
Mossman River via Port Douglas
North Queensland

Reference: Estate of the Late Marie Louise Partridge

Dear Sir,

Your mother passed away on 22nd April this year and Howarth Partners have been appointed executors of her estate of which you are the sole beneficiary. Please find enclosed a copy of her will.

Mrs. Partridge has asked that you be provided with the following information: Your father, William Partridge, died in the year 1898 and bequeathed his entire estate to your mother ... She wished to inform you personally of the content of her will but ill health prevented her from doing so.

This letter has been sent to your last known address. If you are not the addressee shown on the letter please return the letter and enclosed document to the above address.

If you are the beneficiary nominated in the will of Marie Louise Partridge then please contact this office.

You may be interested to know that although the estate has not yet been valued an estimate of its worth is in the vicinity of £500,000.

Yours faithfully
Zechariah Cowan
(Senior Partner)

Winston put the letter on the table, smiled broadly and announced, 'Do you know what this means?'

'We're rich. We can buy the valley back!' exclaimed Juran, hardly able to contain herself. She babbled on, telling how they could spend the money, with every pound going towards the betterment of the Aborigines. She shared wild dreams of her people again owning the land and reclaiming the river. All listened, as much enthralled by her enthusiasm as the goodwill expressed.

Marku marvelled at what Juran said. To buy the land and go back to the old days of living a traditional life would be a dream fulfilled. To her mind this was Mount Demi, her people's protector, coming to their rescue.

Thomas listened with interest, trying to piece together James' history as Juran gave a sketchy account of her father's past. He imagined what £500,000 could buy.

Winston recalled snippets of conversations with James and knew that James came from an upper-class family. Though James had made mention of having been raised in a household with servants and a governess he had given Winston no indication of the extent of the wealth.

Nobody bothered to read the will. The letter was explicit so why wade through all the legal jargon?

Discussion of what could be done with the money occupied them during the weekend, and on Monday morning Juran, accompanied by Thomas, took a buggy ride to Port Douglas to meet with the solicitor. Juran had never met the elderly solicitor before and introduced Thomas and herself before handing him the envelope.

'Howarth Partners,' said the solicitor upon opening the letter. 'High profile solicitors indeed.' He leant back in his leather chair, read the letter carefully and then looked over the top of his spectacles. 'Juran, are you James' daughter?'

'Yes, I was born at our camp on the river.'

'Have you a birth certificate?'

'No, but it's written in my father's diary.'

'And your mother?'

'Yes, her name is Marku and it's written there too.'

'What about the date?'

'Yes, it's all there. I can bring it in if you like.'

'And I presume it's written in your father's handwriting?'

'Yes.'

'That's good. I have his will here written in his hand so that will verify your status.'

The solicitor went to a filing cabinet and returned with a file marked 'James A Partridge'.

'Let's have a look. As I recall he left everything to Marku and, in the event of her predeceasing him, it goes to you.' He quickly confirmed what he had said and closed the file. 'Yes, as I said he's bequeathed it to your mum and in turn you.' He then added, 'Your mum has a reciprocal will which lists you as her beneficiary in the event that James predeceases her.'

'Then we get the money?' asked Juran.

'Maybe.' He cast her a shrewd look.

Juran, mystified by the expression of doubt, sought clarification. 'It's straightforward. Isn't it?'

'Let's have a look and see,' he said, unfolding the will.

Juran took hold of Thomas' hand and held it tightly. It took forever, and when the solicitor looked over the rim of his spectacles with a serious expression Juran thought, *Whatever could go wrong? He has James' papers and says everything is in order.*

'I'm afraid it's not good news,' he said, thumbing the page. 'From what I read, the money is going elsewhere.'

'That's not possible,' blurted Juran. 'The letter says it's ours.'

'That may be so, but there is more to it than that. Unfortunately, James died before his mother and, in that event, the money goes to James' first cousin, a Mr Archibald Paxton.'

'No, it can't be. Read it to me.'

The solicitor read the opening paragraphs:

THIS IS THE LAST WILL AND TESTAMENT OF ME MARIE LOUISE PARTRIDGE of 36 Hancock Street, Kirribilli, North Sydney.

I HEREBY REVOKE all former wills …

He then skipped to the second page and read:

IN THE EVENT that my son James Partridge predeceases me I bequeath the whole of my estate to my nephew Archibald Paxton of …

Juran sat in disbelief, unable to utter a word till the solicitor leaned forward and said, 'Juran, this is a common provision and, unfortunately, you have missed out on the inheritance by less than a month. If James had passed away after his mother then the money would have gone to Marku.'

Juran's world crashed down around her. All her expectations were now dashed, her dreams lost in a muddle of who died when. It was left to Thomas to thank the solicitor and comfort Juran on the way home.

'Too good to be true,' said Winston when told.

Marku took a fatalistic view and accepted that it was not to be.

Juran found herself reading James' diary more often, looking for clues as to the reason for his estrangement from his parents.

Since James' death the plantation had suffered. As the man in charge of field operations, James had attended to all the organising, from what and when to plant, to harvesting and the selling. Thomas' employment as farrier with the police had been terminated following his involvement in the rebellion and now, with the plantation urgently in need of attention, he spent most days toiling in its orchard and fields. He began by riding his horse each day from his parent's home in Mossman but soon found it more convenient to stay at the plantation and had taken up residence in the cottage that Ellen and her children occupied during the time of her estrangement from Jonathan. Marku cooked his meals and, together with Juran, they ate in Marku's kitchen. A routine evolved whereby after the evening meal Thomas and Juran washed and wiped the dishes and then sat on the verandah, enjoying each other's company. Marku, who had always been fond of Thomas, left them alone and busied herself pottering about inside. One evening Juran called to Marku, 'Mum, I'm just going over to Thomas' for a while.'

Marku approved but, as a caring mother, could not help herself and peeped from behind a curtain as, hand in hand, they strolled to Thomas' cottage. When they stepped into the shadow of the porch Marku felt a pang of anxiety. Though she knew that Juran was now a young woman she found it difficult to accept the thought of a man holding her close. She waited and breathed relief when, a couple of minutes later, a lamp flickered to life in the kitchen. The lamp burnt a steady flame for nearly an hour before they stepped from the porch and into the moonlight. They stood as though loitering and then, in what looked like a passionate embrace, they kissed and parted. Marku, not wanting to be found prying, slipped to her room and lay listening as Juran undressed and went to bed in the adjoining room.

Sleep evaded Marku. She lay awake, tossing between thoughts of Juran losing her virginity and what a blessing Thomas would be. She didn't care that he was thirty-three and Juran eighteen. James had always admired Thomas and, with this assurance in mind, she eventually drifted to sleep. The couple appeared for breakfast bright and breezy as though nothing had happened, but Marku noted the telltale signs. Thomas was particularly attentive towards Juran.

After a month of this quiet courtship Juran told Marku that she and Thomas were in love and intended living together. Marku, though surprised at the early announcement, knew in her heart that all would be well and welcomed Thomas into the family. She wished to be the first to tell Winston, Bajal and Nganka and hurried off after breakfast. Winston smiled a knowing smile, while Bajal and Nganka confessed to having seen Juran going back and forth.

Thomas and Juran settled into life together on the plantation, with Thomas taking full responsibility for management of the plantation. Juran continued assisting her people.

PART THREE

STATE BONDAGE OF THE ABORIGINES

Aboriginal housing at the Mossman Gorge Aboriginal mission 1930s.

CHAPTER 44

*T*he *Aboriginals Protection and Restriction of the Sale of Opium Act, 1897* that Charles Benson had spoken about became a Trojan horse, with the real intent being to dispossess Aborigines of their land, segregate black from white and in so doing control their lives. In fact, the Act, apart from reducing the killings, maintained and extended the oppressive policies that had been in place since the arrival of the English. Under this Queensland Government Act Aborigines effectively became wards of the state, with most aspects of their lives supervised by white administrators. Winston's camp soon realised this and opposed the Act in its entirety.

Juran's first battle began in 1897 when the Act was introduced. The local police sergeant questioned James about her parentage and then declared that, since she was a half-caste living in the care of her Aboriginal mother, she was subject to the Act. James argued vehemently, explaining that Juran was his half-caste daughter, that she had been raised in a Christian family and that she was better schooled than any officer at the Mossman police station. He thought the idea so idiotic that he telegraphed Charles Benson, seeking support. Charles agreed and presented a written submission to the Minister, telling of James' success in mediating with the Aborigines and his family's standing within the community. Six weeks later a letter arrived saying that his plea had been granted and that the Minister hereby enclosed an Exemption Certificate in the name of Juran Partridge.

Juran, young, smart, educated, feisty and singular in purpose became an interpreter and mentor for Aborigines facing court, fighting for their rights at every turn. She ignored the provision of the Act that said exempted half-castes must not associate with full-blood Aborigines. Without concern for herself she tussled with the police sergeant, the local Protector of Aborigines, argued with the court magistrate and berated the government for its oppressive and imbecilic laws. She made representation on behalf of dozens of individuals, arguing against the provisions of the Act and pursuing natural justice for her people.

While James had leant towards his mother's gentle personality, Juran inherited the tough traits of her grandfather William Partridge, the famed timber merchant of Sydney. With steely grit she confronted those in authority, questioned their rights and demanded answers. Like her grandfather she understood the power of politics and stayed well connected.

Employment of Aborigines by whites was so tightly controlled it seemed doubtful that the government wanted any Aborigines to enter the workforce. Juran worked tirelessly, finding suitable employers, writing character references for applicants and presenting cases to the local police sergeant. If successful a further problem arose with employers being obliged to deposit the worker's wages into a bank account administered by the police. The worker could only withdraw money with the policeman's permission, and the amounts approved seldom amounted to more than pocket money. No matter that the worker's wife and children were starving. Most of the money never found its way to the rightful owner, being pilfered from accounts by the issue of falsified pocket-money dockets by the local police, and any money not drawn eventually finding its way into the government's coffers.

Travel arrangements were designed to keep Aborigines confined, with permits needed to travel beyond the immediate locality. Details of the date, destination, place of accommodation and with whom, together with a return date, all had to be complied with so as not to be in breach of the Act.

Under the Act a female Aborigine had to seek permission from the Protector to marry a non-Aborigine. Applications were often rejected, and to circumvent this humiliation and denial of a basic human right many Aborigines simply lived with their non-Aboriginal partners, with their offspring branded as bastards.

The most troubling aspect of the Act was the provision relating to removals. The local Protector or other authorised person had tremendous power to remove Aborigines to an Aboriginal reserve or from one reserve to another. Adults and children could be removed at the stroke of a pen, with no reason given to the person being 'abducted'. Adults, rightly or wrongfully accused of crime or petty contraventions of the law, were whisked away. They did not know their destination or if they would ever see loved ones again. Those left behind grieved for loved ones lost. Those from the Mossman district were sent to government reserves or church missions such as Cape Bedford, Mona-Mona, Yarrabah, and further afield to Woorabinda and Cherbourg. All Aborigines dreaded being sent to Palm Island which was known as 'The Black Man's Grave'. The concept of natural justice played no part in formulating the draconian Protection Act. An account given by an Aborigine at the Yarrabah church mission reveals:

> When we look across to the field over there where they keep the horses, Mr. Iven was hiding a boy with lawyer cane. And he was screaming his head off. And we could stand at the fence there. We was singin' out, but they couldn't hear us because we was over this way: 'don't hit that little boy!' He flogged that little boy called Blue John, from Mossman. He run away. He stayed a few days till he feel all right, you know, from the hiding, then he ran away.

Half-caste children fared the worst. Policy makers, hidebound by the chaste values of the Victorian era, hounded half-caste children, snatching them from the arms of their mothers and sending them to mission stations administered by religious groups. These self-righteous missionaries, with no idea of Aboriginal culture, played into the hands of the government, controlling the children's lives from dawn to dusk, pumping them with ideology totally alien to Aboriginal tradition and way of life. Indeed, the Northern Protector of Aborigines stated in a report to parliament:

> Experience continues to teach me that we are working on correct lines in dealing with the transfer of half-caste and full-blood children to the various mission stations and reformatories. Half-caste children should enlist our sympathies perhaps even to a greater extent than the full-blood ones. If left to themselves, the majority of the girl half-castes ultimately become prostitutes, and the boys cattle and horse thieves.

Further to the insidious provisions of the Act, British law, under the guise of *terra nullius*, claimed that all land belonged to the Crown. These once proud people, the custodians of the Mossman River valley, were robbed of title to their land. Their homeland, the land of their forefathers, had been taken away by force, leaving them stateless.

CHAPTER 45

'G erald has arrived,' called Ellen to Frances from the verandah. Frances, now in a fluster, finished powdering her face, checked that her hair was still in place and came to the railing to present herself. Every Sunday had been the same for the past few months, with Gerald Rubenstein coming to court Frances.

'No, Mum, we don't have time for a cuppa,' said Frances as Gerald helped her aboard the sulky. So keen were they to be away that Frances forgot to give Ellen a kiss and instead shouted a goodbye and waved. They were headed to the sugarcane plantation owned by Gerald's parents but no doubt would stop along the way.

Nyulu watched from the garden as the sulky swept along the road, leaving a trail of dust. She despaired, as she had done on previous occasions, when the happy couple departed for an outing that every young couple deserved. Since the introduction of the Protection Act Nyulu had become depressed. She saw herself as a victim, trapped by the colour of her skin. Prior to the proclamation of the Act she considered herself to be white, to stand as an equal with the members of her household and the white community. Never could she have imagined that because of ink on paper her future, her whole life, could turn into a nightmare. She had picked a rose to put on the dining table but now, in a distracted state, began peeling away the petals and letting them fall to the ground, in the same way she saw her life falling apart. Since childhood she had feared the police and now, with their increased powers, she thought home to be the only place that could guarantee her safety. If she became employed by whites a report, wrongly construed, could see her banished to a government reserve. Speaking with a male in the street could have her charged with soliciting and locked away. Even to visit Aboriginal friends elsewhere in the district could lead to her being intercepted and interrogated by the police. She had dreamed of someday marrying a white man but now, with such a union requiring government approval, the prospect seemed beyond reach. All her expectations of a fulfilled life were now dashed, without any prospect of a reprieve. Those of her household, Jonathan, Ellen and Frances, while knowing well the impositions placed on Nyulu and other full-blood Aborigines, said little so as not to upset her. She stayed in the garden for an hour, crying, and when she came back inside Ellen, who had been watching from a window, took her orphan daughter into her arms.

Nyulu's only safe outlet from this caged existence was to visit the Aborigines camped at the bottom her family's property or cross the river to Winston's. She visited both often and found some solace in the company of her own people and those of Winston's camp. Juran understood her situation and persuaded Nyulu to accompany her on some outings in the hope of breaking down the barrier of fear that stifled her life. While Nyulu appreciated this and responded a little she still remained reluctant to go beyond the boundary fence unaccompanied. Her feeling of inferiority dragged her to such a depth that when asked by Frances to be matron of honour at her wedding, Nyulu baulked, saying she was not worthy. Frances, astounded and upset that the Nyulu could speak such words, hugged her sister, told her not to be so silly and proceeded to take her to the seamstress in Mossman to be fitted with a dress for the wedding. All that Nyulu wanted was to be free to map her own life.

Within a month of arriving at Mossman the new police sergeant visited Winston to enquire about the two full-blood Aborigines distributing government rations from his camp. Winston, wanting to establish a working relationship with the newly appointed Protector of Aborigines, sat him down at the table and explained that he was owner of the business, that they were employees and that all the paperwork required under the Act had been submitted. He added that, in addition to Bajal being paid £4 a month by the government, they were provided with accommodation and rations as payment for their services. When quizzed about their integrity Winston referred him to the Minister's office where he said a statement detailing the scope and success of their work could be found.

'Why do you ask?'

'Oh, just enquiring,' replied the sergeant.

Winston thanked him for calling and, although the meeting had been amicable, he thought the sergeant's call suspicious.

Bajal and Nganka, now in their forties, knew every camp site in the district and the whereabouts of almost every Aborigine who had not yet been incarcerated on a native reserve or mission station. The rations they distributed consisted mainly of flour, rice, tinned meat, tea and sugar, and lacked the nourishment needed for good health, leaving adults and children with hat-rack frames and blemished skin. If it were not for the wallabies remaining on the uncleared hillslopes, and fruit and nuts foraged from the mountainous rainforest, they would starve to death. The crammed camps, unsanitary and squalid, were cess pits of disease, with infant mortality soaring to heights greater than in the crowded industrial centres of England. In earlier times they were free of introduced diseases and their annual walkabouts, when they moved from camp to camp, prevented camp sites from becoming soiled. The inspectors who occasionally visited one or two camps in each district most often understated the extent of the deprivation. Their reports, collated into hard-bound copies to be presented to parliament, told of the achievements but not the disasters. The government and, by extension, the public remained uninformed of the real situation in the remote regions.

The Aborigines believed that the police were manifestations of the bad spirits and that they would not be safe till Mount Demi, their spiritual protector, defeated them in a fierce contest of strength. Ritual dance without permission of the Protector was forbidden so they performed in secret, calling on Mount Demi to come to their rescue. Lookouts were posted and their mimicked bird calls alerted them to the approach of what many still referred to as the *buliman*.

Often Aborigines, for self-preservation, hid from the law. With an intimate knowledge of the landscape, alleged law breakers took refuge in the rainforest, with family members ferrying food and covering their tracks. Bajal and Nganka knew of these so-called fugitives and, with Winston's blessing, packed additional food for delivery to the camps involved.

An Aborigine known as Wallaby was apprehended for being 'very cheeky and addicted to drink' and sent to Mona Mona mission near Kuranda. He soon absconded, cut cross-country past Black Mountain, and then followed the Cassowary Range till he reached the Mossman River. His 'cheekiness' led to him being arrested a second time and, to be sure he would not return, the police put him in chains and shipped him seventy miles south along a rugged coastline to the Yarrabah mission. Within a month he was back on the river, having navigated country he had never seen before, swum crocodile-infested rivers and lived off the land. When arrested a third time the police put him before the magistrate to have him imprisoned at Stewart's Creek prison at Townsville. Juran spoke on his behalf in court. She reported that the only reason Wallaby returned was to be with his family, and if sent to prison he would die of a broken heart. She explained further, telling the magistrate that Wallaby was a decent young man who had been led astray. She referred to Wallaby's father, telling how the police had sent him to Palm Island, leaving Wallaby and his siblings with no father figure for guidance. She concluded her plea by saying, 'If he is freed I give you my word that I will keep him in the clear.'

The magistrate gave her a doubtful look and asked, 'How can you give such a guarantee?'

'I will care for him. I have property and a place for him to live.'

'That may all be very well, Miss Partridge, but what happens if he takes to the drink?'

'I have a friend Thomas Brown who knows him well and will keep him sober.'

'Is this Mr Brown white?'

'Yes, your honour.'

'Does Mr Brown live on the property?'

'Yes.'

'And his relationship to you?'

'He's my de facto husband.'

'Have you children of your own?'

'No. We haven't been successful so far but I have an extended family living across the river.'

The magistrate reread the charge sheet, deliberated momentarily and then delivered his decision. 'I find the accused guilty of the offence but, in view of extenuating circumstances, imprisonment is not warranted. A penalty of a twelve months' good behaviour bond is imposed.'

The magistrate had taken into account a recent newspaper report that referred to the search for a lost white boy near Mossman:

BLACKS FIND LOST CHILD

… An army of searchers, including police, residents of the district, and the distracted parents, sought for him all day on Sunday, most of Sunday night, and again on Monday. On Monday night the Aborigines in a camp near Mossman held a sacred corroboree, at the close of which they calmly informed the parents 'No more worry. We bin find that one longa morning.' True to their promise the blacks were on the trail early next morning and two young Aboriginal men, Bailey and George, found the tired and hungry three-year-old near a creek. There was a joyous reunion when the child was returned to his parents, who had been reduced to a condition almost of hysteria and could not be comforted. 'Mummy!' the boy cried excitedly as he ran into the arms of his mother and clung tightly to her, while the mother rocked him in her arms and sobbed, 'My baby, my baby!'

CHAPTER 46

The year 1914 is remembered as a landmark year with the arrival of the first motor vehicle to the district. Having only seen pictures of it in magazines the people looked in wonder. The dealer organised a big parade, as much to advertise his new product as to celebrate the first motor transport in the district. People felt privileged to have a ride in this self-propelled vehicle that did not need a cumbersome steam engine to provide power. To their further amazement this new invention could carry four people and reach a speed of twenty miles per hour on a good road. The dealer shipped the car in because the road via the wagon track to the Hodgkinson gold field proved too steep and dangerous. While people like the teamsters saw the noisy contraption as a hazard to frighten their horses, others readily accepted the modern convenience as progress and ordered one for themselves. To this landlocked backwater of civilisation the motor car represented a show of pride, a symbol that, even though they lived in the wilderness, the people were as forward thinking as those in the cities. Within a few years those from the rich estates could be seen driving to Mossman weekly to shop. The journey to Port Douglas, road conditions permitting, could now be completed within an hour. However, convenient as this may be, the luxury of such travel remained confined to the landed gentry and their families. Others still relied on horse-drawn vehicles or the puffing-billy that rattled along a narrow gauge line between the sugar town and the Port, with overnight stays often necessary to meet the train's schedule.

The Rubenstein family, now a major supplier of sugar cane to the sugar mill, placed an order early and drove about the district displaying their opulence. With Gerald at the steering wheel, Frances by his side and their four children crammed into the back seat they regularly visited Jonathan, Ellen and Nyulu. They also called at Winston's camp where the children revelled in what they perceived as a blackfellows' camp. When reminded that Mummy lived there as a child they conjured visions of her hunting with the blacks and swimming in the river.

Frances, true to her father's tradition, contributed to the Rubenstein's success. With drive and tenacity reminiscent of Jonathan's early years on the river she worked with Gerald and his parents, forging ahead, felling and burning more of the forest that was once home to the Aborigines and native animals. The 600-acre estate, with two Queenslander-style homes—one for Gerald and Frances and the other for Gerald's parents—held a commanding position overlooking the cane fields that swept to the river edge. The workers' quarters, stables and implement sheds, though only a short distance from the homes, lay on the lee of the slope and out of sight.

Many of their permanent workforce of fifteen to twenty men resided on the plantation in slab and corrugated-iron huts, while family men from Mossman either walked or rode horses to and from work. The overseer, a thirty-year-old Englishman named Larry Oswald, managed the day-to-day operations of the property and dined with Gerald and Frances each evening. In keeping with the family's standard he bathed, dressed, donned a necktie and presented himself soon after sundown. At mealtime a maid served the food and then returned to the kitchen where she listened for the tinkle of the bell that would summon her back to the dining room. As head of the household Gerald carved the meat, with Frances sitting at his right, Larry occupying the chair to his left and the children sitting further along. He then handed the plates to Frances who added vegetables and side dressings before passing them on. Following the meal the adults moved to the verandah where they sipped a malt whisky and discussed the day's activity, while the governess put the children to bed. Gerald and Frances thought Larry too decent to remain a bachelor and one evening after he had left they hatched a plan.

Ever since Frances' wedding day Nyulu had remained in a state of confusion. Not a week went by without her being confronted by a reminder that she was black and, by government decree, a lesser person than the whites who passed her by. Jonathan had made vigorous representation on her behalf to the Chief Protector of Aborigines and the Minister for Native Affairs, explaining that Nyulu was an orphan taken at birth, raised in a white household, able to read and write like her white sister, and that she was industrious and thrifty, of sober habits and morals. When Jonathan received the short reply which stated that Nyulu was a full-blood Aboriginal and therefore subject to the provisions of the Act, he immediately booked a passage to Brisbane and confronted the Chief Protector in person. A heated argument ensued during which Jonathan shouted about the injustice and stupidity of the Act and demanded that Nyulu be exempted. The Chief Protector, hiding behind the safety of his desk, defended himself by citing the Act and saying that the granting of an exemption for one would create a precedent for others to follow. Jonathan took umbrage at the pathetic excuse and, as he left the office, he issued a threat that could be heard down the corridor. 'If any policeman sets foot on my place, he'll get a bullet through his head!'

This outburst by Jonathan caused more angst for Nyulu because she thought that she might now be snatched from the street or some lonely roadway and whisked away to an Aboriginal reserve. She also feared that if this happened Jonathan might confront the local Protector and shoot him dead. Fortunately, a confidential memo came through to the Protector at the Mossman police station telling of the threat and that 'in the interest of public relations no police officer is to confront Jonathan Ashton or members of his family.'

Nyulu became so paranoid that she dared not leave the property unless accompanied by Jonathan, Ellen, Frances or Juran. She effectively became self-imprisoned on the property to which her father held title. Each time she heard the fall of horse's hooves approaching the house she panicked, fearing it was the police coming to take her away and that Jonathan would die defending her. She decided that, if this situation arose, she would surrender herself to spare her father who, since she could first remember, had always referred to her as his 'little treasure'. While the others encouraged her to join them on outings she found that Frances understood her better than anybody else. She had bonded with Frances the day she was born, and as children growing up they became closer, revealing everything of themselves and sharing secrets. Those close to Nyulu knew this and it came as no surprise when Nyulu agreed to Frances' invitation for an extended stay with her family.

Aunty Nyulu soon found plenty to do, picking up after Frances' children, playing games in the garden and reading stories to them at night. The children learned to love their aunty who took them fishing and told stories about the Aboriginal Dreamtime. Nyulu's care of the children allowed Frances more time to attend to business and management of the property. When Frances became pregnant again Nyulu assumed more responsibility.

Nyulu breathed more easily. The new situation drew her attention away from previous concerns. Those of the household, with their love and care, slowly healed the wounds of the past. She also realised that being away from her old home meant the police were less likely to visit Jonathan and provoke a confrontation.

Jonathan and Ellen motored over for Sunday lunches, maintaining contact and observing Nyulu's return to the happy person they once knew. Jonathan, now showing his age from a life of hard work, drifted into a reverie on the journeys home, recalling the past and thankful that Ellen had stayed by his side during troubled times. They had always known that Frances would make good. After a visit they would sometimes take photo albums from the shelf and reminisce, tracing photos of the girls as they grew into young ladies.

Larry, now in his eighth year as overseer, earned respect from both the field workers and members of the Rubenstein family. His understanding of farming, ability to manage men and quiet manner guaranteed him a home with the Rubensteins for as long as he wished to stay. Evening meals proved to be a winner, with Nyulu taking special care of her appearance and Larry paying her attention. Among other duties, Nyulu undertook to wash Larry's clothes in the boiler behind his cottage and clean his house. She sometimes left a bunch of flowers in a vase on his kitchen table and, on occasions, he returned the compliment by presenting her with a posy at the evening meal. One Saturday evening Larry asked Nyulu if she would like to join him on a picnic the following day. Nyulu overcame her modesty and readily accepted, saying she would bring the food and drink. She woke before daybreak, rummaged about the kitchen making sandwiches and raiding the biscuit jar. After breakfast she approached Frances in the office, dressed in a single-piece crinoline dress that covered her from neck to ankle, and asked for an opinion. Frances, herself feeling the exhilaration of Nyulu's prospect, suggested, 'What about a sarong?'

Nyulu, with a touch of embarrassment, asked, 'Will that be enough?'

Frances, breaking into one of those cheeky smiles that Nyulu knew well, replied, 'I'm sure Larry won't object.'

Approval meant everything to Nyulu and she began unlacing her bodice before leaving the room.

Nyulu, now dressed in a revealing sarong held up by little more than her nipples, greeted Larry at the door and, at his insistence, showed him into the office where he sought Frances' approval. Frances, impressed by Larry's manners, gave them her blessing and watched as the happy couple headed towards the river with a picnic basket in hand. Frances, feeling tingles of romance, thought of them often during the day, imagining them splashing in the river and hopefully cuddling. They returned at dusk. Larry brought Nyulu inside and then excused himself to go and change for the evening meal. Nyulu, evincing joy that Frances had not seen since their childhood, babbled excitedly about the outing and told how Larry had asked to take her on another picnic the following weekend. Frances felt the thrill of the moment and, with the daring of their childhood past, asked, 'Are you still a virgin?' With tears welling in her eyes Nyulu stepped forward and hugged Frances in a way that Frances understood to mean Nyulu had finally lost her virginity, and to one she loved.

Wedding plans were hurried along when, a month later, Nyulu realised that she was pregnant. Application for Nyulu to marry Larry was made and, given the standing of the Rubenstein family, government approval readily granted. With no thought to colour or race Frances arranged a lavish wedding celebration at the family home, with people of varied walks of life being sent an invitation. On the wedding day Winston sat in a chair by the rose garden and harkened back to the time he sang the girls the ditty:

Three little girls, all in a row.
Black, white and brindle, all ready to go.

The happy throng crowded around for the marriage ceremony and when Nyulu responded to Larry's vow by saying, 'I, Nyulu Ashton, take Larry Oswald to be my lawful wedded husband …' Jonathan cried unashamedly, thanking the Lord for the blessing bestowed on his daughter.

Within a week of their being married the men of the plantation began building a new weatherboard bungalow for the wedded couple. Juran visited the police sergeant, the local Protector, and told how Nyulu had married a British citizen and was therefore eligible for exemption from the Protection Act. The sergeant, knowing of the marriage and that the application would be successful, wrote a letter recommending that the request be accepted. Within a month a Certificate of Exemption in the name of Nyulu Oswald arrived in the mail. Nyulu felt she had been freed from slavery and proudly displayed her 'ticket to freedom' on the living-room wall.

CHAPTER 47

The streets of Mossman came alive each Saturday morning. Shift workers from the sugar mill finished work at eight in the morning and, with pay packets in their pockets, crowded the hotels behind closed doors for an early morning refresher. At 10.00 am, the official opening time, the doors were opened and canecutters flocked in to breast the bars. With standing room only they mingled with others of the labouring class. The plantation owners, shop keepers and other well-to-do businessmen congregated in private bars, away from the noisy mobs.

Winston enjoyed an ale and a yarn and sometimes walked to town on a Saturday to have his fill and stagger home at nightfall. This Saturday he dressed in his Saturday best and, needing a haircut, thought it sensible to attend to this before placing a pound note on the bar of the Exchange Hotel. The local barber, who rented a room on the ground floor of the hotel, nodded for Winston to be seated. The barber shop, with a bookmaker's betting booth through one door and the public bar through another, was used as a corridor, with a mix of men coming and going. Winston, sitting shoulder to shoulder with others on a long bench seat, waited his turn and then went to meet with some river men in the bar. The river men belonged to neither the common labourer class nor the social dignitaries of the district. They lived in shacks by the river, had terrible body odour and were often refused a table in eating houses. Winston, though a gentleman and well attired, preferred to drink with these men who did not boast about how many tons of cane they had cut last week, or their recent business dealings in the town. He walked up to Walter who had come to town with a bunch of bananas on his shoulder and was spending the proceeds.

'Walter,' he called above the din of voices as he approached, 'how about a shout?'

'Sure,' said Walter as he pushed his few pence across the bar to buy Winston a drink.

Walter, a nuggetty, middle-aged river man with an unknown history, lived alone upriver and came to town whenever he could spare a few pennies. He inevitably visited the Exchange Hotel and left when his money ran dry or he could hardly walk. He and Winston became engrossed in conversation and, when Walter's money was spent, Winston kept buying drinks for both of them.

By mid-afternoon the bar room became hot and rowdy, with the occasional argument breaking out over drunken disagreements. A strapping young canecutter dressed in shorts, a white singlet and no shirt had been watching Winston buying drinks and, disapproving of Walter, began taunting him. He referred to Walter's derelict lifestyle and inferred that he had no place drinking in the hotel. Winston ignored this till the canecutter said loudly, 'Go back to the river, you dirty scum!'

'Who are you calling scum!' questioned Winston, taking the reference as being directed to both him and Walter.

'You're one of them too!' shouted the canecutter, stepping in close and unexpectedly throwing a punch.

'Steady on,' cautioned Winston, deflecting the punch with his forearm.

The canecutter then swung a flurry of punches, most of which Winston ducked or blocked. Winston awaited his opportunity and then drove a hard right to the man's head, dropping him to the floor. The canecutter, concussed and disorientated, dragged himself to his feet and stood defiant.

Winston, thinking it no more than a harmless scuffle, said, 'Go home and sober up,' and then turned towards Walter. He had a swig of beer and, as he put the glass on the bar, he was hit from behind with a heavy blow. Winston lurched forward and then turned with his fists at the ready to find himself confronted by two of the canecutter's drinking circle. One crashed into Winston, knocking him off balance, while the other struck at his groin with his boot. Winston buckled from the pain and, as he did, the two assailants punched into him. Winston managed to score a few hits but, being crippled from the kick, he could not match the punches coming his way. The crowd, enjoying what they thought was a regular pub fight, crowded around, with most barracking for the canecutters. Winston, confronting them alone, battled bravely till his body and head could take no more kicks and punches and fell unconscious to the floor. The publican, realising that Winston was seriously hurt, intervened and, with the help of others, carried him to a bed on the back landing of the hotel. His condition worsened rapidly, the ambulance was called and upon arrival at the Port Douglas hospital two hours later Winston was pronounced dead.

Those in Winston's camp could not believe that the patriarch of their extended family had been killed in a pub brawl. Marku, Bajal and Nganka wailed, while Juran sat dumbfounded. With the help of Arthur Brown and Mick O'Shannessy, Thomas arranged the funeral service while Wallaby dug Winston's grave beside Dari's plot. People from both the white and black communities came to pay their respects. He was remembered for many things and, in particular, for the part he played in the rebellion that averted a massacre of the Aborigines.

Fortunately, Winston had insisted on writing his will and, with Juran as witness, they had visited a solicitor at Port Douglas where the solicitor carefully penned the instructions. Winston explained that he wanted to leave the property to Juran but, with the possibility of her Exemption Certificate being revoked and her losing title to the property, he nominated Frances Rubenstein as the beneficiary. A further clause stated that although Frances Rubenstein held title to the land, Juran, Marku, Bajal and Nganka had exclusive rights to the use of the property in partnership till the death of the last surviving partner.

'Sorry. I didn't mean to intrude,' said Frances as she entered the kitchen and surprised Ellen and Nganka hugging.

'It's all right, darling, I'm just a little upset,' replied Ellen, slipping her arms from around Nganka. 'Is Dad all right?' she asked, while still holding Nganka's hand.

'He's very hot. The fever seems to come and go. I'll take in another damp towel and sponge him.'

'Thanks, darling. Nganka and I will be in soon.'

Jonathan had complained of lethargy and headaches for a week and now lay on his four-poster bed in a lather of sweat. A fever had taken hold and the doctor was due to call.

Frances, who had always been close to Jonathan, removed his wet night robe and had sponged and redressed him by the time Ellen and Nganka appeared.

Ellen came to Jonathan's side, held his hand and said, 'We'll have you back on your feet in no time.'

The doctor, a serious man with little time for courtesies, examined Jonathan and found his body covered with a rash that extended to his extremities.

'Scrub typhus,' he announced, while clipping his medical kit shut. 'It's carried by ticks and can result in death if secondary complications set in. It's crucial to treat the fever and keep the patient's temperature down.' He instructed the women on how best to control the fever and, after wishing them well, departed to attend another urgent call.

None of the three women had contemplated the possibility of death and withdrew to the kitchen to discuss the situation. With twenty-four-hour care now required they decided to take shifts, sitting by Jonathan's bed and sponging him when necessary.

Nyulu, though busy looking after Frances' younger children and her own at the Rubenstein estate, found time to motor over to the old homestead each day to see her dad. Those at Winston's camp brought meals across the river daily and attended to milking the goat, collecting the eggs and chopping firewood.

During the next week Jonathan's condition worsened. He lost weight at an alarming rate and could hardly stand to be dressed. Ellen, more so than the others, feared he might not recover and often slept in the chair by his bed rather than retiring to her own room.

The third week saw a continuing decline, with the girls having to lift Jonathan's head for him to drink and bathing him in bed. Nganka, being superstitious and believing in bad spirits, dreaded doing night shifts on her own. Each time a gust of wind blew the curtains or a night bird called she stiffened with thoughts of a *kadaitcha* man, Aboriginal executioner, coming to take Jonathan's life. Early one morning the mournful cry of a curlew drifted across the still landscape, sending shivers up her back. She became anxious, looking about, expecting a *kadaitcha* man to appear at any moment. Another curlew call, this time just outside the window, caused her to panic and leave the room to wake the others.

They came into the room at the graveyard hour just before sunrise to find Jonathan pale and unresponsive. There, by dim lamp light, Frances monitored his faint pulse and, when it faded to nothing and the colour drained from his body, she leant forward and pressed her lips to his as a final goodbye. Ellen and Nganka, greying from age, looked in disbelief as Frances placed one hand and then the other across his body. Nganka held back while Ellen came forward to hug Jonathan and reaffirm her love for him. They then sat in the room with Frances sitting quietly on one side of the bed while Ellen and Nganka sat on the other, sobbing and reaching out to comfort each another. When the early morning rays of sunlight spilt over the ridge and lit the room Frances covered Jonathan with a sheet and ushered the others to the kitchen. She lit the stove fire, put a kettle on to heat and sat opposite them at the table. During the silence that followed Ellen and Frances exchanged glances till Ellen let go of Nganka's hand and quietly asked, 'You know, don't you?'

'Yes,' replied Frances with a knowing look.

'For how long?'

'Since I was a child.' Frances paused and then continued, 'At first I thought they were just friendly hugs but when you locked the bedroom door I wondered … I became curious and one day peeped through the window.'

'Often?'

'Yes, often, Mum. More often than you would like to know. I knew when, because it was always the days that Dad was away.'

'And Nyulu?' asked Ellen, wiping tears from her eyes.

'Not sure. I never told her but I think she would have told me if she knew.'

Nganka, realising possible implications, asked with an anxious expression, 'What about Bajal? Does he know?'

'Yes, Bajal knows.'

Frances then fell silent till Ellen prompted her, 'Did you tell him?'

'Yes.'

'Why?'

Frances looked directly at Ellen and Nganka across the table and said, 'Because Bajal and I were lovers.'

The women, startled and exasperated, stared at Frances in disbelief. 'Yes, Bajal and I for many years.'

'How, when?' asked Ellen, now dry eyed and anxious.

'Remember when we all lived at Winston's camp? I knew you were still getting together there and felt sorry for Bajal so I told him. He was very hurt and asked me to keep watch. Through this we became close and, after a while, he started touching me. As a kid I thought that it was just a game that Bajal liked to play and went along with him. With time the petting became heavier and, when I was old enough, we went further. We did it till I got married.'

Ellen, having difficulty comprehending all of this, asked, 'How did you manage it with everybody in the camp?'

'Easy. We'd go picking fruit or go for a swim.'

'And when we came back home to Dad?'

'Well, at first we found time when I visited, but later I sent messages.'

'How?'

Frances looked shyly at Nganka and said, 'Nganka, remember the times I picked a bunch of flowers for you to take back to your camp?'

'Yes'

'Well, and it's embarrassing for me to say, but that was a signal to Bajal and we would meet down by the river the following day. With him making deliveries it was always easy to find an excuse to leave the camp.'

'And now?' asked Nganka, grappling to come to terms with the revelation.

'No. No more. I've been true to Gerald ever since we were married.' Frances then added, 'Please don't tell Bajal. We all love him and he's not to blame. I shouldn't have told him. It's my fault.'

Ellen sat back in her chair in wonder and said, 'You're the last one I would have suspected.'

Frances, with a wry smile, replied, 'It's surprising what secrets starched crinoline can hide!'

Between the time of this conversation and the funeral nothing more was said, but a mutual understanding and acceptance of the situation evolved, with the accord that it would remain secret.

Jonathan, though he did not achieve his ambition of becoming a member of parliament, nevertheless made a contribution to the district by being a member of community committees.

Following Jonathan's burial on the property Nyulu and Larry, together with their eight children, shifted from Frances and Gerald's plantation to manage the home estate and care for Ellen in the coming years. Soon after their arrival Ellen rewrote her will, bequeathing the family property to Larry because, with the fickle nature of the Queensland Government, nobody could be sure that one day Nyulu's Exemption Certificate would not be revoked, and if she held title to the property it might be returned to the Crown.

Since the time Wallaby narrowly escaped being sent to prison he had lived at Winston's camp and stayed sober. He respected Thomas, saw him as a father figure and learned from him many of the white man's ways. He sometimes accompanied Juran when she visited camps but was mostly engaged helping Thomas with the orchard and vegetable gardens. He remained very much a family man, visiting his family regularly and often having ten or more over to stay for days at a time.

Bajal and Nganka continued delivering rations to the Aborigines and witnessing the deprivations suffered by their people. Apart from the meagre supply of rations the government provided they did virtually nothing to alleviate their plight. Though land had been allocated for a government reserve at the Mossman River Gorge, nothing had been done. This far flung outpost, out of sight and out of mind, cost the government a mere pittance to administer.

The Aborigines lived in camps by the river, sheltering in bark humpies and tin shacks. With hunting and gathering now almost non-existent many relied on menial work where a day's work would earn them a sugar bag containing food and two shillings to spend at the shops in Mossman. Some were reduced to begging, going to the homes of charitable people and lingering close by till noticed. Prostitution continued as a way of life, with women trading their flesh in return for food and favours. Many, under the guise of being housekeepers, lay on the white man's bed during the day and took food home to the family at night. The old and infirm were allowed to die in the camps, with family burying them in the bush graveyard at the Jinkalmu village near the Gorge.

The police continued exercising control with an iron fist, intimidating and coercing the blacks with threats of being removed to reserves and church missions in faraway places. No court order or court appearance was necessary. The local Protector, with approval from the Chief Protector, could forcibly remove individuals without giving them notice. Seizures were most times executed without any warning, leaving bereft family members and relatives in a state of shock and horror. Men and women in chains were led away, not knowing if they would ever return. Children were also taken from their mother's arms and sent to undisclosed destinations, with the only reason given being that it was for the child's benefit. In particular they targeted half-caste children living with their Aboriginal mothers in the company of other Aborigines. Entries recorded in the Removals Register tell of the disregard white administrators held for black people. Demeaning names were used like Tommy Sore Foot, Paddy No 2, Willie One Eye, Sambo and Fat Nellie. Nebulous reasons were given for removals, such as: trouble maker, becoming a nuisance, a prostitute, immoral association with a white man, old, lazy and disobedient, old and unable to work, destitute and undesirable, obscene language. All reeking of colonial arrogance. By 1918 more than thirty Aborigines had been removed from the Mossman district. As a further insult, most newspapers supported this racist policy by failing to report on removals and their consequences. Instead, they devoted their columns to comments like,

> In connection with the sugar industry on the Mossman … Some of the 10,000 blacks that are reported to be on Cape York may be available. It is a pity that so much labour is running about 'wild' and apparently so content with their present state that they absolutely decline to endorse the decree, 'By the sweat of thy brow thou shalt earn thy bread.'

Juran continued dealing with these problems daily, confronting the police and writing to the Chief Protector of Aborigines and the Minister for Native Affairs, complaining of the abuse and pleading that necessities be provided to the Aborigines. On occasions she became embroiled in scuffles with police as they removed so called offenders. The practice of apprehending people for minor misdemeanours and relocating them away from family struck at the heart of Aboriginal kinship. Juran worried about the new generation growing up under the Act. This ration-dependant generation would eventually lose sight of the past and with it their culture, language and identity.

CHAPTER 48

'Melba,' called Juran, standing at the entrance of a darkened room behind the Mossman Hotel.

'Who's that?'

'Juran, from Winston's camp.'

'Come in,' replied Melba, a full-blood Aborigine with a husky voice.

Juran found Melba lying on a rough timber bunk beside a small window propped open with a stick. 'You'll suffocate in here,' she said, opening another push-out window made of corrugated iron. 'Doctor Melville sent me. He said you're having trouble getting your wages from the *buliman*.'

'Yes. I very sick and need the money to see big fella doctor in Brisbane.'

'What's wrong with you?'

'My back. I work for Mr Breen the publican for years and when my back give out from cleaning I ask for my wages he give to the *buliman* but the *buliman* say there's only £20 in my money book.'

'How long you work for Mr Breen?'

'Eight years. Mr Breen do the sums and from what he put in and what I take out there should be £600 but the *buliman* say there's only £20.'

'How much to go see the doctor in Brisbane?'

'Plenty. Nurse at hospital say big trip and doctor cost a lot.'

'How much?'

'She say maybe I have to stay for long time in Brisbane and could cost £100.'

'And if you don't go to the doctor?' asked Juran.

'I bedridden now and maybe I die. I can hardly walk and getting worse. Doctor say, Melba you must see the big fella doctor.'

Juran sat on the side of Melba's bed for another half hour and then took her hand and said, 'Leave it with me.'

Melba, who had become a Christian since working at the hotel, held Juran's hand tightly and said, 'God bless you.'

Juran should have left the matter alone for a day to cool her head but, inflamed by the injustice of the situation, went directly to the police station, asked to see the sergeant and confronted him in his office. She declined the sergeant's offer of a chair and instead remained standing and demanded, 'What's happened to Melba's money!'

'Melba who?' replied the sergeant officiously.

'Don't play games with me. You know exactly who I mean. What have you done with her money?'

'What money?'

'The £2 a week wages she earned, less 10s a week she was allowed for pocket money.'

The sergeant, now on the defensive, replied, 'I'll have to investigate the matter.'

'No need,' interjected Juran. 'Mr Breen knows how much he put in and Melba knows how much she was given. The bank account should have about £600 in it and the piece of paper the duty officer gave to her when she enquired shows £20.'

'Well, if that's what the officer said then that is the balance of her account.'

Juran, with that feisty look that the sergeant had seen before, stared him in the face and blurted out, 'You're a liar!'

The sergeant, taken aback, straightened in his chair and listened as Juran blasted him with a tirade of instances where Aboriginal wages had been pilfered. The sergeant, knowing what she said was true, set to appease Juran in the hope that the complaint would be lost in a pile of paperwork and eventually forgotten. He took a pen and drafted Juran's statement, which she signed after reading carefully.

'When will I get an answer?'

'I don't expect a reply soon. It will take some time to search the records,' he said, making light of the matter.

Three months passed and when Juran revisited the sergeant he produced a memo that stated that the current balance of the account was as advised and that insufficient records were available to conduct a search of earlier transactions.

Juran, in absolute disgust, reiterated what she had previously said about police falsifying pocket money dockets and putting the money into their own pockets. The sergeant simply shrugged his shoulders to signal that as far as he was concerned the matter was closed.

Juran reported to Melba. She cried, unable to believe that the Christian God could let this happen. When the tears dried Juran asked, 'How will you cope?'

Melba, still believing in God, said, 'Mr Breen, he good man, said I can stay here all the time and the pub give me food.'

Juran stayed with Melba till the shock settled and then left, promising to call each week.

At the risk of putting her own exemption status in jeopardy Juran wrote a letter to the Minister, stating her case and boldly asserting that Melba's wages had been misappropriated. She waited for months but received no reply. Juran could have taken the matter to court but chose to let it lapse because the magistrate would, as in previous judgements, favour the word of a white man over that of a black woman. Also, the police, in retaliation, might remove Melba to a distant Aboriginal reserve, never to return. As a consequence, Melba's condition continued to decline till she eventually died, poverty stricken and disillusioned at the early age of fifty-five years.

Marku contracted the dreaded white man's disease known as consumption and when her coughing fits worsened and she began spitting blood Juran took her to the doctor at Port Douglas. The doctor, though sympathetic, could offer no remedy except to suggest she avoid chills and stay away from smoky fires. His suggestion that she be isolated to prevent the spread of the disease went unheeded, with those in the camp continuing to attend to her every need. Her condition worsened and, when confined to bed, Juran slept in her cottage and waited on her constantly.

Early one morning Juran was woken by the sound of her gurgling and struggling for breath. She called the others to the bedside and, when they were assembled, Marku looked around as though saying goodbye and then closed her eyes for the last time. Juran straightened her mother's body and lay her arms by her side, while Marku's son Bajal stared in disbelief. Juran removed the wedding ring James had given Marku as a symbol of his love for her. Nganka stayed by Bajal's side to comfort him.

After a brief talk Thomas saddled a horse and rode like the wind, spreading the word to the black community via bush telegraph and visiting his parents and friends in Mossman to convey the sad tidings. Upon his return he found Bajal and Nganka by the fire wailing and Juran close by sobbing. Wallaby dug a grave beside James' burial site and nailed together a coffin. By mid-morning the following day several tribespeople had assembled and as the hours passed more arrived. The Rubenstein family and those of the Ashton household motored in and parked their vehicles to one side. Townspeople began arriving soon after lunch and by the appointed time for the funeral service the camp was crowded with people bonded together by love for a woman who had stood by her family and moral principles all her life. At Juran's request the local Anglican priest delivered the service. Following this the tribespeople conducted their own service, dancing and chanting to the sound of clap sticks. The rituals continued throughout the night, echoing up and down the river that Marku once loved.

CHAPTER 49

By the 1920s the town of Mossman had coalesced around the sugar industry. Sugar became the mainstay of the district, providing employment and prosperity. During the harvesting season flares of light lit the evening sky as farmers burnt small sections of their cane fields, ready for the canecutters to manually harvest the following day. Wood-fired locomotives criss-crossed the countryside, hauling loaded tramway trucks to the sugar factory situated next to the town. Soot from the factory smoke stack rained on the town and adjoining residential area but nobody cared. The operation of the mill meant money in the bank. Shoppers dodged the noisy cane trains as they rattled along the rail line through the centre of the town. Most of the administrative offices and commerce had shifted from Port Douglas to Mossman, leaving Port Douglas with the prospect of a bleak future.

While all this activity prospered the white people the unseen irony was that it did nothing for the Aborigines, who continued living as hungry fringe dwellers on the riverbank. Nobody, except those of Winston's camp and a few true Christian families, cared about their abysmal circumstances. The landscape also continued to suffer, with cordwood cutters denuding the hillsides of timber to feed the fire boxes of the locomotives and, to a degree, the mill's furnace. The river and nearby reef suffered further from the siltation that accompanied cultivation of the land. This white community, like the rest of the industrialised world, pressed forward in the belief that more is better. Although still cut off from the outside world this valley, hidden away in the far north, became a source of wealth for those with the means of production at their disposal. The days of white overlords riding high in the saddle had given way to men of commerce.

Bajal continued delivering rations but with age catching up he found each year increasingly difficult. Three decades of trudging the valley had taken its toll and he now hobbled between the camps. To add to his troubles his new packhorse often spooked for no good reason. Early one morning Nganka helped him load the pack saddles and then watched as he led the horse away. He planned to visit a camp at Finlayvale and expected to be home by mid-afternoon.

At the main river crossing the horse snorted and reared, refusing to enter the water. Bajal, thinking a crocodile might be present, hitched the flighty horse to a tree and walked the bank both ways, looking for signs. When satisfied that all was clear he looped the rope over his wrist and tried again. After more rearing and fight back the horse took a giant leap, dragging Bajal with him and landing in belly-deep water. Bajal struggled to his feet and held firm to save the load of tinned meat and flour that was destined for a camp that had been without supplies for two weeks. He continued along native paths and around sugarcane fields till he came to a riverside drive that passed through a rainforest. This narrow carriage way, hemmed in by thick rainforest on both sides, caused further problems, with the horse refusing to cross the shadows cast by the forest canopy. With his patience now frayed, Bajal wrapped the long halter lead behind the horse as a britchen strap and took the weight. The horse took a few timid steps and then walked forward warily. Once through this eerie section Bajal settled the horse and proceeded to the Aboriginal camp. He found the families emaciated and hungry, and watching them eating raw flour and gobbling tinned meat he realised he must continue making deliveries.

On the return journey he entered the same riverside drive and proceeded cautiously. Part way through the horse halted and pricked its ears. Bajal thought little of this and coaxed it forward a few more paces before it bailed up altogether and began to tremble.

'Woo. Woo there,' called Bajal, sensing something wrong.

The horse swung one way and then the other, trying to free itself from Bajal's grip.

Unknown to Bajal a Chevrolet roadster with two girls aboard was rapidly approaching from the opposite direction. Jane Worthington, the seventeen-year-old daughter of a wealthy sugar planter, and her rich cousin Tilly from

Sydney, were in high spirits as Jane drove along the dusty road towards Finlayvale.

Tilly had arrived at Port Douglas two weeks earlier by steamer, bringing with her several trunks of clothing, fashion accessories, expensive jewellery and women's magazines for her special cousin. She belonged to the social clique that set the fashion standard for Sydney during the Roaring '20s. As a thirty-year-old she revelled in the Charleston dance craze that swept the world. She prided herself on being one of those women who had torn free from the constraints of the Victorian era to assert herself as an individual.

'The idea is to look seductive,' said Tilly, holding a light chiffon dress against Jane for her to admire herself in the mirror.

'And why would I want to look seductive?' replied Jane innocently.

'To catch the richest man in the district of course!'

Since Tilly's arrival they had spent most of their time in Jane's bedroom, dressing in different styles, applying complimentary make-up and choosing accessories. This morning they had spied a young farmhand polishing the family car on the front lawn and had decided to put their work to the test. Tilly, with her tightly cropped hair, fashioned herself as a woman on the make by applying brash red lipstick, wearing a silhouette dress that left little to the imagination and stepping into a pair of high-heeled shoes. For accessories she chose a long necklace of beads, teardrop diamond earrings and a wrist full of bangles. As a signature mark she carried a long cigarette holder engraved with her name. Jane, a brunette, slim and demure, puddled in indecision till Tilly suggested a pale-blue shift with thin shoulder straps and a hem line above the knee. Tilly then chose for her a colourful headband to highlight her bobbed hair and helped apply lipstick, rouge and eye shadow.

'You ready?' asked Tilly, pulling a crease from Jane's dress.

'You sure?' replied Jane, suddenly feeling coy.

'Of course. Just follow me.'

The girls walked down the hallway and stepped onto the verandah to be in full view of Karl the roustabout, who attended to the livestock and gardens. Tilly wasted no time and called, 'Hello there.'

Karl turned, waved and asked, 'Are you the new girl?'

'Tilly is the name. Jane's cousin from Sydney.' She took hold of her string of beads and moved them about suggestively. She then remarked offhandedly, 'Nice car.'

'Yes, a 1922 Chevy convertible, four cylinder, three speed and painted ox-blood red.

'Do you drive?'

'Not this one. It's Mr Worthington's. All I do is the servicing and polishing.'

To draw his attention further Tilly moved to the railing and lit a cigarette.

'Cigarette?' she called, blowing a puff of smoke his way.

'No thanks. I'm a non-smoker.'

'A drinker then?'

'Yes. I get on the swill most nights.'

'I might join you.'

'Not sure about that. Mr Worthington would have to approve.'

Karl had, in a soft way, signalled that his employment was worth more than a frolic and turned back to polishing the headlights.

Tilly, now revelling in the challenge and not to be outdone, spoke to Jane in a not-so-quiet voice and said, 'He'd be a hay shaker.'

'You think so?' replied Jane.

'Sure do and I'll bet he's got one as big as a policeman's nightstick.'

Jane gulped at the thought.

'Karl,' she called again, 'could you take us for a spin?'

'I'd like to oblige but only Mr Worthington and Miss Jane have that privilege.'

'Well then,' said Tilly, turning to Jane, 'should we ask your father?'

Jane went to the office on the far wing of the homestead and soon returned to say, 'Dad says it's all right as long as I drive carefully.'

Karl folded back the convertible hood and opened the doors as a courtesy. Jane drove off down the driveway and he watched till they disappeared behind a field of sugar cane.

The girls motored about the countryside for an hour before Jane decided to take Tilly along Finlayvale Road to a picnic spot at the foothills of the mountain. They turned from the main road north, travelled along rough gravel roads flanked by lush fields of green, and then entered the corridor of the riverside drive. With Jane at the wheel and Tilly leaning back smoking they sped along the road without a care.

Bajal heard the motor car coming and began to panic. He looped the rope around his wrist and looked for a pocket in the rainforest where he and the horse could stand aside while the car passed. He could find no gap in the dense understorey. He considered running the other way but he would be run down before reaching the open country. If he were to set the horse loose and let it gallop off he would never see the horse or pack saddle again. These thoughts were dismissed when, from around the corner, appeared a red car travelling at thirty miles per hour. He waved and shouted but when this man-made contraption failed to slow he backed the horse against the forest wall and held tight. As the car came closer the horse began to rear and plunge, tangling with the vines and thrashing about. Bajal bellowed for the car to stop.

When Tilly saw them she screamed and held her hands to her face. Jane caught a glimpse through the offside of the windshield, panicked and instead of applying the brakes pushed the accelerator to the floor. The horse, now crazed, leapt forward, taking Bajal with it and landing in the middle of the road. Screams were the last thing Bajal heard before the car collided with him and the horse.

The tangled wreck, with steam spurting from the radiator, sat sideways across the road. Tilly lay semiconscious and groaning on the seat. Jane had been thrust forward, splintering the windshield, and hung impaled by the throat with blood spraying across her and Tilly's dresses. The horse, with its belly torn and innards hanging out, kicked wildly, trying to free its leg from under the car. Bajal had been knocked to the ground and lay pinned under a rear wheel.

Three blacks who had been fishing close by heard the crash and raced to the scene. One stayed to help those that might be alive, another raced along the road to tell the nearest planter and the other, a friend of Bajal's, ran downstream faster than any black man before him to tell those at Winston's camp.

Nganka, Juran, Thomas and Wallaby jumped to attention when the messenger stumbled into their camp, utterly exhausted and jabbering about an accident.

'Where? What?' shouted Juran, trying to make sense of his gabble.

'Bajal! Finlay! Bin hit by car!'

'Is he hurt?'

'Plurry oath. Car run over him.'

Juran, unable to wait for the man to catch his breath, shouted for an answer, 'Is he dead?'

The black man, dripping with sweat and trembling, looked at her with his dark, syrupy eyes and shook his head.

'Was he breathing? Tell me!' demanded Juran.

'I dunno. He bin stuck under wheel.'

At hearing this Nganka shouted, 'No! No! No!' and fell to her knees in a state of shock.

Thomas broke in. 'He's been hit by a car on Finlayvale road. I'll take a horse and go cross-country. Juran and Nganka bring the buggy by road. Wallaby, you care for the messenger.' Within moments Thomas had bridled a horse, swung aboard bareback and left at full gallop. He pressed his heels hard against the horse's hide, urging it forward as he raced upstream, swam the river and continued on to the site of the accident where he was met by a sugar planter and two of the natives. The devastation shocked Thomas. Bajal had been removed from beneath the twisted wreck and lay on his back, staring up into the trees. Jane remained impaled with her blood-splattered body leaning against the steering wheel. Tilly had crawled through an open door and lay bloodied and concussed on the roadway. The horse lay dead, with blow flies milling about. The stench of death hung in the air.

'Is there a doctor coming?' Thomas asked the planter.

'Supposedly. I phoned the police at Mossman who said they would call the local ambulance and a doctor from Port.'

Thomas knelt beside Bajal, took his hand and spoke loudly. 'Bajal, can you hear me!'

Bajal blinked his eyes and murmured something through his lips.

Thomas continued, 'Nganka's coming. We're going to take you to the hospital. You'll be all right.'

Thomas, now close to breaking point, kept talking in the hope that Bajal would stay conscious till the ambulance arrived.

Juran had harnessed a horse and buggy, bundled Nganka aboard and set the wheels in motion. With three miles between them and where Bajal lay she laid the reins hard on the horse's rump. The buggy rocked and bounced and at times tilted precariously as they sped along the gravel roadways and crossed a low-level bridge. On Finlayvale Road Juran sooled the horse harder. Every moment counted. Nganka held tightly, with tears streaming down her face.

As the women approached the riverside drive Thomas heard the galloping hooves and turned to reassure Bajal. Bajal's opened eyes made no movement and when Thomas touched his eyelids to test he realised that Bajal was no longer with them. He shouted for the planter to hold the women back but the moment the buggy stopped Nganka jumped to the ground, pushed past him and fell to her knees beside Bajal's body. She stared at him momentarily, screamed, and then clutched him, not wanting his spirit to depart. Thomas took Juran in his arms and comforted her while she sobbed quietly.

The Mossman police, ambulance and the local undertaker arrived soon after. The ambulance took Tilly to the Port Douglas hospital while the bodies of Bajal and Jane were attended to by the undertaker.

Burials needed to be prompt in the tropics and two days later Jane was laid to rest in the Port Douglas cemetery and Bajal was interred beside the others buried at Winston's camp. Word had spread throughout the valley's Aboriginal community and every able person attended his funeral to give thanks for what he had done for each of them personally. Many of the white community attended and, in particular, Frances who grieved for Bajal, her former lover. Ellen, who had embraced Nganka so many times before, held her close during the service. Juran had difficulty coming to terms with the irony of Bajal's death: an Aborigine born free in the wild eventually meeting his death under the wheels of a white man's contraption. This also marked the end of Bajal's delivery service, with the police taking responsibility for the distribution of rations from that day forward.

Following Bajal's funeral Nganka's life became ruled by Aboriginal belief. She believed that every tragic death was caused by an evil spirit and feared for Bajal's safety in the afterlife. She also believed that the same spirit had prevented her from fulfilling her lifelong dream of her and Bajal having children. To ward off these spirits she burned smoking fires beside his grave continuously, placing branches of green leaves on the smouldering embers to cloud his grave. She sat by his burial plot all day and slept there on the ground by night, maintaining her vigil. Her mind became so affected that some nights she imagined an evil spirit to be present and stoked the fire till the flames licked the night sky. She refused most food offered by Juran and drank water from a billycan by her side. Within two weeks her condition declined, leaving her a mere shell of the person she used to be. The influence of Christian teachings imparted to her since James' arrival could not erase the beliefs instilled in her as a child. Aboriginal custom, the fibre of her existence, reigned over any white man's spiritual teachings. No matter what the white men said or practised, Aboriginal culture took precedence over European notions of spirituality and the hereafter.

Wallaby wanted to call the medicine man but he knew Nganka had willed herself to die and that incantations would not alter the pathway to her final destiny. Other Aborigines avoided her for fear they could be implicated in Bajal's death and find themselves a target for revenge from the *kadaicha* man, the Aboriginal avenger. Juran, having an understanding of both cultures, did what she could to persuade Nganka to see things differently but all words of encouragement fell on deaf ears. Not even Ellen, her lover and confidant for decades, could lift her from the mire of depression that strangled her life. Nganka eventually drifted into a dazed state, a self-imposed trance that she believed would allow her to communicate with Bajal. Once in this transcendental state she refused all food and water and, with Ellen holding her in her arms, she departed to join Bajal in the spirit world.

CHAPTER 50

The economy of Mossman gained further impetus when, in the early 1930s, a road was constructed from Cairns to Mossman, linking the community with the outside world. The seaport town of Port Douglas suffered more as vehicle traffic became the primary means of transport and bypassed the port's shipping services. The earlier vehicle access via the rough Hodgkinson track, where teams of horses were needed to pull cars up steep inclines, ceased operation altogether. With the shire council office being shifted to Mossman and a new hospital at Mossman replacing the old Port hospital, nearly all government facilities had relocated to Mossman. A road link to Daintree marked the closure of an era, with road travel replacing the shipping that had plied the Daintree River since the arrival of the cedar getters. People now moved about more freely, transacting business and socialising, bringing this hitherto secluded valley to the full attention of the southern states and, indeed, the whole world.

One morning Juran sat at the communal dining table of the camp, reflecting about the past, when a lady riding a bicycle approached.

'Hello,' greeted the lady as she rode into the camp.

Juran, with no thought to the lady's purpose, returned the greeting and invited her to take a seat.

'Colleen Brennan,' said the lady, flicking her ponytail to one side and extending a hand by way of introduction.

'Juran Partridge,' replied Juran, taking the newcomer's hand as a courtesy.

The lady, dressed in khaki shirt and trousers and wearing sandshoes, sat opposite and before long captured Juran's full attention with her engaging brown eyes and the Irish lilt of her voice.

'The police sergeant said you might be able to help.'

She explained that she was a Protestant missionary sent by God to help the natives. Juran listened carefully as Colleen told of her past, the souls she had saved and how she planned to help the local Aborigines. What Colleen said made sense and by the time she pushed off on her bike late that afternoon Juran was convinced that, with Colleen's assistance, her people would be able to pull themselves from their mire of destitution and servitude. She discussed it with Thomas and Wallaby and, after careful consideration, they decided to give it a try.

Colleen and Juran met with the sergeant and, to their delight, he readily agreed with the idea of establishing a central camp on the gazetted Aboriginal reserve located at the Gorge. Correspondence passed back and forth to Brisbane and approval was finally granted. The arrangement carried the qualifications that the approval was unofficial, and that no additional government assistance should be expected. The unofficial status of the Gorge mission meant that it avoided the stringent rules that applied to government-controlled Aboriginal reserves and church missions, where almost every aspect of life was controlled. Colleen had charted a prudent course whereby residents of the Gorge mission could enjoy relative freedom and, at the same time, have the protection afforded by their mission being located on a government-gazetted reserve.

Colleen moved her belongings to Winston's camp and settled herself into one of the vacant cottages. Before long she, Juran, Thomas and Wallaby could be seen daily, riding their bicycles through Mossman, going to and from the Gorge. The reserve, located in the shadow of Mount Demi, proved to be an ideal site. They sweltered throughout the summer months with the sound of their axes ringing in the rainforest canopy as they felled the virgin forest to make way for the mission settlement. During the rainy season they erected pole huts clad with thatch made from the leafy fronds of palm trees. When the wintery months approached Wallaby began a crusade, visiting the river camps to convince the natives that life in a central camp would be better, especially with Colleen liaising with the police for the supply of rations and the medical assistance she could provide as a trained nurse. Those in the small, scattered camps agreed and soon began shifting camp to the mission site. Those at the traditional village at Jinkalmu took more persuading. Within a year most had made the move and, by the rainy season of the fourth year, all that remained outside the mission were a few at Jinkalmu, a family group at the river junction and another family on the south branch.

Colleen, with an unshakable belief in God, believed that God provided for everyone and that needs could be met through devotional prayer. She served these 'children of the forest', attending to their needs with little consideration for her own wellbeing. As the need grew an evangelist by the name of Pam Flanagan joined the mission. She lived with Colleen in a tin shack made with flattened kerosene tins and with an earthen floor. Like Colleen she believed that through the Lord Jesus Christ she could harvest sheaves of good from the fields of sin.

Wallaby became a favourite with his people. With his cheeky personality, everlasting smile and strong work ethic he led the way, teaching them the white man's trades of carpentry and gardening. He had accepted Colleen's belief in God and preached in his own language, bringing his people into God's fold. He sang hymns while playing a piano in Colleen's shack but nobody could truly say he had an ear for music. He loved children and, in particular, the three young half-caste daughters of his full-blood niece Polly. He cared for them while Polly worked away on Mondays and Fridays for Mr Fitzgibbon, a bachelor man who owned a small, isolated property. Only Wallaby and a few others knew the full details of the arrangement and that Mr Fitzgibbon had fathered Polly's three girls. Thomas had wondered how Polly could afford to dress the girls so well until one day one of the children referred to Mr Fitzgibbon as 'Daddy'.

Thomas now divided his time between the plantation and the mission, riding a horse to the settlement often to help Wallaby with his projects. Colleen had always wanted a church and now, with the help of Thomas and Wallaby, the posts were in place and pole rafters were being scarfed and strapped across the roof spans. They worked as a team, standing on makeshift scaffolding and lifting the poles above their heads to set them in place. They made good progress and all went well until, one day, Wallaby arrived at Winston's camp with Polly and the three girls.

'What is it?' asked Thomas.

Wallaby approached with an anxious look and Polly lagging behind with the children.

'It's Polly. The police are going to take her and the girls away.'

'What! Away?'

'Yes.'

Thomas, not believing what he heard, set to ease Wallaby's concern and said, 'They wouldn't do that. You couldn't be in trouble.'

'Not me. Polly,' replied Wallaby, waving a hand for Polly to come forward.

'What's she done?'

Wallaby looked at Maggie, Polly's twelve-year-old daughter and, not wishing to discuss the matter in her presence, asked if Juran was home.

'Yes. I'll get her.'

Juran appeared on the verandah and, seeing Polly so upset, came down the stairs and put an arm around her.

Thomas waited a moment and then said, 'Juran, could you take care of the children for a while. Wallaby and Polly have something private they want to talk about.'

'Sure.' She coaxed them upstairs with the offer of a chocolate biscuit.

Wallaby, wearing only a pair of shorts, brushed sweat from his greying temples. 'The police are coming for Polly. They say she's no good because she has three kids to a white man. They're going to send her and the girls to Cherbourg.' He choked on the words and struggled to say more. 'Polly not bad. She's a good mother. Only trying to do the best for the girls.' He then turned to Polly and, seeing the tears streaming from her face, he took her in his arms and hugged her tightly.

Thomas called for Juran to join them and, after leaving the jar of biscuits with the children, she came downstairs. Thomas explained the situation and then asked Wallaby, 'Where did you hear this?'

'Mr Fitzy. He tell Polly today. Said for her to take the children away and hide.'

Thomas then looked at Polly for an answer. 'Yes,' she said, 'he say that he hear a whisper that they are coming to take me away.'

Thomas became defensive and said, 'We'll see about that! You can stay here tonight and we'll find a hideout first thing in the morning.'

Juran cooked a meal and settled the family into the cottage closest to her and Thomas. Thomas' agitation would not settle and, as a precaution, he chained his dog to a tree near the entrance of the plantation. He slept little and when the dog began barking wildly at first light he bounded from his bed and rushed to Wallaby's cottage.

'Quick,' he urged in a low tone, 'the police are here. Forget everything and cut across the river to Ellen's. I'll deal with the police and come over later.'

As Wallaby, Polly and the girls scurried down the riverbank two Paddy wagons roared up the avenue and braked hard in the middle of the camp. A sergeant and five officers jumped out with revolvers drawn. The officers ran to the cottages and searched while the sergeant approached Thomas and asked, 'You know why we're here?'

'No idea,' replied Thomas.

'We're looking for a Polly and her kids. They—' He suddenly broke off when an officer came from one of the cottages with children's clothing in his hand. 'So, they're here. You'd better tell me where they're hiding.'

Thomas denied any knowledge and when the sergeant asked Juran she refused to answer.

With the officers now assembled before him he said, 'Very well. If you don't want to cooperate then we'll take you to the station. He nodded to an officer who handcuffed Thomas. When he turned to cuff Juran, Thomas objected and threatened violence.

'Put leg-cuffs on the male just to be sure,' instructed the sergeant.

The officer took a set of shackles from a vehicle and when he bent down Thomas took a swipe, striking him across the head with his clenched fists.

The sergeant pointed his revolver directly at Thomas. Juran, though upset, remained calm and persuaded Thomas to climb into the back of the wagon, with her following. At the police station they were locked in a cell and, within minutes, the vehicles left again in a hurry.

CHAPTER 51

The police, guessing where Wallaby and the family had gone, drove at high speed to Ellen Ashton's property and came to an abrupt halt. The moment the vehicles stopped the officers piled out with revolvers drawn and surrounded the house. The sergeant moved to the garden gate and shouted, 'Police! Come out with your hands up!'

Those inside stood aghast, knowing that an arrest was about to be made. After more calls and one officer going inside to check for hideaways, Wallaby, Polly and the children were herded to the lawn, while Ellen, Nyulu and Larry remained on the verandah. The sergeant then proceeded to charge Wallaby and his family under the provisions of the Protection Act and ordered the officers to handcuff the adults. The Paddy wagons were loaded. While Nyulu and Larry watched in horror, Ellen slipped back inside the house momentarily.

'Right. That's it,' said the sergeant after the second door had been closed. The police holstered their weapons and were about to board the vehicles when Ellen suddenly reappeared on the verandah with a rifle in her hands.

'Let them out!' she demanded.

The police jerked to attention with the sergeant and two others drawing their revolvers. Nyulu stepped forward and cried out, 'No, Mum! No!' but her plea went unheard. All that echoed in Ellen's mind were Jonathan's words of long ago, 'If any policeman sets foot on my place, he'll get a bullet through his head!'

Larry, realising there was no bullet in the breech of the rifle, shouted, 'It's not loaded. There's no bullets in it.'

The sergeant heard and called to Ellen, 'Mrs Ashton, put the rifle down. Put it down now!'

Ellen, aged and frail, called back, 'Let the children out. They've done nothing wrong.'

'Mrs Ashton, the children belong with their mother.'

'No. Let the children go. I'll care for them.'

'I can't do that.'

Ellen lifted the rifle from her hip and, with the butt under her arm, pointed it towards the sergeant.

The sergeant stiffened and called again, 'Mrs Ashton, put it down, otherwise I'll shoot.'

Ellen's mind raced with thoughts of vengeance. All the police brutality she had witnessed, the resentments harboured, the sight of little children being once again taken away clouded her judgement. If she had to kill each and every one of these pigs to save the children then so be it. With this impulse she raised the rifle and, as she put the stock to her cheek to aim, the sergeant fired a single shot.

The bullet connected her shoulder, pushing her back a pace, where she stood stark and disbelieving before falling to the floor. Nyulu screamed, pulled herself free from Larry's arms and ran to her mother's side. The police officers, themselves shocked at the sergeant's action, stayed by the vehicles. By the time Larry reached Ellen, Nyulu had taken Ellen into her arms, cradling her and murmuring, 'Mother, my mother.' The sergeant came alongside and looked down, trying to come to terms with how this routine arrest had spiralled out of control. There was little that could be done, with blood gushing from the wound and Ellen gasping for breath. The sergeant hurried inside and phoned the ambulance but by the time he returned Ellen had passed away.

Mourners from all over the district attended Ellen's funeral which was held on the family property. Whites and blacks, some with long memories, each put a sprig of wattle blossom into the grave as a show of respect for the first white woman to have pioneered the river. The inquest that followed exonerated the sergeant of any misconduct, citing evidence that he acted in self-defence. The inquest ignored Larry's evidence that he had told the sergeant the rifle was not loaded and that the ammunition was stored separate from the rifle, and that Ellen would not have had time to access it and put a bullet into the chamber.

CHAPTER 52

Thomas and Juran were bailed and let out of jail the following day. They engaged a barrister from Cairns and appeared before the Mossman Magistrates Court the following month. The three charges pending against them were to be heard at the one session. Thomas, dressed in a suit and tie for the occasion, stood calmly on the stand while the charge of complicity was read. After he pleaded not guilty the police prosecutor, an aggressive and uncompromising man, began by outlining the importance of upholding the provisions of the Protection Act and then interrogated Thomas as though he was guilty of a major crime. Thomas, under strict instruction, answered the questions briefly and to the point, not allowing the prosecutor an opportunity to use Thomas' words against him. He treated Thomas with disdain, intimidating him by repeating questions and drawing false inferences, trying to incriminate him. Thomas withstood the barrage, frustrating the prosecutor's questioning and giving him little room to move. Thomas' barrister did not call Thomas to the stand. Instead he tendered character references and a statement detailing Thomas' connection to the Aboriginal community and his contribution to their betterment. He then addressed the court, presenting a series of questions that cast doubt that Thomas could be guilty of the alleged offence. The magistrate listened closely as the barrister posed the questions: Who owned the clothes? Who put them there? When were they left there? Was the accused aware that the clothes were there? What proof is there that the runaways visited the camp? He went further and explained that Mr Brown was often away, engaged in building a church for the Aboriginal mission, on or about the time of the alleged offence. The magistrate, influenced by Thomas' standing in the community and his devotion to assisting the Aborigines, took a short break and then returned to deliver his judgement of 'Not guilty'.

As Juran was an alleged co-conspirator, the facts of her case were the same and so the charge against her was summarily dismissed.

Thomas pleaded guilty to the charge of assault and, to the surprise of the court, he received a minimal sentence of a £10 fine and a two-year good behaviour bond.

⌒

The court case left Thomas doubting the integrity of human nature. Further to this Wallaby, Polly and the children had been taken away, with no news of their whereabouts. Juran's enquiries at the police station and her written request for information had been ignored. Thomas brooded, languishing around the camp, doing no more than necessary and reluctant to visit the mission. Colleen Brennan, also with her faith in humanity shaken, prayed for those taken away and cried when alone. This was the third removal for the year and everyone wondered who would be next.

The posts erected by Thomas and Wallaby stood as a stark reminder of the mindless act until a mission girl dressed in a blue pinafore and a pink ribbon in her hair asked Thomas, 'When will you build God's house so he can stay here and look after us.'

Colleen, who was standing beside the girl with a hand on her shoulder, listening while Thomas fumbled for an answer, said, 'It would do us all good to pray together in a house of assembly.'

Thomas could not turn aside from the pleas and, although it would be difficult to fit the pole rafters on top of the posts without Wallaby and his knowhow, he set to with the help of two other Aborigines. He notched the tops of the posts using a sharp, broad axe and then scarfed the rafters on the ground before lifting and fitting them in position. One post had been notched incorrectly and, while Thomas stood on his scaffold holding his end of the pole on his shoulder and chipping away with the broad axe, the scaffold under the other two men collapsed from their weight. They all fell to the ground, with the rafter being thrown clear, but when they sat up Thomas held his leg and called for help. By the time Colleen arrived with her medical kit bright red blood had soaked his trouser leg. A sharp corner of the broad axe had gashed his inner thigh, leaving a deep wound. She placed a thick pad on the wound and bandaged the leg tightly.

271

'He'll need the ambulance,' she said in a fluster. 'Willie, go quick to the planter across the tramline and ring the ambulance man.'

Pam, unsure of the severity of the injury, said, 'Will he be all right?'

'Not sure. I think he's severed an artery and if so he's in trouble. He needs to be at the hospital now!'

An Aborigine standing nearby broke in and suggested, 'We take him to hospital.'

'How?' asked Colleen.

'On wire bed.'

Colleen, knowing that every moment counted, applied a tourniquet above the wound while the men grabbed a stretcher bed, blankets and a pillow. With the legs of the bed folded up they laid it on the ground and lifted Thomas carefully onto the blanket. Six strong men then took the stretcher, three a side, and left at a trot they knew they could sustain for the three miles to the Mossman hospital. As they approached the hospital the ambulance car careered towards them with its engine roaring at full throttle.

'We're nearly there,' shouted one of the stretcher bearers, heaving for breath and with sweat streaming down his legs.

'All right. I'll go ahead and warn the doctor,' said the ambulance driver before spinning the vehicle in a cloud of dust and scorching back along the road to town.

None of the men had ever been to the Mossman hospital before and when they passed under the concrete archway of the hospital driveway they baulked until the superintendent waved them forward, ushered them up the stairs and into the emergency room.

The doctor quickly concluded that the patient was suffering from acute blood loss and, unless the bleeding was stemmed, he would die. He removed the bandage and dressing and then bunched together a tight wad of gauze that he bandaged tightly to the wound. He then directed staff to take turns at holding their clenched fist hard against the bleed. The tourniquet had to be loosened to avoid necrosis and amputation of the leg which would likely lead to death. Within an hour of Thomas being hospitalised Juran and Colleen arrived. Juran, in a state of near panic, stood by the bed holding Thomas' hand while the staff struggled to stop a weep of blood that continued to seep into the bed sheets. Colleen, with her nursing experience, made her own assessment, recognising that the bright red blood and the continued bleeding probably meant that the femoral artery had been nicked. This, together with his profuse sweating, clammy skin, dizziness and confused state of mind gave her little hope that he would survive. The staff worked courageously into the night, forgetting their personal lives and taking turns to apply pressure to the wound in the hope of sealing the artery. Some prayed beside Colleen and when the Anglican priest arrived more joined in prayer. Soon after midnight Thomas slipped into unconscious, his breathing became shallow and his blood pressure plummeted. At 1.20 am when the doctor pronounced Thomas dead, those in the room sat silent, trying to grasp the meaning of life.

Juran had known Thomas since she was born, as a child, a sweetheart, lover, confidant and trusted friend. She had never thought of life without him and now that he was gone she felt empty, as though something inside her had died. She placed a wooden cross on his grave and enclosed it with a lattice fence. She visited often, weeding around the flowers she had planted and praying.

CHAPTER 53

The police considered the magistrate at Mossman too soft so transferred Wallaby to Cairns where he was brought before a magistrate noted for his severity. Wallaby, a bush blackfellow, understood nothing of the charge of aiding and abetting brought against him. He stood dumbfounded when sentenced to three years' imprisonment at Stewart's Creek prison. Within moments of his being sentenced a burly police officer took him to a cell where he sat for a week, alone, lost and crying, unable to fathom what he had done wrong. The first he knew of his transfer was when a prison guard brought cold porridge for breakfast and said, 'Eat up, Bozo. You're going on a holiday.'

Later in the morning a young police officer came to the cell, handcuffed himself to Wallaby and escorted him to the railway station. They boarded the steam train, stepping into the guard's compartment at the rear of the train. The officer removed the cuff from his wrist and clipped it to the luggage rack above Wallaby's head.

During the seven-hour journey to Townsville the officer and the guard sat opposite him, swapping gossip and sharing sandwiches and a flask of tea. Nothing was offered to Wallaby. In their minds blackfellas only needed to be fed once a day. They arrived in Townsville after dark and stepped to the platform lit by electric light.

The officer transferred his cuff to the wrist of a waiting officer and walked away without saying a word to Wallaby. The new officer, brandishing a nightstick, dragged Wallaby along the platform and out into the open. He then bundled Wallaby into a Paddy wagon and cuffed him to a security rail inside the cab. Upon arrival at the prison he was shoved into a night cell with no food and would wait till a duty officer arrived the next morning. Thus began three long years of hell, with Wallaby treated as a half-wild animal rather than a human being. The food remained poor, his blankets were washed monthly, and the stench of human waste filled the cells. Seldom did a guard speak to him. If it were not for his release into the exercise yard during the day and the company of other Aborigines, Wallaby would have gone mad. Night time was the worst and sometimes when he raged in a state of delirium officers came in and beat him.

Due to his moments of temporary derangement Wallaby was considered dangerous and, on occasions, sent to solitary confinement for days at a time. There were further repercussions when the parole officer disallowed any remission of the time to be served because of what was perceived to be his aberrant behaviour. By the time of his release he was a broken man, suffering mood swings that ranged from uncontrollable anger to crouching in the corner of his cell and sobbing like a child.

On the day of his release he was handed clothes provided by the Salvation Army and told to dress. Without any indication of what lay before him an officer ordered him from his cell and took him to a waiting car where he and the officer sat in the back seat while being driven to the railway station. Upon arrival the officer took Wallaby to the ticket office, bought a ticket to Cairns and handed it to him. He then took a five pound note from his wallet, stuffed it into Wallaby's pocket and, with the parting words 'Behave yourself', he walked off, leaving Wallaby stranded on the platform.

Wallaby had no idea what to do with the ticket or the money. He was stuck in an Aborigine's worst nightmare—away from his country and people, with no one to guide him. He became paralysed, standing stock still, with people rushing by, shouting to one another, and carriage doors opening and slamming shut. The northbound train carried a vacant seat, the one Wallaby would have occupied if someone had cared and ushered him aboard. It would have been his passage to Cairns and then to home where he would be safe with his loved ones. Yet, it was not to be. The train tooted, let out steam, took the load and, with smoke billowing from its chimney and the wheels gathering speed, it drew away from the platform. Wallaby stood dazed as people hung out of the carriage windows waving goodbyes, with those on the platform returning waves and blowing kisses. When the train had cleared the station and disappeared from view a lad porter came up to Wallaby, took him by the hand and said, 'You all right, Sir?'

Wallaby, startled by the touch of a white man's hand, pulled his hand away, looked at the young man's kindly face for a moment and then turned and jumped from the platform to the tracks. The porter, thinking the black man to be deranged, shouted for assistance and then took chase across the rails. Wallaby, though weak from years of abuse, found hidden strength and fled. Others joined the chase, shouting as they followed in hot pursuit to capture what they believed to be a madman on the loose. Wallaby tripped and stumbled as he raced along the lines near the railway workshops. The shouts were heard at the workshops and men there, wanting to help, also ran after him. Wallaby saw them coming and, struck with fear, cut back to the right and on to the lines of an oncoming train. The driver slammed on the brakes and pulled the whistle cord. The high-pitched sound of the whistle and the screeching of brakes terrified Wallaby. With his consciousness now wholly blinded by panic and unable to endure anymore he turned and ran headlong towards the freight train. The engine driver gasped as the sixty-ton locomotive, with a full load of freight, collected Wallaby, smashing his body and tossing his remains aside.

To escape blame the prison report cited Wallaby's unstable mind as the reason for his running amok and committing suicide by throwing himself in front of a moving train. The undertaker buried him in the pauper's section of the Townsville cemetery with no one else present and with no burial rites accompanying his committal to the grave. As a matter of course the police at Mossman were advised by memo. Juran was the first to hear when she visited the police station about another removal and the sergeant mentioned offhandedly that Wallaby had died in Townsville.

CHAPTER 54

Polly and her pretty half-caste daughters found it hard to adjust to life at Cherbourg Aboriginal reserve. Since the day they had been shunted from Mossman in Far North Queensland to this government reserve in the Burnett district of southern Queensland, they had experienced difficulties on a daily basis. They lived in a small wooden cottage at Top Camp and shared the cottage with another woman and her four young children. Polly and her youngest child shared a bed while the other two slept head to toe in another in the same room. With no bed linen and only two blankets each they slept on kapok mattresses and cuddled together for warmth in winter.

They queued at the rations store with a calico bag to collect their fortnightly quota of flour, rice, porridge, sugar, syrup and tea, plus fruit and vegetables when available. Meat remained scarce, being allocated according to work done, with men engaged on projects receiving double that given to unemployed women like Polly.

The so called education program barely taught the children how to read and write with some, after finishing school, still having to place an 'x' as their signature on ration coupons and travel permits. Works programs, where skills were to be taught, failed miserably due to lack of supervision. Women found themselves not progressing beyond the menial tasks of washing, cleaning, mending clothes and raking leaves.

With no opportunity to better themselves those like Polly and her children became institutionalised, living on handouts with no possibility of advancement. To stay out of trouble the children learned early in life to be compliant and not question the authority exerted over them. For them nothing would change and when they eventually passed away they would be buried on foreign soil, far away from family and the spirits of their ancestors.

Polly's eldest daughter Maggie, with her light skin colour and slim body, drew the attention of white men working on the reserve. By the age of sixteen she knew a little about men's desires and managed to stay clear of them till one day a white man working on the reserve put two shillings into her palm and took her behind a shed. He called on her again and again, having his way, till, eventually, he introduced her to white men from the nearby town of Murgon, offering her services at five shillings a time from which he deducted three shillings for himself. Meetings were always after dark, with the men giving false names. Maggie, with her complacent nature and sensuous moves, became a favourite with men from all walks of life: tall and short, fat and thin, rich and poor.

The lady sharing the house became aware of Maggie's night-time activity and, although she said nothing to Polly, she told other black women of the 'rabbit track' Maggie had worn between the house and the shed. Polly overheard mention of this while washing at the communal laundry but, with a family to feed, she stayed silent. There was even some jealousy between the two women when Polly brought home a nice cut of meat rather than soup bones. While Maggie accepted this as a means to survival it came with the risks of contracting venereal disease, becoming pregnant or, worse still, being discovered by the administrators of the reserve. To be caught soliciting, particularly within the confines of the reserve, would see her sent away, probably to the dreaded penal colony on Palm Island. Maggie lived this risky life for five years till one day a white lady from the main office came to her house, called her aside and began asking questions about her movements.

'So, you haven't been seeing any white men?'

'No.'

'Are you sure?'

'Yes, sure of it.'

The inquisition continued for half an hour before the lady, clearly not believing Maggie, said, 'When is your birthday?'

'Next month.'

'And you'll be twenty-one?'

'Yes.'

The lady continued, 'Being an adult half-caste could make you eligible for exemption providing you have a good record.'

'Yes.'

'Would you like to be exempted?'

'Yes, very much so.'

'Have you a place to go?'

'Yes, to my people at the Gorge mission at Mossman. I have lots of relatives there.'

The lady took more particulars and said, 'Leave it with me.'

She returned again a few days later and spoke to both Maggie and Polly, saying that for Maggie's sake and that of the district an Exemption Certificate was being prepared. Polly tried to question why but was cut short when the lady closed her folder and said, 'Maggie could be in serious trouble. Best she gets out of here as soon as possible.'

During the next three weeks the lady visited twice more, asking questions and with papers to sign. Arrangements were made and, two days after Maggie's birthday, a government car arrived at Polly's house. After a teary farewell to Polly and to her sisters and promising to stay in touch, Maggie sat in the back seat behind the lady and was driven to the train station. After the lady handed Maggie her ticket and £10 she said as a parting gesture, 'Mr Shannon will be glad you're gone.'

'Who?' asked Maggie, never before having heard the name.

'Mr Shannon. The shire mayor.'

The train journey, with two connecting trains, took four days and by the time Maggie arrived at Cairns she had figured that Mr Shannon was the fat man with the braces who often got a cramp in his leg.

Maggie settled back into the Gorge mission and, with Colleen Brennan showing her age and slowing, Maggie became her assistant. She also worked closely with Juran, assisting Aborigines and, in particular, trying to prevent removals. Her crowning achievement came when, due to her unyielding efforts, her mother and sisters were allowed to return home and be reunited with family. Maggie eventually married a half-caste and raised a family whose descendants continued to reside in the district.

CHAPTER 55

The draconian *Aboriginals Protection Act* and its amendments that had treated Aborigines as wards of the state since 1897 softened during the 1950s and, with a shift in public opinion and agitation for change, politicians moved towards giving them more autonomy. Aborigines moved about more freely, socialising with whites and finding worthwhile employment. Full-blood Aboriginal children were, for the first time, accepted into public schools.

The 1960s brought momentous change for the Aborigines, with the Commonwealth Government becoming actively involved in legislating to give Aborigines full citizenship and forcing state governments to adopt policies that fulfilled the Commonwealth's objectives.

After much political bickering the Queensland Government made successive legislative changes that culminated in the *Aborigines Act 1971*. This Act, by revoking previous Acts, finally tore away the last remnants of the original Protection Act that had held the Aborigines of Queensland in bondage for three quarters of a century.

Juran lived to see the removal of the legislation that had plagued her people throughout her adult life. Although 113 Aboriginal people had been forcibly removed from the Mossman district during this period the number would have been much higher without her intervention.

❧

After decades of neglect Winston's property had become a shadow of its former self. The plantation lay fallow, with the orchard blanketed by vines, the garden unrecognisable and the pasture land a fire hazard of long grass. The main avenue, the once grand entrance to the first settlement on the river, showed signs of rolling back in time, with trees growing from what was once a well-worn carriageway. The family cemetery, with its seven wooden crosses poking above the grass, carried memories remembered by only a few, and held stories that others would not believe.

Juran's rickety cottage, with its sagging floor and a rusted rainwater tank outside, stood as a ghostly reminder of times gone by. Juran had never owned a motor car and, unable to ride a bicycle any longer, the bike lay rusting in the tool shed. The flood of visitors of many years ago had shrunk to visits by only a few good friends. In earlier years Frances had called regularly but since the death of Gerald and her confinement to a wheelchair she only sent messages.

Now ninety years of age and living alone, Juran spent most of her time sitting in a rocking chair on the porch of her small cottage, listening to the songbirds and the rustle of the trees in the breeze. She often cast back to earlier times, reflecting on her childhood in a communal camp, the plight of the Aborigines and her contribution to freeing them from the white man's shackles. She dwelt on her moments of triumph and wept when recalling the cruelty that had been inflicted on her people. Her greatest regret was not being able to have children to carry on Thomas' family name and continue with the plantation. Sometimes, late at night, demons of the past appeared in her dreams, arousing fears of the *buliman* coming to take her away. On these occasions she left her bed, made a pot of tea and sat on the porch, peering into the darkness.

Jonathan's property across the river had stayed in the family, with two of Nyulu and Larry's half-caste sons managing the estate since their parents' deaths. Frankie, the elder of the two, cherished Aunty Juran, as he called her, and crossed the river three times a week to bring food, chop wood for her stove and check on her. Of late Frankie had become concerned about a decline in her health. Apart from having great difficulty bathing herself with her crippled hip, she sometimes became vague, with limited recall of recent events. In spite of this she had so far declined an offer for her to live with his family in the original homestead. She told him she would rather die in the camp where she belonged. From a young age Frankie had been influenced by her and now devoted much of his time trying to dispel racial prejudice and assimilate blacks and whites as one community.

The summer of 1974 proved to be particularly oppressive. Under a cloudless sky the sun burnt fiercely, browning what would normally be a vista of green sugarcane fields. Light, leafy trash from the fields swirled upwards in thermal currents, restless to spread any spark that might be struck. Black Mountain, many miles to the south, had burned out of control for a week and lay blackened and desolate. The flames, fanned by a strong, south-easterly breeze, now swept down the Cassowary Range, threatening the valley and the livelihood of its residents.

Juran, having experienced nearly a century of seasons in the valley, kept to her midday routine of stirring the embers of the wood stove, putting a kettle on to boil and then retiring to the rocking chair on the porch for a doze. She drifted in the land of her dreams for nearly an hour till suddenly woken by a crackling sound from inside the cottage. The crackle of a fire, normally a comfort to Aborigines, took on a new meaning when Juran twisted around in the chair to see smoke clouding the inside of the cottage.

She heaved up from the chair, taking the weight on her good leg, and steadying herself by holding the porch rail. By the time she made her way down the stairs and hobbled to the rainwater tank, the crackle had become a blaze. The tank tap, clogged with corrosion, took forever to fill each bucket and, after struggling up the stairs and tossing three buckets of water on the fire, Juran realised that her childhood cottage would be lost. In a frantic attempt to salvage personal items she pawed through the smoke, holding the wall of the lounge room for support, and entered her bedroom. With the wall between the bedroom and the kitchen fully alight and suffocating smoke filling the room, she managed to pull free a duchesse drawer of papers and photographs. As she turned to leave her bad hip gave way, crashing her to the floor, strewing the contents of the drawer across the floor and into the flames. She tried to crawl forward to save them but the scorching heat drove her back into a corner of the room. Rafters began to crumble, the iron roof popped and tongues of flame leapt through windows. She pulled herself across the floor in the blinding smoke, feeling her way by the cracks between the floorboards. In the lounge room an updraft of air coming between the floorboards allowed her to gulp breath as she slithered to the porch and then down the steps. Juran took one look over her shoulder and, with all rooms now engulfed in flames, she dragged herself into the garden.

Frankie spotted the smoke. Knowing it came from Winston's he shouted to those at the house, jumped into an old Land Rover, crunched the gears and careered down the paddock, bouncing and kicking towards the river. He leapt from the open cab, streaked along a track through the rainforest fringing the river and burst onto the sandbar where James had first pitched his tent. In the tinder-dry conditions the flames had already spread and circled the entire camp. The orchard trees behind the camp, dead from neglect and a coverage of vines, shot flames sixty feet into the air and billowed with black smoke. The riverbank, standing between Frankie and where he thought Juran might be, gushed and hissed as fire tore through the long grass. The tops of gum trees exploded like fireballs, sending showers of sparks, spreading the fire further afield. Frankie covered his face with a hessian bag, raced to the river and dived in. He pushed through the water to where the track led up the bank but the heat and flames made the way impassable. He shouted to Juran, calling for her to reply, hoping that by some miracle she had escaped the inferno. He shouted till his throat was burnt from radiant heat, reducing his voice to a whisper.

Frankie's brother and some field hands joined him and when the flames settled they raked the way clear and ascended the steps that were originally carved into the clay bank. At the top Frankie fell to his knees, stricken with nausea, leaving it to the others to search through the hot embers. Before long a call of 'over here' told of the grim discovery. Frankie, hardly able to stand, came to the garden plot and, seeing Juran's charred body, he cried out, cursing the world and blaspheming the Almighty.

Those at Frances' plantation had seen the smoke and men from there, together with the Mossman fire brigade, attacked the fire from the main entrance of the plantation. They pushed their way through and found Frankie's men standing there, shocked and in disbelief. Frankie could not stay for the removal of the body. He took himself off into the bush and did not return home till late the following day.

Frances, though shocked and dismayed, retained her composure and insisted on visiting the camp the next morning. Everything was gone. All the memories from her childhood through to later in life had been erased by the firestorm. The orchard and pasture had been reduced to scorched earth, only a few smouldering house stumps and crumpled water tanks remained of the camp site, and the cemetery was recognisable only by the charred butts of the crosses. Moved by this devastation Frances arranged for Juran to be buried in the public cemetery where her grave would be cared for into the future. All were welcome at the funeral, with blacks and whites mingling to pay their last respects to a lady whom everybody owed a debt of gratitude for the good she had done in bridging the gap between black and white.

Frances, as holder of the title deed of the plantation, declared that while she held title the property would be devoted to grazing cattle, with no remnant structures to be removed and the graves maintained. Following Frances' death the property passed to successive generations and, as there was no covenant on the deed specifying her wish, the property eventually went under the plough for the purpose of growing sugar cane, leaving no trace of Winston's camp or its one hundred years of rich history.

In the year following Juran's funeral Frances finished writing her memoir about the lives of her family and those of Winston's camp. Her observations, including coverage of major events and particulars of personal lives, provide a graphic account of European colonisation of the valley. The work, chronicled in detail, corroborates many aspects of life as it is portrayed in this novel and provides a thread for its narrative. James' diary, which had been passed to her by Juran before the fire, has also been preserved. This reference, that includes drawings on the back pages, further validates the information. A special thanks to her descendants who have made the material available. Unfortunately, no plaque of remembrance has been erected to honour members of Winston's camp for their pioneering work and dedication to the Aborigines of the Mossman River valley.

GLOSSARY OF ABORIGINAL WORDS

English translation shown in brackets

Bujur (feather) Father of Marku and elder of the tribe

Marku (wild cherry) Daughter of Bujur. Raped by a man of the Barron River tribe

Bajal (bowerbird) Son of Marku

Nganka (flower) Wife of Bajal

Dari (boxwood tree) Second wife of Bujur and stepmother of Marku

Frances Marra (zamia palm) Daughter of Jonathan and Ellen

Nyulu (feminine) Aboriginal child 'adopted' by Jonathan and Ellen

Juran (alive) Half-caste daughter of James and Marku

Kija (moon) Midwife to Marku when she gives birth to Bajal

Jajin (sacred) Medicine man

Wadi (gesture of affection) Aboriginal lad accused of stealing vegetables

Mawal (bee) Aboriginal father of Nyulu

Bularr (firefly) Aboriginal man who saves a white girl from drowning

Kaba (rain) The young Aboriginal girl raped by Sergeant Caxton

Murramu (dingo) Name of Bajal's dog

Buliman Aboriginal name for police